*For Adam Swift
and Sindamani Bridglal*

By the same author

The Witch of Exmoor

MARGARET DRABBLE

VIKING

VIKING

Published by the Penguin Group
Penguin Books Ltd, 27 Wrights Lane, London w 8 5 t z, England
Penguin Books USA Inc., 375 Hudson Street, New York, New York 10014, USA
Penguin Books Australia Ltd, Ringwood, Victoria, Australia
Penguin Books Canada Ltd, 10 Alcorn Avenue, Toronto, Ontario, Canada m 4 v 3 b 2
Penguin Books (NZ) Ltd, 182–190 Wairau Road, Auckland 10, New Zealand

Penguin Books Ltd, Registered Offices: Harmondsworth, Middlesex, England

First published 1996
Published simultaneously in Canada by McClelland & Stewart Inc., Toronto
1 3 5 7 9 10 8 6 4 2
First edition

Set in 11.5/15 pt Monotype Bembo
Typeset by Datix International Limited, Bungay, Suffolk
Printed in England by Clays Ltd, St Ives plc

A CIP catalogue record for this book is available from the British Library

Hardback is b n 0-670-87240-7
Trade paperback is b n 0-670-87276-8

Contents

THE VALE OF IGNORANCE

Begin on a midsummer evening. Let them have everything that is pleasant. The windows are open on to the terrace and the lawn, and drooping bunches of wistaria deepen from a washed mauve pink to purple. The roses are in bloom.

The meal is drawing to a close. The bowl of fruit has been plundered. A hacked yet noble slab of Cheddar cheese, a flattening liquid disc of Brie circulate slowly on a heavy round grey veined marble slab. The salad wilts a little in its various oils. There are crumbs and stains on the dark pink loose-woven cloth. Dishes are stacked high by the Aga, in full view, should one wish to look that way, for this is a farmhouse dining-room, and it is open plan, on the twentieth-century, more or less servantless model. The painted moss-green walls glow in the fading light. This is England, but Spain and Italy have coloured the dishes and displayed their bowls and plates upon the wooden dresser, adding their cobalt Mediterranean blues and their hot mustard yellows. The wine is French, and the precociously rosy apples are from New Zealand, but the bread was baked here this afternoon, and the gems of lettuces and the dark red veined oak leaves and the splinters of chive are from the garden. Are the grapes from South Africa? It is hard to tell. Let us say that we are in England, in Hampshire, and that we approach, but not too closely, and not it would seem very rapidly, the end of the twentieth century.

Much bread has been baked by Patsy Palmer over the weekend, for her family and guests are in good appetite. They have been walking, swimming, playing tennis. They work hard during the week, in their different ways, and now they are taking their ease and eating slice after slice of solid brown bread. They have already devoured spinach soup and two large free-range chickens and a platter of roast potatoes garnished with rosemary. Now they eat bread, and cheese, and nibble at grapes, and talk.

This is the home of Daniel and Patsy Palmer. Daniel is that light-haired, skinny, freckled chap who is absent-mindedly refilling his own glass from a bottle of claret. He looks lean, hungry and athletic of mind and body, and is wearing jeans, although he must be in his forties. An academic, a civil servant, a lawyer, a diplomat? Something like that. His wife Patsy is plumper than he, though by no means yet fat, and she also is wearing jeans, and above them a navy-blue Chinese silk shirt and an apron with a pattern of ducks upon it. Her hair is short and brown and slightly fluffy. She could be a headmistress, or a gynaecologist, or a magistrate. And those two young people must be their children, for the family resemblance is strong, and their manner at table is offhand and familiar – and in young Simon's case verging on the rude. Emily looks like her father; her hair is a clear red-gold, her eyes a Nordic blue. Simon, too, resembles his father in colouring, and his nose is sharp.

He bites his nails between grapes, and avoids eye contact. A mother – but perhaps not his – would note that he is too thin.

The other women at table are also related to their host Daniel. They are his sisters. You can see that at a glance. Both born Palmer, they are Palmer no longer, for both have married, and both belong to the generation of women who took their husbands' names. Thus Rosemary is now Rosemary Herz, and Gogo (as Grace is known within the family) is Gogo D'Anger. Both the younger Palmers have married out.

Rosemary is the beauty of the family, or so it has always been said, and there is a residue of truth in the saying. Her hair is a light pinkish gold, slightly paler than her niece Emily's, and assisted in tint by her hairdresser. (She is the only woman in the room to give evidence of regular visits to a hairdresser.) Her eyes, like Daniel's, are a challenging intellectual blue. She is the most becomingly dressed woman at the table, for she has changed, after tennis, into a pale lilac soft cotton dress (an interesting choice of colour, but effective) and added some green glass beads to dangle into her freckle-dusted cleavage. Rosemary has style. She could be an actress, or a television presenter, or a journalist.

Her husband, Nathan, is rather a surprise. He is short and squat and fat and hairy and balding and very ugly. She wears him with pride, like a fashion accessory.

Rosemary and Nathan have two children. They have gone upstairs to the bunk room to watch TV or play some computer game. Or so their parents assume.

Gogo is the middle daughter. She is taller than Rosemary and a little heavier in build. (Does Rosemary watch her diet? Probably, though one would not think so from the amount she has eaten this evening.) Gogo's hair, which had been family fair at birth, had turned darker in her teens, as though making a protest against its powerful and problematic heritage, and it is now a dull brown; she wears it tied back with a scarf, for she says that the feel of it upon her brow annoys her. This habit gives her a slightly Bohemian appearance, which she ac-centuates with bright colours − on this occasion, a bold shirt of geometric purple and red, worn over a long orange skirt − but she counteracts this gypsy look with an expression of forbidding severity. She could be called handsome, but not beautiful. She has the Palmer nose. One would not like to speculate upon Gogo's profession, for fear of reprimand or ridicule if proved wrong. (That she has a profession is manifest.)

Her husband, David, in contrast, has a most engaging manner, as though to compensate for Gogo's austerity. He is Guyanese, and he is as handsome as Nathan is ugly. One could gaze at him with pleasure for hours, and many do. He and Nathan get on well. They do not often meet, but when they do they like to talk. They form an alliance against the Anglo-Saxons.

Gogo and David have only one child. He is upstairs, playing or watching TV with his cousins. Or doing whatever it is that children of that age do.

David and Nathan are talking now. This weekend was set up as a family conclave, but David and Nathan agree that they cannot spend all their time playing Unhappy Families. They have already spent much of the weekend talking about the problem − in the pool, on the tennis court, walking in the shrubbery, chopping parsley − and now it is their turn, at least for a brief respite, to talk about something else. The Palmers, tacitly, agree. They too have had enough, for the moment, of what to do about Mother. They are refreshed, by the claret and the roast potatoes. They are willing to play David's game, which he says is called 'The Veil of Ignorance'.

He has tried to explain it to them in simple terms, but some of them are not very quick – or perhaps they are too quick by half, for they keep interrupting him and going off at tangents and having ideas of their own. They are not as docile as his one-time students. But then, they have no examinations to pass, and for them nothing hangs upon the game itself, or upon his approval.

It is only a game. Gogo knows the game already, has known it for years, so she sits back, smiling her sardonic smile, as David politely and charmingly persists.

'No, it's not a question of imagining a Utopia,' he repeats. 'It's more a question of unimagining everything that you are, and then working out the kind of society which you would be willing to accept if you didn't in advance know your own place in it. If you knew you would have no special privileges or bargaining powers. It's a much more modest proposal than a Utopia. All you have to imagine is that in the original position of choice you don't know who you are or where you stand – you don't know if you're rich or poor, able or disabled, clever or mentally subnormal, plain or beautiful, male or female, black or white, strong or weak. You don't know if you're an optimist or a pessimist, a risk-taker or a traditionalist, fertile or in-fertile, straight or gay. Nor do you know if the society itself is going to be rich or poor – pre-industrial, technologically developed, rapidly developing, booming, declining. You can't expect to be yourself, nor can you expect society to be anything you recognize. Your eyes are veiled by the veil of ignorance. And from this position you have to examine the first principles of justice, and decide what they are. If you cling to any trace of your existing self you will find yourself construct-ing a theory of justice and a society that favour you.'

'As these do us,' murmurs Emily, but nobody hears her.

'Let me get this straight,' says Patsy, who has been trying to concen-

4

trate through distractions about bread provision (could they really finish off yet another loaf? – she was damned if she was going to bake at midnight, and she has a busy day on Sunday). 'Tell me again, David. You mean I've got to construct a society in which I would be willing to take my place as the poorest of the poor and the lowest of the low?'

'Well,' says David. 'It's not the whole of the society you have to construct, it's more the principles on which it is founded.'

('I can't see the difference,' murmurs Emily.)

'You could decide', continues David, 'that a small contingent of the very poor are necessary for the proper functioning of society, and that it would just be bad luck – a sort of social sacrifice – if you ended up as one of them. It would be quite hard to argue, I think, that a numerically overwhelming mass of the very poor can constitute a just society, but it certainly has been argued.'

('Not to say practised,' murmurs Emily.)

'I don't see a problem,' says Patsy. 'I can't see how anyone can ever vote for anything other than a society in which there's no possibility whatsoever, however numerically remote, of ending up at the very nasty bottom of a heap. I know I'd end up at the bottom of the heap if there was a bottom. I've never had any luck at gambling. So I'd prefer a nice safe foolproof society, please, where even if I pulled the shortest straw I could still survive quite comfortably. In fact I'd like a society without a bottom of the heap at all. Would that be a practical possibility? Would the rules of the game permit it? Would the earth's resources permit it?'

'In practice, it's very difficult to design a society in which there's no bottom of the heap. Millions have died for it, but no country on earth has managed it,' replies David, smiling his civil, engaging, disarming smile.

'Really? It sounds so little to ask. Such a modest request.'

'You always think you're being modest, Ma,' says Simon. 'It's one of your most persistent delusions.' (He speaks more sharply than his sister, with a more unpleasant edge, but Patsy chooses to ignore him.)

'What I want to know is this,' says Rosemary. 'If it were all worked out, according to David's rules – the universal principles of justice and all that – would anyone dare to press the button and make it happen? If there *were* a button to press, would anyone press it? Would anyone be willing to rip off the veil and open his eyes in the brave new world of Social Justice? Would one risk all, if one were a professor at Harvard instead of a man in a cardboard box?'

(The man from the attic, who has crept silently down the backstairs to help himself to a banana from the larder, listens intently for the answer.)

'Of course one wouldn't dare,' says Daniel Palmer. 'It would mean giving up all this.' He gestures widely and with a lifted eyebrow, perhaps of dissociation, at his lawns, his Aga, his wife, his dissenting children, his deliquescent Brie, his three empty bottles. 'I like all this. I've worked hard for this. Years of my life have gone into all this. Years of Patsy's life have gone into it. I want to see the bay tree reach six foot. Slow growth. You know, slow growth. Why should I press a button and risk losing all of this?'

'You might not lose it,' says his daughter Emily more forwardly, and this time they are obliged to listen. 'You could', pursues Emily, 're-design society *exactly as it is*. Stone by stone, leaf by leaf. You could work out a theory of justice that said it was proper and necessary for the whole of society that there should be such a person as you in such a house as this, and then you could press the button. And you might end up right here, having this very same conversation.'

'The odds against that', says her father, 'are about sixty million to one.'

'So you admit', says Emily, 'that there's no justice – no justification – for our living in this house?'

'None whatsoever,' says Daniel. 'I gave up any hope of any kind of general social justice years and years ago. What I have, I hold. That's my motto.'

'It's a pity', says Simon, 'that we can't set up a controlled experiment. Let David work out what he thinks would be really fair – and then try it for just a year. Then we could press another button and all scamper back home. If we didn't like it. Which I don't suppose most of us here would.'

'You might die in the experiment. A year's a long time,' says Emily.

'You might die in real life,' says Simon. His tone is not friendly.

'If there were a button,' says Rosemary, 'would you wake up in this new world at the same age as you were when you pressed it? Or might you find yourself a newborn baby, or an old person in a geriatric ward? Does the original position make us all the same age, or not?'

'I think you're taking it too literally,' says David, momentarily distracted by the Elgin Marbles, the concept of historical property, and the sugar canes of Guyana. 'It's only a philosophical concept. A hypothesis. There isn't any button.'

'I take everything literally,' says Rosemary, 'even philosophy.'

'And would you wake up', asks Simon, refusing to be diverted, 'with all the memories of a person who had been brought up in the new society? Would they have been implanted, like in that robot movie? So that you could remember nothing else?'

'You would wake up', says David, teasingly, impressively, 'with the memories of a person who has been born into and lived in a society run on the principles of fairness and justice.'

'Wow!' says Emily. 'That is science fiction.'

'Well,' says easy-going Nathan, 'you can count on me to press your button. Any old button. I'd give it a whirl. I can't be bothered to do the redesigning from the first principles bit myself. I'll leave that to the professionals. I'll leave it to my distinguished brother-in-law. I think I can trust him not to introduce a tyranny or a totalitarian state or an elective monarchy or the murder of the first-born or the culling of anyone whose first name begins with an *N*. I'll just take my chance with whatever David and his chums suggest. The odds are I'd end up being someone much nicer than me in an even nicer place. I'd take a gamble.'

'He's a *terrible* gambler,' says Rosemary, leaning over proudly to pat his hairy hand. 'You should have seen him in the casino at Venice. All his chips on the table.'

'Really?' says Patsy. 'I'm surprised. You are a dark horse, Nathan.'

'I like dark horses and long odds,' says Nathan. 'And poker, and backgammon. But I don't get much time for them these days. Rosie doesn't like it, do you, Rosie?'

Husband and wife smile at one another, in not quite convincing collusion. Nathan takes his hand away from Rosemary's, and fishes in his pocket for a crumpled packet of cigarettes.

'Do you mind, Patsy?' he asks. 'I'll go in to the garden if you like.'

Patsy shakes her head, and reaches behind to the dresser for a saucer to serve as an ashtray.

'Smoking is gambling,' says Emily, staring coolly at her uncle. 'It's just a question of luck.'

'A question of luck as to when or whether I develop the fatal cough? Yes, I suppose you're right.'

'In the just society,' asks Emily, turning back to David, 'would there be any smoking areas? Or would it be altogether forbidden? Would there be sexual reproduction? Would there be illness and death?'

'Smoking areas could be agreed. Or not. But the other things would have to carry on as now, I'm afraid. Otherwise you would end up with a society without anything recognizable as human beings at all.'

'How nice,' says Emily, still staring hard at David.

'That might be the only way,' says Simon. 'You could devise this perfectly just system, but then human beings would come along and mess it all up. Much better to redesign the human beings.'

'What a gloomy couple you are,' says David, smiling his charming televisual smile.

'*I'm* not gloomy,' says Emily. 'Simon may be, but I'm not. I'm just being radical. I mean you might as well go back to the original plan. If you're going to have an original position, it might as well be *really* original.'

David is not sure whether she is being quite clever or very stupid. The evening grows late: surely it is time these teenagers went to bed? His own son had politely vanished hours ago, like the good boy he is.

'A society without human beings', says Daniel gravely, '*is* a radical concept.' Patsy permits herself to snigger.

'A society without human beings', says Gogo, breaking her silence, 'is exactly what *she* seems to have designed for herself.'

Nathan and David and Patsy quickly exchange guilty glances: so the game of Unhappy Families is back upon the table. David has done his best to distract, but he has failed. The Palmers are relentless. They could bring any topic home. They could lasso conversations about gardening, or the cinema, or the Hubble telescope, or the sugar industry, or Guyanese politics, or the slave-trade, and bring them home to graze about their mother.

'I mean, for God's sake,' says Gogo. A long pause follows. She has the floor. 'The Witch of Exmoor,' she says, echoing a phrase that Rosemary has tried out on her over their picnic lunch on the lawn.

'It just isn't habitable,' continues Rosemary. 'She can't go on living there. At her age. It's impossible. We all thought the Mausoleum was bad enough. This is a thousand times worse. At least the Mausoleum was in reach of public transport. Well, almost. I think Daniel ought to go and have a look. Show a bit of masculine authority.'

Daniel smiles his thin, dry, bleached smile. His spare face is briefly irradiated by a sad, mocking, uncertain light. His sisters mocked him much.

'Describe it again, Rosie,' he says. He enjoys her recital. He might as well take pleasure from it.

'*Well*,' says Rosemary. 'To begin with, it's vast. And it's hideous. And it's uninhabitable. And what electricity there is keeps going off. And it's about to fall into the sea.'

'It's literally on the *edge* of the sea?'

'On the very edge. Perched. And the drive – well, you can't really call it a drive. It's hardly even a track. It's more or less impassable. Deep ruts. Great pot-holes. Stuff growing out of the hedges. It was bad enough getting down it in the spring. God knows what it's like in winter. And it's four hours from London even if you put your foot down all the way along the motorway. And then all those miles over the moor. There's a sign, written on a piece of cardboard. I stopped to read it. It said BEWARE OF VIPERS BREEDING.'

It is the first time they have heard this detail: they respond with suitable admiration.

'Did it mean it literally? Vipers, literally vipers?'

'I should think so. It looked real snake country to me. You could feel them round about. You know, roots and bracken. I don't know what she thinks she's doing there. She's got no connection with that part of the country at all. If she wants to go native why doesn't she go back to Lincolnshire where she says she came from? Or Sweden, come to that?'

'She always said she wanted to live in the country,' says Daniel.

'Yes, but why choose Exmoor? It can't mean anything to her.'

'Hampshire means nothing to me,' says Daniel. 'But I happen to like it here. I don't see why she shouldn't live on Exmoor if she wants.'

'In a derelict hotel?'

'I thought you said it was a folly.'

'It's hard to know what it is. It's enormous. She only lives in a bit of it.'

'And it's a four-hour drive?'

'At least. It was just over 200 miles on the clock, but the last 60 are a nightmare. And I can tell you it's not very nice to drive for four hours and then have the door more or less slammed in your face.'

Daniel and Gogo like this bit best.

'So she didn't want you to come in?'

'Not really. She kept me out there in this terrible overgrown court-yard. Nettles everywhere. And it was pissing with rain. She had her back to the door as though she was guarding something. I had to say I was dying for a pee before she'd let me in. And then she said, why didn't you stop a bit earlier and pee in the hedge?'

They all laugh at this sally, and not for the first time.

'What was the lavatory like?' inquires Emily, freshly.

'Well, it was clean. But sort of basic. No lavatory *seat*, for example. Nothing extra. Except spiders. Those long leggy ones. Lots of them.'

'Her familiars,' says Gogo.

'No pot plants, no toilet rolls, no little cane tables, no volumes of verse?'

'There was a toilet roll, but God it was damp. The damp there is a killer.'

'And she gave you a slice of corned beef,' prompts Gogo.

'Yes, a slice of corned beef. And a piece of soggy Ryvita. It tasted a thousand years old. There's a cold like mildew down there. It bites. It's full of microbes. Full of fungus spores. It fills the lungs. I can't describe how horribly cold it was. And this was mid-May.'

'She wasn't expecting you,' ventures Patsy in extenuation.

'How could she be expecting anyone if she won't have a telephone?' returns Rosemary.

'Perhaps she really doesn't want to see us,' says Daniel. (This is the kind of thing he says.)

'Well,' says Rosemary, with gravitas, 'that would seem to be the message. She says she doesn't want to see anyone. She says she's too busy. I said busy doing what, and she said she was busy being a recluse. She said it was a full-time job.'

They all laugh, and there is a respect in their laughter, for Frieda has turned the tables on them this time. They are surrounded by friends who complain at length of the burden of visiting their aged relatives, their aunts with Alzheimer's, their fathers grumpy with cancer or heart conditions or gout, their mothers whining of the treacheries of the past: none of them has a mother who does not want to see them. It is against the natural order. What have they done to earn such rejection? Frieda has removed herself from their concern and set off into the unknown. They had seen trouble coming a year or more ago, when she suddenly decided to sell the family home and all that was in it, but they had not expected a removal as dramatic as this. She had sold the big house in Romley (optimistically and falsely described by the estate agents as 'on the borders of Stoke Newington') and purchased a dilapidated thirty-room Victorian castle by the sea.

'But you said she looked well enough,' says Daniel.

'Oh, yes, she *looks* well enough. I think she's lost weight. Well, one would, on a diet like that. Worse than a health farm. God knows where the nearest shop is.'

'I don't see how we can intervene,' says Daniel, who has no wish to be sent off to Exmoor as family delegate. 'She's not doing any harm up there, is she?'

'Not to us,' says Gogo. 'She can't harm us any more. She's done her worst.'

'I wouldn't be so sure,' says Daniel, rethinking his position as a new light strikes him. 'She's only in her sixties.'

'I'm not so sure either,' says Rosemary. 'I told you what she said about remaking her will? She said she was going to reallocate her posthumous copyrights. Is she allowed to do that?'

'Of course she is,' says David D'Anger, roused by this brazen asser-tion of family rights of interest in family money. 'She can do what she wants with them.'

The three Palmers turn their eyes upon him, the dark intruder.

'Perhaps *you*'d better go and see her and find out what she's really up to,' says Rosemary. 'She'd listen to you, David. She favours you.'

'I'd go,' says David. 'I'd go, in the autumn. If you thought it was a good idea.'

His ready acquiescence both pleases and disquiets them. What does David D'Anger hope to gain from a trip to the West Country? There can be nothing to interest him there. Westminster, the West Indies and West Yorkshire, fair enough, he has interests in all of those – but the West Country, surely not?

'You won't like it there,' says Rosemary. 'You should have seen her face, when she saw me getting out of the car. You may laugh, but it wasn't very funny.'

'I'm not laughing,' says Daniel.

'Neither am I,' says Gogo.

'It's no laughing matter,' says Rosemary.

'Money *is* money,' says Nathan solemnly, provocatively. 'You don't want her leaving it all to pay off the National Debt, do you?'

'I'm telling you,' says Rosemary, 'that building's like a black hole.

You don't believe me. It's worse than any of you imagine. It'll probably slide down the cliff and into the sea. And then where will we be?'

Although it is no laughing matter, the thought of their mother sliding into the sea, on a dark night, has its comic aspects. They elaborate, and I am sorry to say that they laugh. And, in conclusion, it is agreed that David and Gogo, come the autumn, will risk the journey and the mildew and the corned beef. They will take Benjamin as peacemaker, they volunteer. How will she be able to alienate herself and her fortune from her own children and grandchildren? (If Daniel and Rosemary have suspicions about this plan, they keep them to themselves.)

Upstairs, in the bunk room, the youngest of those grandchildren, Jessica and Jonathan Herz, are playing with the fast-forward button on one of the house's several video machines. They are trying to find the bit with the child-eating zombies, but they are not trying very seriously: they are waiting, in a state of heightened excitement, for their cousin Benjamin D'Anger to come back from his bedroom with the Game. Many a video nasty have they watched up there in the nursery, for their aunt Patsy Palmer has a professional interest in video nasties and no interest whatsoever in domestic censorship. But none of the videos is anything like as frightening, exciting, wicked and seductive as the Power Game. Jessica and Jon love coming to stay with Uncle Daniel and Aunt Patsy at the Old Farm when Ben is there, for Ben invented the Power Game and they cannot play it without him. He is the Master of the Game, and they wait for him in a slightly fevered anticipation. Will it be as exciting as it was last time? Will Ben let them change roles this time? Will he have made up more of the story, as he promised? He has been mysterious about it all day, for it is a late and secret game, and it has to wait for a certain hour of the night — tonight he had dictated that it should be ten thirty. The minutes have flicked by on the video clock, and now they wait, sitting on the floor in their pyjamas, round the space they have cleared. (They have built a wall of video boxes, in preparation. It is the city wall.)

And here comes Ben, the divine, the lanky, the dark boy. Ben

13

D'Anger glows with darkness. He wears a yellow night-shirt, and he carries in his arms the large box called Decapolis which holds the Game. Jessica (who is indifferent pale and freckled) wets her lips and tugs at the elasticated waist of her pyjamas. Jon sucks a dark ringlet as he sits, cross-legged, bespectacled, alert, the braces on his teeth glinting in the dimmed light. Ben stands there for a moment, with his arms around Decapolis. It looks innocent: a large cardboard box which once held several dozen tins of dog food, for the dull Dalmatian of the house. He lowers it, ceremoniously. The Herz children silently ask him if, in their month's absence, it has been tampered with. They need no words. He shakes his head. He needs no words. It is intact. Emily has appointed herself its guardian. Emily keeps it safe in her bedroom. It lies in the bottom of her wardrobe, and Patsy is too busy or too lazy to disturb it. Emily is proud to be in collusion, though she has never seen the Game.

Now they begin to unpack its treasures, and lay them out within the video city. Their co-operation is unspoken, intense, complete. First they range the old wooden soldiers salvaged by Daniel from Grandma Frieda's house in Romley. They are handmade period pieces from a bygone age, dating from an unknown childhood. Scraps of faded colour cling to them. Then they line the walls of the video city with the little white plaster busts of the unpainted Rajputani riflemen, lovingly made by a great-great-uncle on the Palmer side who had served long years with the riflemen in India. Then they lay down the pieces of blue ribbon that represent the three great rivers, the Oronoque, the Essequibo and the Demerara, and plant by them the realistic little educational plastic trees of oak and cedar and palm and fig and ebony, and arrange the farmyard animals and the cattle. The scale is bizarre, but that is one of the peculiar thrills of creation. They erect the house called Eldorado, the house called Cayenne, and they lay out the Island of the Dead. Decapolis is a four-cornered city: three of the houses are fortified and occupied, and the fourth is called the Siege House of Hope and Despair. Ben will allot them each a fortress within this small kingdom, and then the game can begin.

It takes nearly half an hour to arrange the site to Ben's satisfaction.

He places a lion on a wall, a wolf in a garden, and floats innocent ducks upon the mirror-lake. The materials are heterogeneous – wood, metal, plastic, fabric. There are no prehistoric monsters, for Ben has banned them – they are, he says to Jon and Jessica, banal. 'Banal' is currently his favourite word. Nor will he admit space monsters. 'Everything must be *of the earth*,' he insists seriously. Otherwise it will not work.

Because it is real. Ben can make them believe it is real. Ben animates everything. His power to breathe life into objects is supernatural, and they know it. He says he can stare at a postcard and make its leaves shake, its rivers flow, its ships sail across the sea, its figures walk the streets. They believe him. He cannot do it when anyone is watching, for that destroys his powers, but he can do it. At night, alone, he tells them, he can bring to life the paintings on the wall. How does he do it? He stares and stares until his eyes lose focus, he says, as one stares at a three-dimensional computer picture, and then the picture begins to move. Can he get inside the picture, they ask? No, he can never get inside. He is always outside, staring. His are the eyes that make it move. He can never enter into his own vision. He is for ever without. But he has the power. He has the Magic Eye.

They are nearly ready now. It is all laid out, and waiting. It is waiting for the Breath of Life. There is a fear in their anticipation, for last time there had been many wounded, many tortured, many raped, many dead. Drowned, washed downriver, stuck through with bayonets, hurled from high buildings. How will it go this time?

This time, Ben tells Jessica she must possess as her captain the little Indian clay elephant man called Trincomalee. Her fortress will be Eldorado. Jon must possess the figure of St Joseph, taken from some long dismantled Christmas cake: his fortress will be Cayenne. Ben has allotted himself that icy and treacherous terrain, the Isle aux Morts, and his captain will be Beltenebros, on his horse, Bayard. The Metal Queen will occupy the Siege House. She must defend herself without human aid. If she falls, there will be forfeits. There will perhaps be executions. Does one desire to die, or not to die? It is confusing, disturbing. Death is pleasure. Death is pleasant.

Ben distributes the troops. So many soldiers to each army, so many horses, so many black painted cotton reels of ammunition, and one ambulance apiece.

Ben instructs his cousins to stare hard at the small figures. He begins the incantation. They must mesmerize themselves. Jessica stares at the small painted features of Trincomalee, at the black and white and red and brown of his clay. He bares his origins bravely. His blue turban is striped with a pure band of yellow. Jon fixes his attention on the gaudier St Joseph with his tawdry cloak and his cheap Taiwanese colours. Ben fixes himself upon the medieval knight, Beltenebros. 'Decapolis, decapolis, decapolis,' he murmurs. 'Isle aux Morts, Isle du Diable, Isle à la Crosse, Isle des Saintes.' Their eyes blur. The small figures begin to march across the carpet. Battle is engaged. This is not a pleasant game. The birds of death gather for the corpses. For many games past, the saviour has not come. Maybe he will never come.

Outside in the garden, Nathan puffs at a last cigarette. He has sneaked out. He is still pondering, in a desultory manner, the conundrum of the Veil of Ignorance. From his own original position, as a clever Jewish lad in suburban lower-middle-class East Finchley, he would have found it hard to imagine the details of the world he temporarily inhabits – this lawn, these scented trees, these in-laws, these assumptions. Had the Veil of Ignorance been snatched from his sixteen-year-old eyes, he would have been surprised by this flash forward. He had been ambitious enough – more ambitious then than he is now – but he would not have recognized the significance of the décor of his life to be. Indeed, as he knows, he does not wholly know it now. He treads his cigarette end into the lawn furtively, then furtively bends and picks it up again and puts it in his pocket. Patsy and Daniel are proud of their garden and spend time on it. They talk about it. They even talk about it to Nathan, although they must know that he is a lost cause. The flower culture of the English middle classes pisses him off. The names of old roses make him ill. He knows more brand names of cigarettes and detergents than he knows names of flowers. Yet he likes to be here, for an evening.

He takes another turn along the kitchen-garden wall. It has been

the first really hot day of the year, but a slight dew is forming under-
foot, and a large liquorice-black ribbed slug crosses his path. He peers
at it through the thick lenses of his glasses. There is a slightly unpleasant smell on the air, which his cigarette has not overwhelmed. He
sniffs. It is coming from those pink roses, those small clustery yellow-
stamened pink roses, which no doubt have some very special pretty
title. He approaches them, sniffs more closely. A rotting, fecal, fungal
smell. The smell of old rose, of old England, of old women. They are
probably called the Duchess of Death, or Cuisse de Vieille, or Mar-
quise de la Mort. Do all roses smell so disgusting? Experimentally, he
progresses to a standard rose of deeper crimson, with larger flowers.
These smell quite strongly of cheap soap. Never would Nathan inflict
a scent so crude upon the British customer.

You have not guessed quite right about Nathan. He is not an academic, though that, with those pebble glasses, that meditative look,
those untidy stained baggy weekend trousers, is what he ought to be.
He ought to be a professor of immunology or anthropology, but in
fact he is in advertising, and on a weekday, in his business suiting, he is
more convincing in the role. At weekends he overflows into a kind of
uncontrolled, deliberate grossness. He is crudely and aggressively
Jewish: his large fleshy nose and his broad fingers, his large dark eyes
speak of a rich and oriental world he has never visited, a world a
thousand miles from East Finchley. Hairs sprout, at the weekends,
unrestrained from his chest. They sprout all year round, day and night,
from his ears and nostrils and the backs of his hands. Women long to
stroke his chest, though as far as he knows they do not long to tweak at
his nostrils. He is an attractive man, and he knows it.

He wanders beyond the edge of the kitchen garden into the shrubbery. Here the smell is even worse. It is the sour and woody stink of
elderflower, though he cannot identify its source.

Nathan has harnessed his alpha brain to selling products and, occasionally, concepts, for he is respected and astute, and on the way up
in a flourishing company. As he inhales the verdant rot, and wipes a
glob of white cuckoo spittle from his naked ankle, he contemplates
the myth of rural England which has been so successfully marketed to

the affluent English. And it is not entirely a myth, for it is here, and now, this little wood, these insects, that calling bird. There is some kind of a fit, however clumsy, between the image and the reality. Daniel's farmhouse, more comfortable now than ever in its working days, is hundreds of years old, and this little wood is older than the house. Ancient coppiced woodland. Vegetables have been grown here for centuries, and for centuries roses have scented and corrupted the air. And who is to say that Daniel and Patsy do not work as hard as any farmer? They work.

Marmalades and mustards and jellies with silly little frills and ribbons round their throats, Victorian pillowcases with honeysuckle patterns, 'Home Baked' biscuits from the factory, pomanders, posies, lavender bags, pots-pourri (*pourri* indeed, nods Nathan to himself) – one cannot accuse Daniel and Patsy of falling into many of these consumer traps. They have better taste. They bake their bread and eat it. Why, then, this deep unease? Is it envy? Is it some deeper disapproval?

The rural England of the advertising commercial is superimposed on the palimpsest of the England of Hampshire in the 1990s, and that again is superimposed upon the reality of the past, the unknowable reality of history. The layers of image fade, fuse, fix, peel, wrinkle, part.

Nathan lights another cigarette. The selling and packaging of England. He has taken part in it. He had intended to be an anthropologist, but reading Mary Douglas on the meaning of shopping had revealed to him the light. He had been twenty-one at the time and about to sit his Finals. Suddenly he had seen it all, revealed in the broad rays of the future. Shopping was indeed our new religion. Consumer choice, in a post-industrial society, was our area of free will, informed perhaps by grace. He would participate in the new faith, as priest, as confessor. He would set up his stall in the Temple.

God, how right he had been, how horribly, uncannily right. Nathan the prophet. Even he would not have predicted the degree to which shopping as a full-time pursuit would have caught on in the last fifteen years. The supermarket and shopping centre as fun-fair, family outing, parkland, playground, stately home, temple, youth club, old people's refuge: the shopping arcade as the forum of assignation, rape, abduction, murder, riot. Oh fountains, oh palaces, oh dreams and aspirations! Let us enter those revolving doors, wide enough to take a trolley loaded with £200 of edible merchandise! It is at once glorious and appalling. Is it, he wonders, in his blood? He does not know much about his own blood. His ancestry cannot be traced. His mother would have preferred him to be a doctor or a lawyer. She is timid and conventional and has been much put upon by false images of an alien tribe.

(But perhaps not quite put upon *enough*. Nathan had turned to her one evening – turned *on* her, that's how she put it – and asked her why on earth she had called him Nathan. I mean, what kind of a name is Nathan, for Godsake, he had demanded. I'll tell you what kind of name it is, Ma. It's a *Jewish* name.)

Miriam Herz would have liked her son Nathan to be more like Daniel Palmer. Daniel is a successful barrister, as you might have guessed. He could have been a civil servant, for his manner is mandarin, but he chose the law.

If choice is what he had, if choosing is what we do. Amazing, really, thinks Nathan on the midnight lawn, how we cling to the concept of choice. It is quite clear to Nathan that Daniel is temperamentally disqualified from playing the Veil of Ignorance, because he is quite incapable of imagining a world in which he would not possess a superior and commanding intellect. Daniel knows that in any society he will rise towards the top, so why bother to play with the construction of a society in which there is no top? It is different for David D'Anger, for David, like Nathan himself, is an outsider. An ambitious outsider, living by his wits. His handicap, his blind spot, thinks Nathan, is that he cannot conceive of a society which does not have ambition as its driving force.

Whereas I, thinks Nathan, staring at the nameless stars, I have given up all hope. Good brains I had and a good education, and what did I do with them? I tried to make a bit of money. I married Rosemary Palmer. I had two children. I had affairs with other women. Not much to show for a life. And I'm the only one of us, it seems, who would jack it all in. To float free of all this, to begin again. So heavy we become, and so entrenched. Our feet are stuck in the clay. We are up to the knees, no, up to the waist, in the mud of the past. We have lived more than half our lives. There is no future. There are no choices left. It has all silted up around us. We are stuck in our own graves.

And that mad old woman up on Exmoor, she is preparing for her own funeral. By all accounts she has left one mausoleum for another, and even now is stitching her own shroud. She is determined to make trouble to the end. One cannot but admire.

Nathan is fascinated by the Palmer family and its history. He is fascinated by Frieda Haxby Palmer.

David D'Anger is right, considers Nathan, to tease the Palmers about their complacency, about their confidence that they will always end up on the right side of any shift or redistribution of power. Yet that complacency comes from a source more mysterious than might at first appear. Seen from afar, the Palmers – Daniel, Gogo and Rosemary – might seem to carry the assumptions of the British middle classes, carried on from generation to generation. But they come from nowhere. They have turned themselves into members of the English middle class by sleight of hand. Their manner, their voice, their pretensions – they appear to date back for centuries, but, as Nathan knows quite well, they date back no further than Frieda Haxby Palmer and her missing husband, whoever he may have been. Nouveaux, that is what they are. But totally convincing. It is a mystery to Nathan. How have they managed it? David D'Anger's family is distinguished, and Patsy's is rich: David is of the expatriate intellectual Indian revolutionary aristocracy of Guyana, and Patsy is of comfortable Quaker stock. The Palmers are nobody, they have come from nowhere, but they look as though they have seized the reins of power. They look as though they have been born to this house, this garden, this tennis court. The D'Angers and the Herzes can never be British. They have the wrong genes, the wrong skin, the wrong noses.

The Palmers spring from Frieda Haxby Palmer, the self-elected witch of Exmoor, the daughter of the Fens. A genetic freak of talent, intelligence or mother-wit had elevated her, and her children had slipped quietly up the ladder after her. Now she has gone mad, spun off into space, but they smile still from their perches like smug saints mounting a cathedral coping. As though they had always expected to be there, as though nothing short of revolution could dislodge them. And, as David D'Anger's game had illustrated, that revolution will never come, or not in this millennium. What we have, we hold.

Nathan knows he will have to go in and face yet another late-night discussion about Frieda. Loitering in the poisoned garden will not let him off. Nor does he wish to be spared. He is fond of Frieda, in his way, and like all the rest of them he finds her of obsessive interest. He will return to the kitchen, in the hope that the washing-up is over and the coffee and the brandy on the tray. He takes a final inhalation, as he makes his way back towards the house – he breathes the stink of the bitter cress, the Mermaid rose.

In the kitchen, we find Patsy, covering cheese with cling-film. The kettle boils on the Aga, and there will be a choice of real coffee, unreal coffee, tea, herb tea. This, as Nathan likes to reflect, is the age of choice. Patsy is tired, and she has a busy day on Sunday – she has decided, masochistically she supposes, that she must attend the Quaker meeting, and then she has to rush back and provide lunch, not only for her house guests but also for a neighbour or two. Why does she do it? God knows. She is tired, and Daniel too looks tired. She thinks he may drop dead of a heart attack. He works too hard. They both work too hard.

The washing machine already purrs quietly, but David D'Anger is drying the crystal glasses, which must be done by hand, and wondering where Nathan has got to. Nathan always disappears when there is any housework to be done. Nathan is an old-fashioned bastard, thinks David, whereas David considers himself to be the New Man. There David stands, tea-towel in hand, the New Millennial Black British Man. He has, of course, another label – indeed, he has several others. He is an academic. He is a politician. He is a journalist. He appears on television. He is a parliamentary candidate for a marginal constituency in West Yorkshire, which he fully expects to win. He is the future. But he has astutely allied himself to the clan of the Palmers, which gives him added credibility. He is the coming man, and they will back him.

You will never guess what Gogo does, when she is not being sister, wife, daughter, mother. I had better tell you. There she is, offering the carving dish for the dog to lick clean before she hands it to David at the sink. The dog licks and wags her tail gratefully. Gogo almost smiles at the dog and says, 'Good girl', in a superior but approving tone. She uses this tone to man, woman, child and beast. Gogo is a consultant neurologist at a hospital in Bloomsbury. That disapproving look comes from examining the slices of other people's brains. She frightens her patients and her colleagues. She is an excellent wife for an aspiring politician. Had David D'Anger constructed her from a range of spare sample parts, he could never have come up with anything as convincing as this. She surpasses imagination. Nobody could have invented Gogo. Not even Nathan could have designed a Wife Image as plausible, as venerable, as alarming as Gogo. And she is only forty-two.

Compared with Gogo, young Rosemary, who is forty, is a light-weight, though of course nobody dares to say so, for she takes herself very seriously, and after all she is a Palmer and English and a good deal more respectable in appearance and behaviour than her husband. You were warm when you thought she might be something to do with the media – she is the right generation to choose such a career, and unlike the others she looks as though she may have some sense of what is going on in the ephemeral world of fashion. She probably knows the names of designer clothes, and could tell you which restaurants are in vogue. She knows the language of the day. So you will not be surprised to hear that she is the Programme Co-ordinator for one of the largest arts complexes in the country. She is in charge of a large budget. Theatre, music, art and dance all bow and beg to her.

So there you have them. The dishwasher churns on into a noisier mode, and Patsy puts the kettle upon the tray. Yes, there you have them – Daniel and Patsy Palmer, David and Gogo D'Anger, Nathan and Rosemary Herz – for Nathan has sneaked back in again, his fag ends in his pocket. (He extricates them and drops them, discreetly, into the wastebin – the wrong wastebin, for it is the one Patsy reserves for compost, but how is he to know?) The middle classes of England. Is there any hope whatsoever, or any fear, that anything will change? Would any of them wish for change? Given a choice between any-thing more serious than decaffeinated coffee or herbal tea, would they dare to choose? As Nathan had considered as he walked the lawn, they are all of them already, irrevocably, halfway up to their necks in the mud of the past of their own lives. Not even a mechanical digger could get them out alive now. There are no choices. The original position has been for ever lost.

We have forgotten about Simon and Emily. Where have they gone? They have taken themselves off to the small sitting-room where they are watching a horrible video, one of Patsy's specials. They find it entertaining, but not quite entertaining enough. They yawn. They had talked of having a play with Emily's new computer game, Simcity, but although Emily is game to redesign her last fantasy conurbation, Simon seems to have lost interest. He never wants to concentrate on anything for long. He lacks perseverance.

Simon is at Oxford, at one of the wealthier colleges, reading His-tory, or so his family believe. Emily is still at school, in the sixth form, sitting her A-Levels, and after them, whatever her results, she will take a year off, and her first solitary trip abroad. Simon and Emily are only ankle-deep in their lives as yet. Perhaps not even that. But the mud pulls and sucks.

The dog is called Jemima. She is an elderly, overweight Dalmatian. I don't suppose you need to know that. I don't suppose the Palmers need a dog. But they've got one.

A family weekend in Hampshire. Tennis has been played. They all play, except for Nathan. And, despite all, at this late day, they still play to win.

> *Timon hath made his everlasting mansion*
> *Upon the beachèd verge of the salt flood . . .*

A faint blue line lies on the horizon. Frieda Haxby Palmer stares as it fades. The days are long. The light glimmers on the water. The moon is on the wane. And so is she. She has had her supper of tuna and brine. She lights another cigarette, coughs, refills her glass, and stares westwards. Is that a boat, far across the channel? She reaches for her binoculars. This is the smugglers' coast.

TIMON'S FEAST

Meals less delicious than chicken with rosemary, meals even less delicious than tuna in brine with stale Ryvita, have been consumed on this summer evening in Britain. Up and down the country pre-packed foods, take-away foods, junk foods, fattening foods, slimming foods, ill-cooked foods have been devoured, messed with, rejected, spewed on to pavements and trampled into gutters. Does anybody actually *starve*? Is it necessary for anyone to dig around in wastebins amongst the fag ends? And if not, WHY DO THEY DO IT? Nobody really knows. Opinions range, but nobody really knows. Relative poverty, absolute poverty – these are shifting concepts, as are the conditions hidden behind phrases like 'free range' and 'farm fresh' and 'corn fed' and 'free roaming' and 'fresh barn'. Does anybody really know anything? If we pulled away the veil, what *would* we see?

In her prime Frieda Haxby Palmer had been good – uncomfortably good, but nevertheless good – at the lifting of the veil. She had been a professional asker of unpleasant questions. She had been admired and indeed honoured for this. But now she has gone mad. This is the opinion of her three children.

In middle age, many women go mad. They are expected to. Frieda had survived her fifties triumphantly, only to crack up in her sixties. Is it a delayed menopause, Rosemary has wondered? Had Frieda been an early convert to Hormone Replacement Therapy, and is she now suffering from withdrawal symptoms?

Over their decaffeinated coffee and herb tea, the Palmers, the Herzes and the D'Angers revert once more, repetitively, obsessively, to the subject of Frieda's madness. They had seen it coming, they now claim, for some time, though none of them disputes that her last invitation to Romley had marked a new stage. That evening had been the end.

But there had been a long trail of premonitions, which they now recall, discuss, recall. We must go back with them into the recent past, before we accept her final invitation and set off with her three children to the Mausoleum in Romley for the last supper.

About two years ago Frieda, who had never smoked, or at least not to their knowledge, took up cigarettes. She was seen puffing away, and seen not only by them. She appeared, cigarette in hand, in public, on platforms, in photographs.

This was not good. It was not fashionable. But when Daniel mildly raised the point, she declared that she had smoked a good deal as a girl, had given it up for years, and had now decided she would take to it again. She enjoyed it. It was no business of theirs, she implied. Who knows, maybe she was also snorting cocaine? They worried now that she would burn herself to death in bed, like Barbara Hepworth. Set that hotel on fire and blaze like a beacon, blaze across the water like Baldur on his death ship.

She took up smoking, and she also took up the opera. In her earlier life she had shown little interest in music, but in her last year in London she was to be seen at the Royal Opera House, at the Coliseum, sometimes alone, sometimes with a motley and expensive entourage. Late in the day, late in the century, she discovered Wagner; she even wrote a letter in defence of Wagner which was published in a newspaper. Her children, who knew that she knew nothing about Wagner, read it with suspicion. She might fool the editor of the Letters Page and a few thousand ignorant readers, but she did not fool them. They hoped she would not take up writing daily letters to the papers, though it was, they conceded, a cheaper pastime than smoking and the opera, and considerably cheaper than gambling, in which she also began to express an interest.

Then there was the business with the car. Stuck in a traffic jam for twenty minutes one day in the West End (in Dover Street, to be precise, on her way to collect a painting from a gallery, for another of her new eccentricities had been the rash purchasing of art works), she had suddenly switched off her engine, got out and left the car there, in the solid, motionless traffic. Oddly, nobody had watched her leave.

People do not notice middle-aged or elderly women. It was only when the traffic flow finally eased that her empty silver Saab was spotted there, driverless, abandoned, a ghost car. It created chaos. She had gone on to the gallery, picked up the painting and gone home in a taxi all the way to Romley. When questioned, she said she never wanted to see the car again. Finders keepers, she had offered. But it had come home to her like a pigeon, like a grey gull, and now it roosted whether she wanted it or not, nesting grimly at the sea's edge – or so Rosemary claimed.

But the most alarming manifestation of madness had been her VAT challenge. This had frightened them more than any of her other oddities, for the financial consequences had seemed incalculable. She had taken on the mighty indifference of Her Majesty's Customs and Excise in a court of law. It was an unprecedented action. She had asserted that the VAT inspector's report on her bookkeeping had been ignorant and incompetent, she disputed this forward and pert young woman's assessment of the VAT and VAT status of her Swedish booty, and she refused to charge VAT on certain expenses incurred outside the UK. She insisted that Her Majesty owed her interest, now, not next year, on a year's overpayment. Her accountants had not liked this procedure at all, and had tried to dissuade her: unwise to venture into such grey areas, she was advised. But Frieda, who had taken against the inspector with a vengeance, was determined. She said she was prepared to spend her entire capital and go to gaol for this *cause célèbre*. Let the light shine in the grey areas, she had insisted. Her regular lawyers had refused to act for her, but she had found other lawyers quite willing to take her money: the name of their firm was Goltho & Goltho. The enterprise had proved expensive but not ruinous. She had confronted the experts, and had stood her ground as they shook their heads and wagged their fingers and sneered and talked gobbletalk at her. The original inspector, produced as witness, had been unwisely condescending; neatly suited, smartly lipsticked, with bouncy bobbed hair and an air of implacable self-righteousness, she had tried to make the old lion look a fool. Little smiles, becks, innuendoes. But Frieda had refused to budge. She had got her case up well,

27

and she had argued it well. Little Miss Cockburn Cocksure had been confused and wrongfooted. Miss Cockburn could hardly believe that this was the same shabby old creature she had been to see in Romley. Why had nobody warned her? But, as Frieda argued, Miss Cocksure's ignorance was no excuse. She was not paid to be ignorant.

The case ended in a stand-off. Both sides claimed victory, but the moral victory was Frieda's. A good deal of unpleasant publicity had been generated, and the public was on Frieda's side. She had presented herself as the Little Woman, fighting for justice against the bureaucrat, and indeed for the duration of the hearing had managed to see herself in that light: she had not managed to convince her children of her harmlessness and frailty, and the tribunal had its suspicions too, but even her son Daniel had to concede that she'd had a case and made the best of it. 'I don't like being pushed around, at my age,' had been her explanation for her conduct. 'I don't like pert little nobodies coming into my house and drinking my coffee and talking to me as if I'm a halfwit. Do you know what that woman called me? Frieda! She addressed me as Frieda. On a first meeting. Without a by-your-leave. I wasn't going to let her get away with that, was I?' It was almost enough to make you feel sorry for Miss Cocksure, with her round eyes and her prim pink cheeks and her double-breasted navy-and-white striped jacket and her brass buttons and her silly frilly white jabot.

When the case was over the family heaved a sigh of relief, and wondered what she would take up next. Bee-keeping, bicycling, or yet more litigation? Was she intent on squandering her money? What, they wondered, of their rightful inheritance? They were all doing nicely at the moment, but these days, with pensions so unreliable, the working life so short, the afterlife so long, the private care so expensive, the health service demolished – who could tell what costly interminable terminal care she or they or their grandchildren's grandchildren might need? Had she the *right* to go mad?

Possibly, speculated Gogo, Frieda's mind had been affected by her mother's death. Gladys Haxby, stout and static, had died five years ago – died where she had lived, at a good old age, in the little cottage in

Chapel Street in Dry Bendish where Frieda had been born. There had been no love lost between Gladys and Frieda, and not much pretence of a warmth between Gladys and her three grandchildren. But Frieda had visited regularly, curiously and improbably dutiful, until the end, driving up and down the dual-carriageway, at least once every three months when she was in England. Why did she go? Because she was the only child. (There had been another daughter, but she had died long ago; and Frieda's father had died, of a stroke, in his fifties.) Maybe, suggested Gogo, over dinner in Islington, on the phone to her siblings, at table in Hampshire – maybe Gladys's death had tipped some balance in Frieda? Frieda had been a grim worker all her life, and she had been held in grim combat by Gladys. In Gladys's presence, Frieda was oddly subdued, reverting to a morbid attentive unwilling servitude that suggested what she had been like as a sulky, determined, ambitious child. Gladys Haxby had been a schoolmistress, and in her demanding and irksome company Frieda became once more a pupil, a listener, although she had nothing to learn and Gladys had nothing to say. Frieda, herself no mean talker, fell silent in her mother's presence, as Gladys talked and talked and talked, of nothing. Of herself, of nothing. An unchanging subjugation.

Then Gladys died, and Frieda was set free. This was Gogo's theory. It was the headiness of freedom in her sixties, the late liberation from the guilt of the tedious and armchair-bound old bloodsucker, that had sent her spinning off into space and seventeenth-century Sweden. It must have been on Gladys's death that Frieda had started her last disastrous literary enterprise. None of them had known what she was plotting, for she never talked about her work in advance; ever a solitary worker, she had hidden her typewriter from prying children's eyes, and in later years, when there were none to pry, she had become secretive – and, if questioned, obscure and misleading. She had, before publication, conceded that she had departed from her usual arena to write a historical novel – but that statement, surprising enough in itself, had prepared nobody for the vast, incoherent over-researched baroque monstrosity of her *Queen Christina*. Her children had found it almost embarrassingly unreadable (although Gogo declared it had some good passages), and the reviews had been appalled and appalling. How could Frieda Haxby, social analyst, prophet, sage and sybil, and author of that perennial and influential classic *The Matriarchy of War* – how could Frieda Haxby have written such tosh?

The critics were delighted, and outdid one another in insults. 'Once seen as Britain's answer to Simone de Beauvoir, Frieda Haxby has revealed herself as the heir to Barbara Cartland,' declared one of the Sundays. 'Long a symbol of the austere and high-minded rigidity of the postwar left, Miss Haxby's latest effort throws into doubt all that preceded it,' somewhat ungrammatically declared one of the organs of the New Right, under the heading THE EMPRESS'S NEW CLOTHES. 'Senile ramblings,' posited an old-fashioned new literary review. The kindest comment suggested that Frieda, like George Eliot in *Romola*, had been bogged down by too much historical detail, and hoped (a little wanly, as though the last book the reviewer ever wanted to see arrive in a Jiffy bag was another work by Haxby) that she would soon return to her 'spare, challenging and relevant interpretations of social organizations'.

Frieda seemed undisturbed by this, but how could one tell what she really felt? Patiently, she pointed out that although she had indeed had a long and interesting correspondence with de Beauvoir, she had never been a member of any political party, and had kept her distance from both left and right. She said that she entirely agreed with one critic who called *The Matriarchy of War* an overrated and outdated thesis which did not deserve its reputation – she'd been in her twenties when she'd written it, and subsequent research into the topic of female employment during the World Wars had contradicted or at least qualified many of her earlier findings. It was a book for its time, and it wasn't her fault if people in later decades used it for their own purposes. And as for *Queen Christina* – well, she'd enjoyed writing it, and where was the harm in that? She could write about what she liked. Thus, reasonably, she replied to her interviewers. Her appearance of calm and unruffled detachment did nothing to pacify them. She seemed quite unaware of the nature of the atrocity she was alleged to have committed. She had betrayed nobody. If others had false expectations, if others had waited for answers that she could not or would not give — that was their problem, not hers. They had been misreading her all along.

At other moments, in other contexts, she appeared less reasonable. She suddenly threatened to sue a journalist who had described her as an ageing Peacenik and supporter of the Women of Greenham Common: hadn't he bothered to check that inside and outside the Labour Party she'd made herself very unpopular right through the fifties and sixties by supporting the nuclear deterrent and opposing unilateral disarmament? He'd clearly got no further than the title of her first publication, which, far from proposing disarmament, had described the ways in which women had at least temporarily profited from the wartime economy, and which had regretted the way they'd let themselves be shoved back into peacetime underemployment. The journalist had apologized, in print, for his error, acknowledging that he had confused her track-record as warmonger with that of some of her eminent and more peace-loving contemporaries. She had dropped her threat: the swine wasn't worth contradicting, she decided. Or so she told David, who told Gogo, who told Daniel and Rosemary.

It was Patsy who heard the oddest commentary of all. Driving home late one night from London to Hampshire, about a fortnight after the publication of *Queen Christina*, Patsy had heard Frieda on the radio declaring to some spaced-out disc jockey that the idea of writing the novel had come to her 'as I stood staring at the stone cross with runes near my ancestral home in Dry Bendish in Lincolnshire'. At that moment, as she laid her hand on the ancient monument, she told the young man, she had known that she was linked by blood to Queen Christina of Sweden — scholar, patron of the arts, lesbian, atheist, accomplice of assassins. 'You mean a kind of reincarnation, kind of?' the disc jockey had asked: and to Patsy's surprise Frieda, instead of snapping his head off, had mildly agreed. 'Yes, well, I suppose, kind of,' she had said. And had gone on to talk about the Vikings, and about her earlier research into the eighteenth-century iron trade of Sweden, and her voyage round the Swedish coast in the wake of Mary

Wollstonecraft, and the honour done to her by the Swedish crown for her recovery of a little-known tract of Swedish history. The disc jockey hadn't been so interested in all this, Patsy could tell, but he'd let the old thing ramble. Mad indeed. Patsy had hesitated to tell Daniel and the other Palmers of this damning piece of evidence, but had been unable to resist. Queen Christina, crazy herself, had driven Frieda Haxby crazy.

It was some three months after the publication of this ill-starred work that Frieda had summoned her family to the Grim Feast in Romley. During these three months Frieda had been attacked by historians of the right and the left, by feminists, lesbians, gossip column-ists and cartoonists, by Catholics, Protestants and humanists. *Christina* had managed to annoy just about everybody. Nobody seemed to have read it (for it *was* very long) but everybody knew it was no good, and that it had ruined Frieda Haxby's reputation as a social historian.

So Daniel and Patsy, Gogo and David, Rosemary and Nathan were not expecting a very happy evening when they were summoned to the Mausoleum, to the house that had been the childhood home of the three Palmers.

Let us return, with them, from Hampshire to Romley. A year and a half has passed since the gathering, though it has not faded from their minds.

There the old house still stood, shabby, stranded, archaic, fronting a stretch of municipal suburban greenery that had once been their play-ground, and which was now strewn with litter – plastic bags, sweet and crisp packets, beer cans, cola cans, and, no doubt, if one looked more closely, condoms and syringes. The tragedy of the commons. When they were small, Romley, though deeply dreary and unfashionable, had not been dangerous; but a wash of grief and misery had swept eastwards to it from Hackney and Leytonstone, as its more successful and forceful residents had pushed their way westwards against the tide to Stoke Newington and Highbury and Finsbury Park. Now Frieda's house stood like a beached, bow-fronted galleon fronting the trodden sour and muddy green. On either side houses had been demolished or converted into flatlets or maisonettes, first by the council, and now, since council spending had been suspended, by housing associations. Frieda's house alone stood as it had in the late 1940s when she and their father had bought it. It was a large, wide, late-Victorian, red brick house, four storeyed, with an air of some pretension: the slightly raised ground floor swelled into a curved and monumental frontage far grander than a suburban bay, with a hint of funerary or temple architecture that had prompted the building's pet name – an affectionate name, in its own way, a name bestowed in order to placate the Furies. The Mausoleum, with Frieda as priestess. The three of them did not know if they hated it or not. It was their place. Here they had huddled, and here they had, after their fashion, survived.

What were her plans for it now? Plans she had, they were certain, or they would not have been convened. It was not Christmas. And she had given up celebrating Christmas more than ten years ago. Last year she had flown off to Jamaica. Or so she had said. (Some said she had been seen over the New Year at the tables in Monte Carlo.)

Daniel and Patsy had met Rosemary and Nathan outside, on the pavement: Daniel had spotted Nathan parking his flash red sports car from afar, and had waited, to make a joint entry. They could see Gogo and David were there already, for there was David's sober Honda, by the cracking kerb. They greeted one another in the soft autumn light. Patsy was carrying a bunch of tightly budded lilies, their pods still green and unripe though faintly streaked with emergent orange: they wore a red triangular laminated label which, in anticipation of litigation, declared that their pollen could stain clothing. Rosemary clutched a bottle of champagne. Who knows, she said, as she pecked Patsy on the cheek, there may be something to celebrate? Who knows? And they had all paused on the pavement, looking up at the brooding building, where Frieda had incarcerated herself, and worked and worked and worked, night after night, for bread and butter and glory and the enlightenment of mankind. 'You're right,' muttered Daniel to Nathan, as they ascended the short flight of badly cemented uneven, peeling steps to the front door, and congregated round the Victorian coalhole. 'You're right. There's a plan for an extension to the motorway. Do you think she'll turn stubborn and refuse to budge?'

Nathan shrugged. With the new mad random Frieda, who could tell? She might decide to chain herself to a tree in protest, or she might offer to wield the axe herself.

Gogo answered the doorbell, with a look of warning on her face. They could hear Frieda and David deep in conversation, but there was also a third voice – whose could it be?

'It's that Cedric chap,' whispered Gogo discouragingly. 'God knows why he's here. He certainly doesn't, I can tell you.'

'Cedric who?'

'That politician chappie,' muttered Gogo, her back to the antlered hat-stand, where Nathan hung his umbrella. 'You know, the one before last.'

A pageant of rejected lovers and admirers stretched back through their communal memory, in file, wringing their hands, grinning, sneering, flattering, soothing, blinking, each after his fashion. Portly ghosts, cadaverous suitors. Some had come in the old days with sweets for the children, some had tried to make themselves agreeable. Cedric had been too late in line to bother them, except as an embarrassment. For it is not pleasant to learn that one's mother is having a fling with a government minister, and a grotesque minister, of the wrong party, and of quite the wrong shape.

As we enter the room the contrast between David D'Anger and Cedric Summerson strikes forcibly. Both sit, politely alert, legs uncrossed, leaning slightly forward, on the edges of their broken-down easy-chairs (who knows what may lurk in their recesses, were one to relax and sit back?), both hold glasses of what looks like still water in their hands – Evian, no doubt, or Malvern. An abstemious couple, though Cedric Summerson's complexion does not boast of prolonged restraint. Both are suited and wear pale ties, but there the resemblance ends. Cedric Summerson is not exactly fat, but he is heavy – stout, jowled, red-faced, ponderous. The colour and texture of his skin are unattractive. It is mottled, pitted, veined, at once shiny and coarse. Good living has sent him off like an old ripe cheese. Runnels of decay thread his features. He is turning bad before one's eyes. How can Frieda ever have fancied this monster? Did she, ever, or was it all a rumour? And if it was a rumour, why is he here?

Whereas David D'Anger is beautiful. His skin is dark and clear and smooth, his features are regular, and his eyes glow with an ideal and gentle light. Sweet reason and intelligence shine in his fine brow. His hair curls bravely, whereas Cedric's is thin and slicked vainly back like a Chicago bootlegger's.

Frieda Haxby holds court. She may or may not think she is Queen Christina, but she certainly thinks she is Queen of the Mausoleum. She sits less formally than her two guests, her legs crossed beneath some kind of longish grey garment embroidered with black, which hides her now shapeless body. Her hair is concealed, like Gogo's, by a scarf, and in honour of the occasion she wears her Baltic amber ceremonial cross. She too appears to be drinking water, which is not like her. She greets her family without rising. Cedric leaps obediently to his feet. Hands are shaken. Rosemary, with diminishing confidence, hands over her bottle of warming champagne. Frieda puts it on the table in front of her, and says, 'Not for me, thank you. There's some water in the jug.'

And that is that. Nobody dares to open the champagne, and there is no other drink in sight, apart from a large stoneware quart jug of what seems to be tap water. They serve themselves and sip its thin fluoride kidney-filtered brew.

Has Frieda become a teetotaller? Has she become religious? They settle themselves, nervously, uncertainly, and wait for something to happen.

They wait for a long, long time. It is a deep game. Frieda lights a menthol cigarette and offers one to Nathan. Nathan refuses her offer, lights one of his own, and the others, non-smokers, gaze in greedy envy as they inhale deeply.

It is not possible to query the situation. It has already gone beyond questioning. Frieda, as usual, leads the conversation. She addresses the subject of vegetarianism. She inquires of Cedric the statistics of the conversion of the young to this modish though hardly new lifestyle,

35

and asks him whether he believes red meat is bad for the body and what the evidence is that it may be. Cedric is no longer in agriculture – he is, some think and David knows, something to do with transport now – but he is expected nevertheless by Frieda to be an authority on such matters, and he struggles, in the hostile circumstances, bravely. What can he be expecting? A primitive and summary execution by the tribe for having once dared to tamper with their mother? He speaks of new dietary advice from the Ministry of Health, of the safety of freezing and radiation processes, of the importance of balance in the diet. He speaks of BSE and CJD. What is this? A seminar? A television cross-examination? At what bar does he now stand and where, oh where is his drink?

David D'Anger, as so often, comes off best. Frieda pets him. David drinks very irregularly, and never in public life, so the evening is no hardship to him. He is also, by and large, a vegetarian, and he rescues the sagging conversation by speaking lightly and dismissively of his own reasons for this choice – it is not through religion, he emphasizes, for his family are in origin a quarter Muslim, a quarter Hindu, and half Catholic, 'which would allow me to eat just about anything sometimes'. (He smiles.) But he does not like meat. And a side benefit of this – a political side benefit – is that he offends no one. As he has no principles, he can eat or pretend to eat a little meat if social circumstances demand it. Equally he can decline. 'Nobody is offended by a vegetable,' he says – though even as the words leave his lips an image of that offensive Koran-inscribed aubergine which had caused such a scandal a few years back flashes across his mind. He zaps it, censors it, blots it out, and is relieved to see that he has not transmitted it to any of the other guests.

Frieda is full of praise for his diet. 'You see how well David looks on it,' she says. 'See, how well he looks.'

It is embarrassing, but they are all forced to admire David, as though he were a slave or (in his case more probably) an indentured labourer upon a sugar plantation in the days of long ago.

Sugar too David does not much take, and in this choice he admits to political motives. As nobody seems to be prepared to introduce any fresh theme, David is obliged to continue with a set speech upon sugar. The taste for sugar, he argues, has ruined not only our teeth but also our intellect and our culture. (David himself has dental problems and has been forced to spend a great deal of money on his teeth.) Sugar is bad for the brain. Sugar is imperialism and colonialism. Its history is appalling, and its present is sinister. Of course as a Guyanese-born intellectual he is bound to be worried by the history of sugar. He admires the French for standing out against sugar and Hollywood. He admires the Swadeshi movement in India which rejects Coca-Cola and Kentucky Fried Chicken. He and Gogo are strict about sugar in the home. His son, Benjamin, does not eat sweets or drink canned drinks. Benjie is not allowed baked beans. It's difficult for Benjie to resist peer-group pressure, just as it is difficult for the French and Indians to resist the subtle, the insidious, the pervasive sweetening and Americanization of foods. But the French resist, the Indians resist, and Benjie resists. David says he is proud of Benjie. Benjie may eat the odd Mars Bar on the tube on the way back from school, but he's staunch enough most of the time. He doesn't even *like* Coca-Cola.

Frieda listens with what seems to be approval. Benjamin D'Anger is her favourite grandchild and she makes little attempt to conceal her preference. Moreover, food production has become one of her latest hobby-horses, and she has been responsible for encouraging David D'Anger to interest himself in the subject. Nevertheless, she does not now help David out in his self-appointed social task of entertaining the gathering. David begins to speak in a more and more unnatural tone, as though participating against the clock in some radio quiz competition that awards prizes for unbrokenly boring and undeviating monologues. Son Benjamin exhausted as a sub-topic, David veers off towards the import of expensive inferior American sugar drinks into Guyana. Why import at all when the local fruit drinks are of such high quality? He knows Frieda has heard of the possibility of a legal case over the inaccurate use of the term 'Demerara' as a trade name. It could hardly succeed in the courts, but it might be of use in helping to raise a more combative national consciousness. (Cedric Summerson looks appalled by the thought of a combative national consciousness, even in Guyana, an unimportant and impoverished ex-colony on the other side of the world. To be honest, he is not quite sure where Guyana is – is it in Africa? No, from what Frieda's suspiciously plausible son-in-law seems to be saying, it must be in the Caribbean. Not an island, clearly. Next to Venezuela, perhaps?)

David describes the Demerara case, which has some similarity to Maori land right cases in New Zealand, to Aboriginal protests in Australia. An ancient treaty has been exhumed, a treaty between plantation owners and some sort of local co-operative of indentured labourers, which seems to give a special legal status to the term 'Demerara' and to all products associated with the word. Can this legal status be revived? Daniel Palmer almost forgets his discomfort as he engages his legal brain with this bizarre piece of subtropical antiquarian pedantry, as he searches in the recesses of his memory for the date (1460?) of the treaty which the Germans used to justify their nineteenth-century claim to Schleswig-Holstein. Nathan Herz is equally intrigued by parallels with the successful twentieth-century actions of champagne in fighting off apples, elderflowers and other invaders. As they show interest, David begins to shy off, for he realizes that Cedric Summerson is at last beginning to pay attention, and will certainly not be a friendly witness. Better to keep the cards of Demerara close to his chest.

It is left to Frieda to take up the tale. She points out that most of the sugar now consumed in such dangerous quantities in the United Kingdom comes from her own homelands, not from David D'Anger's. The sugar beets of Peterborough and Bury St Edmunds have long since taken over from the sugar canes of Guyana and the West Indies.

'My father', says Frieda Haxby Palmer, addressing David D'Anger with a dangerous glint, 'used to plough the beet fields, while yours was at Harvard. We're New Sugar, your family is Old Sugar, David. Not that much money came down to us from it, or not that *we* ever saw. Who owns British Sugar plc these days, Cedric? I'm sure you would know, wouldn't you?'

Cedric Summerson, who does know, and suspects that she also

knows, decides to pretend he has not heard the question. (British Sugar, you may wish to learn, became the British Sugar Corporation in 1936, when Frieda's father, Ernie Haxby, was a young man: it became British Sugar plc in 1982, was then taken over by Beresford International, and in 1991 was swallowed up by Associated British Foods plc, a thriving conglomerate which also owns Allied Bakeries, Burton's Biscuits, Twinings Tea, Ryvita and Jacksons of Piccadilly. Nathan Herz knows he ought to know this, but he has become confused with the brand names of Tate & Lyle – who are they? Are they a competitor? And aren't they British too?)

Getting no answer from either Cedric or Nathan, Frieda continues. 'It would be hard to say, David, wouldn't it, which of our forebears might have expected to do better? If you'd been veiled by ignorance, which society would *you* have chosen to be born into? Eighteenth-century England or eighteenth-century Guyana? How would *you* have calculated the odds?'

(Only Gogo picks up the significance of this question, for only goodwife Gogo, at this point, is familiar with its philosophic terminology, with the concept of the Veil. Daniel and Rosemary are later to remember it all too well.)

David smiles, demurs, indicates that the conversation is becoming esoteric, is excluding Frieda's other guests. Clearly they have been over this ground before.

'The D'Angers', pursues Frieda, 'once owned plantations. They worked their way up. They owned a valley full of eagles and they exported Demerara. Isn't that right, David?'

'That's how the story went when I was a boy,' says David.

'Sugar and rum and coffee,' teases Frieda. 'Thousands and thousands of pounds of the stuff. While we lived on whalegut and turnip.'

Her audience grows restless. All this talk of food does not make them hungry, but it does make them nervous. What is she playing at? Is it a game? They cannot have been asked round simply for a discussion. Surely there will be dinner? They have been asked for a meal, but there is little sign of one, though there is perhaps a faint smell of cooking somewhere in the recesses of the house, a stale and not wholly appetizing odour of, is it, onion? Or is onion wafting in from some passing teenager's polystyrene walk-about pack? They cannot have been asked round for a drink, for water is not a drink. Nor could anyone in her right mind ask even her own family to come all the way to the Romley borders just for a drink. *Is* she, they wonder, in her right mind?

She seems to be, for when she judges that they have suffered enough, she makes a move. 'I'd better go and see to the cooking,' she says, disclaiming any help as she heaves herself stoutly to her sandalled feet. 'No, don't come yet. I'll call you when I'm ready. I've got something really special for you. I've had to go a long way to get this meal together, I can tell you.' She smiles at David, with a horrible favour. 'And don't worry, David, I have remembered that you don't eat meat.'

Daniel later claims that it was at this moment that it flashed across his mind that she had some trick in store — cow heels, pigs' trotters, stewed baby — something of the sort. But he did not voice it at the time. Instead they all sat in paralysed discomfort, unable to speak in her absence because of Cedric Summerson's presence. Nathan puffed at his eighth cigarette. What a comfort was nicotine, what a blessing was smoke. David, gallant, game, polite, the glass of fashion and the mould of form, attempted to engage Patsy in a diversionary chat about the video censorship board on which she sat, but Patsy's response was muted. Yes, she limply agreed, the new technology was a worry, but she still thought people greatly over exaggerated the dangers of . . . and her voice almost died away, for she could not be bothered to work out what the dangers of what were . . .

In that large bow-fronted room overlooking the green, they had spent so many evenings: doing their homework, watching television, squabbling, talking, crying, complaining. It had been the family room. Since their departure into their own lives, Frieda had filled it with more and more books, more and more papers. Tables full of papers were dotted about, box files were heaped in corners. Frieda had spewed her work all over the house. Once there had been lodgers upstairs, but now every room in the house was full of Frieda's junk.

She lived alone amongst the unfiled documentation of her past. The room had not been decorated in decades, yet in it now nestled uneasily some signs of late-twentieth-century post-industrial life – a fax machine perched on a pile of old copies of the *Economist*, a photocopier in a dirty white shroud, a cordless telephone crowning a boxed set of the shorter *OED*. Somewhere upstairs she was alleged to have a computer, but nobody had actually seen it.

In the old days, there had been a sewing basket of something called 'Mending' under the window-seat. Frieda had never done much mending, but it had been there – a historical relic, a tribute to her rustic Lincolnshire past. Now, in its place, was a wastepaper basket full of what looked like old tights.

They sat, oppressed, and waited meekly for her command. And at last she called them and released them from the terrible game of statues she had forced them to play. She ushered them through to the dining-room, where the faint wafting of unpleasant cooking smells slightly intensified. The table, however, took them by surprise. The old scarred gate-leg familiar of their youth had been covered, exceptionally, with a cloth – a slightly rust-stained beige linen cloth, embroidered with baskets and garlands of flowers done in not very elegant chain stitch – a Lincolnshire heirloom, no doubt, from Grandma's collection. And at each place setting was a whole battery of cutlery, from the old green baize-lined box – Haxby plate, Palmer plate, none of them knew, and they had never seen it in use. There was a wine glass at each place, and matching side plates from the set which had come out for special occasions, and a dinner plate – each dinner plate covered with a silver cover. Well, not silver, perhaps, on closer glance – they had, perhaps, been bought from a hospital or school dinner charity sale – but, with the overall attempt at formality, they gave well enough the impression of those fancy silver-service bell-jars which pretentious restaurants and clubs favoured in the 1980s. A bottle of wine stood in the centre of the table.

'Sit yourselves,' she said.

There was a placement, a label by each plate.

They sat. She sat. They watched her.

41

Ceremoniously, slowly, with dignity, she raised the lid from her plate. In unison, they imitated her action. Round the table, seven metal covers were lifted. They stared, amazed.

On seven large white gold-rimmed plates reposed what looked like small, shrivelled beefburgers. On the eighth plate, in front of David D'Anger, was a small round display of bright green peas. Nothing more, nothing less.

To laugh, to cry, to eat? They paused. Frieda paused. Never had the etiquette of following one's hostess's lead seemed more relevant.

She pitied them, reprieved them for a moment.

'A glass of wine?' she asked.

A ripple of relief ran through them, as Daniel leapt up to help, surreptitiously inspected the label, lifted the alas already lifted cork. He poured a little of the dark red into each glass. Two more bottles stood on the side. (Do they need a poison-tester, or will she drink herself?)

Frieda picked up her fork. They picked up their forks. She put hers down again. And so did they.

'Now,' she said in pity, 'I'll tell you what you have before you. And you can eat it if you wish. If not, you may proceed to the next course.'

She rummaged in the large black bag hung from her chair arm, produced a piece of paper, put on her spectacles. She cleared her throat and announced, 'What you have before you are Butler's Bumperburgers. And here is a description of what they contain.' She adjusted her spectacles, began to read. 'The makers of Butler's Bumperburgers were fined £2,000 after trading standards officials in Somerset found the product contained no meat. Hot Snax of Middleton, West Yorkshire, admitted false labelling of the burgers, which were made of gristle, fat, chicken scraps, and water from cows' heads.'

A silence fell. Gogo recovered first, as she smartly put the cloche back over her plate. 'Lucky *you*, David,' she said, eyeing his supernaturally green peas.

'I'm not so sure,' said David. 'I'm not so sure at all.' He prodded a pea, pierced it and pointed it in interrogation at Frieda.

Frieda looked approving. 'Clever boy, David,' she said. 'Quite right.'

'But what', asked Daniel, 'can you do to a pea?'

'Sell-by date?' suggested Nathan quickly.

'Clever boy, Nathan,' said Frieda. 'But worse than that, worse than that. These peas were frozen long, long before the concept of sell-by date had been dreamt up. God knows how old they are, but certainly pre-1978, I've been assured.'

'Still,' murmured Gogo, 'all the same, I'd rather have the peas than these things. Given the choice.'

'Say it again,' said Nathan, entering with a professional curiosity into the spirit of the occasion. 'Water from the cows' heads, did you say?'

Rosemary left the table and went off to retch in the downstairs cloakroom, and simultaneously Frieda rose to her feet and started to clear the plates, scraping the brown wrinkled matted fibrous discs into a plastic bag. Conversation broke out, glasses were raised, cries of, 'What's this wine, Frieda? What vintage?' were well fielded by Frieda, as she snatched David's peas from him, but not before he had defiantly, with bravado, eaten at least three. The demonstration was over, and Frieda disappeared into the kitchen and returned with a large dish of macaroni cheese and a bowl of salad. 'Clean plates, I think?' she said, as she took a new pile of the old chipped set from the dresser and began to serve. The macaroni cheese looked delicious. They set about it with gratitude, with cries of appreciation and relief, as they began to ply Frieda with questions about her performance – whom was she testing, and how, and why, and where she had managed to get hold of those beefless burgers, those antique peas? Why had she done this thing to them? Was it, they now dared to ask, an attack upon poor Cedric, upon the government? Had she become a vegetarian? Was she joining an animal rights campaign?

Frieda dished out, sat down, tucked in, refilled glasses. 'Look,' she said eventually, when she had their calmer attention. 'I wanted to give you all a meal to remember. It's our last supper. Our last supper in this house. I've got rid of it. I'm off.'

Where to, they wanted to know, and she told them. To the sea's edge. To the end of the road. They must come and claim what they wanted, before she got the house-clearance men in. There were still old toys, old school reports, old textbooks from Romley Grammar School upstairs. They must make a date.

The move had been coming up on her for a long time, she said. She had grown to hate London. She had come to hate the human race. What was the point of it? 'I resign,' said Frieda, telling her amber beads as though they were a rosary. 'I leave it all to you. To you, Cedric, and to you, David, I leave the politics. You can divide it equally. That's fair. I leave justice to Daniel, who will surely be made a judge soon. Judges get younger every day. I leave education to Patsy, and the arts to Rosemary, and the free market to Nathan, and the health service to Gogo. That just about covers the lot. I've had enough.'

And they saw that although she now smiled and fed them clean food from a large dish, she had gone mad.

Over pudding – a large, unsuspicious nursery apple-crumble – she elaborated. They had heard the story of how she had tried to get rid of the car? They hadn't even let her get rid of it. She was chained to it. Why bother with cars, with roads, with going from place to place? It had all gone wrong. She would remove herself. Urban life was poisonous. The air was impure, the foodstuffs were contaminated. Madness had fallen on the land and she had caught it. People could no longer tell the good from the bad. You only had to look around to see that they were suffering from a terminal disease. They crowded together to die, like a species intent on extinction. Pallid, shuffling, talking to themselves, crazy. Even when they thought they were having fun – and she pronounced the word 'fun' with impressive venom – they were stoking themselves with misery. She had walked through that dreadful little open air piazza in Covent Garden the other day and she had seen people sitting at tables eating food that was garbage. She had seen mould growing on a slice of wet giant quiche. She had smelt vomit, and had then discovered that what she smelt was not vomit but burger and pizza. People were eating food that smelt of hot vomit

44

(sorry, Rosemary, are you feeling better now?), of regurgitated vomit. Like biblical dogs, they ate. She had pursued the burger story, spotted in a tiny four-line news item in the *Independent*, and had taken herself to abattoirs in Middleton and Somerset. She had seen the light. And while in Somerset she had bought a castle by the sea. She had walked into an estate agent's and bought it. And there, alone, she would moulder.

Triumphantly, she lit another carcinogenic cigarette.

'And you think', inquired Rosemary, 'that you will find the countryside full of pure, clean-living, ecologically correct people? It isn't, you know. It's full of burgers too. Even fuller of burgers than Covent Garden.'

'That's as may be,' said Frieda. 'There must be bits that are empty still.'

There was no reasoning with her, they could see. Meekly, they drank their coffee and made their farewells.

Outside on the pavement, Daniel Palmer had attempted a word of man-to-man worldly deprecation to Cedric Summerson. After all, the woman was his mother, and Summerson was a minister. A bad mother, and a bad minister, but the courtesies must be observed even *in extremis*. 'Bit of a Timon's feast, eh?' said Daniel, pressing the little battery of his car alarm. His car winked back at him.

Summerson took it like a man. 'Impressive woman, your mother,' he said, with a not very successful attempt at a twinkle. They shook hands on it.

Summerson walked down the road to his own car. Although he did not know who Timon was, and was never to discover, he knew quite well why he had been summoned. It was her revenge. He hoped the others did not know. He suspected they did not. Clever they might be, but innocent, he guessed. High-minded, ambitious middle-class innocents – except, perhaps, for Nathan. But Nathan had shown no sign of recognition when the words 'Hot Snax' had been mentioned. Nathan had probably never represented any product as downmarket, as obscurely and deviously provided, as *cheap*, as Hot Snax. Nathan was more a Safeway, a Sainsbury man. The trail was not clear. However had Frieda followed it? She was dangerous, as well as impressive. Just as well that she was about to remove herself from society. Just as well that she would, in a court of law, appear as mad as a meat axe. Her testimony was worthless.

Daniel and Patsy had talked of Frieda's craziness as they drove home that night. So did Rosemary and Nathan. But David talked of social justice, while Gogo drove and listened. Those three peas, he knew, had infected him, as Frieda had intended that they should. He would never expel their message from his system. Like the princess on her twenty mattresses, he would be tormented. He was susceptible. Frieda had known this, and she had chosen to offer him this torment. He would not reject it.

'In his *Utopia*,' said David relentlessly, as Gogo drove down the Balls Pond Road at midnight, 'More proposed that butchers should be recruited, as a punishment, from the criminal classes. You would not expect a good man to become a butcher. Fourier went one further and proposed that all unattractive jobs – all jobs that nobody in their right mind would do without constraint – should be simply abandoned. Society would readjust, he argued. Readjust and do without. Kendrick goes one further still and argues that with any fair system of job allocation any society would choose to be vegetarian. No more abattoirs, no more chicken gutters, no more beefburgers, no more cows' heads. Bernard Shaw said we could live on pills and air.'

'Shaw was fastidious,' said Gogo. 'Like you. Like, it would seem, the reincarnate Frieda.'

'I suppose', said David, 'that I'll have to go and visit an abattoir. She was pointing at one in my constituency, I assume.'

'There's no need to be so competitive,' said Gogo, although she knew there was.

'It's not as though I can't imagine what's behind the curtain,' said David. 'I know what's there. That's why I don't eat meat anyway.'

'Nobody was accusing you,' said Gogo.

'I accuse myself,' said David.

'My dear David', said Gogo, 'you should never have left the courts of theory. Now you must enter the dirty world. And what of the sewers, what of the untouchables?'

David put his hand on Gogo's knees. She pressed it. They were set upon a disastrous course, and, like a good wife, a good politician's wife, she would try to stand by her man. He would betray her again and again, not with a call girl or an actress or a pretty PA (though who knows, perhaps with them as well, for with his looks how could he not fall into temptation?) – no, he would betray her for Social Justice, that blind blood-boltered maiden.

David D'Anger is haunted by the fair vision of a just society. She smiles at him. Is this possible, you ask, in the late twentieth century? We concede it was possible for men and women to create, even to believe in such images in the past – as late as the nineteenth century these possibilities lingered – but surely we know better now? We are adult now, and have put away childish things. Dreams survive in academe, at conferences and congresses where students and lecturers and professors still discuss the concept of the fair, the just and the good. But they have no connection with a world of ring-roads and beef-burgers, with a world of disease and survival.

Imagine David D'Anger. You say he is an impossibility, and you cannot imagine him, any more than he can imagine the nature of the revolution which would bring about the world he thinks he wishes to construct. But you are wrong. The truth is that you, for David D'Anger, are the impossibility. The present world which we seem to inhabit is an impossibility. He cannot live at ease in it, he cannot believe it is real. He believes that the other world is possible. He has left the abstract world of reason and entered the public forum. He has hope. He has ambition, but he also has hope. Look at him carefully. Look at him at Timon's feast in abandoned Romley, in Romley left to its own decay. Look at him a year and a half later at that more palatable meal in preserved and enduring Hampshire. At Frieda's prompting he has made good use of the intervening time.

At the age of seventeen, in Guyana, at school in distant George-town, David D'Anger read Plato and Aristotle. They blew his mind.

Into the hinterland of thought he travelled, to Eldorado. Along rivers, past strange birds, carmine, azure, emerald. Mother of Gold, Scum of Gold. He read Sir Walter Ralegh and dreamt strange dreams. The Guyanese are the chosen people of the Caribbean, and David D'Anger thought himself their chosen son. East and West meet in Guyana, they meet in David D'Anger. Rivers, waterfalls, great iridescent fish. Greeks, Phoenecians, Egyptians. At seventeen he possessed the globe.

To know the good is to choose it. This is what he learnt. This became clear to him as a boy and it is clear to him now. He would push the button, he would countenance earthquakes. He would rip away the veil from the temple and force us to choose the good. You know such men are dangerous. He knows that an absence of such men is dangerous.

David D'Anger is headstrong and he believes in himself and his agenda. His certainties have survived every success, and he has been successful. If he suffers from *folie de grandeur*, he has found others who will collude in his folly. Scholar of the year in Georgetown, he was sent to the old country, to study at Oxford. His family, exiled by Burnham, assembled around him. At Oxford he rose, and he continues to rise. He is courted by institutions at home and abroad. Sugar Daddy America and his tin-nippled hard-coiffed Mother Country have both tried to entrap him. Even the many-teated sow of Europe has grunted her overtures. For David D'Anger is a man for whom the time is right. Handsome, clever and black, he is political plausibility personified. His name helps to legitimate many a committee, his presence sanctions many a conference. He can hardly fail to know his worth. Scholarships, fellowships, awards, graces and favours have been dangled before him. Study-centres in grand palazzi on Italian lakes have beckoned him, and so have residencies in distinguished American colleges. (Perhaps there are not yet *quite* enough clever handsome correct black men to go round?) Even poor Guyana has asked him to return, although she knows she cannot afford him. Choice, whatever Nathan Herz may think, seems to glitter before David with a refracted kaleidoscopic brilliance that would blind a less certain man. But David

D'Anger has no intention of being bought or blinded. He thinks he knows where he is going. And if at times there seems to be an ill fit between his grandiose dreams of justice and the bathos of finding himself adopted as a parliamentary candidate for the marginal seat of Middleton in West Yorkshire – well, he tells himself, he is young yet, and uncompromised. He will force a fusion. Everything is going for him. He cannot fail.

Does his wife Gogo believe in him? Probably. It is hard to tell what she thinks. She has not attempted to check his political ambitions, although she knows that the wives of Members of Parliament are not to be envied. She has her own life, her own career. She does not give much away. She seems to approve his position. She reads some of the books he reads, watches some of the programmes on which he appears. She picks up his references, as we have seen. What more is needed? She is English, she does not show emotion. If she loves both her husband and her son, obsessively, fearfully, you would never guess it. She is the most severe, the most Nordic of Frieda's offspring. She and David D'Anger make an unlikely, a striking couple, and they know it. David and Grace, the dark sun and the cold moon. One day, she says, she will travel up-country with him to Eldorado.

In his early days at Oxford, David had been pursued by men, as was to be expected. It was assumed that he would find it diplomatic to surrender. The Master of Gladwyn College himself, a well-known seducer and corrupter of youth, had courted David, and it was widely rumoured that David had succumbed, for the old boy's manner remained remarkably indulgent over a period of years. Small, vain, preposterous, button-eyed, pursy, plump, treble Sir Roy had petted young David: shaking lingering hands one night after a conversazione, he had murmured, 'Such a turn on, dear boy, such a turn on!' – alluding, as David took it, to the conjunction of his own smooth dark skin with Sir Roy's pallid cloistral parchment. This had been at the end of David's first term. Three years later, having safely survived such favours, David D'Anger had announced his engagement, and old Sir Roy had graced his wedding to Grace 'Gogo' Palmer – indeed he had generously held the wedding celebrations in the grounds of his own

Lodge. During the course of the party he had pinched David's arm wistfully and patted his body most intimately: 'Wisely done, my boy, wisely done,' he had squeaked, as he winked and peered with lubricious approval at the austerely suited bride, at the flowing jade-green robes of the bride's stout and eccentric and eminent mother. Had there been some secret pact? Had David D'Anger kissed the arse of the establishment? Nobody knew, or nobody would tell.

Fourteen years now have they been married, David and Gogo, and they have kept the secrets of their marriage bed. They present a united front. They have but the one child, and they will never have another. He is the pride of their life, the apple of their eye. He is a genius. He has inherited all the talent – and there is much – from both sides of his family. He is heir to great expectations.

Frieda Haxby had recognized his exceptional qualities at birth. Well, not quite at birth, for she had been in Canada when he was born, and she had not caught an early flight home to be with him. Benjamin was not her first grandchild, nor she a natural granny. Had Gogo resented the delay? If so, she never showed it. One could accuse Frieda of many failings, but not of preferring her first-born son Daniel to her two daughters. She treated all with equal inconsistency – scattering favours when it suited her, not when it suited the recipient. Until she saw Benjamin. And then things changed. Or so Gogo thought she noted.

Benjamin was six weeks old when Frieda finally made her way to the D'Angers' untidy basement flat in Highbury. Lying in Gogo's arms, he had stared at Frieda, with his large dark long-lashed seducer's eyes, and he had smiled at her, as charmingly as he had smiled at his Guyanese grandmother. And she had smiled at him. 'The divine child,' she said. 'Oh, the divine child.' And Gogo and David had smiled at one another proudly, for they too knew that he was the divine child, he was the darling saviour of the world. They had been amazed by the ferocity of their passion for this perfect infant.

And Frieda had reached out her arms and taken the baby, and he had lain there on her bosom in gracious ease, nestling comfortably, tightening his little fingers round her smooth amber beads. She had walked him up and down the room, singing over him, droning, as she had sung intermittently to her own children. An incantation, a strange, rhymic, tuneless keening. '*Il est né, le divin enfant, Chantons tous son avènement,*' she had spontaneously, inappropriately, blasphemously chanted, as she paced up and down the stripped floorboards, patting the child's round blue cocooned elasticated bottom in time to the beat of the song.

Later, she put on her reading glasses to inspect his face more closely: Benjamin caught at the gold chain from which she suspended them. She read his face, and he read hers. 'Benjamin,' she said to him appraisingly, 'you are the youngest child of Israel, Benjamin. You are the child of War, you are the warrior babe. You are Beltenebros, the Beautiful Obscure.' Who can tell what the child hears? He takes in everything. Has Frieda put a spell upon him, like the wicked godmother?

Gogo will have no more children, for, with the birth of Benjamin, she suffered a prolapse. She wears a metal ring within her. She tells nobody of this, not even her sister or her friends. The ring is her secret. David knows. It keeps her chaste and faithful to David, but does it compel his fidelity to her, or does it release him? She asks no questions, to be told no lies. She does not want to lose David.

David is unfaithful to her with her mother, or so she suspects. And she is right to be suspicious. For years, Frieda has wooed and tempted David. She has sent him notes and postcards, to his college address, to his television address, occasionally to his home address. Now she sends him messages from her castle by the sea. Frieda Haxby knows David's ambitions. She has cast herself as his Lady Macbeth. She knows what tempts him.

LUNCH ON THE LAWN

The morning after the Aga evening, the Sunday morning, Patsy Palmer rises early, unstacks the dishwasher, lays plates and beakers and jams on the table for breakfast, washes a couple of lettuces, puts a casserole of beans and bacon in the bottom Aga, feeds the dog and the cats, sweeps up the remains of a mangled rabbit and throws it out among the nasturtiums, waters the plants, and wonders if she is crazy. Why does she do all this? What is she trying to prove? She is off to Meeting in Hartley Bessborough, some ten miles away, to commune with a God that she suspects does not exist, to ponder her sins which do, to worry about her mother (for she has a mother, the Palmers are not the only family with a mother, though you wouldn't know this if you listened to them, as she is obliged to do) and to pick up, on her way back, Judge Partington and his wife, who are coming to lunch. (Judge Partington has crashed his car into the back of his own garage and is temporarily off the road.)

Patsy yawns, combs her hair, smiles at herself, and eats a slice of toast. She is satisfied with herself and her sins. And she is looking forward to an hour of silence, away from her in-laws. Thank God none of them is religious. It would be the last straw if any of them said they wanted to come to Meeting with her. (Nathan had accompanied her once, out of curiosity. The silence had nearly driven him mad. He had heaved and breathed in restless misery, listening to the rude noise of his own treacherous guts. Never again, he had moaned, upon release.)

Simon and Emily sleep on, as Patsy sets off across the countryside. But David and Daniel are out in the garden, strolling on the lawn, talking men's talk. Gogo and Rosemary watch them from the upstairs-landing window. The virginia creeper coils its little tender tendrils inwards into the house. The corpse of a small bird lies in the creeper's nestwork, staring up at them from dead eyes and open beak.

Gogo and Rosemary do not see it, for they are watching their menfolk. David has hooked his thumbs alertly in his pockets, Daniel's hands are clasped gravely behind his back.

'Daniel's hair's getting very thin,' says Rosemary, after studying him for a few moments.

'So's mine,' says Gogo, patting her headscarf. 'It's the Haxby genes. You seem to have got Palmer hair.'

'Who knows what Palmer hair looks like?' asks Rosemary, and they both laugh.

'Benjie's lucky. David has good hair,' says Rosemary. 'And in the right place too. On top of his head.'

'There are some advantages in marrying a wog,' says Gogo.

David and Daniel are discussing weightier matters than hair loss. Daniel is professing a cultivated ignorance in the face of David's description of a seminar on Cultural Appropriation which is to be held in Calgary in October. David has been invited to attend, and is not sure whether to accept. Daniel has followed with interest David's update of the slow progress of the trade-name dispute on Demerara, which threatens to involve some large agrofood businesses, but the phrase 'Cultural Appropriation' is, he claims, a new one on him. He wrinkles his nose fastidiously, his eyes crinkle into the dryest of dry smiles: like High Court judges who feign innocence of the existence of the Beatles or the Rolling Stones, he feigns ignorance of Canada's leading role in the debate on communitarianism and ethnic minorities. Quebec he has heard of and admits to, but he disclaims any knowledge of the native minorities and their anti-Quebecois stance, and as for the notion that a white man cannot write about or represent in court a black or brown man, or vice versa – well, it leaves him gobsmacked. 'Gobsmacked,' repeats Daniel delicately. (He has picked up some contemporary phrases from his children, and uses them occasionally, in 'scare quotes', in a manner that he hopes is endearing. It works quite well in court.) 'Are you telling me that a person can only represent or speak for that category of person which he or she happens to be? Isn't that rather restrictive?'

'So some in Calgary will argue, no doubt,' says David. 'Others, not.'

'And what do you think about it?'

'Me personally? Oh, I'm so deep into cultural appropriation that there's no way back for me. No way I can get back to cultural innocence. Yet it must be admitted that it wouldn't be to my advantage to admit this in public or let it be known that I think it. My bread is buttered on the other side.' He pauses, continues. 'On the other hand, it's dangerous for me to take the other line to extremes. There's a line that claims that Philip Larkin is a racist bastard because he didn't notice that there were any coloured folk in Hull. Or at least, even if he did, he didn't bother to put them in his poems.'

'Do people argue that?' asks the *faux-naïf* Daniel.

'Yes, of course they do. It's the new white man's burden. He's not allowed to write or speak *as* a black man, but he's damned if he doesn't recognize their existence and their otherness. Damned if he appropriates, damned if he neglects. It's a fine line.'

'And what's the new black man's burden?'

'Oh, the black man has so many burdens, old and new, that they can't be counted.'

They turn at the right angle of the lawn, by the wall of roses, and continue their patrol along the herbaceous border where the giant spurges cluster.

'As a matter of fact,' says David in parenthesis, 'there aren't all that many coloured people in Hull. About 0.8 per cent, if I remember rightly. About the same as in Stamford or Sleaford or Spalding, in the depths of Lincolnshire. You'd hardly expect Larkin to address his poems to 0.8 per cent of the population, especially the 0.8 per cent that don't read poets like Larkin. Or to write about them, come to that. Would you?'

Daniel ignores this argument, although he spots a loophole in it, and pursues the question of David D'Anger's own position.

'So you think it's more useful for you to present yourself as a black man with a particular voice and constituency rather than to speak out on behalf of universal human nature, and all the possibilities of cultural assimilation and neutrality that you so clearly, with all your talents and blessings, represent?' provokes Daniel.

'Look,' says David. 'I know the dangers. Uncle Tom. White nigger. Token black. It's better for me to dissemble a little, to play the communitarian game. Anyway, I half believe it. I *am* black. Well, I'm Indian Guyanese. Black's out, as a word, these days. I'm not quite sure what's in, for chaps like me. I think I'm supposed to say I'm a man of colour. They'll update me in Calgary. On the whole, I think the more detail, the safer. Guyanese born, Guyanese and British educated, Indian ancestry, mixed religious background, won't eat beef, Anglo-Saxon wife, mixed-race son, representing – or hoping to represent – a West Yorkshire constituency with a 3.4 per cent Black–Asian vote and several distinct ethnic communities. Sociologist and politician and father of one. With surprisingly poor teeth, in view of my origins and my personal dislike of sugar. That's me.'

'But tell me,' pursues Daniel, 'to what precisely do they object, these critics of cultural appropriation? These women who don't want men taking up feminism, these Innuits who won't hire a Swedish, Canadian or American Jew to fight their corner?'

'If you ask me,' says David, 'it's all to do with funding. Like everything else, it's to do with money. Most cultural funding these days is based on category, not on individual talent. Don't think I kid myself, I know why I've had an easy ride. Once you're in the saddle, it's easy. But there's never enough funding to go round, and that's why Indians and West Indians and Guyanese and Sri Lankans resent it when white men and women impersonate their attitudes and try to write their books for them and adopt their politically correct positions and get their money to go to conferences. The Northern hemisphere is full of Canadians and Danes and Swedes and Germans busy studying post-colonial culture and digging into old colonial archives in order to get themselves on the next aeroplane out of the rain and down south to the tropical sunshine. *Sehnsucht nach Süde*, that's what Goethe called it. It's a new kind of colonialism. Cultural colonialism. There aren't enough seats at the table, there aren't enough air fares. That's the real problem.'

'But these are the very guys who invented the concept of cultural appropriation, didn't you say? Doesn't it work to their own disadvantage?'

'Oh, no. They're clever, these theorists. They can always invent a new twist to the theory which means they've got to be there themselves, at the next round, preferably in Singapore or Barbados rather than Calgary, to explain it and represent it. On behalf of the benighted disadvantaged tinted folk who haven't yet learnt that it's their duty to reject all representation and represent themselves.'

'Hmm,' says Daniel. 'If you carried one line of this muddle to its logical conclusion, you'd find yourself in a world where you could only vote for yourself. Because only you yourself could speak for the particular bundle of characteristics that you happened quite arbitrarily to be. A solipsistic world.'

'Sometimes I think that's how it really is. But only in my darker moods. In my lighter moods, I pocket the air fare, attend the get-togethers, make friends and influence people. As you observe.'

'You wouldn't ever', says Daniel, stooping to pick up a tiny scrap of silver paper from the well-mown lawn, 'think of going back to Guyana?'

This is a dangerous question, even from a friendly brother-in-law on a Sunday morning in Hampshire, and Daniel knows it. So does David. After a long pause, during which they continue their stately promenade, David replies, 'I was brought up to think of Britain as my home, even when we lived in Georgetown. Most of my family's here now. I'm more use here, or I kid myself that I'm more use here. We were kicked out under Burnham, you know.'

'Yes, I know. You were rebels.'

'We were the wrong race and had all the wrong attitudes. And we weren't safe.'

'You feel safe here?'

David shrugs. 'Yes, I do. I've settled in here.' He smiles, a half appeal. 'And Gogo wouldn't like Georgetown. It's too bloody hot in Georgetown. She wouldn't last a week. She can't even take the Mediterranean.'

'And Benjamin is British,' says Daniel the tempter.

'Benjamin can choose for himself one day. I'll take him to see the place when he's older. I'll take him up-country, to the land of jungle and waterfall. To the land of mass suicide. I've never been up-country myself. And if he likes it, he can have it. I hope we're keeping the possibility open. Gogo and I.'

'Of course,' says Daniel the judicious, 'it's not as though Britain is the seat of empire that it once was. Most of the brain drain goes the other way now, to our ex-colonies. You must have been tempted yourself. As you yourself pointed out, they have more funding.'

'For people in my category, yes, they have more funding. But I don't want to be American. I don't want Benjie to become American. Would you want Simon and Emily to become American?'

'I haven't travelled as much as you,' says Daniel. 'And I've been lucky enough here. Nothing to complain of here.'

'The Americans', says David, 'believe in universal human nature. There's a heroism in that. But they believe that universal human nature is or shall be American. Except when they live in universities, when it suits their interest to think otherwise. Or to say they think otherwise. One can't always tell the difference.'

Daniel stops in his tracks for a moment, to stare at an intrusive rosette of plantain in the smooth temperate English green. Then he remarks, with seeming irrelevance, 'It's bloody hot in Singapore. And in Hong Kong.'

'Maybe it's Guyana's turn next,' says David. 'It must come one day. You know how Ralegh described Guyana? "A country that hath yet her maidenhead." Guyana for the next millennium. Meanwhile, I'll stay here and support the West Indies.'

Daniel, who does not follow the cricket, concedes a victory. Over the garden and the ridge the sun reaches its zenith. Patsy will be back from Meeting soon, her conscience, they suppose, appeased. A smell of slow-cooking beans and garlic and bacon wafts from the open kitchen window towards them. Beneath the pear tree a full-bosomed matron thrush pecks, jerkily, mechanically, at a worm cast, listening from time to time to sounds below the earth. David and Daniel descend three steps to the lower lawn, the sundial and the fishpond. A white lily opens its petals over the water and yellow irises stand in the marge. This is a temperate, a blessed clime, and with global warming may become yet more blessed, at the expense of less fortunate regions. Daniel has done well to remind his ambitious self and his ambitious brother-in-law that Britain is but a small country, although its population is some sixty or seventy times greater than that of Guyana. Its past has been greater than its future, which may or may not be true of Guyana. But its present holds them all. Daniel would keep it as it is, for he profits from its waning empire. David would change it. But he too profits.

They watch the surface of the pond, where pond skaters skim lightly and rapidly over the meniscus in search of their drowning prey. 'Yes,' says Daniel, gazing around his own small kingdom with its ancient markers, as the shadow of time's finger moves towards noon. (His recently purchased genuine antique sundial has been set slightly off true by the man from the attic, and time in his garden is a little slower than time on his cheap, Taiwanese, battery-driven watch.) 'Yes,' says Daniel, 'it is very pleasant here, on a nice day like this.'

In Meeting, Patsy makes a perfunctory attempt to free her mind from its terrestrial anxieties, fails, and then settles down to them, methodically, as the silent minutes pass, as motes turn in the shafts of light that fall through the plain windows of this square familiar building. Two centuries of quiet settle around her, but her brain is full of noise. She worries about her mother in her expensive rest home, about Daniel's mother embattled on Exmoor. She worries about the next meeting of the Video Control and Surveillance Panel and animal abuse films, about the leak over the study window, and about Daniel's heavy workload and his inability to control it. Will Daniel have a heart attack, she wonders? She worries about the Partingtons' lunch in the Aga – will it be cooking evenly? She worries about Simon's unhealthy pallor and his occasional outbursts of unprovoked aggression; will he be rude to Judge Partington? She suspects that the Partington daughter, Sally, has had a fling with Simon: had it ended in tears, and if so, who was to blame? But most of all, she worries about the man in the attic. Will he ever leave? She worries about him more than she would ever disclose. Her public line is confidence, but sometimes she admits to herself that she is, very slightly, afraid. Not of him, but of what he represents. She likes him, and he makes himself useful. But she fears his category. And he limits her control. He cannot be contained in her frame. She will have to get rid of him. It is an unpleasant necessity.

Meeting today is quiet, though towards the end of the hour, as Patsy twists and turns her pearl ring round and round her finger, secretly, beneath her handbag, old Arthur Clifford rises to his feet and says a few words about our friends in Eastern Europe, and quotes some lines from a Czech poet. He sits down again and silence resumes, until the two elders, Jane Farr and Ronnie Taylor, turn to one another and shake hands, in the spontaneous ritual of Friends. Gradually the gathering stirs back into life, little conversations break out, greetings are made, news exchanged. Patsy, emerging from the Meeting Room into the wax-scented well-polished outer porch, with its notices of jumble sales and WEA lectures and cultural events, pauses to speak to Sonia Barfoot, one of the more congenial and eccentric of the Meeting's members. Sonia has been in hospital again, and there is a soft, vulnerable, pained, washed look about her once plump, once pretty features. Her colourless hair is parted in the middle and drawn tightly back from her face and constrained by two tortoiseshell pins. Her scalp shows pink. An expression of bewildered grief lingers in her pale grey slightly glazed eyes, wide open beneath their bald brows, their long colourless lashes. She is wearing a georgette blouse of lavender blue, a creased linen skirt of darker blue. Spinster's colours. Sonia Barfoot is back from the grave, where once she saw God.

'Patsy,' she says, making an effort to smile. 'How good to see you.'

They clasp hands. She must be on drugs, thinks Patsy, there is something wrong with her eyes. Or has electricity once more crackled through her skull?

'You must come and see me soon,' says Patsy. 'Now you're better.'

'You're always so busy,' says Sonia Barfoot calmly, without reproach. 'And I'm not better. Not really.'

'Ring me,' says Patsy, squeezing the thin, blue-veined, old lady's hand. Sonia is not old, but she seems old. She has suffered too much and it has worn her out. Her suffering is not of the body, but of the mind. 'Ring me. I must dash. I've got to pick up the Partingtons. I want to speak to you about my prisoner. Keep well, Sonia.'

And she breaks away, and turns and waves, and walks briskly off to the car park, to health, to worldliness, to good food, to those un-Quakerly bottles of Bulgarian red. (Cheap wine at lunch, expensive at dinner, that is the Palmer rule, whoever the guests may be.)

Judge Partington is nothing if not worldly. Indeed he is gross. He has to sit in the front seat of Patsy's doggy, muddy Datsun, squeezing his wife unceremoniously into the back. And all the way from his mill house by the water meadows to the Palmer homestead he entertains Patsy with tales of the Bar and the Bench. Partington is an opinion-ated, a controversial judge, and his face is flushed with rich living and low thinking. Today he is wearing his country gear – a bursting jacket over an open straining checked cotton shirt, and what looks like his gardening trousers. His wife Celia, in contrast, is provocatively well-groomed, and sports a soft navy and white spotted crêpe silk dress.

He chatters on, as they bowl over the brow of the ridge, past the wind field, and descend towards the Old Farm. Patsy does not care for local anecdotes and does not listen very hard, though she gathers that there is some story about an injunction that Partington is longing to tell Daniel. Daniel, she thinks, will make a better audience – and indeed, there he is, waiting at the gate, as she bumps over the cattle grid. She slips away, having disgorged her passengers, to attend to the lunch.

Gogo and Rosemary have set the garden table on the veranda, and now they all gather, as introductions are made, as sherry and wine are poured. The younger children circle warily, hungrily, wanting crisps and Bombay Mix but not conversation. Simon and Emily know the Partingtons well, for Simon, as Patsy suspects, had once been involved with their daughter Sally, and Emily, in her riding phase, had shared a pony with her; now both Palmer children wish to forget both daugh-ter and pony, but cannot utterly repudiate them, although Simon asks after Sally in a manner that could be construed as either embarrassed or hostile. (Emily does not have to ask after the pony. It went to the knacker's yard some years ago.) There is another lunch guest, an idle rentier from over the hill who has been playing tennis with David and Daniel and Rosemary. Patsy had been right – Bill Partington has a story to tell, and he wants them all to hear. He settles heavily into a garden chair, which trembles bravely under his weight, and embarks upon his tale.

'Late last night they delivered it,' he says. 'This video. Old People's Home, going out on Monday in the 6.30 documentary slot on *Southwatch*. The home wanted it stopped. More importantly the relatives. Gross invasion of privacy. False allegations. Indecent filming. So I told them to send it round to me. Celia and I saw it last night. Disgusting, wasn't it, Celia?'

'*Fairly* disgusting,' says his wife judiciously, as she sips her orange juice and casts covert glances at Daniel Palmer's handsome brother-in-law David D'Anger, who is listening to her husband's speech with unfeigned curiosity. Has she seen him somewhere before? Is he in television? Should she warn Bill to watch his big mouth?

'Botties on potties, that's what it was,' says Partington, and laughs uproariously. 'Botties on potties. Endless shots of botties on potties. Wrinkled botties, hairy botties. And the contents of potties. You can't avoid shit these days. Medical programmes, wildlife programmes, archaeology, stand-up comics – it's all excrement. You wouldn't have got away with it in the old days. Talk about violence guidelines, it's guidelines on shit that we need these days. What, Patsy? Patsy agrees, don't you, Patsy?'

(But Patsy is indoors, carving the joints of the bacon, arranging the slices of pink meat and white fat on the meat dish, licking her fingers, picking out a clove, miles and miles away.)

'So what did you do?' asks Daniel politely. He enjoys Partington's performances and is glad that his career prospects do not oblige him to take them seriously.

'Oh, I slammed on the injunction,' says the merry judge, helping himself to a fistful of cashew nuts. 'Said it was in breach. Nothing *but* breaches, I told them. Can't do that to people. Can't show their bums without asking them. They're not all senile. And guess what? Dick Champer rings me up from the BBC. Direct from the BBC, to complain. Says it's outside my prerogative. Says he'll appeal. He was in a right stew. Fizzing and boiling. Spluttering and choking. Midnight, this was.'

'And the injunction holds?'

'Of course it holds,' says Partington, munching away, his teeth spattered with a white spew of chewed wet nut. 'I'll fix them. I was at Magdalen with Champer. I'll teach him about human dignity. Dick, I said, I challenge you, you show your bare bum on TV, and we'll let it run. You do a bum shot to introduce it, and I'll see what I can do for you. Fair's fair, I said. Do unto others. I've *seen* his bum, and I can tell you it's not a pretty sight.'

'So what will happen?'

'We'll see on Monday,' says Bill Partington, grinning broadly and reaching out his paw for more nuts, but at that moment Patsy appears at a window, a cordless telephone in her hand, and calls, 'Bill! Bill! It's for you.'

He heaves himself up, stumps across the paving stones, leans across the flowerbed, grabs the phone. He yells into it. All of them hear every word. 'Eh? What? The IBA? The High Court? The Minister? What the fuck are you talking about, you arsehole? Ah, come off it, you bum. Fair's fair. You wait, lover boy. You wait. I've known Reggie since I was a boy. You'll get no change out of him. Eh? What?'

As his unseen interlocutor manages to arrest the flow, Bill paces expansively along the terrace, groaning loudly, and listening with pantomime impatience. He starts to tear at the ragged remains of what had once been a fair crop of brown curls. Then he breaks in again with, 'You swine! You bum!'

Celia, her long brown legs neatly crossed at the ankles beneath her pretty soft hemline, rolls her eyes to the almost cloudless sky, and sighs in disassociation. Daniel smiles with undisguised delight. Nathan too is much pleased. Rosemary pretends to be reading a Sunday colour supplement, David buries his head in his hands, and Gogo rises to her feet and disappears into the house. Tennis guest Julian tries to start up a conversation with Daniel, but Daniel does not even notice: Julian is not bad at tennis but his views on anything other than opera are simply not worth listening to, and he wants to hear the end of Bill's tirade.

It comes abruptly, as the outraged dignitary yells a final oath of defiance, and presses the off button. He slams the phone down on the inner window-ledge (thereby dislodging, though he does not notice this, a small vase of sweet peas). He returns to his chair, gleaming with the heat of battle, slumps down again, and says, 'Hope you enjoyed the cabaret!' Then he appears to fall into a sullen reverie, from which Daniel as host feels, after a moment or two, obliged to rescue him.

'Trouble, eh?' he suggests delicately. Bill Partington surfaces, blowing like a sea monster, and re-engages. He tries to explain the legal technicalities of the injunction, the legal technicalities with which Dick Champer seeks to thwart him, but the moment is past, and Daniel manages to divert him to other, less contumaceous matters.

Is it a form of retaliation that brings the demure Celia Partington to raise the subject of Frieda Haxby over the beans and bacon? She has read a piece somewhere during the last week or two – she cannot remember where, was it in a magazine, the *Spectator* perhaps? about the fall-out from Frieda's VAT dispute. It seems that any victory she had claimed had been Pyrrhic, that new regulations were being drawn up to prevent further defences along the lines she had pursued. The grey area was being made light, to the taxman's advantage. 'Not always wise to challenge, is it?' suggests Celia. 'Even when one's morally in the right.'

None of them answers. Celia pursues.

'And is she still up on Exmoor? Has she any plans to return?' she innocently asks. 'Will you be visiting her this summer?'

Solidly the Palmers close ranks. Not a treacherous murmur escapes them. Frieda on Exmoor is as happy as can be, they all agree. Rosemary has been down to see her recently. The house is too large, but beautifully situated. Frieda is taking her time to do it up, but it will be splendid when it is finished. David and Gogo are off to see her next month. They're looking forward to it.

'We're hoping she'll invite us all for Christmas,' says Nathan wickedly. Rosemary sniggers, Gogo looks severe, Daniel opens another bottle of Bulgarian, and Bill Partington belches, loudly, and pats his stained shirt front. The children have disappeared into the shrubbery. The man in the attic has come down to become the man in the garden shed. He too eats beans, shyly.

It is raining on Exmoor. Frieda Haxby Palmer sits in one of the many derelict rooms that look towards the sea, and listens to the rain on the roof. In better days this had been a garden room, where cream teas had been served. She cannot see the sea and the black rocks below, for rain obscures the steep combes. She can see only broken paving and the lawn and the abandoned flowerbeds and nettles and dodder and brambles. She has been out walking and now she dries her bare feet in front of a paraffin stove. (Rosemary had been right. It is wet here even in midsummer. It is almost always wet.) A wet dog dries by her side, and a pigeon sits at her feet in an upturned saucepan lid.

It is not a scene to comfort an anxious or a proud daughter. The room is full of junk. Suitcases, cardboard boxes, packing cases. Books and papers lie open on an old billiard table, on moth-eaten green-baize card-tables salvaged from the building's hotel life. On one, a game of clock patience is laid out, half played and abandoned. On a heavy mock-Jacobean sideboard stand three skulls, two animal (a badger and a sheep?) and one human. Their grim effect is softened by a cracked red Bristol glass vase holding a peacock feather, a skeleton clock in a glass case, and a large alabaster egg – a *nature morte*, not a shrine or a cemetery. Paintings stand on the floor, their faces to the wall against the skirting board, their canvas backs and their labels of provenance exposed. Next to the alabaster egg lies a brown dried orange pierced at a shallow angle by a bone knitting needle. Now who would wish to torture an orange?

Frieda has been out walking this morning to Pollock Wood. She walks in all weathers. The dog, Bounce, has followed her. He is not her

64

dog, but he goes where she goes. Old, black and white, shabby, disreputable, Bounce suits her well. Now he stinks and dries.

Beyond Turgot Common, on the upland, Frieda and Bounce had spotted a dying calf. It was lying in a ditch by a hedge. Its mother was standing near by, watching it and them without any expression of interest. The cow was big, brown, swollen. The calf was a pale dun pink, a naked skinny pink. It kept rearing and lifting its round ugly head from the sodden grass, then letting it slump down again, as though it were too heavy for its neck. Should she let the farmer know? She thought not. The farmer would not care. This much her hamburger research – the research which had brought her to this ditch – had taught her. Farmers do not care. And she did not like the farmer. She did not like his thrumming generator, his barbed wire, his piles of old tyres, his heaps of slurry. Let the calf die in the wet. Bounce had lowered his head, laid back his ears. Bounce put in no plea for the calf.

They had descended then, Frieda and Bounce, into Tippett's Wood, where they had seen a creature yet more dreadful than the calf. It was a sheep. Its matted pelt hung off it in lumps to trail upon the ground. Its wool was yellow-white, and it was stained with blotches of rusty red, the dirty dull red of dried menstrual blood. Its face was thin and shorn and quivering, its body shapeless beneath its ragged outgrowths. It gazed at the woman and the dog in misery. It was the sheep of affliction, the sheep of God. It gazed at them knowingly, then gazed away again. The dog whimpered with a slight fear. The woman stared back, recognizing it, recognizing herself. The scape sheep. It abandoned hope, and limped away, hobbling painfully slowly into the bracken, on its sodden footrot hoofbones. A rotten sheep, a subsidy sheep. The hillside rang with noisy water, and high overhead a yellow Wessex rescue helicopter buzzed, on its way to search for lost travellers.

Frieda walked on through the ancient woodland. It spoke to her of decay, her own decay. The trees were encrusted with lichen, and small ferns sprouted from them, as orchids sprout from the trees of a tropical rain forest. Fungus grew from living holes and dying trunks and dead logs. Grey-white oyster outcrops clustered. Ash, birch, oak and thorn, the old trees of Northern Europe. Some leant from the steep slope at perilous angles, and others were uprooted, reaching their inverted crowns into the air like great matted discs of red ogre hair, of monstrous curling fibre. Twisted faces peered at her from severed, scarred and stunted limbs. She passed the hollow tree, inside which stood a small lake on which a miniature elfin armada might sail. Scale was crazily distorted in this wracked and rent, this Rackham woodland. There was an overpowering smell of rich wet damp and decay. Stumps rose through the leafmould like old teeth. Frieda's tongue joggled her bridgework, and from beneath her loose bridge an acrid, bitter taste seeped into her mouth. It was the taste of death.

Then she had walked back to her fortress, the wet dog following, and now she sits there, amidst the spoils and bones of her history. She listens to the rain. It drums and drums, it ebbs then it strengthens, it gusts, it pours in heavy chains of water from the eaves, it hangs in great drops on the salt-smeared window-pane. It pours and pours, but her eyes are dry. The sky weeps for her.

What is she doing here in her cavern? Well might her children wonder, well might the estate agent and the hamburger men have wondered. Chance had brought her but she has found a correspondence here, and here she has settled, to write her memoirs. Of course she is writing her memoirs. All her friends are writing their memoirs. At her age there is nothing much left to write, or so she might tell herself. (She is not as old as she pretends. She likes to meet disasters halfway, to get them over with.) She sits here, and addresses herself to her final questioning, her last revenge. This must be clear, she believes, even to her dim-witted family. She is here to summon her mother, her father, her sister, her husband from their graves and from their hiding places. As the Witch of Endor raised Samuel to terrify Saul, so she, the Witch of Exmoor, will raise Gladys Haxby, Ernest Haxby, Hilda Haxby, Andrew Palmer. Her nice clean ambitious well-educated offspring will be appalled by their hideous ancestry.

The problems with writing one's memoirs, she has discovered, include not only libel but also the unreliability of memory, the tedium of research. She has so little to go on. One of the vital scraps of evidence she herself burnt, long ago and, she suspects, criminally. There is not much documentation of the Haxbys. One of the attractive aspects of Queen Christina's life had been the careful documentation. Naturally Frieda had not really thought herself to be a reincarnation of Christina (nor in any way descended from her – the Haxbys came from Denmark, not Sweden, as any fool could work out, and anyway Christina was largely of German blood), but nevertheless she now thinks that her perverse and arbitrary obsession with this seventeenth-century monarch must have led her to this, her final quest. Well, she intends it to be her final quest. She is sick of everything and everyone, herself included, herself above all, and she can't see herself embarking on any new ventures after this. After this, she'll let others inherit the chaos.

Christina has given her a good run for her money, and Frieda had enjoyed her company. Frieda had followed Christina, from cauled and hairy birth through arrogant girlhood, through sexual ambiguity and intellectual experiment, through free thinking and strategic conversions, through disguises and masquerades, to her old age in the Palazzo Riario in Rome. Frieda had followed her curious attachment to Descartes, which had in a manner killed him, and she had invented (evidence being lacking) a relationship with her French ambassador Grotius, who had once escaped from prison in a box of books, and who died by shipwreck in her service. There had been much fun to be had with Christina in the colourful, swashbuckling, wide-gesturing seventeenth century, but her readers had not shared the fun, and had completely missed her subtle subtext on the theme of powerlessness and power. Not a single reviewer had even noted, let alone approved, her complex contrasting of the fates of Christina and her illiterate maid. Oh well, so what? 'I care for nobody, no, not I,' sang Frieda tunelessly to her dog Bounce, 'I care for nobody, no, not I, if nobody cares for me.' And the visit to Rome (legitimate research, all expenses offset against tax) had been most enjoyable. No wonder Christina had turned to Rome. It's a fine city.

Frieda had not been lying when she told the disc jockey, between tracks of UB40 and the Wreckers, that she had been moved to think herself in touch with Christina. Late at night, in the Mausoleum, she had had strange fancies. And here, on Exmoor, she has them too. Who is to say that one cannot put oneself in touch with an ancestral past? Her forebears had come across the North Sea from somewhere, as her mother had never tired of boasting, to settle in the flat lands.

Many times she had been to Sweden before Christina attracted her. She has had a long relationship with the country. Sweden had welcomed and honoured her. She had written of its iron workers in a study that had been much praised. And she had once, long ago, been in love with a Swede. They had sailed amongst the little islands together through one fine week of summer, and eaten crayfish on the shore. He had told her she was an honorary Swede, being possessed, as he was, by those famous national characteristics, self-love and love of solitude. He had also worn a dashing small moustache.

The documentation of Christina's life had been picked over by generation after generation of scholars. Her iconography – Christina as Minerva, Christina ruling Parnassus, Christina as Pallas of the North – had provided food for dozens of art historians. Her relationship with the beautiful Belle Sparre, the tragic widow, her bedfellow and confidante, had been subjected to pages of analysis, and so had her feelings for the blond, handsome and moustached Magnus de la Gardie. Had she been in love with him, or with her successor, Charles Gustavus? Each letter, each seal, each tapestry, each painting in her collection, each binding of each book had been catalogued and examined through microscopes. Even her grave-clothes and her decomposed body had been exhumed and interrogated. The epaulets and button-holes, the embroidered cross, the silver mask, the deformed shoulder, the decomposed fibulae, the silk taffeta buskins and the grave-gloves.

Christina had been buried in a gown of white silk with a gold fringe. And the story went that in 1688, on the Christmas Eve before her death, Christina had tried on this new gown, watched by her last late love and protégée, the singer Angelica Giorgini. And an old wise woman who happened to be there at the same time, as wise women often are in such stories, said to her, 'Madame, you will be buried in

68

that dress not long from now.' And so it had come to pass. Christina had died next spring.

Yes, Frieda Haxby had grown fond of Christina, who preferred flat men's shoes and short jackets to white silk, who loved the storm and feared the calm, yet who ended her days peacefully chewing chestnuts with the cook in her Roman kitchen. Occasionally, of a night, when the wind blows (and here it can blow) she fancies she hears the strains of Scarlatti and the clear pure voices of Angelica Giorgini and her sister Barbara, as they sing to the old queen amidst the scent of jasmine. *Sehnsucht nach Süde, Sehnsucht nach Norde.*

As it happens, Frieda Haxby can hear Scarlatti whenever she chooses. The Giorgini sisters and Christina are three centuries dead, but Frieda has Scarlatti on compact disc.

The mortal remains and documentary leaving of Gladys and Ernie Haxby are, in contrast to those of Queen Christina, sparse. Ernest Haxby had been cremated, with a minimum of ceremony; the indifferent functionary had, to Gladys's indignation, got Ernie's name wrong. He had gone to his long home under the name of Edward Haxby. And he hadn't been allowed the hymn he'd always wanted either: he'd often spoken in praise of 'We plough the fields and scatter', but Gladys and the functionary were agreed that this was a harvest hymn and unsuitable for a spring send-off. God alone knows what Gladys had done with Ernie's ashes, but Frieda herself had broadcast those of the mother in the small garden at Chapel Street, amongst the seeding cabbages. She had dug them in with a trowel and stamped on them with a wellington boot. The cottage had been sold. Perhaps it would have been more fitting to write her memoirs in her birthplace, but Frieda had not been able to face such flat psychic hardship. She prefers it here, by the sea. But she has brought boxes of papers, and those she will, in her own good time, if she can bear it, examine.

Is this desire to write her memoirs a desire for revenge, or a desire to salvage her own self? She is not sure.

She remembers one of her last visits to her mother, in Dry Bendish. Herself a woman in her late fifties, her mother in her late seventies, in fair health but poor spirits. Ernie was long dead, dead of a series of strokes brought on by overwork: he had been the deferential farm labourer, cap in hand, put upon by all and sundry. Whereas Gladys, as she had frequently remarked, thought herself equal to the best in the land. 'Put upon by all and sundry', 'equal to the best in the land'. This had been the ditty, this the refrain, spun out remorselessly over the decades. Frieda stands there, in the small hot room that smells of hair, dust, mice and stale biscuits. Her mother talks and talks. Frieda, the tea-tray in her hand, the door ajar, is awash with tea. She is longing to go to the lavatory, her bladder is weak and grows weaker with age. This time Gladys defeats her. Frieda, standing listening to her mother, transfixed by the unceasing flow of complaints about a husband dead, neighbours disloyal, shopkeepers dishonest and life disappointing, finds that she has wet her knickers. Warm wet urine seeps through her black John Lewis elastic knickers and her black fifteen-denier corner-shop tights. Urine runs down her thigh. Desperately Frieda tightens her pelvic muscles, arrests the stream. But her mother's flow continues. Gladys had boasted, still boasts, that her babies were dry by the age of one, but Frieda knows that this was a lie. Frieda is not dry yet. A 55-year-old professional woman bullied into incontinence in a reversal of roles, in a perverse and sadistic seizure of power. Does her mother know what she has done? Does she know of this hidden humiliation? Please, Miss, please Miss Haxby, may I be excused?

Well, she had escaped from Dry Bendish to the sea's edge and this deluge. Will the rain never stop? It cannot, she thinks, pour down so heavily for much longer. All the waters of the western sky have gathered over the high wet land of the moor and have been sucked down to discharge themselves upon its black bosom and upon its upland bogs, upon its clefts and gullies. There is some movement in the darkness and it must lighten soon. Yet still the force of the downpour makes the great drops splash and break on the cracked paving. They rise again into little round fountains, some inches high.

She and her sister Hilda had called these special effects of deluge 'fairy fountains'. No, she corrects herself, not fairy fountains. 'Fairy crowns'. Little coronets of rain-pearls and rain-diamonds. Such an imagination, Hilda had had. That is what the adults used to say.

Can she nail Vampire Hilda, can she drive a stake through her undead greedy pulsing heart?

What can Frieda care for reputation? The last infirmity of noble minds. She is past all that, beyond, washed up. This at least even the utterly self-centred Rosemary must have observed. Why bother to set right the record for those one despises? Let them sink in their own mire. And sink they will, in the sucking mud of meatless burgers, drifting garbage, false coinage, hot vomit, corruption, greed, triviality. Scrambling for lottery tickets, selling one another bad dreams and ersatz merchandise and junk talk and fake labels. Sometimes Frieda thinks it is what they have done to the language itself that has driven her out of reach of her fellow countrymen and women. She had never considered herself a warrior in the battle for pure English, not wishing to ally herself with the High Anglicans, old-fashioned novelists, Oxbridge pedants, failed publishers and sacked editors whom that cause seemed to attract, but of late her recoil from what she heard over the airwaves, what she read in the press, what she received through the post had become so violent that she had found herself moving towards their ranks. Better here alone than make common cause with such dubious friends. There are no common causes left. Each for herself alone.

In her last days at Romley she had listened to the sounds of the city, to the wailing and bleeping of grief and pain and crime, to the waves of the sky vibrating with jumbo and chopper, to the ground beneath her house rumbling with tube and tunnel and drill and screw. And from the radio had spewed words that no sane society could ever coin. Offwat, Offtel, Offsted, Offthis, Offthat. Everything had gone Off, like bad meat. How had these sounds globbed up from the pure well of language undefiled into the tongue that Shakespeare spoke? Even her local library now labels books as GOO and FOO, as ROM and HIS and PAP. Gristle, fat, chicken scraps and water from cows' heads. The Trading Standards chief in Taunton had told her that the chicken carcasses are put in a huge metal container and pressurized until the tatters of flesh left on the bones begin to melt and flow. This excretion is squeezed through the machine's orifices, collected, reconstituted.

This we devour. GOO, FEE, FI, FO, FUM. Our great post-war civilization.

Once – indeed, only yesterday – this rotting world had fascinated her, and she had done her best to investigate it, to squeeze it till it flowed. But something has snapped in her. So here she sits, a queen in abdication, a queen in exile, a queen at the water's edge, an old woman with bad teeth and a weak bladder. They will not ask her back and she does not care. She has had her time. The wells are poisoned now. Even here, the poison seeps. It flows down the channel from the nuclear-power station, and the fishermen catch dogfish with two heads, mackerel that grow legs, lobsters that glow in the dark. Or so they say in the Wreckers' Arms.

She can see the far northern shore, for the air is clearing now. Across the channel in earlier centuries came Welsh coal for the lime kilns of this acid earth, and from the west came contraband from further afield – wines, lace, brandy, decorated steel blades from Toledo. The illegal trade continues, for today bales of marijuana are washed up on the beach. On fine days Frieda can see the pillar of smoke and the plume of flame and the giant's building blocks and towers of the steel-factory-turned-chemical-plant of Aberary. It rises like an enchanted palace. At night yellow lights bead the shore, and the single white eye of the sleepless lighthouse blinks. Freighters and tankers slowly pass. She watches them through her binoculars. She can see further now than when she was younger. She needs glasses to read, but her long vision improves. She does not always like what she sees.

She does not miss London. She does not miss company. She has had too much company. Her early years had been too thin and clear, too static, too flat, and to escape them she had thrown herself into turbulence, as soon as her children released her – and somewhat sooner, in their view. Her middle age had been restless, it had whirled her from project to project, from continent to continent, from bed to bed. Now she wishes to be alone.

Her feet are warmer now. She looks at them with muted favour. She has an ingrowing toenail on the big toe of her right foot which has troubled her all her life. She can see that if she survives into an advanced old age it will become a problem. On her left leg she has a large scar, which she now examines with interest, for it occurs to her that it is one of the few visible messages preserved from her girlhood. It dates from the day that her sister Everhilda Haxby had tried to kill her. Although much faded, it is still prominent. For years she had entered it in her many paged, richly stamped passports and in other documents, under sections headed 'Special Features' or 'Distinguishing Characteristics', until she had realized in the early 1980s that in these days of black boxes and instant incineration a scar, however historic and impressive, would not survive death. She had then taken to entering her dental bridgework. But not many countries ask for such details these days. We are all on computer, or expendable: who can tell which?

(On one of her academic jaunts abroad, in the 1960s, she had woken from heavy sleep to find her lover departed and her passport lying on the hotel bedside table, defaced: he had added to the admitted distinguishing feature of her thigh-scar, in indelible biro, the additional qualities of 'PARANOIA AND INTRANSIGENCE'.)

The scar is important to Frieda. It will appear in her memoirs. It marks the day when Hilda Haxby had tried to kill her little sister Frieda in the old mill by the river.

Frieda now accepts this attempted murder as a fact. She would stand up for it in a court of law. She has forgotten that this interpretation of that long-long-ago incident is very recent. It had come upon her when she was in her forties, and then only at the prompting of an analyst. The analyst had not been analysing Frieda Haxby: they had met quite by chance at a private view of an exhibition at the National Portrait Gallery. Warming white wine in hand, crumbling puff pastry dusting their suit jackets, they had been speaking of sibling slaughter, a topic prompted by portraits of Bloody Mary, Lady Jane Grey, Queen Elizabeth and Mary Queen of Scots. Bloody Mary, her round cheeks girlish and smug, grimly and firmly clutches a rose and a pair of gloves; Lady Jane nervously fingers her own fingers; Scottish Mary rests her hand beneath her right breast above her rosary; and victorious Elizabeth Gloriana dazzles in many poses with ruff and fan and jewels and brocade. Rivalries, hatreds, treacheries gleam from their stiff bodices, their hard bold eyes. And as the analyst spoke of the murderous passions engendered by heritage and court, it became clear to Frieda, in one of those flashes that come only once or twice in a lifetime, that the ladder had not shaken of its own accord. Hilda had tried to kill her, and all had followed on from that.

'What do you think, bird?' Frieda asks the pigeon. It rattles its saucepan lid in response, and cocks its head at her with a look of pure questioning intelligence. She gazes at it with affection. Its red-rimmed eyes pierce, its iridescent blue-green bright breast feathers gleam. Like the dog, Bounce, it has adopted her. At first she tried to chase it away, following her London-dweller's instinctive dislike of this verminous and greedy species, but the bird had persisted, retreating from her waving arms only to advance yet again and again, until she let it into her house, to sit with her. She admires it, she is sorry she tried to reject it. It is slightly lame, and had flown in with a message on its leg. She does not think the message is for her, and does not know how to open the little capsule. Let it keep its message, the message can wait. Now she and the bird are friends. It is brighter than Bounce. It likes to sit in the saucepan lid. She does not know why. Perhaps it reminds it of something in its former life.

Her own former life lies around her in untidy profusion. She must make a thorough search, one of these days, for her parents' marriage certificate. She is sure she had seen it once, amidst the debris she had carried with her from the cottage after her mother's death. She had made only the most desultory attempt to trace her own ancestry through birth and death certificates at St Catherine's House on the Aldwych, for the atmosphere of the building had appalled her – had such places been as disagreeable as this in the old days, when she had worked at Somerset House herself, before she had been able to delegate such tedious work to research assistants? The smell of anoraks and damp jerseys, the slamming of heavy ledgers, the jostling and poking, the muttered consultations, the crush, the queues, the discomfort, the despair. Every twenty minutes the inevitability of theft had been ritually proclaimed. What could these poor wretches have that would be worth the stealing? Who would want their plastic bags and their stubby umbrellas? Their miserable plough-pushing grandparents, their unmarried mothers?

The sight of her own name in the ledger had made her feel slightly sick. Born at 56 Chapel Street, Dry Bendish. Looking for her sister Everhilda and her mother Gladys had been more than she could face. She had chickened out and run away. She would write a record without records. Her last testament.

She will stick it out here. Maybe they will try to come and get her, those devoted children of hers, and carry her off in a straitjacket. Certify her, section her, lock her up and feed her by force. She must patrol her defences, when the rain clears.

Let us return to Hampshire, for it is still wet on Exmoor, and Frieda, although she has been an adventuress in her time, has become a bit of a bore. She does nothing but brood balefully on the past. She dreams too much, and takes her dreams too seriously. She is not good company. She makes little effort to entertain. Her mother and her sister are dead, but she will not let them rest in their graves. There is no reason why we should watch with her. We can take her in small doses. We will leave her by her paraffin stove amidst the paraphernalia of her necromantic arts, as the deluge gutters and dies, as she wonders whether to go down at low tide to hammer some radioactive mussels and winkles from the rocks of the shore for her evening meal. No wonder she is losing weight. But she likes mussels, and is happy to gleam, phosphorescent, into what is left of eternity.

We will go back to Hampshire, and see what has happened at the Old Farm. We will be more welcome there.

It is now the Sunday afternoon of that same long weekend, and the little cousins, Jessica, Jonathan and Benjamin, are upstairs, packing up the Game. They have been bleary-eyed all day, for they had played for four hours the night before; Benjamin had been on super-inventive form. It had been almost too exciting. When will they have a chance to play again? There has been some talk about a joint family holiday in a borrowed house in Italy in early September, but the children do not think it will come to anything. And anyway, the Game belongs here, in Emily's wardrobe. The children are accustomed to their parents pretending to make plans, then doing nothing about them. This summer, the Herzes are off for a week's cruise of the Aegean, leaving their children in Golders Green with their good grandmother; the D'Angers are too busy to get away; the Palmers will be staying in Hampshire through August. Their best bet for a reunion, the little cousins guess, is another crisis over Grandma Frieda. A second crisis would reconvene them.

They wrap the little riflemen and toy animals in soft cotton squares from Patsy's abandoned patchwork quilting, and lay them in their boxes, tenderly. They hope that something awful happens soon, to bring them all together again. Jon and Jess sense that if too much time passes, Ben will outgrow the Game, and then they will never discover its meaning, its dreadful, its unimaginably thrilling climax.

David and Gogo also pack their weekend bags, and strip their pillowcases from their pillows. They are good guests. Rosemary and Nathan, as they pack more messily in the bedroom over the corridor, argue about whether it has been a good idea to delegate the next visit to Exmoor to David and Gogo. Will they drive down and purloin the family silver, the family secrets?

Rosemary has not recovered from her own sense of shock, and is hurt that the others do not take it seriously. It was partly for their sake that she had made the journey, now all they can do is mock.

They gather downstairs, say their farewells. The Herzes are giving Simon Palmer a lift to London, and he climbs into the back of their car with Jon and Jess. Daniel has returned from driving the Partingtons home; Daniel follows the cars along the gravel drive, across the cattle grid. He is taking Jemima for a walk. As he walks, in the summer evening, he thinks about cultural appropriation. The concept sets his teeth on edge. So does the notion of the Veil of Ignorance. It strikes him, as he walks, that David D'Anger is a shocking fraud. A hypocrite, a pretender. Hidden behind seven veils of academic obfuscation, cultural plausibility and good intentions. An intruder, a thief in the night. Daniel is slightly surprised to find himself thinking these intolerant thoughts. What can David have said to irritate him so much? He slows down, pauses, stands still, as the old spotty bitch squats by the path. Can there be any threat to him, in anything David D'Anger has said? No, surely not.

And perhaps that is enough, for the moment, of domestic friction. Let us widen the circle. We need a new character. It is time to introduce the man from the attic, the man from the garden shed.

The man from the attic has emerged from hiding, and now he is sitting at the kitchen dining-table, shelling broad beans. Patsy is blanching and freezing them. There is a glut. He squeezes the pods, and takes out the plump, pale-green embryos from their silvery furred sheaths. He places them in a pudding bowl and drops the pods, already blackening, into a basket on the floor.

His name is Will Paine, and we have not met him before because he is shy. It is as simple as that. Patsy would include Will in family meals, she would happily (indeed with malicious pleasure) force him upon the attention of His Honour Judge Partington, but Will Paine is shy, and she respects his reluctance to be shown off. It is a pity that he would not meet David D'Anger, for David would surely have found him of sociological interest, but there you are: you can't control everything, even if you have the righteous confidence of a Patsy Palmer.

Patsy and Will Paine met in Winchester Gaol, where Will was serving a sentence for peddling grass to the middle classes of Stoke Newington. Patsy had found out all about it, and had been shocked on his behalf. The sentence had seemed excessive for so small a crime, and very unlikely to do him or anyone any good at all. Will is not, Patsy maintains, the criminal type. He is a lost boy, looking for a good cause.

He is half-coloured. He says his father is a Jamaican, and Patsy assumes he is telling the truth. (He is.) He says he comes from Wolverhampton, and here he cannot be lying, for his accent bears witness to his honesty. His mother now works in Bilston, in a factory that makes cot mattresses. She had, when Will was a baby, worked as an office cleaner.

Will is thin, slightly framed, and pretty. His smile is hopeful, his long neck bare and tender. He wears an earring and his hair is close cropped, sitting neatly on his finely sculpted skull. His skin is palish brown, shades lighter than David D'Anger's: he could almost pass for white, were it not for something deliberately exotic in his manner, a cultivated elegance suggestive of the West Indies he has never visited. Frankly, to be blunt about it, he is too nice-looking to be pure-bred English. The pure-bred English are a motley, mottled, mongrel ugly breed, blotched with all the wrong pigments, with hair that does not do much for them at all. The English are clumsy and gross and at the same time runtish. They do not make the best of themselves. Their bodies are thick, their faces either pinched and beaky like mean birds or shapeless as potatoes. Will Paine is a beautiful hybrid, grafted on to old stock. Both his mother and his father are large (his father, now returned to Jamaica, an eighteen-stone bathroom-scale-crushing dashing desperado, his mother sad and spreading from pie and chips and hot sweet tea). Will Paine is slender like an athlete, like a dancer. He is a mystic and he believes in vegetables and stars and cosmic correspondences. Even now he is explaining to Patsy Palmer the properties of the broad bean, which signifies, he assures her, prosperity in the sign of the water-carrier, good health to the liver, and nourishment for the left-hand side of the brain.

'You see the way they grow,' he says, showing her the little white spriglet at the bottom of the cleft of the swollen seam, 'they turn to the left, when they grow. They reach to the light, but the leaves always turn to the left.'

'Are you sure?' says Patsy, who does not believe in humouring the dotty, even when they happen to be ex-convicts under her own protection.

'No, not really,' says Will, smiling disarmingly. 'It's what I read in this book.' His smile is crooked, charming. His front teeth are both slightly chipped, evenly chipped, giving him a sharp, elfin look.

He recants so quickly that Patsy recants too. 'You may be right,' she said. 'I've forgotten all I ever knew about photosynthesis and the climbing habits of plants. We used to grow beans in jars with blotting paper. I don't suppose they do that kind of thing at school now. It's all computers now.' She sighs for innocence lost.

Will frowns, and continues to pod on. He is puzzled by Patsy, who seems to him to be a mass of contradictions. Here she is, like a good housewife, a good earth mother, freezing vegetables for the winter nights, vegetables which she has grown in her own garden and fed with her own compost. (She gets very little help, as far as he can see, from the aged once-a-week gardener.) Here she is sighing nostalgically about her innocent schooldays. And yet she lets her own children get away with murder. Will Paine wonders if Patsy has any idea of what Simon gets up to in his parents' absence? Will, who is now trying to go straight, would always have drawn the line at some of it – asking for trouble, the road to hell. Will has seen it all and he knows. Simon is a mad boy, a lost cause. Patsy does not even notice. And it's not only the drug scene. The stuff she lets them watch, those videos she has lying around all over the house. She must know what's in those nasty little black boxes, because she watches it herself. Doesn't it cross her mind that it might not be *good* for people to watch that kind of shit? Simon and Emily are her own children, and he supposes it's her business if she wants to let them deprave themselves, but he'd been shocked to see that she'd left it all lying around when those other little kids came for the weekend. Luckily they hadn't seemed interested, or he might have tried sneaking the worst of them out of their way, up to the attic. He couldn't sit through that junk himself. No way. It makes him feel faint. The sight of blood, the body parts, the meat.

He had been interested to learn that David D'Anger was, like himself, a vegetarian. He almost wishes he had plucked up courage and come down to say hello, instead of skulking up there with his tranny and his earplugs, instead of eavesdropping down the backstairs. He would have liked to have heard more of that conversation about the Veil of Ignorance. He had eavesdropped through most of David's exposition of John Rawls's Theory of Justice as Parlour Game, and had spent much of the night pondering its implications, wondering if he too, like Nathan, would give it a whirl and go for change. On the whole, he thinks not. He's been pretty lucky, most ways, and has a lot

79

to lose. Being born in Wolverhampton in 1969 had been a cushy number compared with some. Look at those poor buggers in Rwanda. Africa was a fuck-up, man. He couldn't credit some of the rubbish he heard, from Afro-Brits, about their African roots. He could just about get his mind as far as Jamaica, and one day he'd go there, one day he'd go and see where he came from, but as for going all the way *back again*, back through history, back to Africa and the bush and the jungle – no way. The buck's got to stop somewhere. Americans are barmy, Africa's full of murderous violent bastards. You can see them on TV. Give me Wolverhampton, give me Stoke Newington.

But of course no one will give him either Wolverhampton or Stoke Newington. They won't give him anything. When Patsy Palmer chucks him out, as he knows she will, as he knows she must, he has nowhere in the wide world to go. He has nowhere and nobody. He bites his lip, throws the last fleshy integument on to its ripped and slaughtered fellows, and wipes his hands on his trousers. How has he come to this? How has he, a nice chap like him, ended up in such dire, such lost, such *hopeless* loneliness? He knows he is nice-looking, but he does not fancy the blokes that fancy him. Sex unnerves him, he cannot do it. He's frightened of the big boys, the big-time. He's willing to work, but what can he do, who will employ him? Will Patsy be able to help? Has she a plan for him? He looks at her, as she plunges the last batch of blanched beans into iced water, and tries to read her face. Can she be trusted? Does she know how to help, beyond this room, beyond this small daily task?

She catches him looking at her, returns from her own thoughts to him, smiles, says briskly, rather too loudly, as though to a public meeting, 'Well *done*, Will. You're an ace. Be an angel, take the shells out to the compost for me, and the other compost bucket, while you're at it. Five pounds at least, I'd say, wouldn't you?'

No, she does not know how to help.

He picks up the basket and the bucket, and goes out through the back door, past the gumboots and walking sticks and dog dishes, and down the track to the vegetable garden. He wonders how he would make out if he had been born in Jamaica. If he had been born in this house. If he had been born in China. If he were to win the lottery. Would he still be himself, Will Paine?

He tips out the eggshells, the beanpods, the burnt toast, the potato peelings, the wilted lettuce. The leavings of the feast. In America, he has heard say, they throw out more food a day than Africa consumes in a month. If you don't eat what's on the table in an American restaurant it gets trashed, even if it's still in its cellophane wrapper. That's what he's heard.

He doesn't want to live on leftovers for the rest of his life. He wishes he could push a button and send the whole lot spinning round. Level the food mountains, let the wine lakes flow to the sea. He's heard tell of a computer game, where instead of killing monsters or rescuing maidens you could cause famines and gluts. You could play with the distribution of the earth's resources. You could make the desert blossom and parch the rain forest. What would happen, he wondered, if you spread everything thinly and absolutely evenly and gave everyone a bit of everything? Was that what Emily had been hinting at?

He shakes his head. He knows his brain does not work well. It is undeveloped, and he has messed it up with hash, for only when he is high does he feel less than utterly alone. People tell him his IQ is fine, but he knows better. In prison he had started an O-Level course or two, to fill in the time, but he knows he has no staying power. He bends like a reed. His mind bends. He is pliant, suppliant. These English, they are bred to hold on, like terriers. They hold on to their own interests even while they smile and offer shelter. Nothing will dislodge them.

He wonders if Patsy is right to put teabags in the compost. Are they biodegradable? He pokes the decaying mess with a garden fork, levels it, pats it down, conscientiously abstracts a cigarette butt, which certainly should not be there, drops it in the blue plastic bucket called Lucy.

David D'Anger is a traitor. He has joined the English. So says Will Paine to himself, as he walks back to the house. But he doesn't believe it. David D'Anger is a lucky man, that's all, a lucky man with staying power. You can see his mind follow through. Beware of envy, says Will Paine to himself, envy's a killer. He has seen it kill.

It's not right, that he should nurse this aching solitude. True, Simon and Emily speak to him, Patsy speaks to him, even Daniel sometimes nods at him. But they don't rate him, any more than they rate their poor dumb dog. And they're not all that nice to the dog. He's seen Simon kick the dog.

As Daniel, Patsy, Emily and Will Paine eat their friendly Sunday supper of cheese on toast, Frieda Haxby is scrambling in her welling-ton boots over the slanting slate-grey black and purple rocks, clutch-ing a fossil hammer and a kitchen knife. She is after the mussels. She treads with care on the living pebble-dash of limpets and barnacles, for she has just had a narrow escape on her own staircase: she had put her foot through what seemed to be a new cavity, and had saved herself only by clutching the not-so-solid-fake-Jacobean banister. She had cursed herself: that pretty little estate agent, fluffy Amanda Posy from Taunton, had warned her about the stairs, had told her she'd need to get them seen to. (Amanda Posy had not believed that anyone would ever buy Ashcombe. Who could want such a gloomy monstrosity? People only looked around it for a giggle. But Frieda had not been the giggling type.)

Frieda, in her youth and middle age, had been deep into cultural appropriation, into appropriation of every kind. She had appropriated middle-class education, manners, accent; she had appropriated her sister's admirer; she had appropriated a middle-class husband. Then she had moved on to colonize Canada, Australia, Sweden, various campuses in the United States and, through her son-in-law and grand-son, Guyana. She had meddled with them all, with insatiable anthro-pological curiosity. But now her empire was in decline, it had shrunk to this barren strand, this rotting folly, these dark wooded acres, this sunless kingdom by a sunless sea. Frieda Haxby, booted and skirted, picks her way towards the mussel beds. She carries a plastic bucket. She is watched by three crows. They are a faithful three. She knows them well.

The weather has brightened. To the east the swagged clouds are heavy and swollen, but above her opens a bright-edged ragged baroque space of the purest, clearest virgin blue, from which might descend an angel, a grace, a dove. Arrows of golden light pierce from a hidden source, the curtains tinge with pink. Frieda's castle faces north, and the sun leaves her coast early; its sinking rays stream backwards, towards the brow of the moor.

Frieda pauses for a moment, steadies herself, and gazes at the rent gap in the sky, as it widens and pulses itself open like a great sacred heavenly heart. It reminds her of one of the new paintings she has bought, her new Leland, which still stands in the damp, its face to the wall. She has been naughty with her paintings. They will be ruined if she does not hang them, but she is afraid that if she knocks picture hooks into her peeling walls her house will fall down. Leland paints blue-clay earth and skies of terracotta and salmon pink and crushed rose, and from the raw mines of his clay crawl the blobbed and cellular forms of life. He paints evolution.

She must hang the paintings one of these days, she resolves. They cost many thousands of pounds. She is a patron of the arts.

She reaches the mussels and starts to prize them from their lodgings. The mussels are stubborn, but so is she. Slowly she fills her bucket. Not much lives on this shoreline, for it is too stony, but some forms of simple seashore life have colonized it. Brilliant orange lichens, periwinkles, anemones. Further west, there are crabs and lobsters. *Cancer pagurus, Homarus vulgaris, Palinurus vulgaris*. A wash of leathery bladder wrack and thong weed, a sprouting of small succulents with stiff white and dry pink flowers – the common scurvy grass, she thinks, though it is much prettier than its name. On the salt marshes to the east samphire grows, and she has seen there several times on her wanderings a lone white egret, fishing far from home. What wind had blown it here, so far off course?

Palinurus drowned. Or was he hacked to death by pirates? She cannot recall.

She tries not to break the mussels, but from time to time her knife slips. Her hands are bleeding, but they are too cold to feel the pain.

83

Blood and sea-salt mingle. She hacks, and curses. She has broken a mussel shell, and its living body is exposed. She pulls it away from its rock and a lump of its flesh seems to leap from its crushed dwelling place and attach itself like a leech to her bare and bleeding hand. Horrified, she tries to brush off the clinging fragment, but it sticks. It is fierce and hopeful. It will not die. Its flesh seeks a home on her flesh. She scrapes it off with the knife, and it falls vanquished on to the pale purple rock. The mussels in the bucket breathe and sigh. Frieda the murderer turns her back upon the sea, and climbs up the hill.

THE VALLEY OF ROCKS

For the rest of the summer no news comes out of Exmoor. Frieda Haxby is silent. David D'Anger received a postcard from her in late July, with notes on the subsidy-sheep scandal of Somerset and Devon, with information about a new Japanese protein-producing fungus, but it did not require an answer and gave no address. It was posted in Exeter, so either she or some minion of hers is mobile. David has been appointed her conscience: he knows that she expects him to carry on her abandoned work as fleshthorn and neckpain, that she derides his squeamish emollience, his desire to please. But he does not see why he should take on the subsidy sheep of the West Country. There are none, as far as he knows, in West Yorkshire. He cannot take on the whole of the British Isles at her command. He has visited an abattoir, at her prompting, and he will never recover from the horror of it. Does she endorse or deplore the Japanese fungus? It is not clear from her card, which portrays, on its pictorial side, a view of the small church of Oare where Lorna Doone was shot by Carver Doone at the altar. (What is Lorna Doone, David asks Gogo. She enlightens him.)

Does Frieda Haxby have a postal address, a postcode? The house is called Ashcombe, a dull suburban name for what Rosemary has described as a grand Gothic folly, but Rosemary has insisted that it is beyond the reach of any postman's beat. Maybe Frieda collects letters from a box nailed to a tree at the end of the drive? Maybe she drives into the nearest village to pick up her mail? The house is marked on the Ordnance Survey Map, so it must exist. But Frieda has fallen silent. Neither light nor sound emerge from her remote planet.

Daniel, Gogo and Rosemary are too busy with the complications of their own lives to think about her much, but occasionally they are reminded of her existence. Silly-Season reports of a sheep-savaging Black Beast on the moor – a puma, a panther? – give rise to sardonic speculation. It would be just like Frieda to get herself involved with a Beast. Perhaps she *is* the Beast. Another story, about tragic deaths in a dinghy off the Island of Lundy, makes Daniel and Patsy reach for their map, for this, they know, is Frieda's coastline. They look at the swirling frills of steep brown-green contour on the OS map, at the marks of the Roman Fortlet and the Old Barrow and the farm called Desolate.

None of them knows the West Country well, though all have touched upon it and passed through it: now they turn the pages of their papers and read of stag hunts, of hunt saboteurs, of water pollution, of fires in nuclear-power stations, of an outbreak of meningitis in Taunton – is the virus spreading south and westwards from Stroud? And was it in Taunton that Frieda had seen the photograph of Ashcombe in the estate agent's window? They think it was. It was in Taunton that she had run to earth the story of the meatless hamburger, which had caused David D'Anger to take up the unpleasant scent in his adopted constituency of Middleton. Taunton has much to answer for.

Occasional inquiries about Frieda reach Daniel and Patsy, David and Gogo, Rosemary and Nathan. Friends, acquaintances, colleagues, visiting Americans, visiting Australians, visiting Swedes: none of them seems to know where she is. The tone of some is reproachful. This, they agree, must be part of Frieda's plot. She has forced them into the role of Bad Children, and wilfully, playfully, cast herself as a Neglected Mother. They hope that most of those who ask after her know her well enough to discount this storyline. Her agent surely must. Her agent Cate Crowe had telephoned Rosemary to say that to her astonishment she had had some interest in the film rights of *Christina* from some Australian crackpot, and although there would be nothing in it (how could there be?) (well, maybe a few thousand quid at most?) she felt it her duty to pass it on. But although she had written to Ashcombe, no answer had been received. Did Rosemary know if Frieda had a telephone down there? Or a fax? Had Rosemary any idea of what the woman thought she was up to? Rosemary, not best pleased to be reminded of the embarrassing débâcle of *Christina*, yet anxious to keep on the right side of the powerful Cate Crowe, had muffled and waffled her reply about access to Frieda. But she had divulged that her sister Grace would be going down there in late August or early September on a visit. Grace would relay any messages. And Rosemary had rung Gogo and David, to tell them that they must contact Cate Crowe before they headed westwards.

So David and Gogo, during the summer months, collected and listed topics for Frieda. They even wrote themselves an agenda, afraid that the disruptive power of Frieda's presence and the inhospitable extremity of her retreat would, if ever they reached her, scatter their programme to the high winds.

They would tackle Frieda on the subjects of her health, her electricity supply, the safety of her premises, and the wisdom of contemplating a winter beneath the moor. (The floorboards, according to Rosemary, were dodgy.) If it seemed possible, they would raise the subject of her will. They would take a package of letters and contracts and German Income Tax Release Forms from Cate Crowe, and provide a courier service for anyone else who wished to send communications to be delivered into her hand.

This, of course, depended on her willingness to receive them. What if they arrived there and were shown the door? What if she set the dogs on them?

Neither David nor Gogo thought that this would happen. They considered that they would prove more tactful and acceptable visitors than the worldly and impatient Rosemary, who had arrived unannounced and no doubt on high-heels and smelling of Ysatis. The D'Angers would approach in better camouflage. Moreover they would carry with them the talismanic figure of grandson Benjamin, who had always seemed close to her heart. Who could close a door against Benjamin? He had the key to all castles. So they fondly believed.

They encouraged Benjamin to take an interest in their projected outing, and he, a quick and scholarly child, responded eagerly, though he drew the line at reading *Lorna Doone*. They consulted him about the route, and at once agreed when he expressed a desire to see Stonehenge. Of course he could see Stonehenge, and he could also visit the

Valley of Rocks. Would he like to see Wookey Hole and stalactites and stalagmites and Cheddar Gorge? Yes, he said, he would.

Benjamin was excited about the thought of entering a deep cave. He went to the library and took out books on pot-holes, and studied the diary of the man who set the record for spending time alone underground. The world's largest cave chamber is in the Gûnong Mulu National Park in Sarawak, the largest underwater cave is in Mexico, and the largest cave system in Britain is the Ease Gill system in Yorkshire.

Benjamin read about Wookey Hole. In 1935 the caves had been explored with the help of breathing apparatus by a team led by Gerald Balcombe. There was one woman in the party, Penelope Powell, and she had described descending into 'a world of green, where the water was as clear as crystal. Imagine a green jelly, where even the shadows cast by the pale green boulders are green but of a deeper hue; as we advanced, light green mud rose knee high and then fell softly and gently into the profound green-ness behind. So still, so silent, unmarked by the foot of man since the river came into being, awe inspiring though not terrifying, it was like being in some mighty and invisible presence . . .'

Benjamin looked up fiction about caves and tunnels on the computer index in the library. He read Jules Verne and H. G. Wells and even Edward Bulwer-Lytton. He dreamt of caves. One night he dreamt that he was travelling through tunnels that transfixed the earth: if he went onwards, he would emerge in Guyana, in the green-gold of his own land, where there were waterfalls higher than the eye can see, and chasms deeper than man or woman could fathom. In these tunnels beneath the earth a high wind raged perpetually, a source of unharnessed subterrestrial power far mightier than the winds of heaven which turned the silver mills of the wind field on the ridge behind his Uncle Daniel's false Old Farm.

Benjamin was a rich and prolific dreamer. He dreamt that his grandmother Frieda was standing with him at the prow of a boat on an underground river. The river flowed rapidly through a dark tunnel. Frieda was holding high a banner that swirled in the wind.

Benjamin had also been reading Coleridge, recommended by the librarian, who had become involved in his study of the West Country and the Matter of Exmoor. She recommended *Kubla Khan*. She assured him that both Coleridge and Wordsworth knew Exmoor well, which surprised Benjamin, but when he read the notes on Wordsworth's *Peter Bell* he could see that she was right. (He did not think much of *Peter Bell* – a silly poem, about an old man and a donkey, not a patch on *Kubla Khan* – but nevertheless, the Valley of Rocks might be worth a visit?)

It is not surprising that David and Gogo and the friendly librarian and Benjamin's teachers at his local comprehensive were proud of the exemplary little lad. All knew that he would go far, and bent upon him the earnestness of their intentions and their hopes. An imaginative, hard-working child, he was well enough liked by his peer group; the worst they ever did to him was yell, 'You're a stiff and your mum's a stiff!' Or, more briefly and more unkindly, 'Your Mum!' (What this meant, Gogo never discovered.) Swimming was his favourite sport, and he could swim a length under water, but like his father he followed the cricket and loyally supported the West Indies he had never seen. He had plenty of friends, and though the tabled food in the D'Anger tea-time basement was on the healthy side, it was easy enough to smuggle in Snickers and crisps, cans of Coke and even bacon sandwiches. The tea-time minders turned a blind eye.

In short, Benjamin D'Anger was a spoiled brat and a teacher's pet. But so strong was the D'Anger charm, so formidable the stiff Haxby Palmer presence, and so generous the minders, that he was not resented.

(One should not ignore, in this context, the influence of Grace D'Anger. The other parents knew it was good to keep on the right side of Gogo. If their brains suddenly snapped, if their parents started to dodder with Parkinson's or Alzheimer's or encephalitis, if anyone in the family was struck down with motor neuron disease, Gogo was known to be your woman.)

As the date of the excursion approached, Benjamin's excitement mounted. One would have thought an outing to the West Country tame stuff for a child in the 1990s when 40 per cent of families from social classes A and B took two holidays or more a year and to parts of the world more exotic than Exmoor. (A slightly larger percentage of social classes D and E took no holidays at all but they need not concern us here.) David D'Anger himself was well aware of these statistics; more surprisingly, Benjamin D'Anger was aware of them too, for he took a keen interest in his father's interests, and was very fond of statistics of social trends. A regular little John Stuart Mill, young Benjamin. (He had even tried to read Frieda Haxby's classic, *The Matriarchy of War*, but had found it heavy going, you may be pleased to hear.) Benjamin was well aware that some of his own schoolmates had been to Italy, Greece, Turkey, Spain, the Canaries and Corsica; some of them had been to Disneyland. Others had never been further than the PC games shop, the arcade and the lido. He himself had been to Tuscany, Yugoslavia and France. Yet despite these travels, he was filled with an unusual and appropriately childish joy at the prospect of a week's outing to Somerset and Devon. He crossed his fingers, muttered superstitiously to his private gods. He hoped that this time nothing would prevent or delay their departure. Let there be no crisis at the hospital, no excitement on the political horizon. This was a dull time of year. Let it stay dull. Let Benjamin have his holiday.

They were to set off, for a week, at the beginning of September, and David and Gogo had written to Frieda at Ashcombe, saying that they would be in the neighbourhood and thought of dropping in to see her. She was to write to tell them if the particular day they had selected – they named it firmly, suggesting tea – was unsuitable. No answer was received.

Much anxious family consultation took place before their departure. The Herzes had returned from their week on the Aegean, and the Daniel Palmers were stuck in Hampshire, entertaining a succession of house guests. Instructions and warnings were interchanged. Beware vipers, Rosemary repeated. Don't forget to ask if she's signed her German tax forms, urged Daniel.

At last the D'Angers loaded themselves and their guidebooks into their family car and set off westwards along the M3. Merrily they bowled along on their adventures, like characters in an old-fashioned children's story. Mummy, Daddy and Benjie. Benjie, from the back seat, assured Mummy and Daddy that he felt fine, and was not at all sick.

Daddy, at the wheel, fell silent as they passed the pigs of Wiltshire in the sloping fields, rooting in the sunshine amidst the barracks of their curved corrugated huts. Wiltshire seemed full of pigs and soldiers. Lucky pigs, princely pigs. They could wander at will. David D'Anger wondered if he would forgive Frieda for dispatching him to the abattoir and the chicken gutters. The stench and tumbled carcasses remained with him. That had been what she had intended. The scrappy raw-pecked self-abusing fowl and stunned curly-headed bullocks haunted him, as did the pale girls in bloody overalls, the young men with dull eyes. The human factory farm. Pig skin, chopped gizzards, mechanically recovered meat. Cheap and nasty food for cheap people.

Parliamentary candidate David D'Anger thought of his constituency of Middleton as he drove through Wiltshire. His future flock. It was a scattered constituency, of conservative dormitory villages straggling into Pennine farmland to the west, and to the east the dead and disowned villages of the coalfields, leaking red rust into brooks and rivers. Amongst the coalfields had risen the new hangars of Fast Food. Middleton itself was a nothing place, a small town without a heart. The Westerners never went near the old coalfields. Why should they? They drove past them at eighty miles an hour on the motorway. As he drove past these pigs. Nobody ever stopped to see. One world did not know that the other existed. And David D'Anger had been selected to woo, simultaneously, the Black–Asian vote (3.4 per cent and rising) and the middle-class Westerners. The way the polls were going, unless something unexpected happened (which, in politics, it always could) he is sure to be elected. Well, almost sure. Does he really want to be the Member of Parliament for Middleton?

Like most men of politics, David D'Anger is not very good at taking a holiday and forgetting his work. He is not very good at emptying his head of social statistics. He had brought a lot of statistics with him in his suitcase. He had promised himself that he would try to enjoy the landscape and the company of his wife and son. But it was hard to concentrate on pre-history and Stonehenge. He and Gogo managed to reduce even Stonehenge to party politics, to Benjie's irritation – Benjie had come to worship, and there his parents were, chattering on about the National Trust and English Heritage, about the Minister for the Arts, about motorways and the newly appointed and hubristically entitled Director of Stonehenge. What does she think she's going to do, David and Gogo asked one another rhetorically – rearrange her troops in a more contemporary configuration, and order the noonday sun to shine upon a different dolmen? Benjie thought this was flippant, but perhaps it was no more flippant than the unsightly bunkers of public lavatories, the gift-shops, the tea-room selling Solstice Savories and Megalithic Rock Cakes.

Benjamin tried to abstract himself from the temporal, the trivial. This was the heart of England. All around on the magic turf, amidst sheep and crows and dipping wagtails and flint-white molehills, against a swelling green backcloth of lumps and tumuli, small dramas were enacted. A party of smartly dressed middle-aged Japanese women strode purposefully onwards, their sensible neat polished shoes measuring the metres to the next point on their itinerary; they were trailed by their taxi-driver, a local Druid with long dirty yellow hair, dark glasses, faded jeans and a pink shirt. Two travellers from the New Age sat facing the stones, at some distance, upon an embroidered mat: their eyes were shut, their noses were pierced, their foreheads were bound with embroidered fillets, and their legs were gartered with straps of blue leather. They moved their lips in silent prayer. A fat white baby crowed in delight from its pushchair, and a solitary Mid-Western Wordsworth scholar with a backpack opened a pocket edition and read to himself from *Guilt and Sorrow*. An elegant Indian in a green and gold sari seemed to cross herself as the slight wind ruffled her hem and her long hair. A young woman with flowing red Viking hair knelt at the feet of a dark bearded monkish figure and kissed his hand as tears poured down her pale cheeks. Benjamin gazed at these devotional multicultural figures in the Wiltshire landscape.

His interest in Wookey Hole was if anything more intense, and as they drove on, after an unduly protracted pub lunch (how odd of Gogo to order Scampi and Chips in a Basket, she really must think she was on her hols!), he realized that it was going to be a near thing. They had already decided to skip Cheddar Gorge and take it in on the way home (he'd heard that kind of promise before), but Wookey Hole was still on the itinerary. Now it too began to look at risk. Would it close before they got there? Were his parents already tired of sight-seeing? He feared they were about to betray him by deciding to drive straight on to their pre-booked country hotel for a tedious pre-dinner drink. He kept his eye on the car's clock, and managed by secret map-reading and tactful intervention to prevent them from taking a wrong turn near Shepton Mallet. He got them on course again, and urged them on. They were still in plenty of time in his view, but suppose they turned nasty at the last moment?

His heart sank as they emerged from miles of slow narrow minor road and saw the Wookey Hole car park. This was not promising. It was vast, ugly, multilayered and crowded. Gogo groaned, and David said, 'Oh *dear.*' Wookey Hole was clearly a Fun Spot for the Masses, almost as downmarket and repellent as Disneyland. The car clock told them it was already 4.08. Benjamin knew his parents would try to wriggle out of their commitment. 'There's a space!' he cried eagerly, as he saw a tin-green Datsun reverse from the ranks on the tarmac. 4.09 said the clock. David hesitated, and took the metallic Datsun's place.

It was a long walk to the cute fake stone shop that sold tickets, and there was a queue. The next tour was not until 4.30, and the D'Angers were informed it would take an hour and a half. Could Benjamin persuade his parents to hang around for twenty unattractive minutes in order to join an uncongenial throng and walk into the floodlit bowels of the hill, chaperoned by a talkative guide? He put on an expression of stubborn pleading and willed them not to retreat. He wanted to see the inside of the Mendips.

Gogo was for cutting their losses and for moving on, but David, fortunately, had decided to take a sociological interest in their fellow visitors, in their group dynamic. He discovered that the visit to the caves in fact took only half an hour; the rest of the tour was optional. They weren't obliged to traipse round the paper mill and the fun-fair. They'd be out and away by five, in plenty of time for a hot bath before dinner. Benjamin's will prevailed. He coerced and chivvied his reluctant parents across the road, along the path up the hillside, past the flowing stream and the hyena lair, beneath the hanging wood, and marched them to the iron turnstile with their tickets in their hands. (It was, complained Gogo, expensive: an exploited cave, a marketed hillside. Who owned it? It was not clear. Who owns the bowels of the earth?)

Like docile prisoners they waited, like prisoners they allowed themselves to be ticked off and lined up and filed into the cold and dripping darkness. Benjamin tried not to listen to the guide, who was utterly banal; he tried to concentrate on the hanging horseshoe bats, the exotic tropical hart's tongues, the yellow folds of the limestone. They moved from chamber to chamber as the guide described the Witch of Wookey Hole, who had lived here with her little dog and brought ill-luck to the land: look, there she was, frozen to stone by a monk from Glastonbury, and there was her little dog, and there was her alabaster witch's ball.

The Silver Axe flowed silently and very fast, without a ripple to disturb its surface. It was hundreds of feet deep. The stalactites and stalagmites were elaborate, magnificent: they hung in carved amber and ivory curtains, stained here and there with vermilion, ochre and sooty black. They were fretted stone in a cathedral. (A poet called Alexander Pope had stolen some of them for his grotto, the guide informed them.) The hillside above them weighed billions of tons, and nobody knew why the roofs of the chambers did not collapse. Nobody knew how deep the water was. The guide described the green underwater world discovered by divers, and the muddy Cave of Gloom beyond Chamber 24. He recounted that the divers had found another chamber, a twenty-fifth chamber, but beyond that none had ever penetrated. Beyond that was a dive into 'the bottomless void'. Two hundred feet down the abyss 'one brave man' had plunged, but had returned, leaving the mystery unsolved. What lay beyond, in the

94

heart of the mountain? What caverns, what lakes, what waterfalls, and what abiding spectres? Benjamin was deeply impressed. The unknown called to him, the depths invited him. He was enchanted and afraid.

He was less enchanted by the paper mill, which his parents rushed him through at some speed, pausing only to read out to one another the optimistic Heritage version of the past presented by the Brochure ('It is silent now, the great rag boiler. The benches are empty where the aproned girls chattered and giggled while their nimble fingers shredded the bundles of rags, cutting away buttons and hoods and lengths of whalebone . . .') Benjamin was not interested in whether they had chattered or wept, whether they had shredded bundles of rags or their own fingers; he paid little attention as Gogo, her resistance subdued by marketing, underground imprisonment and oxygen deprivation, succumbed to buying some hand-crafted indigo-blue envelopes made from recycled denim. (They were very deceptively packaged, so Gogo discovered, not to her surprise, when she tried to use one three months later.) Benjamin was not interested in all this. He walked through the fun-fair and the Magical Mirror Maze in a daze, thinking of the one brave man who had plunged and returned. This old-fashioned stuff, these hurdy-gurdies and carved horses and penny-in-the-slot machines meant nothing to him, nor, he could see, did they arouse much nostalgia in his parents. 'The whole outfit seems to belong to Madame Tussaud's and Pearson' he heard them muttering to one another, as they tried to find an exit through the Maze and the fountains and the arcades. It was not easy to get out. 'The bottomless void,' he repeated to himself. 'The Cave of Gloom.'

The young woman at the reception desk did a double-take on David D'Anger. He was used to this, but her response was innocent and unconcealed. She received him at first with a slightly hostile suspicion (Indian chap), then with deference (hadn't she seen him on TV?). She clearly couldn't work out whether she recognized him or not (he suspected, as a practised sociologist, that she might be the type to have endured ten minutes or so of *Question Time* or *Newsnight* or *Race*

Watch, just long enough for his features but not his name to register), but she decided to treat him as a celebrity, just in case. And after that, it was plain sailing. He employed the D'Anger charm, she called for a porter, blushed, assured him that she was giving him the room with the best view, and asked if he and his wife would like a cup of tea. Then she shimmered, in a slightly flustered way, at Benjamin, who was carrying a suitcase and a large canvas bag of books and maps and papers.

She was a pretty young woman, with fair hair, a tilted nose, a fair creamy skin, full lips and a visible bosom. She wore a crisp long-sleeved white blouse over a black skirt, belted with a black leather, gold-buckled belt. An English rose. Her name, she informed them, was Felicity, and she was there to help them in any way she could. She blushed again as she spoke. Would they like to book a table for dinner? Would the young man be dining with them? They would find a mini-bar in Room 12, though not in the young man's room (Room 14) next door. Which newspaper would they like in the morning?

Gogo watched this little comedy from a distance. She never interfered with David's conquests. And the girl was a harmless girl, a country – county girl. Not like those sharp-toothed metropolitan vampires at the studio, those ambitious little graduate politicos who offered their sexual services as research assistants. David's vanity deserved appeasement. Let him have it. She could no longer give what he needed.

And in bed that night, as David turned to her, as he now so rarely did, she tried not to turn away. She held him to her. She loved him, for what that was worth, but she was no wife to him. She did not want to lose him, but how could she keep him? Childbirth had traumatized her. She thought of her mother, as David sadly embraced and caressed and entered her, and wondered how Frieda had broken away into freedom. She remembered her grandmother, that sour old bag in Chapel Street, that endless talker, that killjoy: was she herself a killjoy now? Sex did not interest her. She had chosen the head, the brain, the nervous system. An ancestral puritan rural deadness had flattened and unsexed her. She suspected that neither her brother nor her sister was much interested in sex. They preferred status, money, power. How had

Frieda Haxby managed to break away and run off with so many ill-assorted men? Or had they been, as Daniel sometimes hinted, a cover? For status, money, power?

Gogo knew that she had done David a great wrong, through love of him. She had loved him so much that she had been unable to refuse his formal proposal of marriage. But for his own sake she should have denied him. Now they were bound to one another for ever by that child sleeping in the next room. Gogo believed that her husband had once loved her. She hoped that he was unfaithful to her, for if he were not, how hard his life must be. She hoped that David had not killed in himself all the natural man. He too had chosen the head, but his body, unlike hers, could still speak. How could he remain with her? Should she not forgo him for his own good? What was this loyalty that kept him by her side?

An inky flood of sad regret flows upwards through the stranded body of Grace D'Anger, and tears fill her eyes. Her husband folds her in his arms and rocks her quietly. She is beyond his reach, and he loves her. But she cannot return.

(Grace D'Anger's suspicions about her sister Rosemary's marriage are, as you will have noted at once, quite false. Rosemary Palmer married Nathan Herz for sex. Anyone but Grace D'Anger would have spotted that. The suspicions reveal more about Grace than they do about Rosemary.

Her speculations about Frieda are nearer the mark.)

Four days the D'Angers spent on their slow approach to the siege of Frieda in her stronghold. For four days they strolled streets, climbed hills, ate cream teas, drank shandies, inspected lifeboats. They walked across the dinosaur backbone of the clapper bridge at Tarr Steps, they pulled reassuring banknotes from holes in unfamiliar walls. (Holidays in England did not come cheap.) They thought of visiting the Island of Lundy, but could not discover the times of the boats. High up on the Brendons they ate a sandwich in a pub where they met a dog with three legs and a man with none. They were told tales of smugglers and highwaymen. The night was dark over Exmoor and the stars were brighter than in London.

They also amused themselves by making a personal survey of the ethnic minorities of the South West, both resident and tourist, comparing the evidence of their own six eyes with the statistics provided by David's supply of surveys, handbooks and almanacs. I am compelled to say that the D'Angers do this wherever they go. You might think this indicates an unhealthy obsession with racial origins, and you might be right. On the other hand, you might put it down to a natural sociological curiosity. I don't have to have a view on this, I am simply reporting the facts. The latest edition of *The Almanac of British Politics* informed the D'Angers that the Black–Asian population of Somerset hovered somewhere between 0.8 and 1.4 per cent, and personal observation introduced them to a turbaned sheik walking alone on the top of the Quantocks, a family group from Wolverhampton eating fish and chips at Combe Martin, a Q8 petrol station manager, a student group of quantity surveyors of Middle Eastern aspect measuring the beach at Porlock Weir, and a scattering of signs for tandoori take-aways, Chinese take-aways, Taj Mahals and Curry Paradises. The vegetarian curries of West Somerset and Devon were, to David's disappointment, not very good; David needed a curry fix several times a week, which was easy enough to find in London and Middleton, but not so easy in this outpost. David had held high hopes of Watchet, where a consignment of Ugandan Asians had once been billeted, but none of them seemed to have settled. Watchet offered Battered Cod.

No, this was the white man's kingdom. Beaker folk and Belgae, Bronze Age and Iron Age, Celts and Romans, all had been white, or white-ish. There had not been much assimilation or infiltration here. David and Benjamin D'Anger were conspicuous in the crowds. But then, thought Gogo proudly, they were conspicuous anywhere.

On their last afternoon of carefree wandering before their planned assault upon Frieda, they made their way to the Valley of Rocks beyond Lynton. As they left the green car park Benjamin feared that this celebrated stretch of the coast path would prove to be an Old Lady's Promenade, but as they strode on the crowds thinned, and soon they found themselves alone, with black mountain goats skipping like small horned devils above them and seabirds wheeling below them. The path picked its way along the edge of the precipice, and the waves broke on the sterile purple stones. The famous rocks were perched perilously, erratically, in a strange high ridge, in tormented anthropomorphic configurations, as though a scene of great tumult at the dawn of the world had frozen as it cracked. Benjamin could make out a great beaked witch's profile, a goblin's hunched back. These were the bones of the old world. If he half shut his eyes he could make them move, he could make them rise up and drag their buried limbs from the green turf and walk. He could make the ground itself heave and spew forth more boulders. He could open a cavern and entomb these strolling earthfolk for seven times seven years. Darkest night would encompass them. At his will the rocks would tumble, the seas would rise. He narrowed his eyes and the horizon quivered, the grass squeaked.

And then they emerged in Victorian Lynton, and had a cream tea.

That evening they sat together in the bar of the hotel where they had become regulars: this was their second night in residence. (The barman complained that English holiday-makers were not what they were – in the old days a family would settle for a week, a fortnight, a month: now two nights counted as a long stay.) They ordered drinks and spoke of Frieda. They congratulated themselves on having provided themselves with good camouflage. They were seasoned sightseers now, with stickers and souvenirs to prove it. If Frieda wished to cross-question them on their journey, they had their answers ready. How would she receive them? When they arrived at her gateposts, should they send Benjamin in first, like a sacrificial lamb?

They had come a long way for this meeting, and they set off the next day with uncertain expectations. Already in reconnoitre they had passed and repassed the turning that led to Ashcombe, but now they had to accept its challenge. The little narrow high-hedged lane plunged deeply and steeply. Tracks led off it, to Bolt Farm and Desolate Farm and Sugar Loaf Hill, and there were one or two acorn symbols and coloured arrows marking footpaths and bridle-ways. But they passed no walkers and no horses. The lane deteriorated into a track, as Rosemary had said it would, and brought them to a gate called PRIVATE.

Of this too Rosemary had spoken, but she had found the gate closed, and had got out of her car to wrestle with it. Now, for them, it stood open. Was this, they wondered, a good omen? Had Frieda opened it for them? Was Frieda waiting for them now, at four o'clock in the afternoon, like a good granny, with the kettle on the hob? With caution they descended, bumping downwards over cattle grids and pot-holes. As yet there was no sign of the house. They passed a derelict Gothic gatehouse, and continued down through high Victorian rhododendrons and giant hollies and rowans red with bunched berries of blood. The foliage was reckless, exuberant, profligate. And suddenly there before them, below the next turning, was the house, and beyond the house, the sea.

Cautiously Gogo lurched the car forward over the last few yards, and brought it to a halt before a square archway which led through the front (or was it the back?) of a high three-storeyed grey stone building into a courtyard. As Rosemary had warned them, Ashcombe was not a building of much charm. Of all the charming cottages and farm-houses and gentlemen's townhouses of the West, this was surely one of the ugliest. It sat there, defiant and large and out of keeping. Like a mental institution, a penitentiary. Whoever could have built such a thing here, and how, and why? Rosemary said she had thought it had once been a hotel, but had given no reasons for this supposition. It did not look very cosy or welcoming. No Felicity here.

Gogo switched off the ignition.

'Well?' she said.

'*Avanti*,' said David. '*Su forza*.' (He sometimes spoke Italian when he was nervous. It was a give-away.)

'She can't *eat* us,' said Gogo, laughing falsely as she opened the car door.

'Fee, fi, fo, fum,' said Benjamin. He was enjoying himself. He knew by now that she was in there, somewhere. He sensed her. And so it was that, after all, he found himself leading the party. Boldly, he marched beneath the arch and across the courtyard towards a corresponding arch in the far wall: somewhere there must be a door, somewhere here must be the quarters that Frieda had occupied and civilized?

'Grandma!' he called. 'Grandma Frieda! Where are you? Are you hiding? Can you see me? Where are you?'

It was a fine afternoon (how lucky they had been with the weather!) and a clear north light beat backwards up from the sea, which glittered at them through the double arch. They could hear waves upon the rocks and shingle below, and the gentle soughing of wind in small weathered trees. Benjamin called again, and this time, at his call, an ancient black and white sheepdog emerged from a door in the wall of the second arch. It advanced upon him, wagging its tail. Benjamin patted it, softly, for it was a frail and bony dog. Then he followed it into the building. Gogo and David, in the courtyard, looked at one another, paused, then heard him call.

'Here she is! Come along, here she is!'

And they followed the boy and the dog, and there, in the garden room overlooking the lawn and the terrace, where once teas had been taken, was Frieda Haxby. She was waiting for them. She stood, and smiled, with her arm round her grandson.

She too, a hundred years late, was about to take tea. They saw a table, spread with a white cloth, with a china tea-set, with a fluted silver pot and a silver jug and a silver sugar-bowl. There were scones in a heavily gadrooned silver cake-basket and sandwiches upon a blue Wedgwood plate. A fruitcake embossed with almonds and cherries stood proudly upon a cut-glass cake-stand. Thick cream was heaped in a cut-glass bowl. It was a tea.

And Frieda Haxby was wearing her tea-gown. There she stood, shoulder to shoulder with her grandson, in a floor-length gown of radiant midnight blue embroidered with silver. Sequins sparkled on her bodice, and ran in little streamlets down her full soft draped skirt. Silver earrings dangled from the lobes of her ears, and her wispy grey hair was arrested by a *diamanté* pin.

'David, Grace,' she said. 'Grace, David. You have come all this way.'

She sounded moved. What was the old fox playing at this time? Slow-witted, Gogo moved forward as in a dream to peck her on the cheek; David followed her example, with more simulation of conviction.

'I'm *so* pleased to see you,' said Frieda in a gracious, a sociable tone. '*Do* come and sit down, I'll go and put the kettle on. Make yourselves at home. I'll be back in a moment.' And out she glided, with the teapot, in a rustle of silk.

They dared not speak in her absence, for fear of breaking the spell, but they looked around in wonder, and soon they saw that all was not as wonderful as it had seemed. This was a stage set, and you could see into the wings. Only the table and its precious loading spoke of order. The floor was an old, faded, bleached parquet, unpolished for decades, with blocks missing or rising from the plane; the papered walls were stained with damp. The light fittings were askew, and the curtains hung in uneven bunches, tied back by string. The tea-table was spotless, but round the far edges of the vast room stood other tables covered in familiar intellectual Mausoleum clutter – papers, files, cardboard boxes. 'But', whispered Gogo to David, 'it's all quite *clean*. And how much *weight* she's lost. *That* can't be a trick, can it?'

'No,' said Frieda, returning with a reassuringly blackened and mundane kettle and the silver pot of tea, 'I really *am* a lot thinner. That's not an optical illusion, I promise you.' She had overheard them, or read their minds. 'I really can get into this dress. So I thought I'd wear it for you. Milk, Grace? Do tuck in, Benjie. The sandwiches are Marmite and cucumber, not very exciting, I'm afraid. And the scones are Readymix, but I *did* make them myself. Milk, David? Or do you still prefer lemon?'

As they settled in to their tea, she chatted on, politely, civilly. So good of them to come so far. She'd got their letter, but it was a long way to the post-box, and time passed so quickly here. She'd known they'd find her. She'd been looking forward to seeing them. Benjamin in particular. How was Benjamin?

'Fine, thanks,' said Benjamin, his mouth full of sandwich. He could not take his eyes off this apparition of his grandmother. 'Can you get right down to the sea from here? And where did you get that dress?'

'I'll show you round later,' said Frieda, and proceeded to tell them about the dress. She'd bought it – perhaps Grace would remember? – for the Royal Banquet. And she'd worn it just that once, for the King and Queen, when she went to receive her Swedish medal from the Historical Society for her book on the Iron Coast. The dress had cost hundreds and hundreds of pounds, and it had hung in her wardrobe for years, and was now quite out of fashion. So she had decided to wear it 'about the house'. She was pleased with that phrase, and repeated it. 'I wear it', she said, 'about the house.' She paused, then continued, 'And I wear my other evening dress, that green striped silk one, as a nightie. This one won't do as a nightie because the sequins prickle and the shoulder pads get caught round your neck when you're asleep. But the green striped one is just fine for bed. And this is just right for tea.' She beamed at them, happily, and with great benevolence.

Oh hard to say what game we play.

After tea, she offered to show Benjamin round the house. She did not offer to take David and Gogo. 'You two can stay and watch the sunset,' she commanded them, and she set off with her grandson. (The moment Frieda was out of earshot, Gogo leapt up and started to rummage.)

'Watch out for the stairs,' said Frieda to Benjamin, from time to time. 'Watch that step. Careful with the doorknob, we don't want to lock ourselves in.'

The house was enormous. Corridor after corridor, room after room. Frieda pointed out that she lived in a small part of it, but that she liked to know the rest of it was there. 'It's a comfort to me, all this space,' she said, pausing for breath at the top of an attic staircase. 'All these empty rooms. I *could* go into them. If I wanted.' She coughed, a dry smoker's cough.

Benjamin tagged behind her, gazing at claw-footed baths with corroded bath taps, at leaning wardrobes, at tiles loosened by damp, at crops of woody yellow fungus sprouting from cornices, at delicate thin-stemmed lilac fairy caps growing from window-ledges, at black spatters and dustings of mildew. Only a few of the rooms showed signs of recent habitation, and all of those fronted the sea.

In one of the front rooms, on the top floor, he could see that Frieda worked. Here hung a barometer decorated with marquetry shellwork. It registered that the weather was set fair. A large desk to one side was occupied by a word-processor. The walls were covered with postcards, cuttings and messages, stuck on with drawing-pins and sellotape. A table stood in the window, furnished with an oil lamp, a pair of binoculars and a lantern-globe. 'Sit down, sit down, and look at the view,' demanded Frieda, and Benjamin obediently sat and stared across the channel at Wales.

She sat by him, and idly span the globe.

'When I was your age,' she said, 'I thought I'd visit every country in the world. Now I don't know if I'll even visit every room in this house.' She sighed, impressively.

'Do you see boats, Grandma?' asked Benjamin, still gazing through the binoculars, adjusting the lenses.

'Sometimes. Big ones, freighters or tankers, going up to Cardiff, I suppose. And fishing boats. In the summer there's a pleasure steamer called *The Balmoral*. That's quite a sight. There must have been more of that kind of thing in the old days. And they still smuggle, along here. Or so they say.'

'I can see a boat. A little one, chugging. Is that a smuggler?'

Frieda took the glasses from him, inspected the vessel.

'Could be. How would you know? More likely mackerel.'

'Is it deep, the Bristol Channel? Have you ever seen the Severn Bore? Does it go this far?'

'Full fathom five thy father lies,' hummed Frieda, and fished in her sequined reticule for a cigarette. She lit it with a match, and threw the match out of the window.

'No,' she said, 'I've never seen the Severn Bore, but I did see an air sea-rescue. It took hours and hours.'

'What happened?'

'There was a boat out there. I heard what I thought were shots, but they must have been flares. And then the helicopter came. It circled and circled. It didn't seem to be able to get near. I don't know what the problem was. It kept circling in, then circling out. Like a dance.

Like an insect's mating. It didn't seem to be able to make contact. But maybe it did. Then I saw the hull of the boat rise. And the boat went down. And the helicopter flew away.'

'Did it rescue the people on the boat?'

'I don't know. It was too far away. I didn't see the ladder come down.'

'Did anyone drown?'

'Frieda shrugged her huge padded sequined wings. 'I don't know.'

'Didn't you see in the papers?'

'I don't see the papers any more.'

'Didn't you hear on the radio?'

'I didn't hear anything about it. I do sometimes listen to the radio, but I didn't hear anything.'

'So you might have watched people drown?'

'They were too far away.'

'Grandma?'

'Yes?'

'We went down into the caves in the Mendips. Have you ever been down in the caves?'

She shook her head, and he told her about the bottomless void and the Cave of Gloom and the twenty-fifth chamber with no exit. He told her about the one brave man who had dared and dared and failed. She listened, coughing and puffing at her cigarette. She nodded.

'So you want to dive into the bottomless,' she said. 'Yes, of course you do. Well, you go on wanting that. And maybe one day you will come up into the pure air, on the other side.'

'Is there pure air, on the other side?'

'Who knows? They do not come back to tell us. There must be something, or why would we wish to plunge?'

She threw her cigarette on to the floor, and stubbed it out on the floorboards with a high-heeled *diamanté* slipper. She caught Benjamin's disapproving glance, and cackled.

'Don't worry,' she said. 'I won't set myself on fire. This place is so wet, you'd need a few gallons of paraffin to get even a little blaze going. Every night I spend an hour or two with the firelighters. It's hard work, here, keeping warm.'

Benjamin cupped the globe in his hands. Demerara, Cayenne, Isle aux Morts.

'Come on,' said Frieda. 'We'd better get back, they'll be wondering if we've fallen off the battlements. I've just one more place to show you before we go. I'll show you my treasure house. Follow me.'

And she set off, down some backstairs with old bell-pulls, to a room that she called the butler's pantry.

'I don't know if it *was* the butler's pantry,' she said, 'in fact I don't know what a butler's pantry *is*, do you? But that's what *I* call it. I'm in charge here. I call things what I like. Upstairs, downstairs, what I say goes.'

There were drawers, and cupboards, and a sink with copper taps deeply encrusted with blue-green verdigris.

'Look,' she said, opening drawers. 'Here's the family silver. What's not on the tea-table. If they ask you where it is, when I'm dead and gone, you can tell them.'

Wrapped in green baize lay cutlery, candlesticks, sauceboats, ashtrays, monogrammed cigarette cases. A tortoiseshell box with cufflinks. A velvet-lined box with coffee spoons. Pastry forks, fish forks. An ivory-handled ladle. Treasures from a past world.

'These are Palmer pieces,' she said. 'There was nothing on the Haxby side. Nothing to speak of. You never met your grandfather.'

She stated this as a fact, inviting no query.

She opened another drawer, full of a tangle of old necklaces of shell, coral, amber, green glass. 'Nothing valuable here,' she said. 'Don't let them waste time sorting this lot out. There's nothing here. Except' – and she picked out a square maroon plum leather gold-initialled box – 'except this. This is my best medal. It's probably worth something.'

It lay in its ivory-cream satin nest. A ribboned, enamelled heraldic brooch, gold and blue and yellow, with writing upon it, in Latin and in another language he did not recognize.

'Yes,' she said, 'that's probably worth a few bob.'

She fastened the box's little golden hook-and-eye catches, and put it away at the back of the drawer.

'I suppose you're too old for farm animals,' she said, as she opened the last drawer.

She handed him an old Clark's shoe box. He lifted the damp lid. It contained small chunky animals, crudely hand-carved from wood – cows, horses, pigs, sheep. They were carefully arranged, more lovingly stored than the silver and the beads. They were forlorn yet cherished. Benjamin could see that a whole childhood was preserved in that box. He narrowed his eyes and stared at them. They were full of power. He could awaken them. He stroked their blunt heads with his finger.

'They were mine,' said Frieda. 'My father made them for me when I was ill. I was in bed for weeks. He made me a farmyard, and these were the animals. He was a farm labourer, your great-grandfather. He liked the beasts. That's what he called them. The beasts. Though mostly it was ploughing. The sugar beet. And humping sacks.'

She paused. 'I was in bed for weeks,' she said.

'What was the matter with you?'

'I fell off a ladder at the mill. We weren't supposed to be there. We were trespassing. Look' – she pulled up her long skirt, ruching up the fabric to bare her thigh – 'look, there's my scar.'

He stared at the purple-white, shiny, puckered scar on her bluish elderly mottled soft flesh.

'That's when he made me the animals. I was delirious. They thought I'd got tetanus.' She rolled her skirt down again, to his relief; and laughed. 'We called it lockjaw, in those days. Terrible things happened to you if you got lockjaw. Fits and spasms. I don't think I had lockjaw, I'd probably have died if I had. I think I just didn't want to tell. It's a fine scar, isn't it?'

'Ghastly,' said Benjamin, happy to praise it now it was concealed.

'They couldn't stitch it, too much dirt in it. I was delirious. I thought I could make the animals move.'

'And couldn't you?'

She looked at him sharply. 'Well, for me they moved,' she said. 'But I was only a child.'

'One last thing,' she said, reaching into the back of the drawer, and taking out a small japanned tea-caddy. 'Your great-grandfather gave me these too. They were turned up by the plough. He was always hoping to find a golden necklace, or even a coin. Bert Caney found some coins. They're in the museum at Peterborough. But all my father found were these. Do you know what they are?'

Benjamin handled the cool and amber-green, the coiled and wrinkled twists of stone. He shook his head.

'They're fossils. Fossil shells. But the village people called them the devil's toenails. They were two a penny. They were always turning up. But we liked them, my father and I.'

'I like them too,' said Benjamin.

'They're all that's left, of those days,' said Frieda. He was shocked, for tears stood in her old eyes, she blinked, and her firm voice caught and trembled. How could she care for things so long ago? Such small things from so long ago? Was she going to cry? He could not bear it if she cried. But no, she shook herself, her sequins glittered, she was back in the saddle.

'You can't have them yet,' she said. 'But when I'm dead and gone, they shall be yours. I'll add them to my will, if I remember. And to Benjamin, the toenails of the devil.'

She put them back in the drawer, briskly wiped her dusty fingers on her dress, and gathered herself together. 'We'd better get back to your parents,' she said. 'They'll be nosing around in my secrets. So you've liked your little holiday, have you? You liked Funster Dunster and the Exmoor ponies? Have you seen any deer yet? What the brochures call wild-life is good round here. There's lots of it. I'm studying it. Shall I tell you something? It may come in handy.

> Crows are green, rooks are blue,
> Crows are three and rooks are two,
> I may live for ever, and so may you.

Remember that, won't you?'

★

The soul and body rive not more in parting
Than greatness going off.

'Tis safer playing with a lion's whelp
Than with an old one dying.

On the way back to the hotel, the D'Angers reproached one another. They had been hoodwinked, they had performed none of the tasks they had been dispatched to perform, they hadn't reached the first item on their agenda. Rosemary and Daniel would be outraged at their negligence, their inefficiency. They'd forgotten all about Cate Crowe and contracts and tax forms, they hadn't handed over any of the messages they'd been collecting, they hadn't discovered how many acres went with the house, they hadn't found out whether Ashcombe was freehold or whether the land belonged to the Exmoor National Park, they hadn't asked about insurance or electricity or Calor Gas or telephone messages or postal deliveries or drainage. They'd eaten their tea, and that was about it. True, Gogo had discovered evidence that Frieda seemed to be writing her memoirs – a parish history of Dry Bendish, a report from the village school where Frieda had begun her education, a cutting from a school magazine thanking Mrs Ernest Haxby for her war work, a history of the sugar beet industry in Britain – but she hadn't had time to take it all in, and David had wasted the precious half-hour of Frieda's absence by browsing through some Grimm fairy stories illustrated by Arthur Rackham. He had been attracted to these by a large message stuck on top of an old-fashioned well-worn gold-leafed volume, on a pink Post-It, from Frieda to herself, asking, DID RACKHAM WORK ON EXMOOR? ASK JANE.

As missionaries, as detectives, they had been failures. David and Gogo turned to Benjamin for help, wheedling him to rack his brains for details, but he wasn't very helpful: yes, *all* the house was damp, with great mushrooms in places, and she said she'd never been into some of its rooms. Upstairs she had a globe and binoculars and a word-processor. She *said* she'd found a human skull under the floorboards, but she might have been joking. No, he hadn't tried any of the taps for hot water. Had they?

The truth was that, confronted with Frieda in a ballgown, they had been disabled. She had taken the initiative. How to assess what she was up to? She had looked well, but was it natural to lose so much weight so quickly? It seemed stupid to ask if she was eating properly, when she had provided them with such a feast – but what did she live on when no one was watching? *Did* anyone ever watch? Did she know anybody in the neighbourhood? Who was Jane? Was Frieda gaga, was she wandering, or was she in more than her right mind? And did that dog have fleas?

Frieda's step had been sound, her voice clear. She had not faltered or trembled. (Benjamin kept to himself her moment of frailty over the fossils.) If one had met her in a tea-room, in Sainsbury's, at dinner, one would not have suspected any form of dementia. There was nothing certifiable about choosing to live alone on the edge of a cliff. And they had liked the view. On the whole, they agreed, as they drove inland over the yellow and purple moor towards the Egremont, they had to take their hats off to her. She looked just fine. They'd have to bluff it out with Rosemary and Daniel. Tell them to mind their own business, tell them they were lucky to have a mother who wasn't moaning at them night and day, or breathing down their necks, or costing them a weekly fortune in a private nursing home.

Gogo had recognized the dress of midnight blue. Was it madness, to wear an evening dress at tea-time?

So Frieda had bought it to wear in Stockholm, with kings and queens and princes. She had been given one of the highest honours of the land, for her work on the iron mines of Sweden, for her careful reconstruction of Mary Wollstonecraft's epic voyage in search of treasure round the Swedish shore. All of Frieda's projects had been slightly crazy. That was how she had got where she was.

'After all,' said Gogo aloud, 'if you can't be mad when you're old, it's a pity. And I don't think she is mad. I think she's just gone in for some new form of free association. And at her age, what does it matter?'

'What's free association?' asked Benjamin.

'Letting the mind wander,' said David.

'Exploring the subconscious,' said Gogo. 'Bumping around in the dark.'

They drove on in silence for a while, until David spoke. 'Wasn't there some story,' he asked, 'about an older sister who died?'

'In mysterious circumstances,' agreed Gogo.

'An older sister?'

'That's right. Aunt Hilda. Or, as I've just discovered, Aunt Everhilda. I've just seen her birth certificate. Everhilda Haxby. Can Everhilda be a real name?'

It had an ancient, Anglo-Saxon ring to it, they agreed. Everhilda and Frieda Haxby. Little Nordic Valkyries, little warrior maidens, little Grimm girls.

'Do we know what happened to her?' asked David.

'Little pitchers have big ears,' said Gogo.

'Come off it,' said Benjamin. 'You can't use me as an envoy, and then refuse to tell.'

Gogo laughed.

'I'd tell you if I could, Benjieboy, but the honest truth is I don't know. I think she may have committed suicide. Frieda never mentioned her but Gran – my gran, your great-grandmother – she hinted at it once. Something funny happened in the woodshed, but I don't know what.'

'What woodshed?'

'Oh, just a joke.'

'Oh *look*,' said Benjie, forgetting Everhilda. 'Stop, Dad, do stop. Look!'

And David pulled the car in to the side of the road, for there, on the brow of the moor, was a young herd of antlered stags, crested against the evening sun, grouped as for a postcard. Cars were pulled up all along the hillside, as tourists got out cameras and field-glasses. The D'Angers got out and joined the scattered impromptu viewing panel: Benjamin accepted the offer of a loan of some binos. (They were better than Frieda's, he discovered. Hers had been Taiwanese and these were Swiss.) The stags posed, grazed, and raised their noble noses to the evening air.

Gogo and David stood arm in arm, much married, watching their darling boy as he watched the beasts.

'You can say what you like about Frieda,' said Gogo, as the stags slowly began to saunter away, 'you can say what you like. Mad she may be, but she's been a worker. When you think where she started from. It's been a long, long journey.'

'Yes,' said David. 'And I wonder where she's heading for now. Did you notice, she didn't mention hamburgers or sugar or politics once? And she didn't even ask after Daniel or Rosemary until you brought them up. She must have got some new kind of bee in her bonnet. I hope she doesn't let it loose on me.'

Frieda stood by her favourite rock pool in the slanting light. The evening skies of her first autumn promised well. They turned the stones to a sharp, roseate, Pre-Raphaelite pink and purple and blue.

A string of bubbles rose from a crevice at the bottom of the pool. There was always a string of silver bubbles rising from this pool at low tide. They came from the submerged heart of the rock. She thought of a spring near Granada, at the place where Lorca died. She had forgotten its name. There, near the olive grove where the poet was buried, tears of air rose perpetually through green clear water into a tear-shaped well. These drops of air had wept upwards for centuries to prophesy his murder and now they would mourn him for ever.

So they had gone and left her to her fate. To be fair to them, she hadn't given them much choice. They'd enjoyed their cream tea. They'd eaten quite a lot. She had caught Gogo reading Everhilda's birth certificate, and David deep in Arthur Rackham.

The Grimm stories had belonged to Hilda. Frieda had stolen them from her sister. When she was little Frieda had loved the goblins, the princesses, the old men of the sea, the water maidens, the raven brothers, the haunted woods. Yet the stories were often absurd, often inconsequential. Frieda's literal, logical battleaxe of a mind had been bemused and entangled by these tales. She had tried to chop her way through the briars. She did not like nonsense. There was a mystery there, forever beyond her grasp.

She began to pick her way back up towards the house.

There were so many versions of the story, and all of them were false. You could begin it this way.

Once upon a time there were two little girls, and their names were Everhilda and Frieda Haxby. They lived in a cottage on Chapel Street in the little village of Dry Bendish, which stood on the only hill in the flat, flat lands of the east. Their father Ernest was a poor man who tilled the earth and sold his labour cheap and was known as one of the kindest and most foolish men in the village. Their mother Gladys was proud and vain and dreamt grand dreams for her older daughter Everhilda. She loved her pretty older daughter Everhilda, who was fair and delicate, but she was cruel to Frieda, who was plain and dull. She called them Little Swan and Little Mouse.

Mother Gladys was a clever woman, and she was cunning too. She was much cleverer than her poor, quiet, stupid husband, and when he brought them gifts from the fields – a nail, a pebble, a fossil, a horse-shoe – she poured scorn upon them. She read to her daughters the stories of the old gods, and told them that their ancestors had come from far away, across the iron sea, from the land of the Vikings, to this dry inland hummock. She told them they must be warrior maidens, for this world is but a battleground. They must sharpen their brain-knives, or they would be poor and weak like their father. She set daughter against daughter, and daughter against father, for she saw that Frieda prized her father's gifts. Her own gifts were the gifts of brain and book and word. You are my child, little swan, she would say to Everhilda. Let the little mouse play in its straw.

But Everhilda was cunning too, like her mother, and she saw that her sister was weak, and so she made her sister her slave. She wove a spell over Frieda. The two sisters shared a little bedroom under the eves, and at night Everhilda would creep into the little one's bed to subdue her. Poke, pry, lick, scrape. And as she grew older, she told her stories, stories even more frightening than the stories their mother told. She told tales of children lost in woods and eaten by wolves, of maidens forced to marry cruel dark men from the distant Orient, of little girls sunk beneath the bog in the underworld where great spiders dwelt, with dung beetles and centipedes and earwigs and woodlice and mealworms and tapeworms, and froghoppers and scorpions and scarabs and bats and birds of prey. And spiders would stitch open the eyes of the little girls so that they could never close them, but would be forced to stare unblinking and forever at the monstrous world beneath the world.

('Like *this*,' Hilda would say, advancing upon Frieda's bed, and forcing open her sister's eyes with hard little fingers, 'like *this*. And she can never shut them again, and the insects walk *all over her*, they walk in and out of her nose and her ears and her mouth and her hair and her clothes, and they crawl into her body and they lay eggs down here, *in her body*.')

And so the little sisters grew up, and so the little mouse sister whimpered and scuttled with fear. And then a day came when the big sister said to the little sister, 'Shall we go for a walk, down by the river?'

Or the story could have begun this way, of course.

Once upon a time there was a little girl with golden hair who lived happily in a cottage with her mother and her father, and her mother and her father loved her dearly and gave her everything her heart desired. But one day there came a baby stranger to the little cottage, and the mother and the father told the little girl she must love and cherish the little stranger. But the little stranger was a fierce and changeling child, and it cast a spell over the little girl, and forced her to be her slave. Night after night, the stranger child would demand more and more stories from the little girl, and would keep her awake in the long night hours, and the little girl was forced, night after night, to invent more stories, for the stranger child said she would die if once she fell asleep. And the little girl grew pale and weak, while the stranger child flourished.

So one day the little girl said to the stranger child, 'Shall we go for a walk, down by the river?'

★

Frankly, thought Frieda, panting slightly and pausing to cough as she climbed the last short steep flight of steps to the terrace, you could tell the story any old way, as long as you left out most of the circumstantial details. And she's forgotten most of those, as it had all happened so very long ago. But however you told it, you always ended up at the old mill. And after the old mill, the disputed prince.

She could remember the walk to the mill well enough. It had been an August day, one of those interminable days when summer holidays lengthened into tedium, when cabbage leaves turned yellow and fell from their scarred stalks, when wasp-eaten apples dropped to rot in the grass, when village boys clustered behind hedges pulling legs from daddy-long-legs or smoking furtive cigarettes. Much of the summer, Hilda and Frieda frowsted indoors, reading library books, for they were not encouraged to play with the village children, and therefore they were despised by the village children. Gladys, true to her roots rather than to her education and her adopted class, made no effort to entertain her daughters. They bored her and she bored them. The hopeful child's cry of 'What can we do today?' had long been silenced, and sullen, resentful, the girls skulked and sulked. The father saw, and was sorry, and was powerless.

Gladys Haxby had been obliged to give up her job when she was married. That was the law in those days. Married women did not teach in schools. Or not in peacetime.

Three bored women in one small cottage, making the worst of their lives, while Ernie Haxby worked in the fields or at the farm.

And then, one hot day, Hilda had said to Frieda, 'Shall we go for a walk, down by the river?'

Frieda had brightened, like a puppy hearing its lead rattle. She was ready, she was waiting.

They had walked through the village, past the Wheatsheaf and the Post Office and Caney's General Store, down Church Street, and through the churchyard to the lane which led to the river. They knew the churchyard well, although the Haxbys and the Buggs had been chapel. They knew the tombstones, and Hilda had woven stories about the old table tomb which was coming apart at its stone seams. In it lay bones, and worse than bones – virgins buried alive, with their hearts still beating; old men whose hair grew after death to cloak their bodies with a silver caul; babies strangled by their child-mothers at birth. But now the sisters were too old for that kind of nonsense. Even the dead bored them.

They had plodded along the dry path at the edge of the yellow field towards the river and the mill. Frieda had trotted obediently behind. And they had reached the line of pollarded willows that marked the river, and the bridge by the derelict mill.

Their father had once worked at the mill, humping sacks of grain, in its working days. He was a casual labourer, at the beck and call. But now the mill was abandoned, for the river level had fallen. It stood empty. The slatted wooden wheel was still. Their father worked the beet fields.

The mill yard had been turned into an agricultural dump. Old machinery rusted and weeds sprouted. The sisters had often stood there, on the bridge by the river, but they had never entered the mill. But now Frieda followed Hilda on to its forbidden ground, and edged her way through the broken door, and breathed in the white dust. They heard scufflings, vanishings. And they had looked at the ladder. It mounted to the next floor, from which in the olden days, five years ago, the grain was heaved down the chute. And Hilda had said, 'I dare you.'

And Frieda had climbed at Hilda's command, but Hilda had not followed. And then Frieda had been frightened to come down. Coming down was worse than going up. Down she had clambered, over uncertain rungs, past rusty protruding nails, and as she came down, the ladder had begun to shake and tremble. And Frieda had fallen, and in falling she had gashed her leg. It had bled and bled. And Hilda had run off and left her there, and Frieda had limped home, her leg bandaged by a dirty handkerchief, to her mother's certain wrath.

The wound had healed badly, and Frieda had been ill. And her father had made her the animals.

★

Hilda was dead, and Frieda was alive, with a scar on her thigh. So what did it matter, how it all had happened? What did it matter if there was no true story?

'I look to the past because I cannot see the future,' said Frieda aloud, dramatically, to an unseen audience, as she stood upon the terrace, fronting the sea. She fingered the grey stone ivy-bound urn upon the parapet wall, started to pluck at the tenacious white worm roots, the thicker strangle-hold of hairy tentacles. She had meant to replant these urns, but maybe she wouldn't bother.

Once upon a time, and once upon a time. Fairy stories were all the fashion these days, she gathered. Feminist fairy stories, oriental fairy stories. She hadn't kept up. She was out of date. She belonged to another kind of past, a bruising, grim, spartan, wartime, post-war, heavy-weight past. This was the time in which she had earned her laurels. She'd read her Bettelheim, long ago, but she'd lost interest. Anyway, how could you have a character called Gladys Bugg in a fairy story? Everhilda, yes, but Gladys, certainly not!

A couple of years ago, in Monte Carlo, she'd met a writer of romantic fiction, who wrote under the name of Amantha Knight. Her real name was Susan Stokes. She was very fat and very rich. Over a White Lady they had compared their losses at the tables, and discussed the forging of names, the writing of fiction. Was one influenced by names? Both thought it probable. Frieda Haxby, Frieda pointed out, was a brutal sort of name, a fierce name, a hammer of a name. Susan Stokes sounded, Miss Stokes considered, very plebeian – 'which, of course,' she conceded, 'I am.' It gave Miss Stokes pleasure to invent romantic, alternative names for her characters, to give them romantic, alternative destinies. Although, as she pointed out to Frieda, there were only two plots to choose from. One was *Sleeping Beauty*, the puberty myth. The other was *Cinderella*, the tale of Rags to Riches. All romantic fiction, according to Miss Stokes, was a variant on these two themes. Sometimes she wrote one, sometimes the other. Nobody ever got tired of them.

Frieda had granted that she had a point. She hadn't thought about it much since, until, during her removal, she came across the Arthur

Rackham volume which she had borrowed or purloined from her sister. She had reread the stories with curiosity, still puzzled fifty years later by their fractures and caesuras, their banalities and brutalities. A primitive folk mind, forcing all experience into a primitive mould? She had tried to break free, to create new stereotypes, to discover new patterns in the past. Yet what was her own tale but the tale of *Cinderella*? From Rags to Riches had been her story, as it had been the story of stout Miss Stokes.

She and Miss Stokes had agreed that they were rich enough to retire, to live at leisure. (Miss Stokes had a house in Jersey, and another in Tenerife.) Yet they did not wish to retire. 'Boredom is my bugbear,' confessed Miss Stokes, waving at the waiter. 'I get bored when I'm not working. What about you?'

So on one went, but to what end? Frieda would never attend another conference, never give another lecture, never harass another politician or engage battle with another journalist or historian. They weren't worth her attention. Really, on balance, she was very disappointed in evolution. It didn't seem to speed up at all. It seemed to have got stuck. Evolution had broken its appointment with the human race. Or maybe it was the other way round.

The ivy smelt sour on her fingers. She wiped her fingers on her skirt. Woodlice scuttled, dislodged. She had hung her ballgown back in the damp beetle-bored wardrobe. She had enjoyed its airing, had enjoyed the shock on the faces of Grace, David, Benjamin. Once she had glittered, once she had been fine. She had turned heads, made headlines. And what was there to show for it now? A dress hanging from a brass rail.

'I look to the past because I have no future,' said Frieda Haxby.

Frieda Haxby had never been a comfortable woman. She'd never had much truck with comfort, and she didn't see why she should start to seek it now.

On 1 December 1788, Schiller wrote to his friend Korner, when the latter complained that he was not being very productive: 'The ground for your complaint seems to me to lie in the constraint imposed by your reason upon your imagination . . . It seems a bad thing and detrimental to the creative work of the mind if Reason makes too close an examination of the ideas as they come pouring in – at the very gateway, as it were. Looked at in isolation, a thought may seem very trivial or very fantastic; but it may be made important by another thought that comes after it, and, in conjunction with other thoughts that may seem equally absurd, it may turn out to form a most effective link. Reason cannot form any opinion upon all this unless it retains the thought long enough to look at it in connection with others . . . where there is a creative mind, Reason, so it seems to me, relaxes its watch upon the gates, and the ideas rush in pell-mell, and only then does it look them through and examine them in a mass. You critics are ashamed or frightened of the momentary and transient extravagances which are found in creative minds, and whose longer or shorter duration distinguishes the thinking artist from the dreamer. You complain of unfruitfulness because you reject too soon and discriminate too severely.'

Just over two hundred years later, Benjamin D'Anger sent a postcard to his friend Ronjon de Lanerolle. The postcard showed a view of a dark brown mountainous moorland, beneath stormy clouds, lit by an improbably lurid and fulgent sky; it was entitled 'The Beast of Exmoor' and informed the purchaser that high on Exmoor there had been many dramatic and frightening attacks on farm animals, far more ferocious than those made by foxes or wild dogs, and that the savagery had lasted for several years . . . 'it was hoped that the animal would eventually die of old age, but last year brought new reports of mysterious killings so perhaps the original animal has found a mate!' To this message Benjamin added his own: 'Sorry I couldn't get a snap of the Beast. Saw some great stags today. See you next week. Cheers, Ben.'

STEPPING WESTWARD

Daniel

David and Patsy Palmer, Rosemary and Nathan Herz were not
pleased with the report of the D'Angers. Not only were they not
pleased: they were suspicious. It had been unwise of them to encourage the D'Angers to go to Ashcombe. The D'Angers had stitched up
some deal there. They had fixed Frieda's will, and put their markers on
her treasures. David D'Anger had played his black card, out in white
Somerset, and trumped their red. Perverse Frieda, mad Frieda, foolish
Frieda. And they themselves had not been wise. They should have
taken the warning of Timon's feast more seriously. She had showed
her weakness then, in those green peas, in that sweet sugar talk. David
D'Anger had seduced Frieda, as he had seduced their sister Gogo.
Frieda would leave all to that brown boy, that changeling child.

This is not how the Palmers and the Herzes spoke – not at all, not at
all – but I am sorry to say that it is what they thought.

They have little excuse for what you may take to be their greed and
selfishness. You have already seen that they live in affluence. We have
visited the Palmers' house, and so pleasant is it there that we may be
unable to resist going to see them at least once more. The Palmers live
comfortably, eat well, and are surrounded by a cast of extras who
effortlessly reinforce the Palmers' sense of superiority. You might
think they had no need to lay claim to Daniel's mother's riches. But
you have not reckoned with two important considerations. The first
of these is family jealousy, that long-ago, ancient, fairytale hatred
which means that a brother does not like his sisters to gain at his
expense – particularly when those sisters are not themselves in need.
The second is the more immediate legacy of the last twenty years.
Greed and selfishness have become respectable. Like family jealousy,
they are not new, but they have gained a new sanction. It is now
considered correct to covet. And Daniel is covetous. I am sorry to

have to say this about a man who seems so generous, so agreeable, so drily distanced from all things ugly, a man so free with his tennis court and his wife's cooking. But it is so. He is covetous, and he is mean. And he practises a profession, let us remember, in which base motives are more frequently encountered than fine motives.

Nor should you take Patsy Palmer at face value. She seems a very nice woman, but has she bothered to remember to invite Sonia Barfoot to tea? (Do you remember Sonia Barfoot, that bleached manic-depressive visionary full of lithium?) No, she has not. Has she taken any steps to find any more permanent niche for Will Paine? No, she has not. She has got bored with him, and quietly evicted him. This was perhaps unwise of her. Has she noticed that her son Simon is spaced out and half mad? No, she has not. Patsy is a Mrs Jellyby, she likes problems that are not her own, and when they come too near home she rejects and denies them. That's a bit harsh, but why not be harsh? And she too condemns the D'Angers. Daniel and Patsy Palmer collude in condemnation. Daniel thinks David is deliberately ripping them off; Patsy suspects Gogo is deliberately ripping them off. That's how it goes.

Patsy has had her eye on her share of Frieda's money. She would not admit it but would not deny it. Her own mother is still alive, and is costing much in up-keep. She is in a flat, converted for the disabled. She has round-the-clock nursing. The family home was sold to pay for this, but Patsy's mother costs nearly £500 a week. Patsy has three brothers. Patsy's quarter diminishes week by week. Frieda's money would come in handy. And there must be money: *The Matriarchy of War* is still in print, after forty years. It's a set text. Other titles also survive. Patsy does not welcome the thought that the income of these Works might be diverted to Benjamin D'Anger. What about Simon, what about Emily? What if Daniel drops dead of a heart attack? These are the thoughts of Patsy Palmer.

Let us move on to Rosemary and Nathan Herz. We have not yet seen them on their home ground, so let us join them in their ultra-modern flat on the South Bank, overlooking the Thames. It is on the sixth floor of Ceylon Quay, off Rochester Square, near Southwark Bridge. It is late October, and Rosemary and Nathan are watching television in their vast split-level lounge. Jessica and Jonathan are asleep in their modern bedrooms. It has already been noted that Frieda's children are not homemakers. They were not brought up in a tradition of homemaking. Daniel owes his considerable comforts to capable superwoman Patsy, and to a counterfeit, college-acquired, Middle-Temple-reinforced and slightly ironic vision of himself as country squire, a vision as compulsive as it is archaic. Gogo and David live in a colourful but not uncongenial turmoil, a turmoil reflected in many a middle-class professional British household up and down the land: their chosen careers do not demand (and indeed, in David's case, almost counter-suggest) any excessive investment in bourgeois décor, and Gogo leaves her clinical instincts in the clinic. So they live in a mess. It is different for Rosemary and Nathan. They inhabit a designer world.

Their flat, purchased at an inflated price in the late eighties, is a fine example of negative equity, pretension, technology and gadgetry. Its walls display inestimable art works, its drapes swish at the touch of a button, its sanitary ware is of the first water. The settee upon which they now recline cost a mere £4,000, and can adjust to many angles: the glass-topped table on which Rosemary rests her shining lustre-smooth crossed calves is customer built. The very coffee-cups are bespoke, from a visiting Japanese ceramic artist for whom Rosemary had once found a space. The wall lights are almost the very latest in uplighting, oblique lighting, dimmer lighting and slow fades. The television-set itself bears witness to the approaching millennium, for it is unobtrusively tuned in to every channel in and under the sky. Six tall sunflowers stand on the floor in a white pot, and from diagonally opposite corners of the room blink two small red angry ever-watchful eyes. If the beige curtains were open (which they are not) you would be able to see a magnificent view of the floodlit, neon-lit Thames. You might think, from looking at this room, that either Rosemary or Nathan had a pronounced and confident liking for the modern, but you would be wrong. It is because neither of them has any certainty of taste at all that they live like this. This apartment makes all their decisions for them.

You might think that Rosemary, working, as you have been told, in Arts Administration, might find herself misplaced in her career, if it is true that she has no taste. Wrong again. That's why she's quite good at it. (But not *so* good at it that she doesn't feel the snapping at her heels from time to time.)

They look quite cosy together, Nathan puffing away at his cigarette, and nursing a substantial post-prandial brandy, while Rosemary (and this is a bit of a surprise) works at a shapeless piece of crochet. They are watching a programme on one of the innumerable competing current-affairs cross-examinations that besiege and enrage the nation nightly. They are watching it because there, damnit, is their blasted brother-in-law, the sinisterly photogenic filmstar of race relations, David D'Anger. Nathan, as we have seen, likes David, but he is as suspicious of him as his wife admits herself to be. Rosemary is suspicious because she thinks David is probably a self-seeking bastard. Nathan is suspicious for the opposite reason. He suspects that David D'Anger may, after all, be a good man. After all, somebody's got to be. He may be as high-minded as he seems to be. How can one tell? He looks and sounds so plausible. Would even God know, if there were a God? Probably not. What will it take to catch David D'Anger out for being what he is?

On screen, the talk is of income distribution and the concept of relative poverty. D'Anger is good on this topic, they have to admit, and the others make such blisteringly idiotic remarks ('I prefer not to talk about inequality but about income difference' – that one must be a classic) that they make David sound like the soul of sweet reason. And David's statistics are beautiful. Elegantly, he bowls his fast outswingers; he is the Imran Khan of politics, the well-dressed aristocrat of the sophisticated political game. David plays the Rowntree Report, the United Nations, the European Court of Human Rights, the latest findings from the Child Poverty Action Group, and an incident he'd observed on the tube on the Northern Line between Chalk Farm and Camden Town. (David, one has to admit, has a brilliant line in grass-roots and pavement anecdotes, all of which perforce go unchallenged and unrivalled by his opponents, for none of them, as David manages to insinuate, has ever travelled by public transport. David works the tubes and buses himself partly in the way of research, but they're not to know that.) On this occasion, one of David's adversaries is Milo Barking, a notorious little drunken pundit-whippersnapper, whose hard right-wing line is that all compassion is fake, and not only fake, but debilitating, corrupting, deceitful and dishonest. 'Let's admit it,' says this white-faced rat, 'we're all a lot better off than we were in 1979, and we know it, all this talk about poverty is just a new version of Golden Age nostalgia for the Bad Old Days because all you poverty lobbyists see yourselves out of a job in a few months' time – '

'Oh, come on, Midas,' says David, smoothly intervening in an infuriatingly conciliatory and forgiving tone, 'we can't all be as clever and lucky as you, I mean we can't *all* strike it lucky with every take-over bid, we haven't got your *nose* for it, you've got to spare a thought for us poor sods who have to earn our livings, and those of us who can't get a job for love or money, and those of us who've got nothing better to do than spend forty-eight hours a week watching prigs like us on TV, reassuring us by telling us how rich we really are. We can't all be winners, you know, some of us have to be the mugs.'

Young Barking looks furious, with real not fake fury, for it is known to some viewers at home and to all in the studio (except that harmless female priest) that his last business venture had hit the skids and was about to be declared bankrupt, and that that was why he was on this TV show, trying to pick up seventy-five quid with expenses and a bit of face. The chairman and producer hover indecisively, wondering whether to encourage Milo Barking to reply and D'Anger to pursue, but decide against it: there was libel in the air, and anyway they feel sorry for Barking, who is bound to make a brilliant comeback. Anyone could go bust, it wasn't his fault he'd been taken for a ride by the big boys. They cut to the female priest.

At home, in the belly of their waterside white elephant, Rosemary and Nathan exchange glances. They know the inside story of Barking's financial disaster, but wonder how the hell David D'Anger got to know these things. He'd come a long way since the innocent days when he was teaching Politics and Philosophy. Sinister, really.

'I suppose,' says Rosemary, winding up her ball of scarlet wool and piercing it with her crochet hook, 'I suppose he has a whole team of researchers, sniffing out the dirt for him. Is that how it works?'

'Don't ask me,' says Nathan. 'I didn't think he could afford that kind of back-up.'

'Doesn't it all come with the job?'

'He hasn't got the job yet.'

'Oh, come off it, he's got lots of jobs.'

'I don't know anything about it,' says Nathan, who has in fact heard a rumour that David D'Anger has been seen once too often lunching with a neoGothic miniskirted redlipped Fleet Street floozie; he hopes to prevent himself from passing this poisoned nugget of gossip on to his wife, as it is quite likely to be untrue, and even if it were true, why upset or, more likely, gratify Rosemary? Nathan feels a solidarity with David. Gogo Palmer D'Anger is frigid, marmoreal and self-righteous. He rather hopes David is having a fling. He himself has had a few, as David knows: nothing too serious, nothing marriage-threatening, but pleasant in their way. He has had his secrets. One he keeps.

'I'm off to bed,' says Rosemary. She reminds him that she has to catch an early flight to Glasgow. She hovers, her hand on a lightswitch.

'OK, OK,' says Nathan. It never ceases to annoy him, the way she will announce the obvious, the way she seems to expect him to follow her to bed. What does she suspect? He's grown up now, he can sit and watch TV all by himself if he wants. He sits out the current affairs for a few moments more after her departure, switches off as the conversation turns to drugs in athletics (Nathan, like much of the nation, is by now in favour of a Drugs Olympics, and to hell with fair play), and then opens the curtains, heaves himself to his feet, opens a slice of window, and steps out on to the split-level balcony. This is his view. He has seen smarter views – new ones, downstream, from some of the more recent developments, and old ones, upstream, along the Upper Mall. But this is his. He likes it. It is Southwark, it is real. The Thames is very low tonight, and a dank smell of wharfmud rises to his sensitive nostrils. He sniffs, inhales.

There is London, to right and left of him, glittering with religion, art and commerce. From this distance, in this obscurity, London looks fine. Dickens would think things had come on a long way since the days of the bodysnatchers and the river rats and the suicides. The skull-dome of St Paul's still looms across the water, bleached and fluted white-blue in its floodlight, and to either side of it Nathan can see towers and spires. Over there, somewhere, though he cannot see her, stands Justice with her sword and scales. And over here, on what he thinks of as his bank, there is development – a reconstructed Elizabethan theatre with a grass roof, converted warehouses, shopping malls, office towers, museums, clinks and tourist pubs where once Ben Jonson and Will Shakespeare drank. Maybe it is all fine, maybe Rat Barking is right to hymn the rising tide of prosperity. Maybe Rat Barking is right to point out that the Poverty Lobby is always with us, and that it is self-serving and self-perpetuating. Those same old caring faces do pop up again and again, as they rotate from Campaign to Campaign, from Charity to Charity, begging from and bleating at the hard-working wealth-creating rich. Nathan's never had all that much time for the Poverty Lobby, although he has been known to chuck a fist full of fivers (fluttering, pale blue and pink silver-threaded fivers) at the beggars beneath the bridge. (One of the beggars once had the cheek to hold a fiver up to the light, to see if it was real. Maybe it's true that beggars are getting aggressive, dangerous?)

Most evenings, when he is at home and can get rid of Rosemary, Nathan comes to look at this view. He cannot leave this place. He would like to, but he is bound to it. The water is low tonight, it slaps at the wooden piles and fenders.

Nathan is convinced he will die shortly of a heart attack. Most of the time he considers this to be more or less inevitable. His father had died at the age of fifty-four, and so will he. Nathan has insured and assured and double-indemnified his life, so that's all right. Everyone will be fine except himself, and as he'll be dead, he'll be all right too. Or so he tells himself.

Nathan's mother can't think why he and Rosemary and the children want to live South of the River, in an area with an E in its postcode. Your grandparents, she tells Nathan, worked day and night to move west. To her, Nathan's expensively converted apartment with its river view still stinks of poverty and the old East End. Nathan's mother hasn't moved with the times. She won't even eat food with an E in it. She is shocked to hear that Nathan and Rosemary eat out most evenings and, as often as not, apart. When do the children get a proper meal? Do they live on snacks and microwave dinners?

Nathan cannot leave the river. Occasionally Rosemary suggests that they move, for she is not so fond of the area, some of which remains dismally undeveloped. She says she does not like to get out of her car at night, even in the underground car park. She says she does not like the dark menace of the streets – the hints of portcullis, guillotine, noose, spike and chain that linger on like instruments of torture in the ancient architecture. She does not like the embattled river, with its heavy dredgers, its rusting buoys. But Nathan stonewalls. It is convenient, and they cannot afford to move, he says. They must wait for the rest of the neighbourhood to improve, for the market to shift, he says. But his real reason is other.

Nathan cannot leave because he holds a ghostly tryst with this stretch of the Thames. Here, in the dark water, not far from where he now stands, young Belle was drowned.

Belle was drowned when the pleasure boat, *The Marchioness*, went down, sunk by *The Bowbelle*. Belle had been partying. And now she is dead. Fifty-two drowned. Belle was the last of the list.

Belle was twenty-six when she died. Nathan had adored her. He thought she was the most beautiful girl he had ever seen. This was ridiculous, as by advertising standards, she was nothing special. And yet, he repeats to himself like a mantra, she was the most beautiful girl I ever saw.

She had worked for the firm, and her work had been lowly. But all had adored her. Her laughter had rung out, down corridors, over telephones, in the lift, through the walkways of the open plan. Her face was as open and as glorious as the sky itself. She was radiant. Her wide brow, her brown eyes, her chestnut hair, her cream-pale skin. Her skin, so supple, so innocent, so untouched. She had broad shoulders, full soft breasts, white hands, careless clothes. She was a radiant, art student mess. Cheap bangles, crumpled shirts hanging out over her trousers, not-so-little laced boots (she had big feet). She wore rings on her fingers, and punning bells in her ears, which jingled when she shook her head. Dull men smiled when they saw Belle, and unhappy women unfolded their secrets to her. Belle was fearless, and she rejoiced them with her escapades. She could walk safely through the city night. She charmed the lonely from the edge of tenth-floor sills, she led the wicked to safety, she disarmed the mugger and bought drinks for the homeless and the mad. She knew the pubs, the manors, the estates.

Nathan had propositioned her, one evening, as they descended late in the thick-carpeted static-thrilled office lift. He'd offered dinner, he'd thrown himself upon her mercy. And when she had taken in what he was offering, she had laughed and laughed. Then she had shared the joke. 'But *hey*, Nathan, didn't you *know*?' she had said, laying her lovely white hand, with its slightly bitten nails, upon his. 'Didn't you *know*? I live with Marcia. I never *ever* go out with men. I couldn't go out with a *man*.'

As she took in his expression of surprise, which he had been unable to disguise quickly enough, she threw an arm around him and violently patted his back. 'Oh, I'm so sorry, Nathan, you *didn't* know, I thought *everybody* knew,' she had cried. And of course, the moment he knew, he knew. She was, as he in that instant saw, of the essence of camp. That was how she made her way through life so gaily. That laughter, that tireless patience with all comers, that indiscriminate good nature. To her, all the world was one glorious joke, and although at this moment the joke was on him, he was invited to share it. So he took her out to dinner anyway, and over a platter of smoked fishes and brown bread and butter they continued to rejoice. They consummated their affair with a wicked froth of egg and cream and sugar and Grand Marnier, and then they kissed and parted and Belle whisked home to share the joke with Marcia. Nathan thenceforth adored Belle.

She was his mistress, his daughter, his friend, his salvation: she was the bride of all the world. His heart sang whenever he saw her, whenever he heard her lovely, unlikely, beautiful name.

And then, one night, outside his window, Belle and fifty-one others had drowned, while out on a pleasure trip. The whole office went into mourning for Belle. It was not possible that she was dead. As easily might one extinguish the sun itself. Stunned with disbelief, her friends and colleagues exchanged bewildered words, clubbed together for a wreath, attended her funeral. There was an inquest, then another inquest. It emerged that Belle's hand, at the command of the coroner, had been severed after death, for purposes of finger-print identification. When Nathan heard this he thought he would die. Belle's hand, with its little wrist, its bitten nails, its cheap and innocent and silly rings. Belle's hand on a block.

Surgically removed, the coroner said. Severed, he meant.

Now, whenever he gazes at the dark water and thinks of Belle's hand, his eyes fill with tears. And thus he knows he is still human. She has left him this enormous, this generous gift. He sometimes feels himself to be a mean small man in a mean small world, indifferently married, indifferently unfaithful to his wife, and intermittently bored by his work. He has made bad choices and shored them up with worse. But he can weep for Belle. The tears which her name and her white hand induce are most precious to him.

The dark water beneath him stands still. It is on the turn. The river has drained to the marshes, and soon the sea will flood back, silently. The salt will surge back, pulled by the moon, to merge with the fresh river waters of the land, there, beneath his window, where Belle died. It is a twice-daily miracle. 'Belle,' he murmurs. The waters tremble as they meet. How *can* she be dead? Is her death too some profound and beautiful joke? As inexplicable, as lovely, as her short and blessed life?

Will Paine stands by the roadside on the M5, at the Gordano Service Station Exit, his worldly possessions in a canvas bag. He is thumbing his way westwards. Since Patsy Palmer kicked him out, he has not fared well. Now he looks back to the summer he spent with her at the

Old Farm as to a Golden Age. Had she really fed him, and given him pocket money, and given him a bed in the attic? He cannot understand why she had ever been so gracious to him, and repents that he has at times thought ill of her. He regrets too that he never warned her about Simon, who is going crazy. Either Simon is out of his mind with the wrong kind of drugs – Will Paine is an expert on good and bad drugs, and is wary of the difference – or he has a mental illness. Or both. Simon will end up feeding himself to the lions in the zoo, or murdering a stranger in a tiled underpass. Simon has the city sickness. Will has seen its symptoms many times. Pallor, fever, anger, palsy, fear. The glancing over the shoulder, the demanding with menaces. Will should have warned Patsy, who has been good to him, but he had felt it was not his place. He had not dared. Once he had tried, but Patsy had not been willing. So he is walking away from the problem, from the memory. He is heading for the west, away from the city.

He's had an easy ride so far. One golden Beetle, driven far too fast by a crazy bald young man and his girlfriend, had brought him all the way from Chiswick. They'd been a laugh. They'd laughed all the way, and shared their cheese and chutney sandwiches. The young man was off to see his mum at Portishead. His mum lived in a maisonette on an estate. Life was dull in Portishead, but they'd be able to stick it for a couple of nights. His mum's cooking was diabolical. He'd warned Sal. The curse of the microwave. Plastic bags in the box. You wouldn't think you could get it as wrong as she did. You'd think it was foolproof, wouldn't you? Oh, come on, said Sal. You wait, said the young man.

Will Paine envies them. They know where they are going. He told them he was going to see a friend in Cornwall. But he hadn't got a friend in Cornwall. He has only a shadow of a plan. The days are getting shorter and colder. It is autumn. The summer is well over. He'd heard there were easy beds in Totnes. He'll try Totnes. Perhaps.

He stands on the slipway, facing the west. A steady stream of cars and lorries passes him. It is early afternoon, and there are a few hours more of daylight. He thumbs mechanically, half-heartedly, in a semi-trance, as he thinks of his months inside, of his months with Patsy. He is determined never to see the inside of a gaol again. It had turned his delicate stomach. He thinks of the bit of luck that was Patsy. She had come his way by chance. What had that meant? He thinks of David D'Anger, and all the talk he had overheard. Sometimes, in a dream, he has thought of appealing to David D'Anger: they were both, after all, Caribbean. At some remove, but Caribbean. He has seen David D'Anger on television, he has read him in the papers. He even knows Middleton, which is only fifty miles from his own home town. He had worked there for a couple of months one summer, packaging Cheese and Onion Pasta Twirls, and sleeping in an official council squat with a group of students from Sheffield University. He could almost consider himself one of David D'Anger's constituents. Would it be an abuse of hospitality, to approach David D'Anger? D'Anger must get spongers all the time.

Will Paine thinks of the just society, which has placed him by this roadside, and sent Sal and Steve off to a cosy council estate supper of cling-film-impregnated sliced brown beef with cold gravy; which has driven Simon Palmer into some needled nightmare; which has placed Benjamin D'Anger in a well-run North London comprehensive, the closely supervised darling of both his doting parents; which has set his mother to work on a machine that seals the plastic coating of babies' mattresses, and deprived 8 per cent of its members of any employment at all; which has decreed that some should be non-executive directors of companies on vast salaries, while others should teach small infants or drive long-distance lorries or wipe the tables in the service stations of the land. It is all a mystery. He thinks of poor Prince Charles, a victim if ever there was one, hangdog, depressed, brooding, gloomy, derided, fallen from grace. Will feels very sorry for Prince Charles, who has drawn one of the shortest straws of all. Being a royal has probably always been a bum deal, but these days it's dire. He thinks of Frieda Haxby, of whom he has heard so much gossip, alone in her castle in the west, alone with all her empty bedrooms.

He stands there dreaming, his thumb idly extended, as the sun sinks slowly before him. He manages to feel quite lucky. And lucky he is, for as he lowers his hand to reach into his pocket for a peppermint, he hears a voice calling. A small white van has pulled over, and its driver is leaning out of its open window shouting at him. 'Hey, you there, d'you want a lift or not?'

Will jumps to, jumps in. His chauffeur is a middle-aged weather-beaten sixties survivor with long thin straggling hair. He says he is a heating engineer, and he talks relentlessly. Will is a captive audience. Hitch-hikers cannot be choosers. The heating engineer talks about the weather, about the refurbishment of the service station, about VAT, about the government. Will sits quiet and says nothing. It soon becomes clear that his new friend considers himself to be some kind of anarchist, and that he hopes Will will sell him some grass. Will is depressed to find that he can be suspected as a potential dealer or carrier even as he stands on a slip-road in the middle of the country-side: no wonder he had found himself doing three months inside merely for carrying a stash for a friend from one pub to another. Does he really look like a pusher? Obviously he doesn't look innocent, or this nutter in his noisy little cart wouldn't have stopped for him. Would the nutter have stopped for David D'Anger? But David D'Anger wouldn't have found himself hitching along the M5, would he? David D'Anger's got a nice metallic silver-blue Honda, and his wife's probably got another.

In time, unprompted by Will, the conversation drifts from the Somerset police and the Home Secretary to Glastonbury and New Age travellers. Trevor has all the obsequiousness of a bore who wishes to captivate and placate his listener for ever, but Will, who has man-aged to indicate that he has no dope upon him, is not forthcoming with views on King Arthur and the Criminal Justice Act. He gets himself dropped off at a service station just beyond Taunton. Thence he gets a quick lift to Tiverton, where he spends the night in a room over a pub, and, in the morning, takes stock.

Tiverton is a dump. Will Paine is surprised. He had thought it would be a pretty, West Country market town, full of smiling county people and expensive shops, but it is hilly and grim. Most of the shops seem to be selling second-rate second-hand clothing in aid of obscure charities. The population looks grey and elderly and idle. Will walks along a pedestrianized High Street, through a car park or two, round a market precinct where nothing is happening at all. There is nothing for him here. Where are all the wealthy folk of the soft rich south? Clearly they do not hang out in Tiverton. Will decides to move on. He will hitch north, up over Exmoor, to Frieda Haxby. He will offer his services to Frieda, as gardener, handyman, cleaner, fortune-teller. He can read the Tarot, though he doesn't let on to everyone. Frieda might find a space for him, for a while.

He has a composite image of Frieda, assembled from evenings of eavesdropping, from studying the dustjacket of the ill-starred *Queen Christina*, from family photographs stuck in a collage on the wall of the downstairs cloakroom at the Old Farm. She is rich and famous and eccentric. She might take a fancy to him, who knows? She might disinherit that pampered little D'Anger boy in his favour. Her castle might be stuffed with rich jewels. She had been wearing jewels in some of the family pics – emeralds, pearls, diamonds. Maybe she will bestow them upon him. With such fantasies he entertains himself, as he works his way across the moor.

His last hitch is with a load of doomed cattle on its way to an abattoir. The driver, a taciturn and kindly man, is reluctant to deposit Will Paine by the roadside so far from human habitation, but Will, who has studied the maps, knows that this is the right spot to dismount. He has been evasive about his destination, muttering something about joining some friends with a caravan. The driver wishes him good day. The cramped cattle low. Will Paine sets off along the high coast road, looking for his turning.

And there it is, a sign to Ashcombe. The track plunges down from the road, steeply, past high banks of leathery sprawling rhododendrons. Will shoulders his bag, and starts the long descent. It is late afternoon. The sun sinks to the west.

Frieda Haxby is playing patience at a large dining-table which she has lugged to the garden end of what had been the dining-room. The room has long, mullioned windows, and now the bleeding sun pours through their lights on to her cards, her glass of whisky, covered with a postcard against the wasps and flies, her guttering cigarette, and her expanse of papers. From time to time she breaks off from her game to make a note, to turn a page.

Will Paine can see her clearly, through the windows. She is on view. He is concealed in the shrubbery. He has lost his nerve.

The descent had been much longer than he had expected, and he doubts if he'll ever have the strength to climb back up again. It's almost vertical. And he'd been unnerved, on the way down, by nature. There had been squawkings and rustlings in the woods. Distant dogs had barked. He had heard a strange beast's roaring, far away. He had passed a stone hut with a padlocked door and conical towers from which a dull thrumming noise seemed to emanate. He had gone under a gateway, surmounted by a heraldic lion and two griffins, almost overgrown with ivy. He had been through a gate marked PRIVATE. He had seen the sign of the vipers. He had heard the melancholy rattle of waves on shingle far below, and the secret voices of contending brooks in the undergrowth. He had flanked the empty walled kitchen gardens.

He had crept down to the large house, quietly. It was much bigger and grander than anything he had imagined. Rosemary Herz had been dismissive about it, had made it sound like an old ruin, but it was imposing. It had turrets and battlements and a belfry and a rambling roof system which he had viewed like a bird from the path above. So steep was the drop from the path that he felt he could have jumped on to the roof with one bound. The gardens had once been formal, and the map of their former glory was still plainly visible.

Will Paine is frightened. This place is too much for him. It is spooky. He wishes he hadn't come. How on earth is he going to introduce himself to this mad old woman? She won't be very pleased to see him, now or ever. On the other hand, it will take him a good hour and a half to get back up to the road, and nobody will pick him up at this time of night. He squats back on his haunches in the leaf-mould, and thinks hard.

Frieda sighs over her patience. It is her fourth deal this evening, and this time it looks as though it's going to come out. For some reason this makes her feel she has been cheating, although she doesn't think she has. Maybe she hadn't shuffled properly?

She has made yet another attempt at her memoirs. Maybe it is another false start. She does not, these days, find writing a pleasant process. She has never enjoyed it much, and looks back now at the facility with which she produced her early work with admiration and disbelief. How had she done such things, burdened as she was with children, husband, sister, mother, and a viper's knot of hatreds? And not only hatreds. There had been other passions, hard now to credit. Ambition must have been one of them, or she would not have been able to lift herself out of the rutted mud. The ambition was her mother's, inherited, transferred, a deadly legacy. Had anything been her own? Had even her husband been her own, or had he too been a legacy?

By writing it down, she hoped to make sense of it, but perhaps there would be no sense. She could not hope to forgive, or to re-capture. Love turns to hate by the inexorable law of entropy, but never, thinks Frieda Haxby, can hate ever by the most monstrous effort of the memory or the will be turned back into love. As this landscape, these woods, this body, this country will never be young again, so will hatred never dissolve and be remade as love.

Impossible, to look back and make sense of love, that destructive, inconstant passion, that seems at times so good. But it is not good, whatever the priests and poets say, it is neutral at best, and at worst a killer. Sexual passion dies, that is well known, but so do all other affections. Frieda Haxby tells herself that she does not care for her children, or her grandchildren; she has outgrown them, as years ago she grew out of her love for her mother and her sister. (She cares a little for Benjamin D'Anger, she reminds herself, but only by way of experiment.) They are grown, they may manage without her. They are no longer part of her. She did her best for them, but her best was not very good.

She came to dread her mother, and to hate her sister. She came to hate her husband, but that, she believes, is a common story.

She thinks of the laws of living and the laws of dying, of that severed blob of orange flesh from the sea that had clung to hers. So tenacious, so unformed. And here she is, so complex, and so tired. She has lost that simple will to grip. She turns the cards.

The personal decays from us, leaving us with no memory of it, although we know that it has been. But it was at its strongest nothing more than an evolutionary trick, a spasm of self gripping to a wet rock. We were born without meaning, we struggled without meaning, we met and married and loved and hated without meaning. We are accidents. All our passions are arbitrary, trivial, a game of hazard, like this game of patience which I now play.

Napoleon on Saint Helena. Turner painted him on his last beach, against a red sunset, in exile, staring at an ill-placed, an improbable and outsized rock limpet. He called his piece *The Exile and the War.* So stand I, looking back.

Here comes the knave of clubs, Le Vicomte le Nôtre, stout and bewigged; Frieda lays him upon the lap of Marie-Leczinska, Queen of Hearts. This is too easy.

(Out there in the shrubbery lurks the Knave of Wolverhampton, working out his approach. This is a complicated building, facing several ways. He does not wish to startle Frieda Haxby by creeping up on her from the rear. But from which direction would she *expect* a visitor? She cannot receive many. Though her grey Volvo is in better working order than he had expected. It is newly washed and waxed. She is not a prisoner here.)

Frieda turns a few more cards, then suddenly sweeps them all in, stacks them, shuffles them, and begins to deal again. She pulls towards her a page of text labelled DOC:MEM8 and stares at it as she deals. It reads:

'I first met Andrew Palmer outside the Rising Sun at Bletchley Park in 1945. It was just before the end of the war. I was still at school. He was in uniform. So was I. He had been sent to meet me by my sister Hilda.'

This statement is true, as far as it goes, but it does not go far. Frieda draws a little sun on the page, in red waterproof de luxe uniball micro, and adds rays. Then she inks in the sun's orb. She tries to remember

Andrew Palmer as she had seen him then, sent to her with Hilda's dangerous blessing. Handsome, heroic, yellow-haired, in his RAF bomber jacket.

She'd been too young to be allowed in the pub. He'd led her back to Hilda's billet. She'd been thrilled by Andrew. Well, she was only sixteen, and there was a war on. Should she blame herself for what had happened? Or should she blame Hilda for setting it up? Or should she blame Andrew for weakness, for vanity, for taking advantage, for playing sister off against sister? There hardly seemed to be any point in blaming Andrew Palmer. He'd been a bit player, a nobody. The father of her three children. The pieces had all been in place before Hilda had met Andrew. Before the war broke out. Nothing was Andrew's fault. She could see that now. Is he alive or dead, she wonders, or is he still skulking in the Orient? Last heard of in Singapore.

Reduce, reduce. Everything dwindles, everything shrinks. A blue ballgown hangs limp on a brass rail in an Oxfam shop. It has had its last outing.

Those had been the days of clothing coupons. She had married in a white dress cut out of parachute silk. The days of peace and austerity. But why bother to remember all of that? Tinned cream, tasting of white chalk paste.

Andrew wasn't even seriously interested in women. That had been one of the ironies. He had destroyed one, and done his best to destroy another, but he hadn't wanted either of them. He had run off to Ceylon with a German film-maker. Andrew had been a clever boy, a mathematician, a talker, a spark. A weak and pretty face, as she now remembered it. He'd been a trouble-maker. He had loved trouble. Vain, dependent, narcissistic, androgynous. What had he thought he was playing at, with the Haxby sisters? They were not his style. They came from a different, a bloodier, a more matriarchal mythology.

The three Palmer children had shown little curiosity about their absent father. They had smelt dishonour and wanted none of it. Frieda has warped them all by her silence. It is too late now to advertise for Andrew Palmer, to set the detectives on to him. She sometimes wonders if he has followed her career. Hard to remember that she had once suffered over his infidelity and his disappearance. Although he loved trouble, Hilda Haxby's death had been too much for him, and he had run away with Otto Weinberg, who made movies about oil-wells. A coward and a traitor. Maybe he was long dead.

It hardly seems worth recalling his successors in her affections. Yet at the time they had been important to her. After Andrew, she had favoured more fleshly men, men of substance. Some of them had died corpulent deaths. Some lived and flourished – the Swede still sent her postcards from his many conferences, and recently an ageing Irish lover had written to her, out of the blue, after two decades of silence, asking if she remembered the night they'd spent together in Heidelberg so many many years ago. Did she remember that they had ordered Steak Tartare, not knowing, in their innocence and ignorance, what it would prove to be? And had she been sick in the night because of the rawness of the steak, or because of him? Could she please let him know? It was important to him.

And, her memory thus prompted, she had recalled in detail this long forgotten night. They had arrived late at the inn. Neither then spoke German, and tourism had not then invaded the Rhineland. The menu had been uncompromisingly German, and they had ordered steak, expecting at worst a chunk of charred tough meat with large white boiled potatoes. But there on their plates had reposed a small dome of red raw flesh, surrounded by a necromantic circle of strange little chemical pyramids of peppers and spices – green, red, black, yellow, crystal white. A golden raw egg yolk in a halved eggshell had topped each frightening bloody pap. They had stared in mutual alarm, yet they were hungry, and had eaten bravely and stubbornly, ignoring the condiments, consuming the meat. After the meal they had taken themselves to their room, where they had found their bedding as foreign, as unaccommodating. A high wooden bed, a rigid bolster for pillow, a feather duvet of vast sighing dusty mountain ranges for their covering. It had taken courage to plunge into that structure, but they had forced themselves, for their desires had been overwhelming. And then, when what had to be done had been done, Frieda had got up and taken herself to the bathroom and vomited up the lot. The meat, the beer, the man.

How could she have forgotten this disgraceful episode, and why had he remembered it? She wrote back, warily, telling him that as far as she could recall it had been the unfamiliarity of the repast – had there not been sauerkraut on the side? – that had produced her nausea, not his sexual activities. But she would not go into more detail until he told her why he wished to know. And he had written back, from Bellagio, saying that he wished to set the record straight. 'I am writing my memoirs, here in Bellagio,' he had informed her. 'And I wished to know the worst. So write to me again, Frieda sweetheart, and tell me all you know.'

She had replied tersely, on a postcard: 'I'll leave you out of my memoirs if you leave me out of yours. That's a fair offer. F.H.P.'

And indeed she had so far left him out, and all the others: at this snail's pace she would never reach him, even though he had figured so early in her amorous career. (Her German, now, is quite passable.)

Is she the same person as that woman who had sweated and moaned with multiple orgasms in that vast antique Germanic feather bed? Is it this body that had eaten that meat? She sometimes wonders. The problem of continuity perplexes her. Has she split off for ever from that rapacious, relentless girl who had devoured and spewed out Andrew Palmer, after screwing three children out of him? A memoir should establish continuity, but sometimes she wonders if the links exist. Can she be held responsible for crimes committed so long ago? Can Hilda? Can Andrew? Were they the same people then as they are now? Hilda is long dead, so her mortal being has stayed the same, fixed at the age of thirty-two in her final act of cruelty, of selfishness, of Pyrrhic victory, of who knows what fleeting angry despair. But Andrew – is he, if he lives, the man who fathered the children, the youth who flew an aeroplane and got back alive, the boy whose grandfather had served in India? Would they recognize one another if they were to meet now? Is any of their flesh the same as that flesh that touched, and rubbed, and fused?

And what about teeth? Surely these teeth are the same teeth? She runs her tongue against her bridge, lifts it, joggles it. She still has most of her own left. She detests her bridgework.

Her mother, Gladys Haxby née Bugg, had been keen on continuity. She had invoked Vikings and Norse gods and longships. She had claimed for her children a Nordic inheritance which, who knows, may well have been fact, not fiction. The Haxbys and the Buggs must have come from somewhere. Frieda and Hilda had imbibed a good deal of dubious folk history from their mother, a package of disinformation from which Frieda had been rescued by an exceptional history teacher at Scalethwaite Grammar School, a teacher whom Frieda, if she were more generous, could credit with much of her later success. It was Miss Mee, not Gladys Bugg Haxby, who had set Frieda on a true course. Nevertheless, Frieda owes some of her intimations to her mother. She has had moments of ancestral recognition, when facing a certain combination of blue sky and low golden grassland and blue water, when laying her hand on an old stone, when gazing at a brown furze upland, or an iron crag, or a fjord. She had not been lying when she had told the disc jockey about her mystic moment by the runic stone.

In recent years, Frieda has taken the trouble to check some of the fanciful notions which her mother had imparted. And she had discovered that there had been Haxbys in Lincolnshire and South Yorkshire and Cambridgeshire for a few centuries, though none of them had been in any way remarkable. Ernie Haxby had been a farm labourer, not a Viking. The Buggs had been Lincolnshire folk, and Frieda had been pleased to note that the word 'Bugg' – Danish, Old Norse? – was said to mean crooked, swollen, bulging, officious and proud. Pleased also was she to discover that one of her mother's favourite grammatical constructions, involving the strongly stressed terminal preposition, was derived from the Scandinavian: every time Gladys declared, 'If you don't stop crying I'll give you something to cry *for*,' she was recalling the linguistic roots of her race.

Oh, yes, there had been an inheritance. A handful of phrases, an old colouring book of the Norse gods with sub-Burne-Jones illustrations, very badly inked in by Hilda. A pre-war rag book of nursery rhymes.

A rare Bank Holiday outing to Bayard's Leap, near Sleaford, with her father, to see the marks of the leap of the famous horse. (Ernie had brought her home from the fields a lucky horseshoe once. She had it still.) And Frieda had been drawn to the north – to its words, its music. (Wagner, so late in the day, had been a revelation.) Why else had she been so dangerously attracted to the Iron Coast, and to Queen Christina? She can blame Gladys and her blood for this.

But what, Frieda asks herself, is all this mish-mash of the past? What does it *mean*? Can she stick it all together, or is it too late? She thinks it is too late. Each time she sorts out one strand, others entangle her. The world must spin on. Europe has had its day. Better to cut the links, better to stop thinking, better to liberate the young, to set them free. Well, she has done her best to see to that. She has made her will. They won't like it one bit.

Frieda Haxby, an old rationalist, an enlightened one, a lateral thinker, has come here to get rid of thinking and of reason. And here she has heard voices and dreamt dreams. She is trying to will herself into another medium.

She gets up, crosses to the sideboard, pours herself another three fingers of Scotch, adds a dash of water from a brown jug. Will Paine watches her intently. He cannot hear what she is saying, but he can see her lips move. She is talking to herself.

She sits again, and begins to move the cards.

She is speaking to herself of her dreams.

She had dreamt, the night before, both of evolution and of death. In the evolution dream, she had watched one of the little nameless fish that come up with the high tide clamber out of the water on to the shingle. It had grown legs, as does a tadpole, then had risen on its haunches, and grown larger, and hairier, until it was larger than a man. In her dream she had labelled it 'a dangerous species'. Fierce, grim, hairy, primitive, it had loped off into the woods, and she had woken, pleased with her dream logic.

The second dream, the death dream, which came towards dawn, had been less pleasing, and more realistic. She dreamt of her friend Patrick Fordham, the actor. He was dying, and he was holding court upon his deathbed. Frieda had been solemnly received at the ceremony of farewell. Patrick was bald and emaciated, and he knew that he had precisely one day to live. The next day he would die. He was surrounded by monks or courtiers, obsequious, attentive. They ushered her into the presence. Patrick was lying on a draped litter. She forced herself to bend over him, to try to say something meaningful, on this, the last day of his mortal life. What could one say in the presence of certain death? She had uttered, 'You know how much our friendship has always meant to us, Patrick,' but to her horror he gave a horrible little sneer in response to this speech. Then she bent over him, and kissed his bare skull, knowing that this was what she had to do, and he winced and turned away and said, 'I'm sorry, I'm so tired, I'm so tired.' And Frieda knew that she had offended, and indeed she herself had offended herself, for both her words and her action had been hollow. She had valued his friendship, but not much, and her reluctance to kiss that diseased skull had been more powerful than her affection. But she had to stand there, as his attendants discussed his imminent death, and the disposal of his body. He would be buried the next day in Tadcaster, and his body would lie there for a year and a day, and then it would be transported to its final resting place at Bury St Edmunds. To Frieda's surprise Patrick seemed to find this information soothing, more soothing than he had found her own efforts, and she despised him for taking comfort from it. The pomp of his death – for clearly there was great honour in lying for a year and a day in Tadcaster – had reassured him. Even here, with less than a day to live, he had been pleased to find himself surrounded by ceremony and flattery. He who had played the king would die deceived like a king.

As Frieda had stared at his bone-thin death face, she saw that his skin, before her eyes, was taking on a different colour. He was turning turquoise. Not corpse green, but a bright, strong, burnished, ornamental turquoise, like a Mexican deathmask. He had willed himself to mineral and metal. Frieda turned away from him, and woke.

But the dream had stayed with her, as clear and as uncomforting as truth.

'AIDS and leprosy, status and vanity,' she says to herself, aloud, as she turns up the cards. Why does she dream so much of death? Her dreams are omens sent from the other world. Does she fear death? Patrick is only sixty, but she believes that her dream means he is doomed. Is she also doomed, and is she afraid? She cannot find it in her to think that she is. Patrick had been afraid, but she thinks she is not.

Resignation, indifference, despair. Calm of mind, all passion spent.

Of course, in a novel, she tells herself, this is the moment at which she would discover herself to have a mortal illness, an illness which would inspire her with a new desire to survive, to triumph over the Black Ace. And she has been coughing rather a lot lately.

It is not an illness that stalks her, but Will Paine from Wolverhampton. He has been round to what he takes to be a front door, and knocked. He is not surprised that she does not answer: how could she have heard him? He tries a sidedoor, in the wall of the arch, the door that Benjamin had discovered. It stands half open, and looks promising. Again, she does not answer, but he has roused an old, mild, shabby black and white sheepdog, which approaches him, wagging its tail, lowering its head in deference, showing the humble whites of its eyes. Will is nervous of dogs, but manages to pat this one: the dog cringes gratefully and lets out a very low servile whine.

Will is at a loss. Shall he enter the house and track her down, noisily announcing his presence as he goes? Would that count as trespass, as breaking and entering? Is it illegal to walk through an open door? He decides it would be wiser to approach from the garden side. And so it is that Will, closely followed by Bounce, finds himself crossing the expanse of tufted grass that was once a lawn, towards the window where Frieda Haxby sits. And still she does not look up.

He is obliged to tap upon the window.

Frieda looks up, sharply: so she is not deaf.

She sees a young dark handsome elfin stranger with a bare short-cropped head, an earring and a carpet bag, wearing a denim jacket and a white T-shirt bearing some half-concealed slogan. He is tapping at her window-pane.

She certainly does not look afraid, notes Will nervously: she looks furious. There may have been a passing flicker of alarm, but it is replaced by a glower of angry and haughty indignation, the sort of expression that middle-class people reserve for beggars and travelling salesmen selling ironing-board covers and yellow dusters and absorbent floor cloths made of industrial shoddy. Maybe she thinks he *is* a travelling salesman?

He mouths at her, through the glass: 'Are you Mrs Haxby?'

Her expression changes from defensive contempt to a wary wrath: this, she decides, is some mad fan, come all the way to Ashcombe to annoy her. But she crosses to the window, opens one of its large damp-swollen wet-rot reluctant panes, and stares down at him as he stands below her on the sunken lawn. There, with him, stands Bounce, bowing and grinning, putting in a mute plea for this luckless companion in misfortune.

'Mrs Haxby?' says Will, in his utterly distinctive Black Country nasal twang.

'*Miss* Haxby, in point of fact,' says Frieda, ever pedantic, standing on ceremony. 'Or *Mrs* Palmer. If you prefer. What can I do for you?'

Will Paine coughs, clears his throat. 'I wondered – I just wondered – if there's any work going?'

This question seems to annoy her. 'Of course there isn't,' she snaps. 'Whatever kind of work would I need, down here?'

Will stares around him. It seems evident to him that a lot needs doing. There had been a lot to do at Patsy Palmer's, and her place had been as neat as the Archbishop of York's compared with this wilderness.

She is about to show him the door, and he hasn't even got in yet. The thought of climbing that fucking great mountain back to the A39 brings sweat to his brow and a lump to his throat. He tries again.

'I'm a friend of your grandson Simon. And of Emily,' he says, stretching a point or two.

He has her attention now. 'Oh, are you?' she says, relenting slightly.

'I spent a bit of time in the summer with them,' he embroiders.

'Oh, God,' says Frieda. 'I suppose you'd better come in.'

'How do I get in?' he asks.

The scene is ridiculous.

'Oh, I'll come and get you,' she says. 'You stay where you are.'

And he stands there, patting Bounce hopefully, until she appears, round the corner of the building. The sun has sunk behind the hill, and the air grows colder.

She lets him in. She offers him a whisky. He declines. She makes him a cup of tea. He does not much like tea, but he accepts, out of politeness. She offers him a £20 note. She wants him to go away. She wants to be alone.

'Nobody ever gets this far,' she says, as he drinks his tea. 'You gave me a fright, knocking on the window like that. Nobody's ever been here except the Jehovah's Witnesses. They made it. You have to admire them, don't you?'

'I'm not a Jehovah's Witness,' he says. He pauses, tries again. 'I'm sorry,' he says. 'I didn't mean to intrude. I just thought you might have some odd jobs.'

'I like to be alone,' says Frieda.

'And I thought I ought to tell you about Simon,' says Will, improvising.

'What about Simon?'

'He's not well,' says Will, in a tone of pity and censure. 'He's on crack. And worse. He's cracking up.'

'Oh, is he?' says Frieda, taking another swig of her stiff whisky. 'Well, that'll teach him a thing or two. And how's little Emily?'

'Emily's OK, so far,' says Will cautiously.

'What do you mean, so far?'

Will shakes his head and says nothing.

'So social worker Patsy took you in, did she? And then she kicked you out? Well, she's bigger-hearted than me. I'm not even going to take you in.'

Will Paine looks forlorn, and sniffs. He reaches for his bag. The dog, seeing the defeated movement, whines in sympathy. The homeless homing pigeon rattles its tin lid.

Frieda concedes.

'Oh, all right,' she says. 'Just one night, mind you, and off with the dawn. And don't bother me. You're not to bother me. I'm not much of a one for conversation. I like my own company.'

Will smiles, his face irradiated. He's a very nice-looking boy.

'Just a bed for the night,' he says. He knows he is in with a chance. He's very good at not being a nuisance. Or so he thinks.

A BEAST IN VIEW

Autumn advances, and a date for the next election is mooted. It will be in the spring. David D'Anger pays many visits to his dentist and works overtime. He is ubiquitous. His party pledges this and un-pledges that. David speaks on social justice and race relations and the food industry here, there and everywhere. He even speaks on social justice and race relations in Middleton. Gogo D'Anger continues to study the neurological conditions of an increasing number of cus-tomers and to complain about the decreasing funding of the National Health Service. Her private practice grows. She and David D'Anger ensure their own health privately and at some expense. David finds he cannot insure his teeth. As he doesn't in principle approve of insur-ance, this pleases him. But it doesn't please him very much.

Benjamin D'Anger studies the causes of the Second World War and writes an essay on the Romantic poets and opts to take geology as a subsidiary subject. He draws crystals and synclines and anticlines and lies at the bottom of the bath each night in deep water, seeing how long he can hold his breath. His breath control improves.

Patsy Palmer surprises herself by finding she is obliged to view a porno video which makes her feel slightly uneasy. She had thought she was past such niceties. She also surprises herself by finding herself in bed with a chap from the Home Office. She can't think how it happened. She hopes Daniel Palmer will not notice. He does not. Daniel Palmer is involved in a protracted case concerning pollution in the River Wash, a river which flows through South Yorkshire, Derby-shire, Staffordshire and some of Cheshire. Nobody seems to want to claim it, but somebody will have to.

Little Emily Palmer is far away in Italy, where she is, in principle, learning Italian in Florence; in practice she is hanging out, and very happy with it.

Simon Palmer is not so happy. He has bad dreams. He dreams of toads and crabs.

Nathan Herz dreams nightly of the white hand of Belle. She torments him by night and comforts him by day. He has never learnt to swim. He is afraid of deep water. Her white hand beckons him.

Rosemary Herz runs around too much to notice anything. She is busy working out lottery schemes, millennium schemes. The rapid triviality of her life is exhausting but it keeps her from thought. She has successfully numbed all introspection, all reflection. Her life glitters with surfaces. It has no darkness and no depth. This is the way she likes it.

They are all too busy to think much about Frieda Haxby, and have to be called back into line rather sharply by Cate Crowe.

Cate Crowe has been to the Film Festival in Lisbon. She had not attended this increasingly glamorous annual event in her capacity as literary agent, but in her new role as partner of Newbrit filmstar, Egg Benson. The Egg's new movie, *Crates of Ivory*, was being premièred, and Cate Crowe had dropped all at the office to accompany him. The Crowe was herself something of a glamour-figure, a *Vanity Fair* trader, and she felt quite at home amongst the stars and starlets. Famed for her ability to drive a hard bargain, and her Marlene Dietrich legs, she justified her trip by telling herself that somebody had to keep an eye on the high-earning Egg, who was given to intermittent bursts of spectacular misbehaviour, and by assuring her partners that she would keep her ear to the ground to see if any talent was zumming along down there.

Cate Crowe had never been to Portugal before, and she liked it. She particularly liked the hotel where she and the Egg were installed, high up in the hills at Sintra: palatial, enormous, and fit for royalty. Vast empty frescoed rooms ornately furnished and full of floral masterpieces led down to yet more vast empty frescoed rooms, and there late at night she and Egg would wander, astonished, like children in a fairy story, like dreamers in a *trompe-l'œil* opium dream. Though both had struck the jackpot in life, neither had been reared in luxury, and this whole edifice seemed insubstantial, magical, like a filmset that would be dismantled at any moment before their eyes. Yet it was real. The marble was solid, but the space was not. Usually it's the other way round, as they both have discovered.

The films on show at the festival were not so easy on the eye, for the fashion of the year seemed to be for black humour, violence, decapitation, dismembering; cannibalism featured not only in the Egg's own movie but in several other pieces from small nationalist movements through Europe and beyond. There was a Scottish film of singular ferocity. (Cate Crowe had already seen this movie in London, and hadn't understood a word of its dialogue; the Portuguese subtitles were a great help, even though Cate couldn't speak Portuguese, and whoever wrote them deserved, as she said several times, an Oscar.) The Croatian and Romanian contributions were also on the cheerless side, and Cate resolved to play truant and skip the rest of the official programme, apart from the banquets and parties; she'd have one last shot, and condescend to attend the film about which everyone was talking. Then she'd take herself back to the real world of the Palácio in Sintra.

The buzz film of the year, *Dangerous Exchanges*, was scripted and made by a young, unknown, art-house Australian called Claudia Cazetti. It was a philosophic fiction about time travel, in which a group of characters was granted the opportunity of residence in any period of the pageant of history: they were invited to choose, then had to test the consequences of choice. The joke was that they all kept making silly mistakes like forgetting to specify what age or class or even what species they would belong to, and in the end they all got sick to death of their own stupidity and opted for the one remaining choice – to die, or to be reborn as themselves in exactly the spot they'd started from, the spot from which they'd been so keen to get away in the first place. This was Brisbane, 1996. (They all chose Brisbane rather than death: all but one.) Cate Crowe couldn't follow the intricacies of the plot, as she'd had several glasses of Portuguese red before settling down to the viewing, but she admired the costumes and the special effects, and was much taken with the performance of the principal actress, who played the Fairy Godmother in charge of the exchanges. This actress, as everyone had been saying, had star quality. She was cool, icy, intelligent, superior. She surveyed the panorama of history and the follies and littlenesses of man with a divine indifference. She was rumoured to be Cazetti's lover. She looked a bit like Greta Garbo.

It was when the name of Garbo surfaced in the sludge of Cate Crowe's memory that she remembered where she had seen the name of Claudia Cazetti. It wasn't just the sympathetic alliteration that made it seem familiar: it was Cazetti who had faxed her, months ago, about the film rights in Frieda Haxby's *Queen Christina*. Hadn't Garbo played Christina, a thousand years ago? Cate Crowe knew she'd better get hold of Cazetti. She'd better get hold of Haxby's book. There might be something in this after all.

Cate Crowe had never read her client's latest work, and had felt little need to do so. She hardly knew Frieda Haxby, whom she had inherited from Bertram Goldie, an older member of the firm, now retired. She had regarded Haxby as a sleeping investment, a quiet, steady-little-earner whose 10 per cent from those old classics, *The Matriarchy of War*, *The Scarecrow and the Plough* and *The Iron Coast*, was well worth harvesting, and whose lighter works (a heterogeneous mix of popular sociology and rogue political pamphleteering) had proved surprisingly resilient. But she hadn't read *Christina*. She'd read the reviews, and that had seemed more than enough. Maybe she'd been wrong?

It wasn't easy to get hold of a copy in Lisbon. Cate got on the phone to London and told her assistant to dig out the letter from Cazetti, and then set off in a taxi to scour the bookshops. After two hours of unsuccessful trawl, and risky parking, on tramlines and cobbled streets and precipices, her driver suggested the Biblioteca of the Instituto Britanico, and there indeed she found at least a trace of a copy: the librarian said she had purchased one, but it was out. On further investigation, she discovered it had been out for some four months. Could it be recalled instantly, asked Cate. The librarian seemed unhappy at first, but, succumbing to Cate's air of urgency and high talk of film, she agreed to ring up the borrower, a Miss Parker-Sydenham, who lived, as it happened, in Sintra, just down the hill from the Palace Hotel. Cate herself spoke to Miss Parker-Sydenham, who sounded abashed at having kept the book for so long, and agreed to allow Cate to call round and collect it. 'I've *nearly* finished it,' she repeated, apologetically, several times.

Cate took the obliging taxi all the way back to Sintra and went to wrest her client's novel from Ms Parker-Sydenham's keeping. The lady proved to be not the tax-evading expatriate Salazar-supporter that her name had evoked, but an impoverished English-language teacher aged thirty who came from Huddersfield. 'I'm awfully sorry,' she said, yet again. 'Don't apologize to *me*,' said Cate, and swept off to the hotel with her trophy.

She didn't have time to tackle it that night, as the Egg rolled home in a right state and needed some handling, but the next morning the sun shone pleasantly enough for her to sit out with it in the gardens below the lemon grove. Two hours into the text, after much skipping, she thought she could see what Cazetti had seen in it. At the very least, there was a fine vehicle here for a leading lady, and plenty of opportunities for feminist deconstruction of the past. Lesbianism and espionage, rape and assassinations, art and abdications – what more could you want? Amazing that the subject hadn't been snapped up before. Clever old Haxby. Cate Crowe, retrospectively, grew indignant with the reviewers. What had the ignorant little oafs been complaining about? This was a cracking good story, plenty of action, glamorous settings, strong characters. Was there a part for the Egg? Not really, for the Egg was hopeless in any kind of classical role – he was a bald brute of the nineties, he'd never be able to play Gustavus or Magnus. (His attempt at Jane Austen had been risible.) But the absence of Egg in the script was the only defect Cate Crowe could see, and she was full of plans as she made her way in from the lemon grove to see if the man had come round yet.

On her way in she was arrested by the concierge at the desk, a squat and swart and elderly man of some dignity.

'Miss Crowe,' he said, 'I see you are reading a book by our old friend Miss Haxby.'

Cate was surprised and pleased by this recognition: she gave him the book to inspect. He turned the pages carefully, and paused over Frieda's portrait on the back flap.

'Yes,' he continued. 'Miss Haxby was a regular visitor here. Also members of the Swedish royal family. Also we have received Agatha Christie and Marguerite Yourcenar and Sir Angus Wilson.'

Cate explained that Miss Haxby was one of her most distinguished and valued clients.

'A very nice lady,' said the concierge. 'And how is Miss Haxby? We have not seen her for two-three years now. She used to sit here in the garden to write. Maybe it was this book she was writing.'

Cate said that as far as she knew Miss Haxby was alive and well and living quietly in the country. Writing, it was rumoured, her memoirs.

Frieda Haxby's memoirs seemed a more interesting proposition today than they had seemed yesterday. So did Queen Christina. Cate resolved to pursue.

Cate Crow's fax from Portugal reached Rosemary Herz on a bad day. She had arrived late at her office after spending an hour at the Nightingale Hospital undergoing various tests: a routine health check for insurance purposes had recently revealed startlingly high blood pressure which had required further investigation. Today her blood pressure was still up. Were these two freak results, or was there something wrong with her? And if so what could it be? She was not overweight, and she did not smoke, she drank only moderately. Surely Nathan was more of a high blood pressure candidate than she? But his was said to be steady and low.

Stress she did have, and this news had caused more of it. Her Private Patients Policy already cost her a fair sum, Jonathan's school fees had just gone up, there was talk of removing tax relief on various parts of her pension. Worse than all of that, her job itself was at risk. She had been sitting pretty for three years and had lulled herself into a sense of security. But there had of late been turmoil in the arts world. Resignations, sackings, venom in the press. Robert Oxenholme, one-time Minister for Sponsorship, had denounced the vacillations and pusillanimity of his own department and taken himself off to Bologna for a year to write a book. It was all very well for some. Her budget had been cut and cut again, and her Board was said to be very unhappy about hostile publicity for the last season's programme. There had been a particularly controversial installation involving live molluscs and crustaceans which had been deplored by some as cruel and by others as political. She had been called to meet members of the Board to review the situation. Maybe she would be asked to leave. Should she ring up her accountant to ask advice on redundancy pay? Probably not. Every time she rang her accountant it seemed to cost her three hundred quid plus VAT.

This situation was enough to give anybody high blood pressure, that invisible and intangible complaint. Could she feel it coursing round her body, throbbing in the veins at the back of her neck, knocking like a death drum in her temples? She was far too young to suffer from such an ailment. This the specialist had implied, as he probed her genetic inheritance. Did high blood pressure run in the family? Did her mother and father suffer from it? This question in itself was enough to make her pulse race. How could she tell this expensively neat old boy that she had hardly known her father, and that her mother had gone mad? Was her work stressful, he had inquired. Yes, she had said. Yes.

Rosemary, reading her morning's post, drinking a strong black coffee brewed for her by her PA, heard echoing in the back of her memory some words from an otherwise forgettable Leader of the Opposition at some party conference nearly two decades ago. What was it he had said? 'I warn you not to fall ill, I warn you not to get old'? It had been a fair warning. Was Rosemary right to suspect that even her PA had looked at her this morning with a certain levity? Were people talking about her, laughing at her, waiting for her departure? Treachery was in the air. Would she come back from lunch and find her desk cleared, her paintings stacked with their faces to the wall? Would she find herself dispatched to Hadrian's Wall, or jobless altogether?

And here, freshly arrived, was a fax from Cate Crowe, asking about her mother. 'I really need to get in touch with her urgently,' said the blotchy curly sleek fax paper. 'Have you any suggestions? Did your brother-in-law ever manage to make contact with her? I'll be back in London tomorrow, do get in touch. I need to speak to her soonest. I need a signature.'

Rosemary stared at this communication with a baffled irritation. Was she her mother's keeper? More to the point, was she one of her mother's heirs? It would be very handy if Frieda were to pop off and leave a tidy three-way fortune. Who knows what she might be worth?

This was an ignoble thought, but Frieda, in Rosemary's opinion, had done little to induce a warmer regard in her children. Frieda had hated her own mother, and now was hated in turn. Frieda had alienated her children from their father, had brought them up unsuitably. Rosemary had little idea of who her father had been, what he had looked like. Had he been a red-faced, choleric, pressurized man? She thought not. He had been a mathematician and a drinker, a weakling and a runaway. Or this was the picture of him that Rosemary, on slim evidence, had formed.

The three Palmer children had never talked about their father, had never discussed why he had disappeared while they were still in their infancy. Daniel, the eldest, had set the tone of reticence. He could not bear to hear his father mentioned. The girls had not dared to speak of him. The subject was taboo. And Frieda too had kept her silence.

It would be trying to inherit high blood pressure from so absent a parent. Frieda herself had never suffered from it, as far as Rosemary knew: but why should she know? Of what had Frieda's sister Hilda died? Frieda's own father had died of a stroke. Perhaps it was the Haxby blood that had broken the little vessels in her eyeballs and treacherously weakened the muscles of her heart.

Rosemary, at her desk, was in mild shock, which intensified into something near panic. She did not want to be ill. She had never been a hypochondriac, had never suspected herself of any ailment. This made the shock the worse. She was untrained in anxiety. Should she ring Gogo and ask her what high blood pressure in a forty-year-old might mean? Or did she prefer not to know the worst? The specialist had told her she must go back to the clinic the next week to be fitted with an ambulatory monitor. If news got out that she was not in perfect health, she would be sacked at once.

Cedric Summerson had been the blood pressure type: you could tell it from his complexion. Frieda had fancied beef-coloured men. Several of the uncles who had featured in their childhood had been red of face, including the most dominant of them, who had lasted a good eight years or more. He, like Cedric, had been stout, solid, flesh-ly. He had been rich and important and he had brought gifts. Uncle Bernard from Austria. He had been jowled and guttural, heavy and clever. He had been a philosopher and a philanderer. He had many children of his own and several wives, but he had nevertheless seemed anxious to spend his evenings in the Mausoleum in Romley with Frieda. He had helped Daniel, Gogo and Rosemary with their homework from time to time. He liked children, and they had liked him.

Rosemary had not thought of Bernard for years, and recognized that there was not much purpose in thinking about him now: who-ever was responsible for her condition, it could not have been Ber-nard. He was genetically innocent. Innocent, and dead. He had died three years before, and had been buried with pomp. Frieda and two or three widows had attended the Memorial Service at St Martin-in-the-Fields. Rosemary had seen Frieda's photo in the papers, on the steps, arm in arm with one of the widows, unsuitably sharing a joke.

Frieda had been a scandal, in the days when scandal was less common than now. And she continued to be a scandal. Rosemary looked at Cate Crowe's fax and wondered what to do next. In the olden days one could have sent Frieda a telegram. Rosemary was just old enough to remember the days when telegrams were little yellow serious messages instead of large Occasional Greetings Cards that take just as long to arrive as normal mail, and a good deal longer than a fax. Was there money involved in Cate's cry? It smelt like it. Could she send a courier down to the West Country to summon Frieda? Could she alert the local police? Or perhaps she needed a lawyer, a detective? Could Frieda be cajoled into a signature? And if she couldn't, could Daniel take on power of attorney?

During her lunch break, eating carrot and nut salad with a plastic fork from a disposable plastic box, she investigated. Her PA (a well-trained young woman) had obtained telephone directories of Somerset and Devon, for it had occurred to Rosemary that there was no need to send a motorbike all the way from the metropolis. Even rural England (and it had, as she had driven through it earlier in the year, struck her as ridiculously, almost pretentiously rural) must have dispatch riders. And yes, here they were, two yellow pages of motorcycle and van couriers, promising urgent speedy fully insured distance-no-object twenty-four-hour same-day nationwide conveyance of documents, parcels, packages, even livestock. One could dispatch a hamster or a goldfish, or, as a hospital had recently done, to in her view excessive public opprobrium, a dead baby.

No problem there, but what should she send to Frieda? A copy of Cate Crowe's fax, perhaps? That would let her out of having to make up any verbiage. She looked at the fax and decided that it wasn't quite suitable. There was something insufficiently deferential in Cate's wording – nothing overtly offensive, just a general lack of the obsequiousness that Frieda seemed to think her due. Rosemary would have to rephrase it slightly, make it sound lucrative, tempting, important.

Was there any hurry? Should she wait for Cate to get back to England with more details? Should she consult Daniel and Gogo?

She could feel her blood chugging, blooming, swelling. She tried to breathe deeply, calmly. She recited a bit of a mantra she had once picked up in a yoga class, and stared at the Henry Moore sheep on the opposite wall. The sheep stared back with their silly saintly faces.

The young man on the motorbike buzzed happily along the high coast road, through the bracken and the gorse, past the nibbling sheep and a small herd of Exmoor ponies, sheltering from the prevailing wind in the lea of a high wall of beech hedge. It was a wild clear day, with high clouds over the channel: a dramatic day. The road was a switchback and he took the bumps and curves at a reckless speed. It was good to be out of Exeter, and moving fast. This was an important mission. He was bearing a valuable document, marked CONFIDEN-TIAL: DELIVER IN PERSON TO ADDRESSEE. The route had been marked for him in shocking pink Glow Pen by Mr Ffloyd on an OS map. Terry wasn't all that brilliant at map-reading but he could tell that he was off to a remote spot, off the beaten track. He had been told to track down Miss Frieda Haxby, to force her to acknowledge his package, to compel her to sign for it, and if possible to extract from her some kind of answer. This struck Terry as quite a lark. His engine revved and roared as he overtook a G-reg Renault and a tractor.

The descent to Ashcombe slowed him down. His machine skittered over stones, bumped over ruts, churned up mud. He was almost at the bottom, almost at the sea's edge, when he saw the roofs and bell-tower of the big house, just below him. There was no sign of any habitation, no smoke curling, no post-box stuffed with circulars nailed to a tree. It was desolate. Ferns sprouted at him from high banks. Boughs thrashed. It was getting darker, though it was only midday. Rain was on the way from Cornwall. He was dry and warm inside his windproof leathers, he was buckled and badged like a knight errant. A secret skull and crossbones was stamped upon his black shirt, and beneath his black shirt his snake tattoos rippled.

This was a wrecker's coast. Two summers ago he'd had a few drinks in The Wreckers' Arms, just ten miles back on the headland. The pub had been hung with trophies. Planks with inscriptions, brass lamps, old manacles, a pair of painted wooden hands from a wooden ship's figure-head. Terry and his mates had had a few pints, then smoked a few joints amidst the hot bracken. Bliss. The unmanned lighthouse had winked and turned.

Terry Zealley parked his bike in the weed-choked courtyard and stared up at the bleak façade. Then he marched boldly towards the nearest door, and knocked. He pressed an old white button of a bell but could hear no answering sound within. He knocked again, then advanced, tried the sidedoor, shouted. He could sense there was nobody here. The old bird had flown. He skirted the side of the house, as Will Paine had done before him, making his way to the front lawn that faced the sea. Again he shouted and his voice sounded thin in the wind.

One of the long, low, mullioned windows had blown open, and was swinging and creaking. This was odd. Terry Zealley crossed the lumpy grass, and peered in. He could see a large table, laid with various objects, including a bottle and glasses, and several smaller tables, some also littered. It looked, as he was later to tell his mates, like the *Marie Céleste*. It was creepy. Again he shouted, into the damp interior. He could have climbed in, easily, over the low window-sill, but instead he went back to the sidedoor, and tried it. It was unlocked. He went in.

The house smelled of dereliction, but there were signs of recent occupation. Muddy boots in the hallway, a raincoat and a stick hanging from a peg, tins of dog food in a cardboard carton, a new-looking Calor Gas *bombe*, empty milk bottles, a plastic bag of wine bottles and fizzy-water bottles that looked as though they were awaiting a trip to a bottle bank. Terry backed out again, to explore the courtyard, the back regions. There might be somebody hanging about in the outhouses. In one of them stood an old grey Volvo, with a broken wing mirror. It was unlocked. He opened the door, sniffed. It was stale, a smoker's car. A tin of boiled sweets sat on the dashboard, with a spectacle case and a box of tissues. Nothing remarkable there.

As he slammed the car door shut, hoping and fearing that the noise might attract attention, he heard a low whining, and saw, approaching, an old thin black and white dog. Terry, born and bred in a Devon village, knew that kind of dog: a scrounger, an outcast. He whistled at it, and it approached, its ears flat, eager, but keeping its distance. It would not come near his offered hand, but crouched, looking at him with its head tilted. Terry started back towards the house, but the dog did not want him to go. It looked at him and whined again, a mournful supplication, then stood up and set off towards the garden, stopping to see if Terry were following. Was it trying to take him towards his mistress's body, his mistress's grave? Was she lying in the woods out there with a broken leg?

Terry followed the dog, which led him down the shrubbery and through a gap in a hedge to a lower level of neglected kitchen garden and crumbling walls. The ground was thick and wet with autumn leafmould, and puffballs and parasols sprouted from the decay. Brambles thick with berry clambered and caught at him. Flies buzzed, for this was a sheltered spot, and somebody had been burning garden rubbish – he could see and smell the remains of a large bonfire. He approached, kicked at the charred sticks. It had been a large fire, for the blackened circle it had left was some five feet across. Grey-black logs, partly consumed, and soft mounds of finer ash. Terry kicked again, and ash rose into the air. Looking more closely, he could see the remains of what looked like thick wads of papers, whole boxes of papers, which had been heaped on to the pyre. Was it a recent fire? Was it his imagination, or could he feel a faint warmth? He kicked again, and fancied that a single spark flew upwards. A fire like that could smoulder for days.

The dog seemed satisfied with his inspection of the embers, and now suggested that Terry return to the house. Terry was not sure what he was meant to have noted; had the dog been indicating the scene of a crime? And were those mussel shells and splinters of bone that he could see in the ash part of the crime, or were they the remains of an innocent barbecue? He bent down, picked up a shell, rubbed it on his trousers, inspected it. It was neatly hinged, cross-rayed with brown and purple. Empty, sucked dry. It told him nothing. He followed the dog back towards the building.

He went in again through the sidedoor, and made his way down a long corridor to the large room he had seen through the open window. And there he found more clues. An abandoned meal, laid on the large table, with knife, fork, plate, a half-empty bottle of wine, a half-empty wine glass full of drowned flies. The end of a loaf, dusted with blue mould. A hard and shining cheese rind, a brown and withered apple paring. A bowl of winkle shells. An open book, propped against a kitchen-roll. Terry stared, sniffed, prowled. He discovered a clock patience, half played. A board laid out with coloured counters for a game which he did not know to be backgammon. A dried orange skewered with a knitting needle, and an atlas, open at the Americas. Spooky, definitely spooky. A little brass pot full of burnt-down joss sticks. A three-cornered pub ashtray full of cigarette ends. And, if he wasn't mistaken, a half-open matchbox full of the weed. He picked it up, sniffed cautiously. Yes, of course. And a packet of Rizlas. Somebody here had been smoking substances. A rum old lady. And where the hell had she got to?

Miss Frieda Haxby: Deliver in Person. Easier said than done. He smelled sorcery, he smelled witchcraft, as he was to tell his mates. He was tempted to open the package, to see if it contained a contract with the devil, but knew better than to risk his job by tampering. There weren't many nice jobs going in the South West, for an enterprising lad like Terry Zealley.

The skull gave him a turn. He hadn't spotted it at first, in the clutter of bric-à-brac, but eventually it managed to catch his eye. It stared at him from its deep eye-sockets, grinned at him with its four remaining teeth, warned him from its blaring absent nostrils. Yellow and pitted and slightly marked with grey and pink, it held its place for ever. What were those cracks in its cranium? Those stitched seams joining the plates above where its ears had been? Those deep slanting eyeslits? Had it ever lived, and how had it died, and why was it here?

Terry went out into the courtyard and ate one of his tuna and mayonnaise sandwiches. He didn't want to eat in that house. He'd thought he was hungry, but somehow it didn't taste as good as he'd expected. The Crosskeys Garage usually sold a good sandwich, but this wasn't up to the mark at all.

What to do next? Should he ring Mr Ffloyd on his mobile? Should he ring the police? Should he poke around a bit more in the hope of finding a corpse or a haul of grass?

Terry nosed around. The sandwich had restored perspective. He'd always wanted to find a dead body. Well, who hasn't?

He made friends with the skull, picking it up to speak to it: he was alarmed when its jaw dropped off, but he managed, guiltily, to re-assemble it so it looked just the same as before. He inspected the little bird and animal skulls that surrounded it. One was a sheep's skull, he thought, one a badger's. There were some curled horns, and a few feathers. Had there been voodoo, had there been slaughtered chickens and dancing goats, had there been hanky-panky? He rather hoped so. He went upstairs, boldly, and followed the sound of humming (a refrigerator? a corpse in a freezer? a dehumidifier?) to discover Frie-da's workroom. There was her word-processor, switched on, and speaking quietly and patiently to itself. The screen was blank, but there was a line of pale green flickering writing at the top of the screen which said EYEBOX PC 2000 8.3.1990 LAST USED 00.00.00 CURRENT INTERRUPTED. TO RECOMMENCE PRESS ENTER. TO DISCONTINUE PRESS ESCAPE.

Terry found the keys marked ENTER and ESCAPE, but thought better of pressing either of them. He did not understand computers. This whole thing was getting out of hand. How long had that ma-chine been patiently waiting for its mistress's return? Did it know where she had gone? Did it contain her farewell message, her suicide note?

He looked around him, found the globe and the binoculars, switched on the light in the globe so that all the nations of the earth and all its oceans glowed with blue and green and brown and desert gold. Importantly, from the look-out post, he raked the horizon through the powerful binoculars.

A small fishing boat chugged along westwards, over a grey and choppy sea. Was it a drug-carrying vessel, part of an international plot? Was the package for Miss Haxby a summons from her Godfather? Two tons of cannabis had been seized off Ilfracombe the month before, from a thousand-ton merchant ship called *Proteus*, on its way from Morocco. It had been a big story in the local and national press. Had Miss Haxby been the mastermind behind the fleet of bogus fish vans lined up to distribute this sinister loading? Was it from this very window that Miss Haxby had flashed her secret signals? For here, by the globe and the binoculars, stood a large, heavy waterproof torch, and an old-fashioned paraffin storm-lantern. He was surely on to something here.

The house was far too big to search, but on the way down he easily found what must have been Frieda Haxby's bedroom. A double bed, with a duvet heaped upon it, and piles of books and papers on the bedside table. A sea view. Another torch, a packet of cigarettes, a lighter, heaps of clothes upon a chair, several pairs of shoes lined up not untidily. No corpse in the bed: he lifted the duvet to look.

Frieda Haxby would never sign the document that he carried in his plastic satchel. She had vanished, to avoid it. She had gone for good. She was dead. So who should he ring, the police or Mr Ffloyd?

Of the two, the police seemed the more attractive option, the one which would yield him the most entertainment. He'd never had occasion to dial 999 on his mobile. *Could* you dial 999 on a mobile? Maybe mobiles didn't recognize real emergencies, maybe they only recognized privatized emergencies, financial emergencies. Well, now was the time to find out. Terry Zealley settled himself in the courtyard, in a sheltered corner where he thought reception would be good. He'd got his map reference ready. He was looking forward to his stint in the witness box. He punched in the magic numbers, and waited for a reply.

'Disappeared,' echoed Gogo.

'Yes,' said Rosemary, distraught, on the verge of unseemly laughter. 'Disappeared. Vanished. A missing person. Or a Misspers, as they seem to be called in the West Country. They've got the coastguards out, searching the seaward side of the cliff. And the local constabulary are going through the house.'

'Jesus,' said Gogo. 'How fucking inconvenient. Have you told Daniel?'

'I've left a message for him at chambers. He's in court.'

'He won't be best pleased when he hears.'

'You're right there. Can you imagine?'

'Do the police know who it is they're looking for?'

'I don't think so. She didn't have much of a social life up there, I don't suppose.'

'Better keep this out of the press.'

'Don't worry, I'm not going to put them on to it.'

'What had I better do? Ring Daniel this evening? When does he usually get out?'

'God knows. He's probably aiming to get back to the Farm, but this may stop him.'

'One of us is going to have to get down there.'

'It's *five hours*. I'm telling you. I suppose it's lucky it's the weekend.'

'Lucky?' snorted Gogo, and laughed.

'Gogo?'

'Yes?'

'I've just discovered I've got roaring high blood pressure. What does that mean?'

Gogo paused, changed tone. 'Oh, nothing, probably. Work pressure. Wonder we haven't all got it. Don't worry. Look, I can't talk now, I've got a patient waiting. I'll ring you this evening. I promise.'

How gratified Frieda Haxby would have been had she been able to witness the consternation with which her family greeted the news of her vanishing, had she been able to hear the messages that ran backwards and forwards along the wires on that Friday night! Such touching distress, such urgency of response. Not all mothers would have created such a stir. How impressed she would have been by the speed with which her three grown and busy and important children managed to shed their weekend work and leisure engagements in order to hunt her down upon the moor!

It took them, it is fair to say, a whole evening of renegotiations, during which they spoke not only to one another but also to the West Somerset Police, the Devon Police, the Exeter Express Dispatch Service, the coastguard in Swansea (why Swansea? – they were not sure, but Swansea it was), Cate Crowe, and the old-fashioned family solicitor, Mr Partridge, whom Frieda had sacked over the VAT affair. They even spoke to Terry Zealley. They cancelled guests and

163

rearranged meetings and collated their diaries and took money out of their banks. They left instructions with PAs and secretaries and clerks of chambers. Daniel personally rang to apologize to Sir Noel for letting him down over the briefing. It was a damn nuisance, said Daniel tersely to Patsy, as he packed his bag on the Saturday morning, but he couldn't afford not to go. Could he?

They were able to disguise their concerns as anxiety, and anxiety indeed was what they felt – why examine its springs or its quality too closely?

Daniel drove: Rosemary and Gogo sat together in the back. They had not travelled in a car together like this for many years. If ever. Would it have been easier had they brought one of the in-laws along, to dilute the thickness of their emotions? By unspoken consent they had agreed to travel alone, the three of them, leaving their spouses behind to guard the home front. Each had insisted that it would be unfair to involve those not of the blood in such a quest. Each had known quite well that shame and fear and greed, not selflessness, had inspired this prohibition. Patsy, David and Nathan were not fit to see the Palmers *in extremis*, they were not to be allowed to witness the ignoble chase. They would track Frieda down by themselves, and the three of them would confront her, alive or dead, without the help of marriage partners. This was an internal business, a family affair.

It was Gogo's view, which she expounded over a snack at the Gordano Service Station, that Frida was alive, and well, and had done a runner. It would have been just like her, she said, biting into an egg and cress baguette, to have left a false trail. She had faked a disappearance, and would turn up laughing in Monte Carlo or Uppsala or Rio.

'This is disgusting,' said Rosemary, opening her ham sandwich to look for the ham. A thin ragged half-slice lay, flattened in a smear of mustard. 'Shall I take it back and ask for another?' she asked Daniel.

Daniel shrugged. He was eating, unaccountably, a slice of pizza, and drinking an apple juice.

Daniel was of the opinion that Frieda had broken her leg in the woods, and would, by the time they arrived, have been discovered in a state of maximum distress and inconvenience – either dead, or dying.

Rosemary agreed that something horrible must have happened, but favoured a death by drowning. 'I think she may have fallen into the sea. It's right on the edge, and a steep cliff. And she was always a walker.'

All three of them contemplated the tiresomeness of a missing body. How long did it take for a missing person to turn into a missing body? How long would it be before they could prove the will? And where was the will, and what would be in it?

All three were united in a suspicion that whatever she had done, she had done it to annoy them. They did not state this baldly, but many of their asides, as they dried their hands in the jetstream in the Ladies, as they discussed which motorway exit to take from the M5, as they gazed at the willows bending over the Somerset Levels, might have been taken in that sense. Had she not for two or more years now been pursuing a policy of irritation, of aggression? They supposed that policy to be directed largely or wholly against themselves: it did not often occur to them that they did not loom as large in her life as she in theirs. They were unwilling to admit other, non-dynastic, non-familial motivations. They were understandably unable and unwilling to think of the tracts of Frieda's life which lay before and beyond their know-ing. They feared these tracts – the dull ploughed furrows of her child-hood, the swelling adolescent foothills of her career, the hidden and mysterious folds and valleys of her marriage to their father, the thickets of her scandalous romances, the public peaks and craggy coastlines of her ambition. She had been writing her memoirs: on what scrapheap, in what vault, on what agent's desk lay those in-criminating documents today? Had she mapped the past, and if so, to what end?

Daniel and Rosemary assumed a deathwish, for what else, they argued, could the dead-end Ashcombe represent? And if death had come her way it was no more than she had asked for. She had gone to meet him halfway. Only Gogo dissented, and she with half her heart. Gogo was the last to have seen Frieda alive, and she described now the apparition of Frieda in her blue dress, shining like starlight. She had seemed – well, said Gogo carefully, she had seemed quite *well*.

But it must be remembered that Gogo, professionally, saw the ill, lived amongst the ill. Frieda had not trembled, Frieda had not stumbled or jerked her head or spilt her tea or fumbled for words. Her hand had been steady, her speech clear. No palsy, no paralysis had possessed her. And to Benjamin, she reminded her brother and her sister, to Benjamin Frieda had been very kind.

The name of Benjamin was not welcome in the car. It fell coldly, and Rosemary shivered, while Daniel turned up the heater. Neither of them wanted to hear of Benjamin's reception at Ashcombe. They feared the worst. Jealousies, exclusions, favours, competitions. Betrayals, thefts and alienations.

Darkness fell early even in the west, and Daniel turned on the headlights. They had agreed to pick up the keys to the house from the police station in Minehead, an unnecessary formality as the police had conceded that the house seemed to have been standing open to intruders and the elements for days, if not for weeks. They approached the neat brick suburban thirties building with apprehension, wondering what news could await them there: a discovery, a trail of clues? But the officer, apologetic, told them that no trace of Mrs Haxby had been found. They had searched the wooded areas, but had found nothing. 'It's very dense, very steep,' said PC Wainwright. 'It could take days.' The coastguard had been out, but no bodies had been reported. There were no signs of forced entry at the house, no evidence of foul play. They'd taken away one or two items for examination, but there'd been nothing suspicious. (He did not like to mention the cannabis to these three disconcerting Londoners: it had looked to him and to his boss as though the old lady had been smoking it herself, but this seemed so unlikely that he didn't like even to raise the matter. He'd let someone else deal with that one. If she had been having a puff, who cared? If they found outhouses full of the stuff, that would be another matter.)

The boss had thought of shutting the house off and refusing the keys, but had decided not to bother. No point in over-reacting. There might be all sorts of innocent explanations. Mrs Haxby might have had a sudden call to go to London. She might have had a visitor and gone off with her to town. She might have gone on holiday. He gathered she was a professional lady. She wouldn't be pleased to come back and find her absence had been treated as a crime. Nor, it had occurred to him, would she necessarily be very pleased to find her keys had been handed over to her avenging family. But that wasn't his problem, was it? Next of kin is next of kin, in the eyes of the law. And Mr Palmer said he was a lawyer.

Mrs Haxby was a professional and an eccentric. Exmoor was full of eccentrics. Would a normal person want to live alone at a place like Ashcombe? Ashcombe had a bad reputation. Nobody normal had ever lived at Ashcombe. In its hotel days, it might have had one or two normal guests, but they hadn't stayed long. And the manager had been barking mad. So had the proprietor, and so had the retired admiral who had built the place. It stood to reason that anybody who lived alone at Ashcombe might well wander off alone. Nothing illegal in that.

So PC Wainwright and his boss Sergeant Wiggins had reasoned, as they washed their hands of responsibility, and handed over to Daniel Palmer, Grace D'Anger and Rosemary Herz.

The trio drove on, with Gogo now at the wheel, and Daniel by her side. Daniel had been further downcast by the news that Ashcombe lay right on the county boundary, and that if Frieda had wandered from Somerset into Devon, if her corpse was washed from Somerset to Devon, her case would be at the mercy of two police forces, the subject of two files of paperwork. How characteristically inconvenient of her to live on a boundary, he remarked, as he peered into the gathering gloom. She always liked margins, said Gogo sharply, as she swung off the main road and down the steep descent.

Daniel was deeply shocked by the house. Neither Rosemary's warnings nor Gogo's emendations of those warnings had prepared him for this Victorian Gothic asylum. It offended all his instincts for comfort, for order, for maintenance. The degree of decay and dilapidation appalled. The smell stopped his nostrils. How could this ever have been kept up, how could it ever be restored? What impulse of folly had built this folly here and abandoned it here, at the sea's edge? Its very position clamoured with offence.

Gogo and Rosemary were almost amused by his horror, but they too were overwhelmed. The abandoned house had grown yet more sinister, it loomed darkly above them into the lowering afternoon night. Was Frieda in there somewhere, trapped in a closet, imprisoned in an oak chest? The police said they had searched the house, but had they? Frieda's last supper still stood upon the table: the winkle shells, the glistening oily yellow rind, her open book. (Unlike Terry Zealley, they register the title of the book, and register it with surprise: Frieda seemed to have been reading a Mills & Boon romance called *The Sweet South* by Amantha Knight.) And there were objects familiar to them from Mausoleum days – the skull, the skeleton clock, the alabaster egg, the vase of red Bristol glass. They were instinct with foreboding. So Frieda had moved from one folly to another, from one mausoleum to another. From the grave to the grave. What life had she had, and where were its joys now? Where was she now? WHY HAD SHE COME HERE? Had all come to this? Or was this some endgame prank?

Their flesh crawled, shrivelled and listened. Rosemary sat heavily on an old basket chair and dropped her head into her hands. Her heart was beating loudly, for she too was marked for death. She was worn out, defeated. Gogo crossed to the window and stared out across the darkened garden towards the sea, the indecipherable scrabble of the interminable sighing of the water. She stood transfixed, like a dead person, like a statue frozen. She could hear her own blood. And Daniel, thinly, leanly pacing, came to a halt before the backgammon board, so neatly laid, before the game of patience. So she had wasted time, so she had eked away the dull long hours.

The skeleton clock had died when they were small children, in the heavy stifled fatherless shame of Romley. It never struck the hour. Time had stood still. They had lived in a house without a man, and Frieda had worked like a man. Frieda had taught Daniel to play backgammon. Night after night, during his lonely, freakish boyhood, he had played backgammon with his mother for an hour before bed. He had forgotten this. In turn he had taught his sisters, and they too had played. Did they remember? Did they now, like him, recall?

Daniel had tried to make for himself a rich light life without these grim shadows, yet here he stood, trapped. All three of them were motionless, silent, exhausted. The air was heavy. They could not move. She had brought them to this cave and turned them to stone.

Rosemary, the youngest, was the first to break the spell. She groaned, tightened her fingers in her red-gold hair, clasped at her skull, rocked back and forth as though to wind herself up into motion, and made a gurgling sound in her throat, as though she were a sybil about to speak after long silence.

'Shit,' said Rosemary. 'Jesus fucking Christ. I can't fucking *take* this. Do you think there's a *drink* in the house?'

Daniel, who found, to his surprise, to my surprise, to your surprise, that his eyes were prickling with tears, was the next to move. He laid his hand upon the pack of cards, turned one up. It was the three of hearts. 'I gave her these,' he said, perplexed. 'I bought her a couple of packs when I was killing time in Luxembourg. I can't think why. Look, they're the kings and queens of France.'

'Well done, Danny boy,' said Gogo bravely, turning back from the window, attempting the normality of sister scorn. 'Clever lad.'

But her voice shook a little, as though she did not trust it to find its register. She picked up at random black Marie-Antoinette, La Dame de Pique, and stared at her blue and silver dress, her blue and silver hair, her white aigrette.

'A *drink*,' repeated Rosemary. 'She was never short of a drink.'

And they jerked into action, opening cupboards, sniffing the dregs in the half-empty bottle (a perfectly good 1995 Chablis, noted Daniel, gone to waste), tripping over piles of papers, turning on switches to lamps. Some of them worked, and some did not. They found glasses, and, in the bottom shelf of the mock-Jacobean sideboard, a fine array of bottles – gin, whisky, sherry, vermouth, Marsala, cherry brandy.

'She'd stocked up for Christmas,' said Rosemary, her spirits rising as she poured herself a large Scotch. 'Gogo, whisky for you?'

'Who's driving?' asked Gogo, as she accepted a tumbler.

'Who cares?' said Daniel. 'Cheers, Cheers, Rosie. Cheers, Gogo. Cheers, Frieda. Can you hear us, Frieda? Are you out there listening?'

And the three of them stared defiantly at the dark windows, at the glimmer of sea and distant shoreline beyond, and they raised their glasses and they drank.

There had been a crime, but this had not been the scene of it.

Gogo knocks at Rosemary's bedroom door, hears a tap running, hears her sister call, 'Hang on a minute, I'm coming.' Rosemary appears, in a shining white satin night-dress and a sage-green silk kimono, smelling of aloes. She is ready for bed. Gogo sits on the bed. There is nowhere else to sit, for Rosemary's hotel room is small and cramped, and the only chair is covered with Rosemary's discarded clothing. Gogo's room is bigger, a double overlooking the sea. The sisters had thought of sharing, but had not been able to face it. 'I snore,' Gogo had said dourly, to discourage Rosemary, who had herself been trying to think of good reasons to sleep alone. Gogo, the elder, had claimed the best room.

The hotel is an old coaching inn, perched on the cliff above the coast path. It boasts Fine Sea Views, but it is too dark to see them. It has known better days. Gogo, David and Benjamin had lunched there in the summer, eating scampi and chips from a basket. And Frieda Haxby too, it appeared, had lunched there. The elderly barman remembered her. He brought the subject up himself, as the three Palmers sat in the dark brown bar at a small round oak table, looking at the menu and eating Bacon Twirls. News of Frieda's disappearance had spread along the coast, from headland to headland, from beacon to beacon, from pub to pub. For a recluse, she had aroused a fair amount of interest. Nor, it now seemed, had she been as reclusive as they had thought, for the barman, a grey-haired, moustached, melancholy, gentlemanly figure, who smoked perpetually, even while pulling pints, claimed that she had been in for lunch with another lady. They came in once or twice, for pensioner's lunches, on a Thursday. A good value lunch – roast and two vegetables, or fish and chips, for £3.50. They'd seemed to enjoy it. Of course the weather had been a bit better, last month. They'd sat out, on one occasion as he recalled.

He took a morbid interest in Frieda's disappearance, probing for more details. He volunteered that he could tell they were family, there was a likeness. (Gogo's expression of stony refusal at this suggestion was a wonder to see, and Rosemary got out her pocket powder compact to effect an instant cosmetic alteration.) Yes, they all knew she lived alone at Ashcombe, and had heard she was writing a book. About the Vikings, he'd been told, but he wouldn't know about that.

Daniel ignored the Vikings and ordered a baked trout, then asked if the barman knew the name of the other lady. No, he didn't. He thought she came from inland, from Exford way, but he couldn't say for sure. About the same age as Mrs Haxby, she would be. This, he had added, was a popular part of the world for retired people.

Gogo, sitting on the edge of Rosemary's bed, takes up this theme. 'A popular part of the world for retired people,' she echoed. 'And Frieda, out for a cheap pensioner's lunch. Do you really think it can have been her? And who on earth can she have been with? She didn't know anybody round here, did she?'

'God knows,' says Rosemary, applying cream of almonds to her hands and elbows. 'God knows what she got up to when we weren't watching. But it doesn't sound very likely. Still, he did seem to know where the house was. So I suppose it might have been her.'

'Daniel says we've got to look for the will tomorrow,' says Gogo. 'I think that's a bit crude and premature, don't you?'

Rosemary looked sharply at her sister, through the dressing-table mirror.

'Well, he is a lawyer,' she concedes. 'Do you think Frieda made him an executor?'

'I'm sure she didn't. He'd have known if she had. He's been on to Howard Partridge, you know. Didn't he tell you?'

Rosemary shakes her head and starts to brush her hair.

'He didn't tell *me* either, but Patsy did,' says Gogo.

The room is hot and full of the smells of Rosemary's nightly rituals, which overlay the older smells of tobacco. This is a heavy smoker of a

hotel. The two sisters are rarely in such proximity, for they now inhabit larger spaces, so that even when they are together, they rarely
find themselves as close. It makes them physically uneasy. They are
troubled, as though something is expected of them. And it is. As
Rosemary too settles upon the bed, high up on her pillow, her back to
the crushed rose padded button plush velvet bedhead, and tucks her
knees under the top sheet, Gogo at the bed's foot speaks again.

'Did Frieda ever speak to you about her sister Hilda?'

Rosemary shakes her head. 'Why do you ask?'

'I just wondered. What happened to her.'

'She never mentioned her. Do you think she can still be alive?'

'I don't suppose so. We would surely have heard something if she
were.'

'I don't know about that.'

'She'd have kept in touch with Grandma, surely.'

'There was some quarrel,' says Rosemary flatly.

'It's surprising that Frieda was so loyal to Grandma, really. Considering,' says Gogo.

'Considering what mean old cows they both were,' says Rosemary
with more energy, then, gathering strength, rushing at the fence,
rising, clearing it. 'Considering that we don't know whether our own
father's alive or dead.'

Gogo is silent. Rosemary is silent. These words have never been
spoken between them. They have followed Daniel's prohibition, and
of their father they never speak. He has been written out of the text of
their lives. It is as though he has never been. Unmentioned for so
many years, he cannot now be invoked without a great tearing and
rending.

'Oh, God,' says Gogo. 'I can't face all this. I want to go home.'

'It's not going to be as easy as that,' says Rosemary, with a small
note of satisfaction in her voice. She is pleased with herself for having
braved Gogo, braved her father, braved the past. She has said the unsay-
able. She has cleared the fence and now, for a mile or two, she leads the
field.

★

172

No will is revealed by the Sunday search of Ashcombe, but other useful and interesting items come to light. Daniel, Gogo and Rosemary find the butler's pantry and the family silver and the toenails of the devil, and they locate the boxes which contain Frieda's genealogical research. There had been a bonfire, but not of these papers. They discover her word-processor, which is no longer attempting to speak to them, for one of the police visitors, disliking the waste of electricity, had thoughtfully turned it off. Rosemary, who understands such machines, turns it on, and brings up a list of what seem to be Frieda's files. This, they agree, may be vital, but the labels of the files are, like the labels of all such files, cryptic. It will take them time and some luck to unlock the secrets of the box, and they are not calm enough to try.

Not many communications seem to have reached Ashcombe from the outside world. A request to fill in the Electoral Register, a couple of religious pamphlets and an appeal from the Lifeboat Association lie neglected on a window-sill inside the front porch, together with an opened Jiffy bag addressed to Mr F. H. Palmer. This Daniel investigates, and finds that it contains a booklet called *The Householder's Guide to Radon*, fifth edition, published by the Department of the Environment, and an envelope containing a letter from the National Radiological Protection Board addressed to Ms Frieda Haxby Palmer. Daniel scans the letter rapidly, and notes that it had thanked his mother for her co-operation in testing her home for radon, and advised her that, if her detectors had been accurately placed according to instructions, they recorded, when corrected for seasonal variations, 'an average radon level over the year of 850 Bq m-3. As this is above the Action Level, it is advisable to reduce the level as soon as reasonably practicable.'

Daniel replaces the Jiffy bag on the window-sill, and pockets the letter, without drawing it to the attention of his sisters. He will ponder its ominous implications later.

They also discover a highly coloured postcard of Mount Teide on Tenerife from one Susan Stokes, correctly addressed and including a post code, which says, enigmatically, 'Doing a Sleeping Beauty at the moment. Great fun. What about you?', and a letter from a Mr Glover in Yeovil, thanking Miss Haxby for her great kindness in looking after his prize pigeon Paula. Paula has returned home safely (to join Peter, Paul, Priscilla, Pansy, Posy, and all the other Pees!) and is now restored to full health, thanks to Miss Haxby's care: he had taken the liberty of enclosing the introductory leaflet of the Royal Pigeon Racing Association, and a copy of *Homing World*, in case her experience of sheltering Paula has led her to think of keeping pigeons herself!

What is one to make of these small fragments of an Ashcombe-based social life? They present Frieda Haxby as an innocent pensioner, a responsible citizen, almost as a good neighbour (though Yeovil, it is true, is fifty miles or more away): there is nothing here to suggest that she might be, or have been, either more or less than the nice if slightly eccentric old lady into whose contours the barman at the Royal Oak had tried to squeeze her.

And what is one to lift, of her leavings? Should they take the box files, the computer, the silver? They have not time to explore further, and they are afraid that if they take their spoils, even in her own best interests, she will arrive screeching like an avenging angel, clouded in wrath. 'Do you *remember*,' says Rosemary, giggling nervously, 'how *cross* she used to get when we went into her room when she was working.'

'Yes,' says Gogo, 'and how we were always ignoring her. We were always interrupting her. God knows how she got anything done.'

'She worked nights,' says Daniel. 'She had a will of iron, and she worked nights.'

As they hesitate, in the butler's pantry, they hear a loud knocking at the door, and jump guiltily, like thieves. Rosemary returns the Swedish medal to its box, Gogo shuts the lid of the tarnished Palmer cutlery, as they hear a door bang, and footsteps approaching down the stone corridor. A man's footsteps, heavy, deliberate: they sigh with relief.

The detective inspector is clearly not satisfied with their answers, although he is very polite. Nor do they themselves find their own answers satisfactory. They sit in the drawing-room and try to explain, but of course they cannot explain.

Why had Mrs Haxby Palmer (he'd got that right, for a start, which was improbable) decided to settle in this part of the world? What had first brought her here? Had she intended to stay? What were her connections?

Their replies sound thin. They are unable to say why she had chosen to live here. They agree that the house is large, for a woman alone, and in bad repair. As far as they know, she has no connections here. (Shall they mention that friendly pensioner? As they have never met her and do not know her name and doubt if she can exist, it seems unwise.) How did she come across the house in the first place?

They look at one another, unhappily. They have not had time to collude, and Mr Rorty knows it. Daniel is getting irritable; he dares not risk showing it, but his sisters can tell. They do not know whether they want Daniel to assert himself or not. After a pause, he does.

'She saw it advertised in an estate agent's window,' Daniel says, a little coldly.

'In Taunton?'

'We understood it was in Taunton,' says Daniel, even more coldly.

The detective inspector does not ask what she was doing in Taunton, but his silence, his attentive expression, ask the question for him. This time it is Gogo who answers.

'She was in Taunton in search of a meatless hamburger, we believe,' she says provocatively. She has had enough of being intimidated. Mr Rorty looks even more quizzical, so she pursues. She tells him the story of Frieda's investigation of the meat-free burger, of her visit to the Trading Inspector in Taunton, of her interest in the firm that made Hot Snax. She does not tell him about Timon's feast, but the memory of it fortifies her, and she can see – all three of them can see – that she has made a wise decision in expounding Frieda's case. Mr Rorty listens with interest. The story is ludicrous, but he does not appear to find it so. Mr Rorty makes notes in his notebook.

'And so,' concludes Gogo, 'finding herself in Taunton, at one stage in her quest, she saw the picture of the house in the shop window, and she bought it. That's the kind of woman she was. I mean, is.'

Mr Rorty is mollified by this confession of idiosyncrasy. Yes, he knows Mrs Haxby Palmer is a writer, and appreciates her need for solitude. Writing her memoirs, you say? How interesting. Now can they, as her family, think of any reason why she might have chosen to disappear, of her own free will?

Dumbly, they shake their heads. Are they suspects, accessories?

He thanks them for their co-operation. The search will continue, and he will let them know as soon as there is any news. Meanwhile, if they will get in touch with him if they hear anything from Mrs Palmer, he will be most grateful. He hands them his card.

As they part, in the courtyard – they are keen to see him off, for they wish to assert that this is their territory, not his – he asks them, casually, 'Is your mother by any chance a smoker?'

Gogo, again, takes it upon herself to answer. 'I'm afraid she is,' she says with disapproval. 'She took it up late in life, but yes, I'm afraid she does smoke.'

'Why do you ask?' says Daniel suspiciously.

'Just checking,' says Mr Rorty. 'Checking the possibility of in-truders, that's all. Somebody had been smoking, and there are butts in the garden, that kind of thing. Butts down on the beach. But from what you say, it was probably just your mother. Not many people walk along here.' He grins, collusively. 'Too steep for most folk, isn't it?'

And off drove Mr Rorty, congratulating himself on not having mentioned the fact that in the next cove three plastic-wrapped bales of high-grade Moroccan cannabis had been washed up earlier in the week – the second big haul in two months. It didn't seem as if the old girl had had anything to do with it, but you never can tell. She's cer-tainly been smoking the stuff, but that was another matter. That was her own affair. She'd chosen a fine and private place to do it, and it looked as though, wherever she'd got to now, she was beyond prosecution. It looked like it was just a coincidence. He'd tell the local boys to get the dogs out on Monday. You could rot for years in this undergrowth.

★

At the end of the next week, an Identikit impression of a young man was posted up outside the police stations of West Somerset and Devon, and released to the local press. A copy of it was also sent to each of the Palmer family. Daniel Palmer opened his over breakfast, and silently handed it to Patsy. She looked at it for a cold moment and said, 'That's Will Paine.' The backs of her wrists prickled, as they did when she'd had a near hit in the car.

Frieda Haxby Palmer had been seen with the young man in Exeter, in Minehead, in Ilfracombe, in Bideford and in Westward Ho!

The photofit was an excellent, an unmistakable likeness. There was Will Paine to the life: his sweet smile, his short cropped hair, his symmetrically chipped teeth. His dark skin. There aren't all that many black men in Exeter, Minehead, Ilfracombe, Bideford and Westward Ho! According to D'Anger's almanac, there were 0.8 per cent in most of these places, though Exeter boasted 1.45. Not much in the way of cover. And anyway, Will Paine had the kind of face that stayed in the memory. He was such a nice-looking boy.

'I don't believe it,' said Patsy. 'I don't believe there was any harm in him.'

Daniel looked at her with that ironic expression which had thrown panic into the prose of many a hard-boiled witness. It seemed on this occasion justified.

'What do they say?' rallied Patsy, ready to spring to the defence.

'Wanted for questioning. In connection with the disappearance of. And with cash withdrawals from various cashpoints.'

Patsy breathed sharply. 'So he stole her cashcard. That's not the end of the world.'

'Nobody said it was. It's what he did with the body that's of interest.'

'Oh, don't be ridiculous,' said Patsy. 'You're not suggesting he murdered her, are you?'

'Somebody seems to be,' said Daniel reasonably.

'I don't believe it,' repeated Patsy stubbornly. But, of course, she did. And, dutifully, like a good citizen, she rang Mr Rorty and spilled the beans. She owned up to an acquaintance with Will Paine.

Reports from the witnesses who had drawn such a damning likeness of Will Paine were confusing. He had, it is true, been seen in the company of a grey-haired, large-nosed woman of middle height; she had been wearing an old Persian-lamb jacket, grey trousers and wellington boots, and he a leather jacket and black trousers. The couple had been spotted together in the vicinity of several cashpoints. But at no point did he appear to be threatening or menacing her: indeed, one observer, a female taxi-driver in Westward Ho!, alleged that it had been the other way round. The woman had been pushing the young man towards the bank and urging him to insert the plastic card he was holding. He had appeared reluctant.

The police officer had tried to talk Mrs Boxer out of this statement, but she had been immovable. The woman had been pushing the boy. He had looked nervous and ill at ease. Yes, she was quite sure that this was what she had noticed.

Mrs Haxby Palmer's bank statements had been examined, and, bafflingly, had showed no cash withdrawals at all over the relevant period. Monies had been paid in, on a monthly basis, from her agent, and there had been one or two small debit transactions – £20 for petrol at the Crosskeys, £40 for a meal at the Hunter's Inn, £15 from a stationer's in Exeter. Yet witnesses swore that they had seen slabs of banknotes clicking and gliding out of West Country walls.

Mrs Haxby Palmer had a balance of £34,000 in her current account. Roland Rorty was not convinced that this was evidence that she was involved in drug trafficking. He thought it more likely, from the profile he was compiling, that it indicated a degree of financial insouciance characteristic of an unworldly intellectual. Perhaps Mrs Palmer had never heard of deposit accounts and interest rates. Or maybe she was so rich that £34,000 was, to her, peanuts. Either seemed equally possible.

Not surprisingly, Will Paine had vanished too. He was nowhere to be found. Nobody came forward from North London to claim him, even when Patsy had handed over what she knew of his curriculum vitae. Remarks about his strong Midlands accent had already widened the search to Wolverhampton, but his mother, if she had noticed the inquiries, remained mum.

It was all most unsatisfactory.

After a couple of weeks, Goltho & Goltho disclosed that they were holding not only a copy of Mrs Palmer's latest will, but also the deeds of Ashcombe House. They were quite willing to co-operate with family pressure to view the will. She had left everything, apart from a few small legacies, in trust to her grandson Benjamin. The trustees were to be David D'Anger and her old friend Lord Ogden.

Gogo, hearing this news, was struck with a chill of fear. It could not, nor it would not come to good. Daniel, hearing this news, resolved to challenge the will, for his mother could not have been of sound mind when she made it. Rosemary, hearing this news, felt faint with mean rage. As she happened to be wearing an ambulatory blood pressure monitor on this day, fitted to her arm at 8 a.m. that morning by the Nightingale Hospital, the mean rage was registered by the most impressive lurch in its readings.

So nobody was pleased with Frieda's gesture, and nobody was quite sure what it meant.

David D'Anger, who had been taking the line that Frieda's disappearance was none of his business, found that it was his business after all. Why had she done this to them? Why had she put them to this test? And was it legal to appoint him as trustee without even asking him?

Gogo and David had decided to protect Benjamin from the gossip and speculation surrounding Frieda's disappearance. So far this had been easy, as it had not hit the national press: Frieda's fame had not been of the sort to command tabloid headlines, and the police had been discreet in their inquiries. None of the witnesses they questioned had ever heard of her, so the damage had been limited. Could this go on for ever? No, of course not. Soon Benjie and the world would have to know. His innocence was threatened.

Jon and Jess Herz found out because they heard their parents shouting at one another about it, but it did not mean much to them as they had not seen Frieda for years. They had not been favourites. They could not think why Rosemary was so worked up about it. They preferred their Golders Green granny. Simon Palmer no longer took any interest in family affairs, but Patsy, wracked with guilt, had confessed to Emily over the telphone that Will Paine had somehow tracked down Frieda on Exmoor and made off with her.

'What do you mean, made off with her?' Emily's cool voice had asked, as Patsy nervously paced the bedroom with the cordless phone. 'Do you mean they've eloped together?'

This new interpretation struck Patsy as a saving notion: she clutched at it.

'Well, maybe they have,' she said. 'I hadn't thought of that.'

'He was a nice boy, Will Paine,' said Emily. 'He wouldn't hurt a fly.'

'That's what I thought,' said Patsy, weak with the relief of avowal. 'But I think I may have been wrong.'

'Never,' said Emily. 'He won't have hurt her, I promise you. They've probably run off to Eldorado.'

'I hope you're right,' said Patsy.

And she told Daniel that evening, that he'd better not rush into anything hasty over Frieda's will. She might still have the last laugh.

'She'll have it anyway,' said Daniel irritably. 'But I take your point.'

Will Paine's fax to Patsy put paid to this line of comfort. It came not from Eldorado but from Jamaica, and in Patsy's trusting view it exonerated him, perhaps alas, of all blame. Will Paine had heard, he would not say how, that he was being looked for, and although he had no intention of coming home and getting into trouble he did want the Palmers to know that he hadn't robbed Frieda. They had done right by him and he wanted to do right by them. He had left Frieda alive and well, standing on Exeter station, waving him off on the 11.31 a.m. to Paddington. He had, it's true, a bagful of money which she had thrust upon him, but he had never asked for it, had repeatedly tried not to take it, and while he could not say he did not now want it, he had not got hold of it by unfair means. Frieda had assured him she did not need it.

'She give it me to get rid of me,' read his fax. 'She said it was American money from a special bank account and not wanted because of tax reasons. She persuaded me to take it and I swear that is the honest truth. I bought an airticket and came here to seek my father. Please tell the police I am an innocent man and get them to take the poster down, I don't want my mum to see it, she has enough trouble. Please tell Mr D'Anger that Mrs Haxby said to say it was just redistribution. I pestered Mrs Haxby but that is the worst I did. She let me stay on to help in the garden. There are blackberries in the freezer, but the electricity goes off too often, so they may be off. We had some good times and she taught me blackgammon. But then she got tired of me being around all the time and wanted me to go.

'Please tell Mr D'Anger that it's not possible to open your eyes take off the veil and wake up a different person just because of different place or money.

'I hope Mrs Haxby has not come to harm. She liked to walk to Hindspring Point above the old kiln and it was a dangerous walk. Bless you Mrs Palmer, you were a stroke of real luck to me.'

Patsy, reading this, wonders how much luck she had brought Will Paine, if any.

She believes every word of his fax. It has the ring of truth. But will the police believe it? Will Daniel believe it? Should she keep it to herself? She does not trust Daniel not to tell the police, so instead she rings David D'Anger and reads him the text. She can hear that David is as much at a loss as she.

'I can't see what's to be gained by telling the police, can you?' she suggests to him. 'They'll never take his word for anything.'

'You could check out the kiln and the blackberries,' says David.

'I'm not going near that creepy place,' says Patsy. 'It sounds like hell. I've always hated Devon.'

'Then we'll just have to wait and see what happens,' says David. He too is not keen to persecute Will Paine, whose presence he cannot even remember, and whose personal messages baffle him. Can he once have been an extra-mural student at an evening class, years ago?

David compromises. He puts it to Gogo that Gogo put it to the police that she has just remembered that Frieda had mentioned a walk to the old kiln. Gogo obliges.

Will Paine hates Jamaica. The only lie he had told to Patsy had been that he had come here to seek his father. His father was, as far as he knew, in New York, and Will had no desire to see him. His father had terrorized his mother and frightened Will Paine. Will has come to seek his fatherland, and he does not like it much. He wishes now that he had gone to one of the other islands, or to Guyana. But he had chosen Jamaica. It is a slum, or the bit of it he's found is a slum. The dogs bark, the bananas rot, the heat is a killer, the room is full of bugs, and he has seen a snail as big as a football. He can't get used to the dollar bills, and knows he has been cheated. His delicate stomach has been upset. He is neither one thing nor the other here. He is not a tourist, but he has no job. Where shall he drift next? How long will the money last?

He had told the truth about the money to Patsy. Frieda had bought him off. He hadn't wanted to leave so soon, he'd liked it at Ashcombe. He'd liked the woods, the rosehips, the blackberries, the elderberries, the chanterelles, the little black *trompettes des morts*. Frieda had told him where to look, and he had fetched bagsful for her. He had been happy and light of foot among the bracken, and on the narrow path to Hindspring Point. He had found liberty caps for her, on the upper grassland, and had taught her how to make a magic-mushroom stew. He had bought her weed and they had smoked together. They had eaten winkles and played cards and backgammon. They had listened to the roaring of the stags in rut, and to the crying of the gulls. But then she had been tired of him. 'I want to be alone now,' she had said one night. He had pleaded in vain.

She'd taken him off, the next day, to town. To several towns. She'd got a new plastic card which she could put into the holes in the wall, which she said connected with an illegal bank account in America.

She said the money was useless, she couldn't declare it, she couldn't spend it. He could have it. It was money for free. Free as blackberries and chanterelles. Look for the symbol, she said, and it was there – a symbol he'd never noticed before. MIDAS, next to ACCESS and VISA and all the other logos. And the money had spewed out, in town after town. English money. All over Exmoor. She got over-excited. She had laughed as one bunch fell to the pavement and began to blow away. She stuffed it into her coat pockets, into her bag. People took notice, people stared, he tried to restrain her but she didn't care.

'Let's just get *rid* of it,' she said, as she drove on to the next machine. The system had seized up, finally, in a small town – more of a village, really – on top of the purple moorland. Their last stop, and the machine refused to give. It blinked angrily, and swallowed the card for ever.

'Damn,' said Frieda happily. 'They've caught up with us. Oh, well, never mind. I've got you enough to be going on with.'

He'd tried to refuse it, but she hadn't let him. 'You're doing me a favour,' she said. 'You're making an honest woman of me.'

And she'd forced it on him, and had driven him, the next day, to Exeter, to the station.

'That's it,' she'd said. 'That's the end. I don't want to see you back here again.'

She hadn't wished him luck, but she had waved as the train pulled out.

That was his true story, and he was sticking to it. But who would believe him? He has been turned into a joke, a fraud. He too is a missing person. He will have to lie low, perhaps for life. He wonders if Patsy will feel it her duty to hand over his letter to the police. He wonders if he can be tracked down electronically through the fax machine in Kingston Korner Kommunications. He wonders about the laws of extradition. He wonders if he will ever feel more at home here. Is he Jamaican, is he a Wolverhampton man, is he a North London man? Is there a place in the world for him? This question had not arisen during his brief scamper in the bracken. Is he a man of the woodland? What is it that threatens him now?

★

Benjamin's life is also under threat.

When Gogo had first heard, in garbled version, over the telephone, the terms of Frieda's will, she had known that some bad thing had happened, irreversibly. What it was she did not know, but it had happened. Like a road accident, an illness, a breakage. In that moment she knew that the future had changed. She was not sure if David also felt the breath of fear. At first she did not dare to ask him.

For what was it that seemed so ominous in this good fortune, this windfall? It would annoy her brother and sister; it would be natural for them to be annoyed. But this perhaps could be put right, with time and tact. (Not so easy, if Daniel pursued his notion of disputing the will, but maybe he would drop it. Maybe they could reach some compromise.) Gogo was clear in her own conscience that she had never sought to influence Frieda in any way in her own favour or her son's. The idea was ludicrous. As soon might one seek to influence the tides or the weather or the traffic on the M4. She believed that Daniel and Rosemary would believe her on this point. They would not blame her personally, surely? And even if they did, she could learn to live with the disapproval of her siblings.

Her fear attached itself to something other, some unknown shape.

Neither she nor David had any notion of the size of Frieda's estate, were she truly dead, and were it truly to come to Benjamin. They hardly dared to mention it between themselves. The fact that she had disappeared with £34,000 in her current account seemed to them, as it seemed to Roland Rorty, inconclusive. £34,000 was in itself a tidy sum for a schoolboy to inherit, but there was the possibility, indeed the likelihood, that it represented buried treasure. And what of that terrible house, and the royalties from Frieda's books? What, come to that, of the film rights of *Queen Christina*? It was all too burdensome, too uncontrolled. It would ruin them all. What had Frieda been playing at? What should Gogo say to Benjamin? What had Frieda herself already said to Benjamin? Had grandmother and grandson entered into some unholy pact?

David was also worried about the implications of this shower of gold. The D'Angers had successfully disposed of their own small fortune, back home in Guyana (though it was rumoured, as ever in such families, that some portion of the family estate awaited reclamation – a bauxite mine? a tropical valley? a plantation?). The D'Angers had not abandoned their homeland and survived the Burnham years to find themselves as heirs to the spoils of an English ploughman's daughter. David had been unfairly favoured by fortune already: she had heaped upon him the gifts of beauty and intelligence, and was she now to add to these the gross injustice of unearned wealth? All his adult life David had been striving to redress the injustices of that initial over-lavish distribution, and now fate had come in like a bad fairy in the shape of Frieda Haxby, to make his position yet more untenable. David had a position on capital gains tax, he had a position on inheritance tax, as he had once had a position on private dentistry: was it fair to test and to try him in this way? Had the testing of the D'Angers been Frieda's dark intention? Or had she been merely randomly irresponsible?

You will note that it did not occur to Gogo that Frieda had been affectionate, or generous, in the making of her will in her grandson's favour. Nor did Gogo see the inheritance as a blessing. Make of that what you wish.

The memory of the house at Ashcombe, during this first week or two, pressed down upon Gogo, hung over her like a storm cloud. What had her boy done to deserve to be threatened by this gloomy pile with its midden full of shells and bones, its black fungi, its long-plundered Old Barrow, its leaking radon? Her boy was bright and beautiful, he was the future. This dump was the pit of the past out of which we may never never clamber. It sucks at our ankles, it pulls off and eats our shoes, it drags us under. Gogo went to the Bloomsbury Public Library in her lunch break, and found, in the dark nineteenth-century dinner-smelling gravy basement of Topography, a County History, which told her that Ashcombe had in its grounds an old leper colony as well as an old kiln. She shuddered. She was not superstitious, but she shuddered. And she discovered worse than that, worse than the lepers and the radon. She discovered rape and murder. She rang the estate agent in Taunton, to ask if she could speak to the young woman who had first showed Frieda round Ashcombe – hoping that in some way she could normalize Frieda's aberration, hoping to turn Frieda back into a harmless nature-loving eccentric who had chatted her way round the battlements in the spring sunshine with gay Amanda Posy. And the estate agents told her that Amanda Posy was dead. Twenty-seven, and dead. Had they not heard? Amanda Posy had been killed by a man posing as a client. She had shown him round a house up in the woods behind Luxborough, and he raped her, throttled her and buried her in Treborough Tip. A copycat killing. A newsprint death. There had been a spate of estate agent killings and abductions. Amanda Posy was one of several.

Gogo was appalled by this discovery. It prompted her to action. She rang Daniel, who was staying up in Matlock, and asked him how he was getting on with the question of probate. Had he managed to get a copy of the earlier will out of old Mr Partridge? Were there reasonable grounds for disputing the Goltho & Goltho will? She very much hoped there were.

Daniel, not sure what Gogo was playing at, but eager to exploit what seemed to him to be an excess of generosity on her part, confirmed that there would certainly be grounds for disputing Goltho & Goltho, who were known in the profession for practices both sharp and slack, but that Mr Partridge was not very happy about releasing the terms of the former will until death and cause of death were established.

'*Not* a very good situation, at the moment,' said Daniel, with a hint of question in his tone. If he got Gogo to agree over the phone that Frieda's last will and testament was unfair, would she stick to it, and would her opinion stand up in court? But Gogo had jumped quickly to the next stage.

'But until we see the other will, how can we be sure it's not even worse? She might have left everything to the Cats' Home. Or to the Exmoor National Park. Or to that ghastly chap Cedric. I'd rather Benjie got it than Cedric.'

Daniel said nothing to this, though he noted it. He promised to pursue the solicitor. He promised to ring Mr Rorty about the progress of the investigation, to check if the paths to the old kiln had been thoroughly searched.

'And one last thing,' said Gogo. 'That computer she had there. I think we should remove it, don't you? Who knows what might be in it? Rosemary says she knows how to work it. I think we should get it back to London.'

Can you feed your will to the Internet? Can you send it through Cyberspace? Can you send your money out to the stars?

The news of his good fortune seeps through to Benjamin. He overhears conversations. His cousins telephone him. At first it does not seem to affect him much, but slowly he begins to sink. Imperceptibly, the poison fills the bloodstream. He grows silent at home and in class. He rejects his food, he bites his lips anxiously. He is wary and withdrawn. Mrs Nettleship, his class teacher, notes the change in his behaviour, but puts it down to adolescence. Boys do get moody at this age.

Fools' gold, fairy gold. Lying awake late one night, sick with anxiety, Benjamin remembers that withered orange on Frieda's cabinet. The bone needle had been stuck through it, from Britain to Guyana. She had skewered him, transfixed him. What is he to do? What has she demanded?

His aunt Rosemary is ill also, though she has not yet found a way of pinning her sickness upon Frieda. The prim and dapper doctor is interested in her case but has not yet come up with an explanation. He gazes at the lurches of the print-out of her erratic pressure chart with a neutral expression of respect. He sends her to clinics where she offers her arm for the extraction of vials of blood and her urine in small jars for testing. He prescribes pills and tells her to eat less salt. Rosemary cannot tell from his demeanour whether hers is an everyday problem, or whether she is on the eve of kidney dialysis. He has shown an excessive interest in her kidneys. She assumes there must be something wrong with them. She does not confide her fears to anyone. She tells herself that she has two kidneys, and that they cannot both be failing at once. Can they?

Rosemary is a fastidious woman. She greatly dislikes the feel of alien fingers upon her body, the sight of specimens of her own body fluids in bottles. The blobs of cold jelly upon her wired breasts and heart disgust her. Her heart throbs with indignation. She can see it pulsing angrily like a green volcano on a television screen. She dreads that she will be asked to mount a public treadmill. She is a Private Patient, but not all processes are private. She does not trust the clinic's procedures. She has heard too many cases of mixed results, mislabelled diagnoses. Every news bulletin on the radio brings some new medical scandal. One is at the mercy. She takes to writing her name in large print on every piece of paper, every test result, every ECG or Blood Test Request. She does not trust the numbers.

Rosemary's spirits are not good, but she conceals the causes of her short temper. Her husband Nathan sympathetically assumes that she is worried about work, for he is worried about work himself. He and his firm have taken on a brave task and he is not sure if he is up to his part in it. Renfrew & Wincobank are to update the corporate image of the National Health Service.

'Update' is the word that is used: 'alter' is what is meant. It has become clearer, as we approach the end of the twentieth century, that we cannot afford a National Health Service for everybody, all the time. Some may have kidney transplants and some may not. Some may have their varicose veins tended, and some may not. Some may live to be ninety, and some may not. So we must alter the perceptions of the people. We must adjust their expectations. We must encourage private health insurance. We must persuade the community-minded, the socially aware, the meddling middle-class egalitarians, the David D'Angers of this world, that it is their social duty to save resources by paying into the pockets of insurance companies, in order to release funds for the sick and the poor. We must teach the poor and the sick that they cannot have what they want. We must reassure the rich that they have a right to have what they want provided that they pay so much for it that the surgeons, the anaesthetists, the pharmacists, the insurance brokers, the insurance companies and the shareholders all get what they want too. And they want a lot. They want at least ten times more than the hotly disputed, oft-rejected and as yet fictional Minimum National Wage. Some of them want and expect a hundred times as much. This makes health care very expensive indeed, and ever more inaccessible. There is no justice, no equity in this situation. Nobody would choose this if their eyes were veiled by ignorance, for each of us knows that we may pull the short straw. We can't all imagine being poor, but we can all imagine being disastrously, expensively, pro-hibitively ill. Nathan's powers of invention and persuasion will be stretched to the limit.

Nathan Herz finds himself curiously depressed. He knows he ought to find the gross effrontery of his brief to deceive the nation a chal-lenge, but it doesn't inspire. Building up the corporate image or iden-tity of an insurance company, or a shipping line, or a bank, can be amusing. But health is depressing. However many suggestions for happy images of healthy children and smiling nurses and hotel-foyer-receptionists he generates, Nathan cannot forget that his own father died in his fifties, after a short life of overwork. He died on a street corner. Many of his blood had died in the camps. Thinking about Health turns Nathan's thoughts to Death. For however you package the whole thing up, however many Healthy Smart Cards and Credit Points and poster campaigns and little TV ad-dramas you invent, Death is where it ends. If you're lucky, you can afford to die in a clean bed. If you're not – well, there's the street corner. Man goeth to his long home, and the mourners go about the streets. Ecclesiastes 12:5. An atavistic Jewish melancholy seeps through Nathan, and at times he enjoys it. At least it is better than all this febrile pretence that we are all having such a good time and will have it for ever. Looking around a restaurant at the munchers, he thinks to himself: in thirty years most of you will be dead. You can chomp away, but you can't devour Death. If you pay those spiralling insurance costs, you may be able to die pri-vately, on individually ground mince and personalized liquidized slops, but it's going to cost you a packet. And you may not be able to afford even that.

He finds himself wondering how it will be for him. He cannot help wondering how it was for Belle. Slow, sudden, hopeless, hopeful? Had she struggled or had she gone under quietly? He wonders if Belle had been Jewish. He knows nothing of her family, nor does he wish to. Belle had been a happy soul. She hadn't been rich, or famous, or extravagantly talented, but she had been happy. So it could be done. But how?

Nathan and Rosemary are not happy. Would winning the lottery make them so? Would a successful challenge to Frieda's will make them so? Rosemary begins to think that nothing can make her happy again but the purchase of some new kidneys. They are not yet available for sale either on or off the National Health, but Nathan will surely be able to get round that little problem for her. He can recover the trading instincts of his ancestors, and buy some in from Bangladesh. Surely any husband would be glad to do that for his young and pretty wife? It is not much to ask. Quite a small organ. Quite a young wife.

Nathan dreams he is back in Venice, a city he loves above all others. The water of the canals laps upon the mossy steps. The steps lead down, oh so easily, so graciously, with so sweet an invitation, into the water. The water laps and sucks, sucks and laps. The green weed stirs and rises, rises and falls, like tresses of green hair. Steps of yellow, grey and pink, scooped by age, scooped and fretted by the ceaseless gentle tide. One could step into eternity. One could embark from these steps for the Orient, for one's Long Home. Nathan loves canal paintings, marine paintings. Canaletto, Guardi, Turner, Claude Lorrain. The little frisking waves of the harbour, the steps, the temples, the prospects, the far horizons. We have said that Nathan has no taste, but that is not true. He does have taste, but he does not have taste that he can afford. He does not like modern paintings. He could put up with a Hockney swimming-pool and palm trees, but what he wants are Canaletto, Guardi, Turner, Claude Lorrain.

He wakes, with the sound of the Thames lapping in his ears beyond the double glazing. He has always loved the water's edge, although he cannot swim. He wakes, and wonders: could he market, not life, not health, but death? Could one take upon oneself the challenge of changing the corporate identity of death?

He thinks of Frieda Haxby, in her kingdom by the sea. Her coast is too wild for him. She has drowned in too savage a spot. He prefers the city steps.

Benjamin D'Anger's health deteriorates. Gogo takes him to the doctor, who can find nothing wrong. Perhaps he has been working too hard at school? He takes his schoolwork so seriously, for a boy of his age. He should get out and about, enjoy himself more, not frowst indoors over his books.

Simon Palmer is not in good shape either. He has not been home since the summer, so nobody has noticed the change. Nor would they have been able to interpret it, had they seen him. His tutor notes that he's not been turning in any essays recently, indeed hasn't been seen round much at all, and resolves to have a word with him about it, but he himself is in the middle of an expensive divorce fuelled by a drink problem, and he never gets round to it. He drinks a bottle of Scotch a day instead, and thinks himself heroic.

Emily Palmer, far away in Florence, worries about her mother and her grandmother. She is fond of them both. But what can she do about it? She alone is of the hope that Frieda is alive and well. She imagines Frieda sitting in a bar in Georgetown in the sweltering heat, or travelling upriver amongst the piranha fish and jaguars to see the mountains of gold. She thinks this would be admirable. She herself has for some time taken the line that family life is destructive, and she has decided to detach herself from it. And if Grandma has done the same – well, good on her.

Daniel Palmer cannot be so relaxed. The demands of river pollution prevent him from devoting too much time to Frieda, but he pursues old Howard Partridge, who had been Frieda's solicitor for many decades, who dated back to the days when Andrew Palmer had been upon the scene. (Daniel, unlike his sisters, has authentic though not very reassuring memories of his father. Meal-times of shepherd's pie.

A walk along a towpath. A visit to a museum. Walt Disney's *Fantasia*, at the Romley Gaumont.) Howard Partridge, now retired, is an old stonewaller. He has not forgiven Frieda for pursuing the VAT case against his own advice and for coming near to winning it. He cannot resist pointing out to Daniel, over the telephone, that the consequences of Frieda's legal action against Customs & Excise have been unfortunate for other clients who have found themselves in her position. Far from establishing a helpful precedent, she had caused HM Customs & Excise to close a useful loophole. And no, he cannot divulge the contents of her will without proper authority. I am the proper authority, Daniel is on the point of saying, but then it occurs to him that maybe old Partridge knows more than he'll let on. Maybe he is in touch with Andrew Palmer. The possibility of this shocks Daniel, and he puts the handset down with a sick dismay.

Some news, after days of waiting, comes out of Exmoor. The cliff paths above and leading down to the old kiln have been searched, without success – no corpse, or signs of disturbance there, apart from a few cigarette ends and the wrapping from a Kit-Kat. But Mrs Haxby Palmer's friend Jane Todd has turned up and been interviewed by the local police and by Mr Rorty. She is upset about her new friend's disappearance and simply cannot account for it. She would be happy to come up to town to talk to the family about Frieda, as she can well imagine how worried they must all be feeling. She has to come up to town in a couple of days to see an exhibition and attend a lecture at the Cochrane Gallery: would they care to set a time to see her?

Daniel, Gogo and Rosemary agree that they are all intrigued by the existence of this Exmoor friend. Who can Jane Todd be, and how can she and Frieda ever have got together? Patsy, who has spoken to her on the phone, says that she sounds very pleasant and very ordinary. 'You know, just ordinary. Not Mummerset or anything. Just ordinary.'

This is even more curious. Daniel regrets that he cannot make lunch on the day in question, but both Gogo and Rosemary converge upon the ordinary little Italian restaurant in St Martin's Lane which Rosemary has selected as an appropriate meeting place. They get there early, to be ready for their guest, and are discussing kidney transplants when they see her approaching their reserved table. There is no mistaking the lady from Exmoor. She is wearing a good suit in a bold grid of bobbled green and heather tweed, enlivened by a sporting scarlet fleck. She has polished brogues, and a felt hat with a feather in it. She carries a highly polished maroon leather bag with a gold clasp and a gold chain. She is autumnal, and her face is delicate and soft and wrinkled and faded. She smiles at them vaguely, sits herself down, introduces herself, as she accepts a gin and tonic.

'I'm Jane Todd, from Exford,' she says. 'This is so worrying. So very very worrying. I *did* like your mother. Such a nice woman.'

Her vague smile flitters, pleasantly. She has sharp blue eyes, pepper-and-salt hair, and gentle folds of becoming chin. She butters her roll vigorously.

She had met Frieda, she tells them, in a pub in Simonsbath. Both had been taking lunch while sheltering from heavy rain. She herself had been out walking and collecting specimens – 'I do a little botanizing, just as a hobby' – and had been examining an ivy-leaved bell-flower through a hand lens when Frieda had introduced herself, and asked the name of the plant. They'd got chatting, and Jane had been most interested to learn that Frieda lived at Ashcombe, for she'd known the house in the old days. She could remember it as a hotel, and then again when it had been inhabited, briefly, by a Mr Silver from Vermont. They had talked about the house, and its curious history, and Frieda had asked her to come round for a drink one day. And so they had become friends. They'd had lunch out together several times – they'd discovered another pub which did a cheap Thursday lunch for pensioners, and thought its landlord needed their support. Frieda had been interested in Exmoor stories, and she herself had known the area all her life, though she'd lived abroad for years. Yes, she was widowed, and retired there now. Frieda had been to her cottage on a couple of occasions, and admired her botanical drawings. Jane Todd was interested in botanical drawing, had built up her own collection, was off to see this new show at the Cochrane. The flora of Alberta. With a talk by Montague Porter. Frieda had known quite a lot about flora. But of course, they would know that, wouldn't they?

Gogo and Rosemary, making their way silently through their *penne all' arrabbiata*, had exchanged glances. Was this woman that Jane Todd knew really their wayward monster mother? Jane Todd made her sound quite usual. But then, on closer examination, Jane Todd herself was not as usual as she looked. It emerged that her husband had been an explorer – yes, an old-fashioned sort of explorer. Jane had travelled with him on many occasions. She could say she had seen the world. She and Frieda had exchanged travellers' tales.

Jane Todd could not believe that Frieda had simply vanished. The last time she'd seen her she'd been so well. They'd had their lunch, then gone for a walk through the woods to the County Gate, talking of Arthur Rackham, and fairy stories. They'd both been brought up on Rackham. Then they'd gone on together to Minehead to look at the charity shops. They'd discovered that they both enjoyed nosing around in charity shops. Frieda had been most impressed by the quality of the stuff you could find in the West Country. Not that she wanted to *buy* much, for both she and Jane had reached the age where they had enough stuff to last them a lifetime – but they liked to look. Frieda had professed herself interested in the economics of this new barter system, this late-twentieth-century rural by-product of an unprecedented mixture of affluence, indigence, unemployment, underemployment and a crazy rating system. Frieda had said that she was thinking of writing a book about it. So they called their visits 're-search'. Jane would report her findings to Frieda, and Frieda would report hers to Jane. 'Now look at my hat,' commands Jane Todd.

They look at her hat.

'I got that from the Spastics,' says Jane Todd proudly. 'You wouldn't have guessed that, would you?'

'And my bag,' continues Jane Todd, 'is Cystic Fibrosis.' They gaze at her bag. It shines and swells.

Oh dear, laments Jane, she would miss Frieda. There weren't so many like-minded people on Exmoor.

She was so sorry she'd been so long getting in touch. She'd been in Cornwall, visiting a friend who'd just had a hip op. She only heard the news when she got back. Oh dear what a worry.

Jane Todd did not look very worried. Her morbidity quotient seemed surprisingly low. She was much more interested in pink toothwort and monogrammed silver teaspoons and second-hand hand-knitted Fair Isle pullovers than in sudden deaths, drownings, suicides. She was a very unprying person. When asked if she herself had a family, she hardly seemed to know the answer. Yes, she thought she did have a son and a couple of daughters and a few grandchildren, but she couldn't quite remember where they were these days. Or that was the impression she gave.

Gogo could see that this indifference would have appealed to Frieda.

They agreed, after her departure for Paddington, that her evidence was little help. She could testify to the fact that Frieda, on recent sightings, had seemed cheerful and of sound mind, but that got them nowhere. It could perhaps be used in court to try to establish that Frieda's last will and testament was not the ravings of a mad old woman of the moor, but they would leave that to Daniel to pursue. Should it come to that. Both had noted that Jane Todd had made no mention of a houseboy called Will Paine, or of any other inhabitants or visitors to Ashcombe. Frieda and Jane had seemed to dwell in a remote, unpeopled, fantastical world, detached from human history by age and much wandering, content with trees and rocks and roots and bell-flowers.

Jane Todd, at the Cochrane Gallery, listened intently to the lecture on the flora of Alberta, and watched keenly as slide followed slide. It all went in one ear and eye and out the other, but for the space of an hour her eyes were pleasantly occupied by saskatoon and choke-cherry, by monkshood and harebell and gentian, by scarlet mallow and snow buttercups and mountain forget-me-not, by Indian paintbrush and asters of purple and gold.

THE CAVE OF GLOOM

Frieda's body was recovered three weeks later, washed up twenty miles along the coast off Rampion Point. For more than a month she had ebbed and flowed with the steep tides of the Bristol Channel and the grey swell of the wintry Atlantic. To Lundy she had drifted, and back again, to rest at last on a rocky promontory, at the foot of the iron cliff. Mackerel in the salt water and seabirds and ravens and crabs on the shore had feasted upon her. Her prophecy came to pass, for she was identified not by the scar on her thigh but by the bridgework in her skull. Her scar had been sucked and nibbled away by countless plucking mouths. Her bridgework, loose though it was, had not been washed away. It clung to her jaw. Obstinacy and paranoia had perished, with all other qualities, but the bridge had hung on. The coastguard at Ilfracome, who recovered what was left of Frieda Haxby Palmer, had known her at once. He had been on the look-out for her. He had felt she was coming his way. He had programmed the charts of tide and wind and weather, and had expected her to come to him. He had waited, and she had come.

He had to send a man down the cliff on a rope's end to collect her. She was bundled into a bodybag, and hoisted up amidst the crying gulls. He rang the police of both counties, wondering which would claim her. Somerset prevailed over Devon, and Somerset rang Derbyshire to inform Daniel Palmer.

There would be an inquest, Daniel told Gogo and Rosemary.

It is not pleasant to think of one's mother so long in the icy sea. Even Frieda's undutiful son and daughters felt the force of this, and could not inhibit their imaginings. But for Benjamin, her heir, her chosen one, the news was ghastly. He took to his bed and would not, could not move. His teeth chattered as with a high fever, although he was as cold as any stone. Gogo sat by his bedside and wept.

There was no hope now of concealment. The newspapers picked up the tragedy, and picked up Frieda's connections. The well-prepared obituaries were long. Her rogue reputation was assessed and reassessed. Reporters rang Patsy and Nathan and David D'Anger. The story of Will Paine reached the press, and for a while the Identikit drawing resurfaced. Had Frieda Haxby Palmer been murdered? Had she been pushed off a cliff? Had she jumped off a cliff? Journalists made their way to Ashcombe and described it in Gothic prose. It made a good story. The names of Cedric Summerson and one or two others in high or public places were stirred into the brew. Had MI5 been involved? Or the CIA?

None of her family welcomed these attentions, and indeed they were not well meant. David D'Anger was accustomed to finding himself the target of the right-wing, but not to finding the chaste and austere name of his wife dragged into the attacks; nor was he at all happy with some of the innuendoes about the private aspects of his working life. Nobody had yet dared to call him a playboy of the media, or to link his name with that of Lola Belize of CNN, but he could see danger ahead. Nathan was not best pleased by mocking references to his occupational practices (lunches, dinners, clubs and nights on the town), and Rosemary knew that, for her, this was it. The arts were on principle loathed by most of the press, and as a representative of the arts she was savagely derided: she would not be forgiven for the attention she had unwittingly drawn to herself. Daniel, whose case, like the Wash itself, wound on for ever, assured them from Cheshire that the whole business was a storm in a teacup, that Frieda's death would be forgotten in a week, but privately he prayed that there would be no more incriminating faxes from Will Paine.

So far the three Palmer children had stuck together in the face of this unwanted exposure, but all sensed that this solidarity could not last. Gone were those pleasant weekends of tennis and conversation in Hampshire, those West End theatre evenings arranged by Nathan Herz, those inconclusive but pleasant plans for weeks in Italy. There would be no family Christmas this year: Christmas would never come again in its old form.

Frieda had ruined it all. Jessica and Jonathan knew that they would never play the Game again. Disaster had come upon them.

Old Howard Partridge no longer had any excuse for not digging out Frieda's penultimate will, but when he produced it it solved nothing. It posed yet more problems, as Daniel, who had first sight of it, knew he should have known it would. It had been no less arbitrary and malicious than her last: indeed in many ways it was much worse. She had named as her executors her recently retired but still sprightly literary agent Bertram Goldie, and Lord Ogden, a heavy-weight legal bruiser now enjoying a comfortable autumn life of overeating as Master of Grotius College in Cambridge. (Daniel, seeing Ogden's name in the document, recalled that Frieda had sat on the Ogden Committee on something or other – Equal Opportunity? Industrial Espionage? The North Sea Bed?)

Goldie and Ogden had been her executors, and the will which they had agreed to execute had left £20,000 to each of her children and to each grandchild a thousand pounds. So far, so good. But she had left the rest of her estate and all her copyrights in trust to her son-in-law David D'Anger, for the purpose of re-establishing the D'Anger family claim to the Valley of the Eagles, and establishing therein the Just Society, to be founded on the principles of social justice, as discussed. There was a lot more about this Society and its trustees, in small print, along with mentions of the Demerara case and the restitution of economic and cultural rights in Guyana. There was even a mention of the Boston Tea Party. Daniel was so enraged by all this codswallop that he could not bring himself to read it carefully, and he could see at a glance why Howard Partridge had not wished to divulge it. How could any reputable lawyer have allowed himself to be a party to such a document? What could old Ogden have been thinking of? What had David D'Anger been up to? If this wasn't a sign of undue influence on an unsound mind, then it would be hard to know what was. The prospect of young Benjamin D'Anger winning the lot began to seem almost acceptable, in comparison with this deliberate, money-wasting nightmare. Daniel does not believe in concepts. He believes, or so he thinks, in people. And Benjamin is, at least, a person.

There is no way of keeping the contents of this document away from the other family members, although Daniel has been the first to see them. Daniel is not sure how to dress them up. He is in a cruel dilemma which he begins to think the wicked Frieda must have foreseen. Shall he go for the second will, on the grounds of its superior clarity and sanity, or for this earlier garbage, on the grounds that there is more money in it for him and the Herzes, and that a subsequent appeal could successfully challenge the excessive D'Anger share and hand it back for equal redistribution amongst the next-of-kin? Would a successful challenge to the first will reinstate the disqualified second will? These are complex legal points.

~~David~~ *Daniel* decides to be bold and to speak to Nathan. Nathan is supposed to be a practical man, a man of business (though Daniel has at times had his doubts about this). He rings at seven in the morning from his Holiday Inn in Chester, and reads out to him the offending paragraphs. To his dismay Nathan laughs heartily, though not very happily, and says that although he could do with £20,000 right now, he can't think that all that Just Society nonsense could stand up in a court of law. Yet he agrees that it would simply waste Frieda's posthumous income if they were to challenge it. Better to let Goltho & Goltho give it to little Benjie, says Nathan. He's a nice boy, maybe he'll help us out in our old age. 'The Just Society,' repeats Nathan, with finely dramatized incredulity. 'She might as well have left it to the Conversion of the Jews!' And is it possible, he pursues, after a moment's pause, to leave your money to a cause that doesn't exist?

Daniel, who has been lying awake for most of the night, tossing in his flat tight sheets, watching the red digital clock flick soundlessly onwards, has his answer. 'Yes,' he says with neat precision. 'Yes, it is. Bernard Shaw left his to a new alphabet, remember. And Old Hutch Hutchinson of Derby left his to found the London School of Economics. Shaw's will was successfully challenged, but the LSE is there all right. It was cobbled together by the trustees over a breakfast party near Godalming, if I remember rightly.'

'But come off it,' says Nathan. 'The Just Society! What a freak idea! Now if she'd wanted to found a Society for the Promotion of Social

199

Justice, that would have been different. *Everybody* says they believe in Social Justice. The words mean nothing. But the Just Society? Whoever heard of such a thing?'

Daniel is not sure if this is helpful, but it is smart. The wording is indeed such that it would be hard to sanction any monies being handed over on its terms by David D'Anger to the Labour Party or any other known organization. Can David himself know what is meant by the Just Society? Is it some agreement between David and Frieda? Had they cooked this up together? (Daniel dimly remembers that there had been some bending of the terms in the Hutchinson–LSE case – hadn't Hutch originally left nothing to his family, and everything to the cause of Socialism? Was it Sidney Webb who had sorted that one out to everyone's satisfaction? Or was it that unworldly lunatic Shaw again?)

Nathan, on the end of the line by the Thames, is now wide awake, and is beginning to take a keener interest in the philosophical and legal conundrum which Daniel has sprung upon him. He unhelpfully reminds Daniel that the Ethical Society and the National Secular Society and the Philosophical Society and the British Humanists and even the Gay British Humanists are all *bona fide* organizations, probably even charitable organizations, to which one could legally leave one's entire fortune, though it is hard to know how ethics or secularism or philosophy or humanism would benefit from such a bequest. And is justice a concept more vague, more immaterial than ethics or humanism? It would be odd if it were, says Nathan. How would one set about founding a Just Society, Nathan begins to speculate – would it be a society *for* justice, or a society to *discuss* justice, or a society that *practised* justice? Had Frieda's will spelt any of this out? Perhaps the Just Society could spend its time playing variations on the Veil of Ignorance? How had Sidney Webb got the London School of Economics off the ground? How had he got from a breakfast party at Godalming to bricks and mortar in the Aldwych?

'By lectures,' says Daniel tersely. He is beginning to regret interesting Nathan in this topic. 'He set up courses of lectures.'

'Well, there you are, there's your answer. Frieda's money could all be spent on lectures on social justice. Or on social justice research projects. I bet they cost a pretty penny.'

'I can't think that was quite what she had in mind,' says Daniel.

'Anyway, whatever she had in mind, she seems to have thought better of it,' says Nathan. 'She decided to give it all to Benjamin instead.'

Daniel's breakfast has arrived, on a tray. He pours himself a cup of coffee, his mind beginning to meander from Frieda's wills to his river case.

'It sounds to me', says Nathan, 'as though we'd better let Benjie scoop the jackpot. With as good a grace as we can muster. I'm going to buy myself a bonanza break of lottery tickets today. Do you play the lottery, Daniel?'

'Certainly not,' says Daniel with austerity.

'Well, keep me briefed,' says Nathan.

Daniel rings off. Daniel eats his cooling eggs.

Daniel, it should be understood, is a man of probity. He is, if you like, a Just Man. But his is the justice of the law. He is a man of the law. He dislikes muddles. In part of his mind he knows that it is unlikely that David D'Anger had suborned Frieda Haxby in the hope of personal gain. Nevertheless, he will never trust David D'Anger or his sister Gogo again. They are contaminated by his mother's caprice.

His river case has disclosed a startling amount of contamination and corruption. Pollution, greed and dirty money have been flowing through four counties. Infection has run downstream, killing fish and decency, gathering momentum, until it flowed into the dirty sea. There have been lies, there have been legal evasions and tax evasions. There have been gestures and posturings. One of the alleged polluters has been seen recently on television, dashing down a clear tumbler of water taken from the River Wash as it flows through the backyard of one of his factories. 'The champagne of Staffordshire!' he had declared to the camera. Daniel does not like this kind of posturing, which has become so popular in the television age. It has corrupted us all. It had even corrupted the austere Frieda. For what had Timon's feast been but a gesture without cameras, borrowed from the minister who fed his daughter on hamburgers for the entertainment of the nation?

Daniel drinks his metallic orange juice, and takes himself to the bathroom to shave. As he gazes at himself in the mirror he wonders if he is beginning to resemble his father.

Had Frieda committed suicide, and if so, what was the law relating to the estate of suicides? Daniel does not believe that Will Paine pushed Frieda off a cliff, but he thinks it possible that Frieda may have jumped. Death by misadventure, the inquest had concluded, but what if Frieda had known herself to be fatally ill? Might she not well have jumped? Daniel has now had time to study the letter that Frieda had received from the National Radiological Protection Board at Didcot, and has discovered that the radon level at Ashcombe, calculated at 850 Bq m-3, is way above the national average of 20 Bq m-3 and way above the danger level of 200. Her house had been full of Radon's daughters. No wonder the NRPB had urged action. The DoE pamphlet had also stressed that 'cigarette smoking, which is the dominant cause of lung cancer, aggravates the risk of lung cancer from radon exposure'. Frieda had taken up smoking, she had lost weight, she had developed a cough. Had she therefore jumped into the sea? Such a leap would have been in character. She had a habit of taking precipitate action, of meeting trouble before it met her.

Daniel has not disclosed the radon information to anybody. The letter had stated that it was confidential, and would not be disclosed to anyone else without written permission. Nevertheless, the legal implications had sprung to Daniel's mind as soon as he had seen the label on the Jiffy bag, and the last sentence of the letter confirms his suspicions. It had instructed Frieda that tenants, landlords and owner-occupiers of radon-infected dwellings should consult p. 4 of the *Guide*. This stated that an owner-occupier had no legal obligation to disclose the results to anyone, but that such a person 'should take advice about contractual matters'.

Daniel decides not to disclose anything to anybody. Or not yet.

Who would wish to buy Ashcombe, with or without its radon?

★

If Gogo D'Anger had shivered at the news of Frieda's second will, the Goltho & Goltho will which left all to Benjie, David D'Anger is struck with horror and guilt at the news of the first, which had left so much to The Just. For he has been directly responsible for this madness. Innocent of intent, as he himself and he alone knows, but nevertheless responsible. The perils of conversation, the dangers of philosophy, the pitfalls of speculation! Many hours over the years he had spent in discussion with Frieda Haxby, but it had never occurred to him that she took his ideas seriously. He had assumed it was all a game. She had never seemed to condone his interests. Indeed, she had mocked them, had made fun of them. And now she had called his bluff. She had asked him to press the button. At least, to be fair, she had thought of asking him to press the button. And then she had given him up and thought better of it. She had given him up, as he now gives up himself. But with what disastrous consequences! He had so prided himself on his Palmer alliance, he had cherished his friendly relations. But Frieda Haxby had sown perpetual dissension like dragon's teeth. She had set her family at war.

He replays his encounters with Frieda, and she appears before him in her protean forms. Girlish in Indian print, as she walked down the towpath past the houseboats near Nuffield in Oxford, on the day that he and Gogo had announced their plans to marry. (She had taken a piece of bread from her large bag to feed the ducks.) Stout in green silk at his wedding in the gardens of Gladwyn, champagne in hand, holding court to dons and divines and assembled D'Angers from three continents. Eating a plateful of spaghetti in their Highbury flat, and holding the infant Benjamin in her arms as she uttered prophecies over him. Appearing with David himself and an MEP and a Minister of Agriculture on a programme about British sugar production. Accompanying David and the Minister round the sugar factory at Scalethwaite, inspecting steel silos amidst the fetid smell of cooking beet. Celebrating her sixtieth birthday at a large party at the Conservatory at the Barbican amidst tropical plants and orchids – the nearest I could get to Guyana, she had joked.

At Timon's feast in Romley. In her tea-gown at Ashcombe.

And now, most vividly, most ominously returns to him the memory of another meeting. She appears to him as she had appeared on that ill-fated night three years ago – three years, four years, five years ago? – in Toronto. He had not even known she was in Canada, let alone in the same building, and had been startled to see his mother-in-law emerge from the make-up room of the space-age television studio where he was waiting to take part in a live TV phone-in on communitarianism and multiculturalism in Quebec and the UK. There she was, Frieda Haxby herself, curiously highly coloured, her grey hair puffed by eager fingers into a great crest. She had greeted him with a screech of delight, and informed him that she herself was to speak about the sensational discovery of the Swansberg Stone, an archaeological find which, if its runes proved authentic, would push back the date of Viking settlement in North America by some hundred years. She was as proud of this stone as if she had discovered it herself, as if she had been one of the first Viking seafarers to cross the Atlantic. And she was proud too of her glamorous son-in-law. How pleased they had been to see one another, amongst the alien crowd!

Though David, as he explained to Frieda in the back of a Beck cab on their way to the Harborfront Hotel where both were staying, did not find Toronto alien. It allowed for him, as it allowed for the many. David D'Anger admired Toronto and Trudeau. Toronto had received over the decades Vikings and Vietnamese, Guelphs and Ghibellines, Italians and Indians, and had made them all welcome. Toronto was a young city, it had no old age, no middle ages. It had made its own contracts. How fortunate, to start so late in history, without the baggage of Britain. So they had mused, as they sat drinking in a slowly revolving bar high above the bright lights, the lake, the islands. They had talked of post-colonialism, of Guyana, of vanished empires, of rising empires, of the Pax Americana. They had talked, alas, too much, of too many things – of communism and perpetual revolution, of socialism in one country, of Stalin and Trotsky, of Cheddi Jagan and Forbes Burnham, of Coleridge and Pantisocracy, of the slow death of the vision of the just. Oh, it lingers on, David had said, this vision, artificially protected by university grants in departments of political

204

theory, but nobody believes in it any more. Capitalism and the free market had triumphed. Only a poet or a fool or a philosopher would speak of justice now.

The bar revolved very, very slowly, almost imperceptibly, as they drank their way through the night. And Frieda had probed him about new theories of social contract, about the possibility or impossibility of conceiving of a society as a closed system isolated from all other societies. Could one set up a just state in isolation? And could it survive? How quickly would it deteriorate? Would human nature itself change if society were changed from the roots? Could one eradicate the motive of greed? And is envy, as some philosophers have argued, an unnatural by-product of inequality? Or is it innate? And if innate, is it useful?

Frieda had been taken by the idea of an experimental society, as others had been before her. You'd need time, she had concluded, in order to see it work through the generations. Time, and an isolated location. Guyana, she pointed out, would do well. Surely Professor Challenger could have discovered the Just Society up the Oronoque, instead of the dinosaurs? Wouldn't David himself like to have a crack at it? This she had asked him, on top of the Harborfront Hotel, after a third of a bottle of Scotch, and he had said yes. Who would have thought that this conversation, and that fatal phrase, would have lodged in Frieda's maverick imagination? Whyever had he told her about the Sixth Form Society he had founded at school, of his attempts to re-establish it at Oxford! It had only been a talking club, a discussion group, a game. They hadn't meant to *do* anything. Had they? How could she have even thought of leaving money to the Just Society? As soon finance yet another expedition to raise the *Titanic*, or to dive for pirate gold amongst the hammer-headed sharks of Cocos Island!

David D'Anger knows that the Just Society is an impossibility, that his brain cannot even conceive of it, as it cannot conceive of heaven or of hell. But he does not like to know that he knows it. He does not like to know that mankind and womankind are envious, greedy, violent and insincere.

They had gone late to their beds, that night in Toronto, high, drunk, over-stimulated, jet-lagged. Had their difference in age been less embarrassing they would have slept together. At least David had been spared that memory. He knows that Frieda would have been willing. But the rest of the night had been bad enough. He had felt the whole room revolve as he lay in bed watching the revolving stories and advertisements and self-advertisements of CNN. Was a Just Society, he remembers thinking then, and thinks now, any more improbable than a society which runs on a diet of 'stories' about plagues in India and wars in Africa and serial killers in Idaho? To the repeated accompaniment of a ditty sung by an animated cartoon cash register which tells us that 'Jingle bells mean Christmas sells'?

Well, yes, the answer was that it was. The cash register sings the true tune.

David lies awake in bed, as Gogo lies asleep beside him. (Benjamin too is awake, although David hopes he sleeps.) David mourns the lost trust of Daniel and Patsy Palmer, of Rosemary and Nathan Herz. David mourns the death of hope. He has been forced to indict himself, and now all his family know of his failure and his folly.

He had meant no harm by speaking to Frieda of Eagle Valley, where the vast endangered harpy-eagles breed. Whatever had possessed him, to turn the loose cannon of Frieda Haxby's powerful will towards the Just, towards the D'Angers, towards Eagle Valley? Had he been boasting of his heritage, as she had boasted her mystic links with the Swansberg Stone, with Queen Christina of Sweden? What tosh, what junk! Yes, he must have spoken of Eagle Valley, or she would not have been able to mention it in her Ur-will. Does it really exist, out of family mythology? David has never been there, nor has any other living D'Anger. The D'Angers are scattered round the globe – in Africa, Canada, Australia, India. They have peopled the world, but none of them has ever dared to visit the interior.

So twice five miles of fertile ground
With walls and towers were girdled round:

And there were gardens bright with sinuous rills . . .

The D'Angers do not know their ancestral land. Politics drove them out, and now they live in perpetual diaspora.

> *Weave a circle round him thrice,*
> *And close your eyes with holy dread,*
> *For he on honey-dew hath fed*
> *And drunk the milk of paradise . . .*

David tries to lie still, as he summons up those forests, those waterfalls, those circling birds. The land of many waters. Pterodactyls, dinosaurs and monster fish with shining scales of pink and blue and silver. The red god and the maiden with the knife. The crab, the cave, the sacrifice. In the Guyanese savannah, in the year of our Lord nineteen hundred and seventy-eight, some nine hundred believers had died, had died willingly, at one man's command. Could not at one man's command nine hundred live?

The forests and waterfalls fade and dissolve, and David sees instead a dream-image he knows and fears and tries to keep at bay: it is of one small puny deluded stick man, far away and far below, pulling and pulling at a vast heavy carpet of cloth. He is trying to drag it towards a peg, a hook, another seam of cloth? The cloth is as large and as heavy as the globe, and on it stand all the peoples of the globe, weighting it down. The tiny figure hawls and hawls, and strains and sweats, but the cloth does not shift or give. The figure is himself, and before him are all the rich leaden vested interests, all the dead weight of traditions, all the conglomerates and agglomerates and multinationals and conurbations, and behind them the multitudes of the thin starving sufferings. There is no hope of moving this mass. He has neither the brain nor the strength. He might as well let go. It will make no difference if he lets go. But if, by some superhuman miracle, he were to drag it even a centimetre, he knows he would have done well. So he cannot let go. Maybe all that the utmost of his effort can achieve is this terrible tension, without which the whole cloth will retract and unravel and unwind, and, like a released rope, uncoil at a speed which will destroy all in its violence? He must hang on, he must hang on. But he cannot hang on.

Benjamin, along the corridor, lies awake. He is afraid to sleep, for his dreams are terrible. He dreams he is drowning in the lake in the Cave of Gloom. He fights for breath, he surfaces, but there is no surface. The roof of the cave is under the water. There is no space, no air. He drowns, and the fish nibble at his toes and fingers – little tickling nibbling fishmouths. His flesh frays, turns white, dissolves, shreds off. He is phosphorescent decay in the water. He has murdered his grand-mother, and for this crime he must die.

He fights to lie awake. He wishes to die. He wishes it were over, that he need struggle for breath no more. Let me let go, he prays. Dear God, let me go, let me depart to the Island of the Dead. He knows such prayers are sinful.

What is the sin he has committed? It is in the Game. He should not have meddled with those powers. He should not have assumed those powers. Now he has lost them for ever. He can no longer animate the inanimate, for he can no longer animate himself. He has invoked bad spirit, black spirit. He promises God, he promises Jesus Christ of the Christians, that if he lives through this night he will renounce all his kingdom. He will recall his subjects and lay them all to rest.

His mind burns, his skin burns, the night prolongs into torture. Will it never end? Shall he creep for comfort into his mother's bed? But he cannot, for he is a wicked boy. He must remove himself, before he kills them too, as he killed his grandmother Frieda. He cannot creep back into his mother, for he is a child no longer. Something frightful has happened to his body. It is not man, it is not child, it is monster. Will the long night never end? He counts up to a thousand, up to two thousand, up to ninety-nine thousand. A long dead march of numbers. But why should he wish for the morning? The morning will bring no relief, the daytime no respite.

Gogo is in a fever of anxiety. Something must be done, but what?

Benjamin is fading before her eyes. He too now has a fever: his temperature rises to a hundred and four, to a hundred and five, and sweat drops off his thin body through the sheets and the mattress to the floor. Glandular fever, scarlet fever, viral meningitis? She summons her GP, and blood samples are sent off for urgent testing. She sits rigid, like a plaster statue, by his bed, with a yellow pudding bowl of cold water and a white cloth upon her knee. *Mater dolorosa*, thinks David with a pang, as he sees her vigil. Then wishes the thought undone. The wooden cathedral of his childhood had been brightly coloured, and so too remains Gogo, even in grief, though her colours are less tawdry than those of the madonna – a dark red skirt, cinnamon shirt, a dark draped plum scarf wound around her head. Benjamin lies rigid, staring at the ceiling, occasionally covering his eyes with a bony crook of elbow. Gogo keeps the lights dim. Benjamin's lips are dry.

Gogo cannot keep vigil day and night, for she has to go to the hospital in Bloomsbury, the clinic in Maida Vale. She rearranges her patients as best she may, but she must keep most of her appointments. She knows she is no longer functioning well. She does not listen closely as symptoms are described, her mind wanders homewards as she examines the X-rays and scans of the nervous systems of strangers. Will Benjamin's illness show up on a screen?

A hired hand sits by Benjamin when Gogo is not there. David too cancels much of his life, and hovers, helplessly. Shall they insist on Benjie's being taken into hospital? You would think that with their joint expertise they would be able to ride the system, to insist on a private wing, on a short cut to instant health, but they are curiously inept in the face of crisis. They do not want to let their only one out of their sight, out of their home. The fever lasts for only a couple of days, although it seems like weeks, and it vanishes as mysteriously as it arrived, leaving Benjamin as he had been before he overheated – listless, apathetic, withdrawn. All tests have proved negative. There is nothing wrong with Benjamin. There is everything wrong with Benjamin.

This is not Gogo's field. The nervous system is her field – the cervical nerve, the somatic nerves, the cranial nerves, the gyri, the sulci, the cerebellum, the spinal nerves and the sympathetic chain. Benjamin is sick not in the nerves but in the spirit. Neither Gogo nor David know how to reach his spirit. They tempt him with delicacies, they bring him books, they install a television by his bed. He does not eat, he does not read, he does not watch, except while his parents are watching, from a residual politeness. When questioned, he says he feels cold. Sometimes he mutters to himself, 'I can't *do* it, I can't *do* it,' but when they ask what it is he cannot do he turns his face to the wall and will not say.

Gogo rings up a friend at the Tavistock to ask about childhood depression. David rings his mother in Birmingham and asks her to come up to London. Perhaps one grandmother can right the wrongs of the other.

Ronjon de Lanerolle, Benjie's best friend at school, is prompted by his elders to come and see Benjie. The visit is not a success. Ronjon is puzzled and irritated by his friend's lack of response to any of his conversational gambits, and ends up glumly watching an Australian soap opera on Benjie's bedside TV. He cannot wait to get away. Nevertheless, he promises to come again soon.

It is Benjie himself who asks after his cousin Emily. It is the first sign of curiosity he has shown for a week. Gogo rings Patsy, and Patsy says that Emily is, as it happens, on her way back to England for a friend's eighteenth-birthday celebration: shall she ask her to ring Benjie? Gogo unburdens herself a little to Patsy, though she is too proud to show the depths of her anxiety. Patsy is sympathetic. She confesses that she has her own worries about Simon. His tutor says he seems to have dropped out of everything and he has run up enormous bills at the college buttery and on his bank card. Daniel has had to put a stop to his son's credit. What can Simon be up to? Surely, Patsy asks Gogo, he can't be on drugs, can he? He wouldn't be so stupid, would he? Gogo's silence replies.

Emily comes to see Benjie on the morning after the schoolfriend's birthday party in Crouch End. As we have seen, she is fond of Benjie, and is proud to be requested. She had been happy to play big sister to this charming boy, had treasured his confidences. The role of Nurse

Emily appeals to her, but when she sees Benjamin, hunched in his bed, she is alarmed. This case is beyond her. He holds her hand as she sits by the bed. His hand is dry and hot and thin. He looks like a little fledgling bird, a poor wounded bird, a bird blown off course. A little finch.

'What's up, Benjie Boy?' she asks as cheerfully as she can. At first he shakes his head and will not speak. After a while he mutters, 'Grandma Frieda. What happened to her? They won't tell me.'

'They don't know, Benjie,' says Emily. 'She's dead, but they don't know how it happened. That's why they haven't told you. They're not keeping anything from you. Not that I know of.'

'She drowned,' says Benjie.

'They think she fell,' says Emily.

'Do you know what she told me?' says Benjie. 'She told me:

Crows are green, and rooks are blue,
Crows are three and rooks are two,
I may live for ever, and so may you.

What do you think it means?'

He has to say it again, before Emily can take it in. She ponders. 'It's some kind of spell,' she says. 'But it's a good spell, can't you see? It says she'll live for ever, that she's not dead at all. I kind of believe that, don't you?'

Benjie shakes his head but he looks very slightly cheered, before he plunges back into melancholy.

He makes Emily promise that she will go to the Old Farm and collect the Power Game for him and bring it to him in London. Emily had not been keen to go to Hampshire, but for Benjie's sake she consents. He seems to think it is important. He doesn't want to see Jess and Jon, though. He makes this clear. They mustn't know. They will hate him now.

Emily assumes this is something to do with the legacy, but doesn't know how to respond to his fear. Shall she tell him that she herself doesn't want a penny of Frieda's gold? No, better not, better not even mention it. She pats Benjie warmly, as warmly as one can pat an unresponsive little bundle, and as she makes to leave the sickroom a thought strikes her. 'I say, Benjie,' she says, 'you know, crows *are* green and rooks *are* blue. Well, sort of. They're both black, but they have a different sheen. It's one of the ways to tell them apart. It's quite a useful little rhyme. Do you think she made it up? I've never heard it before.'

'Emily,' he says, as she stands on the threshold. 'What are harpies? Are they birds?'

'Sort of birds,' says Emily. 'A sort of mythological bird. With claws.'

'Sort of eagles?'

'Yes, sort of eagles,' agrees Emily, for the sake of agreement. She has never heard of the harpy-eagles of Guyana.

Then Emily goes downstairs to report on Benjie to Benjie's other grandmother, Mrs D'Anger from Georgetown and Edgbaston. Emily has no recollection of having met Mrs D'Anger Senior before, though she thinks she may have done when very small: she had been illogically expecting some sort of ample Black Mama figure and is surprised to find Clarissa D'Anger to be considerably less grandmotherly in manner and appearance than Frieda Haxby. Clarissa D'Anger is smartly dressed, sophisticated of manner, and, despite her five children, trim of figure: she has not a grey hair in her head, and her red high-heeled shoes are dauntingly, dangerously chic. She now offers Emily a cup of tea, and listens with her head cocked alertly on one side to Emily's bulletin. 'Poor child,' she says, and reveals that in her view Benjamin's problems spring from having been sent to a neighbouring comprehensive: he would have been much better off, in Clarissa's view, at Westminster, or, if David would insist on state education, at the William Ellis. 'The state system just doesn't work,' says Clarissa, 'I'm sure it would if David ran it. But he doesn't. Why sacrifice your own child? Such a clever boy. They just don't give his mind enough to bite on. All this project work, it just gets them in a muddle. The quality of teaching is terrible. Where were you, dear? You and Simon both went to Winchester, didn't you?'

Emily mutters that Winchester doesn't seem to have done them all that much good, and makes her excuses. She backs away from this ambitious, tailored, dark-suited, well-spoken interrogator. She feels suddenly hungover and shabby. She has failed the test.

Clarissa D'Anger blames the educational system for Benjamin's breakdown. David and Gogo blame themselves and Frieda. David's friend the poet finds another interpretation.

David's friend the poet is a Guyanese writer called Saul Sinnamary, and he and David have known one another for most of their lives. Both have risen through the systems of both their countries, and Saul leads now a life of global restlessness. He has a reasonably salaried and tenured appointment at a distinguished North American college where he teaches for a few weeks of the year: the rest of his time he divides, as his CV diplomatically puts it, between England and Guyana. He is a little older than David, and less ambitious, or so he claims. He and David meet from time to time, when Saul is passing through Britain, and they meet now, in a pub off the Aldwych. (Saul has been recording for the BBC World Service in that imperial monument, Bush House.) David is anxious to ask Saul about the Valley of the Eagles, for unlike himself, Saul has visited the Interior. He has kept his links. You can tell that from his poetry. It is all in there. Gold and waterfalls, myths and fish, bauxite and basalt.

Saul does not know the Valley of the Eagles, but he has been to the Kanuku Mountains and the Makarapan Mountains, he has seen Lake Amuku, and he has seen – or he thinks he has seen – a harpy-eagle. A bloody great big bird, huge talons, monkey-snatcher, baby-snatcher. A threatened species. A protected species. *Thrasyactus harpyia: Harpyia destructor.* 'Protect the poet, protect the eagle,' says Saul Sinnamary. 'They won't last long.'

Saul Sinnamary is of the opinion that Benjamin D'Anger is suffering from exile. Although he was born in Britain, he is suffering from exile. He needs the ancestral images. So, in Saul's view, does David.

'We can't live here,' says Saul, over his pint of Murphy's. 'We need to get back for a fix. When were you last there, man?'

David shakes his head.

'Your boy,' says Saul, 'he needs to see where he came from. To get in touch. Western medicine is no use to the Guyanese mind. What use are Freud and Vienna to us?'

'For fuck's sake,' says David. 'We came from India, not Guyana. And your lot came from Africa, or so you say. How far back do you want to go? To *homo australopithecus*? The Olduvai Gorge?'

Saul Sinnamary insists that he knows what he is talking about. He is a romantic poet and he knows about the effect of landscape on the soul. Jung is a better guide to the psyche than Freud, even though he was a Swissman. Mountains are more use than sex, says Saul. Well, at least as much use. Saul should know, he's seen plenty of both in his time. You take that boy of yours back home for a break, he'll be a changed man, says Saul. And take that white nerve doctor wife of yours with you. She'll love it there. You can take her the easy way if you like, but take her. Take her to the gazebo on Kaow Island, Fred's brother's wife's family are in the catering there. I know, I've been there. It's paradise. A bird should fly home, man. We are homing birds.

David listens to Saul with respect, for this is a man with a human face, a man who loves his own children however far away they may be. Maybe what Saul says has truth in it? Should he go back to Guyana? Take Gogo and Benjamin on a holiday, on a luxury tour, to see the harpy-eagles and the rufous crab hawks and the blood-coloured woodpeckers and the saffron-crested tyrant manakins and the great-billed seed finch and the cayenne jay? Saul is something of a bird man, and he has in his wallet a crumpled, dog-eared checklist of the birds of Guyana which he has ticked off – 362 species in two weeks, bio-diversity run mad, says Saul. Who sponsored his trip, inquires David. 'I gave poetry readings, man, all the way up the Essequibo,' says Saul. 'I lectured them on Caribbean poetry, on Derek Walcott, on flora and fauna, on myth and legend. I caught the *pocu* and the *basha* and I helped to cook the rice. They'd never have made it without me. I lectured them on the novels of Wilson Harris. Every trip needs a poet. You've got to get off to the interior, to save yourself. You've got to get out of the cement and the city and go up river.'

'You lectured them on Wilson Harris? Who were these bird fanciers?'

'They were a captive audience, my friend. It was me and Wilson Harris or the piranhas and the electric eels. They survived.' Saul laughs. 'Did you hear that story about Wilson Harris at the 1970 Guyana Republic Celebrations? How he lectured on the continuity of man and nature, on how we're all rivers of fluid locked up in our skin casements, how we need to flow to the sea? I hear it was some lecture. It baffled them all. It inspired one of the greatest sentences Andrew Salkey ever wrote. You look that up one day. That's what you politicians need from time to time. A voyage into the interior.'

David assures Saul Sinnamary that he will look it up. Saul's speech has set his mind careering. Saul promises to call in one day, to bring Benjamin his book on South American birds.

Saul has been much taken by the story of Frieda's double-dealing double will. On the one hand, he points out, it's one hell of an old-fashioned plot. Wills, legacies, inheritance tax, capital gains tax. A real old nineteenth-century property plot. ('This is a real old-fashioned nineteenth-century country,' murmurs David.) On the other hand, it's an archetypal exile's dream plot, a twentieth-century transmigration plot. The family jewels buried in the garden of the homeland, awaiting the return of the exiled prince. Return to St Petersburg, to the Polish estate, to Harbin, to Riga, to Kashmir. Reclaim the jewels, the coalmines, the sugar plantations, the aristocratic titles, the deeds. The herd of cattle, the cinammon tree. Forget that, advises Saul. Forget the property. Birds, rivers, they are the truth of the soul. They are free. They are our great allies.

'So you don't think I should try to reclaim the Valley?' says David.

Saul shakes his head. What is possession? What are politics?

'If you gave me the whole of Guyana, I wouldn't take it,' says Saul. 'I want to be free to come and to go. Dreams of justice end in the abuse of power.'

'Who said that?' asks David.

'I did,' says Saul. 'I, Saul Sinnamary.' They both laugh.

'Remember Jonestown, man,' says Saul. 'The Reverend Jim Jones, he called himself a socialist. He tried to set up the Just Society.'

David had thought of this, as we have seen, and has wondered whether Frieda Haxby had been aware of this appalling precedent, this disastrous experiment in social engineering and utopian hubris. On 20 November 1978, the Reverend Jim Jones from Indiana had ordered the 900 members of his People's Temple to commit suicide, and obediently they had swallowed lethal draughts from a cauldron of sugar-sweet Kool-Aid and cyanide. There, in the Guyanese savannah, on the rich wet land surrounded by rain forest, they had perished. The just, the egalitarian, the communist society, founded in defiance of US capitalism and the nuclear arsenal on 27,000 acres in the North West District. Jones had believed himself to be Lenin reborn, and his American followers (80 per cent poor black and one lone seventeen-year-old Guyanese) had believed in him, to the gates of death. They had died, suffering from athlete's foot and other skin diseases. They had rotted in the hot rain. The ideal city, with its corrugated huts, its sophisticated electronic radio and closed circuit TV, its foot-rot, its home-grown vegetables. Even now it has its apologists.

And what of Michael de Freitas, alias Michael X, alias Michael Abdul Malik, a conman on a smaller scale, a power-crazed crackpot who had briefly been the Black Power darling of the Western World? His commune was in Trinidad, and he had been its Prime Minister. He had grown coconut, limes and mangoes, produced milk and manure and propaganda, but then he had taken to drinking blood and murdering his recruits. He had ordered the death of a white woman, and she had been buried half alive in a pit of dung. He had fled from the crime to Guyana, where he had at first been received in style, but as events caught up with him he had gone on the run, had gone into hiding with some ten-dollar notes, some tins of sardines and some biscuits. He had hidden in hotel rooms, in Georgetown, in Linden, then made off into the interior, towards the south-west, barefoot, demented, through the anthills. He had ended up at a thatched shelter called Bishop's Camp, and there, as he babbled of planting green fields, the police had found him. They had flown him back to Trinidad, where, three years later, in 1975, he was hanged. That was the end of commune leader Michael X. These were not good precedents. Michael X had no apologists now.

David D'Anger shivers as though someone had walked on his grave, and takes another gulp of his black Irish beer. Saul is staring round the crowded pub, at the mixed races and faces of London town, with a half-smile on his handsome face. David watches him. Bleed, bleed, poor country. Benjamin D'Anger lies fretting and staring at the ceiling, and Frieda Haxby reposes in a small urn in Patsy Palmer's kitchen, on the shelf above the Aga, among the split peas, lentil and haricots. Will Paine counts his dollars and his pound notes in a darkened room in Kingston. Simon Palmer hallucinates, and walks the hard shoulder.

Saul Sinnamary declines another beer. He must be on his way. Saul is off to Singapore next day, for a conference on post-colonial literature. He'll be back in a week, he'll remember to bring Benjie the bird book, he promises. Promises, promises.

They walk out into the London night. A beggar crouched in a doorway in a filthy flock-seeping sleeping-bag mutters a ritual request for change, but they ignore her. They walk along the Strand together, to Charing Cross tube station. The climate of Singapore is not dissimilar to the climate of Georgetown, Guyana. It is tropical, hot and wet. It too stands on land reclaimed from the sea. In fact, if you stuck a needle through the earth in Singapore, it would come out in Guyana, more or less. Singapore aspires to the skies, a twentieth-century miracle, a model for all Asian city-states. It is rich and clean and wired up. It has self-flushing lavatories and an air-conditioned subway and many television stations and an authoritarian regime. Both David D'Anger and Saul Sinnamary are thinking this at the same time, as they walk along past the gauntlet of the white beggars, but they do not say so.

At the entrance to the tube, they part. They embrace. 'Don't you worry about your boy,' says Saul. 'I'll come and see you when I get back.'

David is cheered by this encounter. Saul's speech about the birds and Wilson Harris offers hope. He changes trains at King's Cross, and on the Victoria Line he decides that he will suggest a Guyanese Christmas to Gogo. If it's not too late to book. It will take Benjamin out of himself, give him something to look forward to.

But when he gets home he finds he may be too late. Benjamin has been rushed to hospital. He has been found unconscious, face down, in the bath. He has tried to drown himself. Or so it seems.

On Benjie's bedroom floor lies a torn cardboard box labelled CHUM, a heap of wooden soldiers, some white plaster models crushed into smithereens, some plastic animals, a broken mirror and a hammer. Children's toys, the end of childhood, a massacre.

David absorbs all this from the hired hand, summons a cab, arrives at the hospital, fights his way through to the bedside on the twelfth floor. Intensive care. Benjamin is wired up, monitored. But he is breathing, and his eyes respond to light.

David and Gogo sit side by side in the waiting-room through the darkest night. They hold hands, they wait. There are no reproaches. There is a solidarity in their suffering.

Benjamin recovers. He can have been out for only a matter of seconds, of a minute. It was Gogo who had found him, visiting the bathroom to replace the soaps. The bathroom door had not been locked. Indeed, it had been ajar. She tells David this, for it is a message of hope.

Has there been brain damage? They are told there has not. They believe what they are told. Gogo is a professional, she has watched the monitor. They would not lie to her, it cannot lie to her. Benjamin shows none of the seven symptoms of brain damage, brain death.

Benjamin is apologetic. He had not meant to cause such trouble. He tries to explain, though they try to spare him his explanation. He looks so old and so small and so sad. He says he has been practising holding his breath. He wants to be a diver, to explore caverns. It had only been a game. A silly game. He had been practising for weeks, trying to break his own record. He had counted up to four hundred. He must have slipped. He is so sorry.

He can come home soon.

Gogo, in the hospital's coffee-shop, cannot stop crying. She never cries, but now she cannot stop. Tears flow from her eyes and her nose and she hardly bothers to wipe them away. David holds her hand.

Where has their Benjamin gone to? Who is this person who tells them that he has tried to drown himself as a game?

Will Paine is homesick. He wants to go back to Hackney, to the Old Farm in Hampshire, to the Pasta Twirl factory in Middleton, even to primary school in Bilston. He'd rather be in Winchester Gaol than here in Jamaica. He thinks of Ashcombe and the bracken and the roaring stags and the blackbirds and the gulls. Frieda Haxby has cut off his retreat. Her Midas money has sent him into exile. Nobody wishes his return – except, perhaps, for the police, who may still have some questions for him to answer. He has read of Frieda's death in the English papers. So she had slipped from the coast path. She was not the first to have done so, as the papers also say. But who will believe that she was not pushed? And why should she have slipped? He should never have left her that small supply of grass. He should never have left her to stew up her magic mushrooms. But she had taken to the grass. She said it was good for her liver.

There is plenty of weed in Jamaica. You can smell it on the hot air day and night. But Will does not feel at home on this dangerous island. He wants a respectable life. Here he drifts and wanders. He is afraid. He cannot make judgements here. At least in England he had known how to avoid being at the bottom of the heap. Here he does not know what the heap is made of, or where its bottom may lie. He remembers prison scare stories about yardies, about the Jamaicans on Death Row. There is still a death penalty, here in Jamaica. The Queen of England, shame on her, must sign the death warrants. At least he is more free than the Queen.

He dares not surface yet. He sews some of Frieda's cash into his jacket lining. He is surprised that nobody has caught up with him, for he had travelled on his own papers. Perhaps he has not yet been identified. Perhaps Patsy Palmer and Daniel have kept what they know to themselves.

He wonders how Simon Palmer fares. He himself is not in an

enviable position, but he would not change places with Simon Palmer.

Will Paine is lonely. He would like a friend, but he does not know who he can trust.

It is easier to get out of England than to get back in again. This he knows.

'I wonder,' wrote the young Charles Dickens, when contemplating emigration as a proper response to an incoming Tory government, 'I wonder, if I went to a new colony with my head, hands, legs and health, I should force myself to the top of the social milk-pot and live upon the cream! . . . Upon my word I believe I should.'

Gogo D'Anger has never had much time for therapists and analysts, for witch doctors, shrinks and counsellors, though she has friends who wear these labels. She calls herself a physician, and has tended to regard those meddling with the mind and the psyche as amateurs. Even psychology and psychiatry she treats with suspicion. But now, like many before her, she is humbled, and forced to seek for help. Benjamin, it is clear, is suffering from some form of depression. Is it endogenous or reactive, and does it matter which it is? Is it wise to put a boy of his age on psychoactive drugs, and is there any alternative? And if drugs, which drugs? Benjamin has never been manic, as far as his parents know, but maybe even they have not observed him very closely? David and Gogo ask around, and discover to their surprise that half their friends, for no very obvious reasons, are on Prozac. They are of the Prozac generation without knowing it. But nobody has any clear advice about the medication of the very young.

Neither of them likes the idea of their boy swallowing substances. Substances may poison him for life. There must be some other way to reach him. Since the incident in the bath, they have watched him day and night. He has promised, wearily, that he will not try holding his breath under water any more, but can they trust him?

Gertrude Cohen had been a friend of Frieda Haxby's, but that does not necessarily disqualify her from being the wisest woman in Europe.

220

She responds to their appeal, and comes round to see them, although she says she is now old and retired. She is like a caricature of what such a woman might be imagined to be. One of the most eminent of the 1930s refugee generation, she has written several books on child development, on child psychology and on child psychotherapy. Her accent is guttural, her eyes fierce, her hair grey and wiry and wild. She stares at them through spectacles tethered to her bosom by a gold pin and a gold chain. She had opened her career with a study of separation, loss and survivor guilt, and in later years had specialized in adolescent depression and – though they do not mention this – adolescent death. She had worked with the terminally ill child, with the suicidal child. She has been into the caverns of the mind. She has seen grief and torment. There she sits, drinking China tea with lemon, a wise woman who has been into the underworld and led others up to the light of day. They gaze at this old woman, whom normally they would I fear have regarded in benign and superior amusement. They gaze at her in a mixture of awe and hope. They throw themselves upon her mercy.

Gertrude Cohen listens patiently, a withered sybil. She has heard all the stories of all the world before. All parents think their child the brightest and the best of the sons of the morning. David D'Anger and Grace D'Anger are Everyman and Everywoman. They tell the strange tale of Frieda's wills, and here Gertrude Cohen shows them the favour of looking more than usually alert – for this is a variation, she concedes. Frieda had been an original. Gertrude Cohen looks at Frieda's daughter Grace with a glimmering of professional respect, as though acknowledging that Gogo had done well to stay alive and gain qualifications and get married and hold down a decent job. Gertrude Cohen accepts another Marie biscuit, which she nibbles with her evenly white false front teeth.

Then Gertrude Cohen plunges them into gloom by declaring that she is far too old to practise. It would be wrong for her even to set eyes on Benjamin. But she is sure they were right to refer the case to her. (They brighten, like good students praised in class.) She would like to recommend that they take Benjamin to see a colleague of hers, now practising at the Jameson Clinic. This colleague would be a most suitable person, in her view, to interview Benjamin. Of course, she cannot speak for her colleague, as her colleague is much in demand and may not be able to take on any more cases at the moment, and they will appreciate that even in the event of an acceptance the treatment may be long. (It will also, she implies, be costly, though she does not spell this out.)

David and Gogo nod, meekly, gratefully. They wait for the magic name of the designate, the successor. Gertrude Cohen inscribes it on a page of a notebook, which she tears out and hands to them. It reads

> Lily McNab
> 18 Dresden Road
> Maida Vale
> London NW8

Miss Cohen has also given them a phone number, and the address of the clinic, which is in St John's Wood.

David and Gogo stare at this scrap of paper with an unjustifiable degree of faith and expectation. The very name of Lily McNab reassures them. They thank Gertrude Cohen profusely, and ask if they can ring her a cab. Not at all, she says, quite tartly. She is quite capable of walking to the station. Can David drive her to the station, they ask. Certainly not, she says. Exercise is good for me, she says, and off she marches to Highbury and Islington, on the stick-like and slightly bandy legs that have walked her into Dachau and out of it, that have walked her into the night and out of the night and now will walk her unbowed into the vale.

David does not believe in private medicine. Gogo does not believe in psychoanalysis. But they both believe in Lily McNab. They have no choice.

Before we meet Lily McNab, let us return, briefly, to the Herz household by the river. We suspect all is not well with the Herzes. Jessica and Jon are fine, and we don't have to worry about them: let's say that they are lucky in their choice of genes on the Herz side, and although they have inherited the Palmer colouring they have also received a fair amount of natural optimism and gregariousness from their Golders Green gran. They have been only mildly affected by the expurgated news of Benjie's illness, for they had sensed he was growing out of them anyway. It's a pity, but that's how it is. They have not been told about their mother's condition, and they have not guessed that there is anything wrong with her, for they are accustomed to her short temper, her vagaries, her busyness, her exhaustions, her absences. They are enjoying the relaxed reign of a particularly amusing non-live-in paid minder called Chantal, who collects them from school, cooks their suppers, takes them to the movies. Chantal is a laugh. She lets them stay up all hours while she chats on the phone to her boyfriend in Beirut. We can forget about Jess and Jon. As Chantal herself, unmindful of their fate, so often does.

Rosemary demands a little more of our attention, for her situation is more complicated and more developed. Although she feels no physical effects from her medical condition, her mental unease increases, for it is clear that her suspicions have been correct. There *is* something wrong with her kidneys. Is it serious? The specialist will not commit himself, he hedges his bets. He annoys Rosemary by returning once more to the subject of her ancestry. He seems to wish to insist that she has inherited degenerate kidneys. As Rosemary's mother's kidneys have by now been eaten by the mackerel and the dogfish of the Atlantic, there is no way of inspecting them for clues, and Rosemary is obliged to state quite bluntly that she cannot inform Mr Saunders of the cause of the death of her father, Andrew Palmer. Indeed she cannot confirm that he is dead. And she has no intention of digging around in the family gene cemetery for the kidneys of her grandparents. The Palmers, she bluffs, had been military men, and a lot of them had died of malaria and dysentery and alcohol in India. Smart diseases, positional complaints. The Haxbys had gone in, less smartly, for strokes. He can make of that what he will. It is up to him to sort this out. That is what he is paid for.

Mr Saunders finds her a tricky and unsympathetic customer. He could almost prefer the days when patients were patients. He'd been paid nearly as much, in the good old pre-market days, and he'd been treated with a lot more respect. Respect is worth something. Respect is a positional good.

Rosemary wonders whether to confide her fears to Nathan, as most wives would. But she is not most wives. And Nathan is in unreceptive mood. His position in the firm is embattled, and he is abstracted. He and his team seem quite unable to come up with anything brilliant or new on the Health Marketing Plan. It is all cliché, all pastiche. He wonders whether it would be possible to break out completely, to think the unthinkable, to start marketing not by reassurance and innuendo but by full frontal fear? A Black Campaign? Skeletons, diseased organs, skulls, scare stories? Or what about extending the lottery to spare parts, kidney machines, fertility treatment, hip replacement? He tries this out on Rosemary, who is usually receptive to his darker jokes, but she seems curiously unamused. In vain does he insist that we all know quite well that it's done by lottery anyway, and has been, discreetly, for decades: she's been strongly in favour of the lottery money for the arts, so why should she disapprove of Bangladeshi kidneys by lottery? She makes it clear that she does not wish to continue this conversation. He can't see why she's being so squeamish, and is not in a position to guess that she is wondering if she has been correctly advised that no private insurance on earth would cover the cost of long-term renal dialysis. She has not yet had the courage to inspect the small print of her own policy. And no, she does not agree with Nathan that we will, by the end of the century, solve the health service crisis by introducing legalized euthanasia. Demographically, it's a cert, insists Nathan. It's got to come, so why not go for it now? But Rosemary won't listen, and neither will the punters or the electorate. Purgatorial flames are already big business, argues Nathan. The American way of death. Forest Lawns. Oh, shut up, says Rosemary pettishly, feeling her pulse flutter.

And Nathan himself can't find much consolation in these fantasies. Can he be losing faith in the market?

Nathan loves the lottery, he is a heavy investor in scratch cards and lottery tickets, he doesn't think much of the dull puritanism of Daniel and Patsy Palmer, of David and Gogo D'Anger, who disapprove of the whole damn thing. But he doesn't think his number is going to come up. So far he's only made twenty-five quid back, and he's spent hundreds. What he'd said to Daniel, about his pressing need for £20,000, had been less than the truth. He needs more than twenty, he needs a hundred grand. Nathan Herz is in trouble. He has forgotten to charge a client, for a bill of £120,000; a year has passed, and now he dare not send in the bill, he dare not own up to his colleagues. He's not been a criminal: just bloody stupid. He has been lying awake at nights with worry, listening to the lap of the Thames. He is getting stale. He is making mistakes. He hears whispering behind closed doors. Rosemary thinks she is for the axe, and Nathan is beginning to think he is for the high jump: from being a two-income, high-earning, upwardly mobile family, they are about to become a no-income, on the skids, debt-ridden casualty. Can this be so?

And Nathan is beginning to think he had never been a real achiever. (He is too subtle, too clever, he tries to console himself.) That summer he and Rosemary had been guests on a week's cruise of the Turkish Aegean, invited by the richest of the rich. Fabulous money, unimaginable money. Nathan had been unnerved, unsettled, and so had Rosemary, though she had tried not to show it. They had been invited by Greta and Bob Eagleburger, patrons of the arts, friends of Rosemary's. Greta painted on Sundays, Bob bought. Theirs was the yacht, theirs were the Braques and the Dufys and the Hockneys that hung on the walls of this floating emblem of good taste. For the Eagleburgers had an eye, they had bought well. Bob Eagleburger had an eye for Rosemary, but Nathan could tolerate that: it was the *grande luxe* that pissed him off. *Luxe, calme et volupté.* Servants, champagnes, diamonds. And a fucking Turner, a real Turner, in the Circe Lounge. Generous, were the Eagleburgers, to their little crew of sponging impressionable guests: generous, and mean with it, for they sometimes made them sing for their suppers. The rich are like that. They can make demands. The Herzes and the Spensers had sung to their tune. Even Harry Danzig, lord of unnumbered acres of barren Scottish moorland, had jumped at their bidding. Lord Danzig's demeanour was impenetrably civil and servile, as he accepted Eagleburger largesse, as he toiled round ruins and tinkled old dance tunes on the piano and entertained with indiscreet tales of royalty. The Spensers had been less docile: once Nathan had caught a subversive smirk of astonished disbelief on Sandy Spenser's face at the appearance of yet another far-fetched miracle of cuisine. But Sandy was a sculptor: he could afford to smirk. The Herzes could not. They had to toe the line.

Nathan Herz knew he would never be in the big league, but he had not realized, until he set sail with the Eagleburgers, that he was a pauper. The rich are different from us. And in the last decade, they have become more and more different. The rich have got richer and richer. Nathan knew he could not afford to keep that yacht afloat for half an hour, for five minutes. Yet until that invitation, until that cruise, he had thought himself to be doing well. His confidence had gone.

Nathan wanders round the perfume department of Selfridges on the Thursday evening that Benjie D'Anger is rescued from the bath. He is looking for a birthday present for his mother, but he is dreaming of the Turner in the Circe Lounge. It had been of a beauty to break the heart. An unfinished oil, of a rocky Mediterranean shore, with caves and a natural arch topped with a brush of trees: in the foreground, on the beach, strayed dimly painted figures, emerging from stone and sand and sea as though from the ancient forms of time itself. And across the blue and emerald water the faint sketched shapes of antique ghostly ships. Gold, amber, aquamarine.

His mother would not want a Turner, so that's all right. She is the easiest woman in the world to please, and Nathan has always enjoyed buying her gifts, for she is delighted by any small female treat – by soaps, salts, sprays, oils, lotions, perfumes. And Nathan loves the cosmetic halls of the large department stores. Selfridges has a grandeur, a dignity that the new out-of-town malls will never achieve. Its Corinthian pillars, its carved cherubs, its brass plaques, its bronzed marble, its Egyptian sphinx-lions, its pigeon-netting, its lofty lifts, its history. A woman here may be queen for a day, a man may be a prince, a benefactor. He enjoys chatting up the sales girls, as they lean forward with their glowing pellicles and sexy clinical uniforms, fluttering their long false lashes at him, dabbing or squirting fluids on to the back of his hairy wrist. He sniffs the scents of Arabia, the distillations of rose and cat and whale. He has the keenest sense of smell. He is a sensuous man. The perfumes glow gold and blue and amber and crystal in caskets and chalices, in ziggurats and phalluses, in pearls and cubes and apples of clear and cut and bevelled and frosted glass. Their names are the names of Temptation, Obsession, Possession, Frivolity. This is the apotheosis of presentation, the triumph of form over content. Minimal dabs of exorbitantly expensive cream and jelly reside in elfcups magnified by prisms, enclosed in deceitful phials, emprisoned in false-bottomed boxes. Who wants No Nonsense packaging? The package is the product.

Salesperson Tricia Chang insists that the Principessa Venier is the best of this season's new perfumes. She daubs, Nathan inhales. He cannot really get a proper whiff of the Principessa, he complains, for he is already too bespattered by the newest names from Chanel and Guerlain, from Cabochard and Klein, from Lancôme and Armani: would Tricia happen to have a spare clear inch or two of her own personal skin to test it upon? He likes the deep sea-green glass of the container, the long old-fashioned scent-bottle slim column of it, the under-watery pearl of the stopper. Could she oblige? Honey-skinned Tricia smiles, with her curved mahogany-red lips, and stares at him with widened, skilfully outlined, china-and-white-and-cornflower eyes: then she modestly lowers her lashes, opts for her left wrist, sprays it, extends it across the glittering counter to the gallant frog-like Nathan. Nathan takes her hand, smells it, breathes her in.

The Principessa Venier and Tricia Chang do not smell good to Nathan. They smell of dankness and drains. He inhales again. Has some sinister chemical reaction taken place? The Principessa smells of death in Venice. Nathan looks up sharply, at Tricia's waxy cherished blandly smiling face: she is not mocking him, she has not turned into a deathmask, she has not begun to decay before his eyes. But this, this is Belle's little dead hand he is holding in his. He squeezes it, and breathes again, sorrowfully, the putrid odour of river water. Tricia is now pulling her hand back again, aware that the quality of his grip has changed from flirtation to desperation. This attractive, ugly middle-aged man is in crisis, she can tell, and he relinquishes her member with a sigh of profound sadness, and shakes his head. No, he cannot say he likes the Principessa Venier. Nor would his mother like it. It is too dark for her. He wants something lighter – something more ? – he searches for a word. More floral? suggests Tricia, sympathetically. She is used to dealing with incompetent, wordless men. Yes, more floral, agrees Nathan meekly. The spirit has gone out of him, the fun of choice has abandoned him. He lets Tricia choose for him. She selects a short list of three, but cannot recapture his interest. He allows her to sell him a small flagon of Vie en Rose, which reminds him of those overpowering synthetic pink roses in Daniel's garden at the Old Farm; Tricia assures him that it is very popular with the more traditional older lady. Tricia Chang wraps it in shiny gift wrapping, and seals it, and ribbons it, and teases its ribbon into butterfly bows and corkscrew spirals, and encloses it in a gift baglet. She does her very best with the packaging. She feels she has failed this mystery man, this man of moods. When he has gone, she covertly sniffs at her rejected hand. She cannot see that it smells bad. She likes the Principessa. But perfume is a tricky, a personal affair. It is, as she has been told on a course she once attended, as much of an art as science.

Nathan boards a cab and on his way home he broods once more on money. He is rich enough to buy his mother a birthday present fit for a duchess, but he is not rich enough to be able to buy his way out of trouble. The lights of Oxford Street glitter garishly. Jingle bells, Christmas sells. The taxi, avoiding roadworks, makes for Blackfriars Bridge. On impulse (is that the name of a perfume?) Nathan asks the cab to stop on the far side, on the Surrey bank. He descends, and then he descends. He makes his way down steps to the water's edge. He thinks of Belle.

He walks under the bridge, past a panorama of painted tiles taken from prints of old designs of Blackfriars. He is not thinking of old London. He is thinking of Roberto Calvi, God's banker, who had hanged himself by a yard of nylon rope from a pile of scaffolding beneath the north side of this bridge in 1982. Or was he murdered by the Pope's henchmen, by members of a Masonic Lodge? Calvi was carrying a crudely forged passport, and his pockets had been stuffed with foreign banknotes and ten pounds of stones lifted from the grounds of the City of London School which Jonathan Herz will soon attend. A good old-fashioned revenge tragedy, here by the water's edge, so near the stones of the Rose, so near the thatch of the Globe. *Mutatis mutandis.* There had been two inquests.

The arches of the bridge curve and soar, the traffic above thunders and rumbles. Road-works are in progress, somewhere up there – when are they not? – and strange lumps of cladding and loose heavy dirty swathes of industrial-weight polythene protrude and dangle and flap in the night air. Grey and black, black and grey, a fine nocturne. They have cleaned this stretch of riverside walk, have tamed and ur-banized it, but nevertheless Nathan notes piles of greywhite birdshit and feathery filth, and a heap of red rags abandoned by a nesting beggar. A browning banana skin lies on top of the red rags. The little heap is eloquent – a still life, a dead life. The brave red cries out.

Nathan strides out eastwards along the reclaimed Jubilee pathway, watching the lights dimple and glimmer on the tide. A police boat cruises purposefully downstream, and a little commercial launch ad-vertising advertising buzzes towards him from Southwark. *The Bow-belle, The Marchioness.* Belle drowned, Frieda Haxby drowned, Robert Maxwell drowned, and Calvi hanged himself where he could dangle in the water.

Nathan Herz, with his glossy oblong gold-corded gift bag and his sober briefcase, stares up at the high brick fortress wall of the power station and at the moon lying drunkenly on her back in the Novem-ber sky. Swags of cloud are lit silver-blue by the moon's aura. Lottery money will transform this power station into an art gallery, but as yet there are few signs of development. Barbed-wire, weeds, demolition, desolation, solitude.

A flight of steps draws him down to the water's edge. He stands on the margin. The tide is rising. His executive shoes gleam black against the oily black. He listens to the sucking and the sighing. The wash of a midstream wake ripples towards him, but he does not step back from it. It laps upwards, splashes his shoes: it subsides and withdraws. He takes one step down towards it, tempting the next wave, but it does not rise again.

The water sighs, and Nathan sighs, and a seagull cries. Roberto Calvi had been strung up for one and a half thousand million dollars, and brought down the Banco Ambrosiano of Milan. Robert Maxwell had gone under dragging the pensions of thousands in a string of silver bubbles after him. Young Nick Leeson brought down Barings Bank for seven point seven seven seven billions of yen. Nathan Herz is not in their league. He is a small trader. A man of the past, not a man of the future. Or so he thinks, on this sad night.

Now we may return to Lily McNab. You remember the name of Lily McNab, child psychotherapist? We have not yet been introduced. We have several possibilities with Ms McNab. Is she a scholarly grey-haired owl-spectacled Scot with an Edinburgh accent? An imported American from New York? A Belsize Park matron who walks regularly upon the Heath with a small dog? A lipsticked lesbian from Leeds? She could be any of these characters. We had better take care, in our choice of attributes for Ms McNab, for it is a fact that there are fewer than 350 child psychotherapists in the whole of the United Kingdom, and we do not wish to be sued for libel if Lily McNab should fail. (It is a curious fact that the United Kingdom, which indulges in delightful hot-flushed orgies of re-crimination and sentimentality whenever a child is conspicuously abused, injured or foully murdered, has refused to finance the long, rigorous and expensive trainings of these 350 – but that is by the way.)

All that we know of Lily McNab, until we are ushered into her presence, is that by some means she has raised the money for this training, and that she must be younger than Gertrude Cohen, who recommended her. But as Gertrude Cohen is in her eighties, that leaves space for speculation. Lily McNab may be in her sixties. Whoever she is, she has what might be considered a daunting assignment in taking on the D'Angers and their son. But she has been trained, we may assume, not to be daunted.

We stand on her doorstep in Dresden Road, and locate her doorbell. Already she begins to materialize, for her terraced house is neat, white-painted and well-maintained, and it has windowboxes with flowering plants in them on the upper floors. It appears that she also has lodgers or partners, for there are other names on other bells. This is an expensive district, and smarter than the area where the D'Angers live. Lily McNab cannot be poor. Will she have a receptionist? Will she open the door herself?

Gogo and David stand and wait. They have come together to confront their saviour. United they stand.

Yes, this is Lily McNab who ushers them in. She is tall, bespectacled, large-featured, in her forties, wearing a rust-coloured trouser suit and a cream silk roll-necked sweater. She also wears lipstick. And she is black.

Well, perhaps not *black* black. More a lightish brown.

David D'Anger hopes that he has not done unto her what has so often been done unto him. But he cannot be sure that he has not.

It will emerge, in the next weeks, that the parents of Lily McNab were Indian Jews from Calcutta. She herself was born in Calcutta but has been educated in Scotland. Her birthname was Gubbay. She is married to a barrister called Jeremy McNab. She has an indefinably hybrid accent when she speaks, and her voice is low and husky.

Is this heritage of any relevance to her profession, to our story, to the fate of Benjamin D'Anger? Has Gertrude Cohen, as David instantly suspects, deliberately matched Benjamin with Mrs McNab? And if so, why? And was it wisely done?

Only time will tell. As Lily McNab explains, as the D'Angers already know, there is no miracle cure. If Benjamin is willing to come to see her – and there will be resistance, it is normal for there to be resistance – then she will see him.

The D'Angers drive back to Highbury with hope in their hearts. They have taken action. Surely love and money can save Benjamin.

★

Will Paine has found himself a job. He has flown east from Jamaica to Trinidad, to cover his tracks, and has been taken on as a cleaner by an American-owned hotel. He has struck lucky. Nobody seems to want to fuss too much about his papers. He has changed his name, and now calls himself Robert. He answers to his new name smartly, and works hard. He sleeps in a room the size of a broom cupboard, and hides Frieda's money in a sock in his travelling bag. He daren't try to bank it. He's afraid of banks, as his mother was before him. He's changed some of Frieda's money into dollars, and he's spent some of it on airtickets, but quite a lot of it is still in the very same pounds sterling that had leaped from the cash stations of Exmoor. What if the notes are marked?

Will Paine has found friends to hang out with, to smoke a joint with. One of them is a bellboy and wears a red uniform with gold braid and his name on a metal badge. His name is Marvin. Will also knows Marvin's girl, Glory, who works as a masseuse and studied alternative medicine at nightschool. These are nice friends for Will Paine. Marvin is political and talks about Black Power and whatever happened to it and why the Caribbean isn't doing as well as it should. Glory is more into New Age mysticism and thinks that all will be well. Will Paine is interested in what both of them have to say. Sometimes he too speaks. He does not tell them about Frieda Haxby, for she is his secret, but he tries to describe David D'Anger from Guyana and Highbury, David D'Anger, parliamentary candidate for a sprawling constituency in West Yorkshire where Will had once worked in a pasta factory. He attempts, not unsuccessfully, to convey the concept of the Veil of Ignorance. They discuss their own initial positions and whether they would have altered them if they could. They agree that the institutions of society favour certain starting places over others, and that these advantages provoke especially deep inequalities. They affect one's initial chances in life, and all subsequent chances. Marvin and Glory believe they have been disadvantaged, and are puzzled by Will Paine's view that he himself has had a good deal of good luck. They are even more puzzled by Will's assertion that, according to David D'Anger, none would urge that special privileges should be given to those exactly six feet tall or born on a sunny day, or special disadvantages imposed according to the colour of one's skin or the texture of one's hair. As far as they can see, such preferences are being urged, not to say practised, all around them every day.

David D'Anger, they agree, must live in a rum world. He has clearly had far more advantages than any of them and they have turned his brain. He has had too much luck and it will do him no good in the long run. They all agree that some of the guests at the hotel where Marvin and Will work do not seem to have earned their leisure and their wealth by any recognizable concept of merit or desert. Justice as fairness hardly shines out in the Mayfair Hotel. Some of the women – well, it's hard to imagine what they can have done to get themselves where they are. Can they have been very very good in their past lives? Surely that's not what the Buddhists mean – that if you're very very saintly and live on brown rice with a begging bowl dressed in orange you'll be reincarnated as a waddling fat-arse with a loud mouth and fuchsia earrings?

Glory says they are thinking on the wrong plane and that she doesn't envy these poor ladies at all. She wouldn't at all like to be fat like that. They can't help it, says Glory. They don't like being fat any more than you would like it, she tells Will and Marvin.

Marvin diplomatically changes the subject and says he likes the Japanese. The Japanese, unlike some, are always very civil to him. People make fun of them, says Marvin, but they are a very polite people. And they tip well.

Benjamin will be a long time mending, and Frieda's testaments will be long in the proving. It had not occurred to Frieda or her lawyers that her grandson might not long outlive her, might choose to drown himself in his bath during the period of probate. Better lawyers than Goltho & Goltho might have been forgiven for overlooking such a possibility. Had Benjamin died on that November night, what would have happened to Frieda's money? It does not bear thinking about. He will live to inherit. Lily McNab will guide him back to life. There is hope for Benjamin. He has deep problems, deep delusions, but he can be brought to the surface. Benjamin D'Anger manages a sort of ghostly smile for Saul Sinnamary, who arrives from Singapore, true to his word, bearing a bright book of the Birds of South America, of coloured plates of great expense and beauty. Saul sits by Benjie and turns the pages. They come to the picture of the whip-poor-will, the goatsucker, a night bird related to the European nightjar with (Saul reads), 'large eyes and cryptic plumage'. That's us, man, says Saul to Benjie. Large eyes and cryptic plumage. And listen – Saul reads from the accompanying text, a quotation from an eighteenth-century traveller from Yorkshire, who had defended the poor humble bird from its dark, its criminal reputation. Saul reads, Benjie listens. Saul reads very well: he has had a lot of practice.

'The prettily mottled plumage of the goatsucker, like that of the owl, wants the lustre which is observed in the feathers of the birds of the day. This makes him a lover of the pale moon's nightly beams . . . His cry is so remarkable, that having once heard it, you will never forget it. When night reigns over the immeasurable wilds, you will hear this poor bird lamenting like one in deep distress. A stranger would say it was the departing voice of a midnight murdered victim, or the last wailing of Niobe for her children . . . Suppose yourself in hopeless sorrow, begin with a loud high note, and pronounce "ha, ha, ha, ha, ha, ha, ha", each note lower and lower, till the last is scarcely heard, pausing for a moment or two betwixt every note, and you will have some idea of the moaning of the largest goatsucker in Demerara. Four other species articulate their words distinctly, crying "Who are you, who who who are you" or "Work away, work work work away" or "Willy come-go, Willy Willy Willy come-up" or "Whip-poor-will, Whip-poor-will, Whip-poor-will".' Saul reproduces these cries with haunting, heart-breaking melancholy, and concludes, in Charles Waterton's words, 'You will never persuade the negro to destroy these birds, or get the Indians to let his arrows fly at them. They are birds of omen and reverential dread. They are the receptacles for departed souls. They haunt the cruel and the hard-hearted master. Listen again! Listen! "Ha ha ha ha ha ha ha . . ."'

Saul's fine rendering of the cry of the nightjar-goatsucker is so moving that he begins to cry, for he is an emotional chap, easily distressed; Benjamin too begins to sob, and they sit and hug and weep. Saul wonders if he has gone too far, but he believes in tears, he believes in emotion, he thinks the Guyanese half of Benjie has been repressed, it will do him good to weep and wail. As he sits there, hugging Benjie D'Anger, he decides he could write some bird-poems, try some bird-poem-readings. If they affect a larger audience as they have affected this boy, he will be on to a good thing.

When Benjie has sniffed and blown his nose, he looks a lot more cheerful, and more alert. He wants to know who wrote the bit about the bird, and Saul looks up the name and dates of Yorkshire squire Charles Waterton, and promises to investigate further. He wants to know if Saul really knows about birds, and Saul is cornered into modesty. For all the hundreds of species he had ticked off on his checklist, he admits he can only recognize, unaided, a dozen or so. 'Poets are cheats, Benjie,' he says. 'You remember that. They get drunk on words. They like words and sounds. Some of them use their eyes, but a lot of them only use their ears. Have you heard of Sylvia Plath?'

Benjie nods. (Odd, thinks Saul, how all conversation with Benjie seems to plunge of its own accord towards suicide and death, but he ploughs on.)

'Sylvia Plath,' says Saul Sinnamary, 'was a great poet. But she couldn't tell a rook from a jackdaw.'

'How do you know?' asks Benjie.

'Because she said so.'

Saul has struck a lucky subject. He confesses that he himself, like Plath, is bad at British birds, all of which look much the same to him, and Benjie is able to recite Frieda's little rhyme. Saul is delighted with it. He repeats it, writes it down. He can do something with it, he thinks.

The solitary egret walks through the salt marsh.

Benjamin studies the plates of the book which Saul Sinnamary has entrusted to him, and discovers from a footnote that Charles Waterton had most improbably been married to the granddaughter of an Arawak princess from Guyana. David D'Anger, also true to his word, remembers to track down the reference by Andrew Salkey to Wilson Harris's lecture in Georgetown in 1970, and he finds it: Salkey, studying the audience at this event, noted of Guyana's once and future Premier and long-time Leader of the Opposition: 'Dr Cheddi Jagan interested me most. For a man who has had to deal, variously, with the wily, rhetoric-laden representatives of British Imperialism and with the cryptic vocabulary of the infiltrating priests of the State Department and the CIA, and also with the Minotaur of Guyanese Party politics with their gelignite of opposing races, a man, in other words, who should know his metaphysics from his materialism, if only because he has had to distinguish between the contrasting mysticisms of Hinduism and Mohammedanism, between the language of Marx and the message of the American millennium, and between the call of Fidel and the killing signals of Macmillan and Sandys, poor Cheddi seemed more bewildered, dislocated and beaten, during Wilson's lecture and afterwards than at any time in his long political Gethsemane!'

Saul had been right. There was a sentence. There was Guyana. Poetry and politics. But what had Guyana in the 1970s or the 1990s to do with the expatriate D'Angers? Cheddi Jagan has returned to Freedom House, but Ashcombe, not Eagle Valley, is the D'Anger problem now.

And what of radon-reeking Ashcombe, what of the secrets of the Haxbys?

Gogo has no interest in them. Her world has narrowed to the small round of Benjamin's convalescence. She wakes to worry, she falls asleep to worry. For David too the world has narrowed. The condition-of-England, the condition-of-Guyana, and the conditions of post-colonial cultures worry him yet, but they worry him less than the condition of poor Benjamin. David's dream of himself as a small stick figure vainly dragging at a vast and heavy carpet has given way to a new vision: he sees the scales of blind and bloody justice held aloft, and in one round burnished dish stand all the heavy peoples, in the other a thin boy. They balance, and the brass bowls tremble. Would he sacrifice the peoples of the world for that child, the Inquisitor asks, the Devil tempts. It is no question, but the vision will not go away. Let us save the one before we try to save the many, a spirit whispers. It is no question, answers David D'Anger to the spirit. But his answer rings thin. What has he been missing, what have his statistics left out?

Cate Crowe has no such preoccupations. To her the whole Ashcombe débâcle has been an accursed nuisance. An entertaining nuisance, at times, but nevertheless a nuisance. She wants a signature on a contract, she wants a percentage. There is a possibility of serious money here. The film rights of *Queen Christina* wander in some kind of limbo, and other contracts and tax forms need urgent attention too. Can it be right that a sick sub-teenage boy is to answer for all these decisions? Nobody seems to know who is responsible for what. And those memoirs that Frieda Haxby was said to be writing – where are they? The obituaries had hinted at interesting liaisons, at unlikely friendships. Had Frieda written anything saleable before she plunged to her watery grave? Is there a typescript at Ashcombe, or in a safe-deposit in Exeter?

Cate Crowe nags, phones, faxes. The Palmer family prevaricate. Yet the Palmer family know that somebody should go to Ashcombe soon, to sort out the papers, to rescue objects of value. An agent has been put in charge of sealing doors and windows against the winter, but one cannot trust a man from Taunton with a literary estate.

Which of them shall we send? Whose turn is it now?

As Rosemary observed in our opening pages, it's one hell of a long way, and since she said that, the weather has been getting worse, the nights longer, and the distance no shorter, although there is a new by-pass round one of the villages on the A39. Rosemary refuses to go: she's done her turn. Daniel is still too busy with his river case. Gogo can't leave Benjie. Patsy doesn't see why she should, and, although one of nature's meddlers, she dares not meddle in this. It is agreed that Nathan, even if he were willing, could not cope with the Englishness of Exmoor. And David D'Anger, who has most reason to go, knows that he cannot. Innocent or guilty, he is no longer trusted by the Palmer clan, and a visit to Ashcombe, even if he could spare the time, would confirm his collusion with Frieda, would exclude him for ever from grace. (If he is not already so excluded. Daniel has not spoken to him since the reading of the wills.)

Whom does that leave?

The finger begins to point at Emily. She can easily be reclaimed once more from Florence. She has passed her driving test and is young enough to enjoy driving. She has already demonstrated herself to be an unusually mature and independent young woman. She can be bribed and controlled. She has a lot more sense than Simon, and anyway Simon can't drive. She can take a friend for company if she wants – she can take her brother Simon for company if she wants – but it is Emily that shall be dispatched. She has always taken a balanced and friendly view of Grandma Frieda. She can go and sort it all out.

Emily accepts the suggestion without protest. Once again she is flattered by the faith which others have in her, though she wonders in passing if she has been cast too readily for life as a responsible adult. She says she'd be happy to go alone. She does not say that she would hate to go with Simon, cannot think of a worse companion than Simon.

Everyone is delighted with her. She is flown home Business Class, and sips champagne and nibbles canapés over the Alps. She is becoming a seasoned traveller.

Daniel and Patsy press upon her money, keys, advice, a mobile telephone. She must spend the night in comfort in the best hotel the coast can offer, and ring them – they give her multiple, variant numbers, for they will do anything but go there themselves – if she has any queries. She must bring away any portable valuables, and Frieda's computer. On the way back, she should report to the estate agent at Taunton, who has offered to provide some kind of surveillance of the property. She must not walk along the coast path. And, says Daniel repeatedly, with unusual paternal solicitude, she must *not* stay in the house too long, getting cold and damp and breathing in the mildew. She must wrap up warm.

Emily is pleased and amused by all this attention. She is impressed that she is being offered Daniel's BMW instead of Patsy's muddy Datsun.

On the night of her departure she rings Benjie, because she knows that Benjie knows some of Frieda's secrets. Benjie, she thinks, sounds dreadful, his voice mean, flat and pinched, but he manages to say that there is some stuff in the butler's pantry, some wooden animals in a shoe box and some old fossils. They are for him. He wants them. She'd better bring them now or they'll get chucked out, he says.

He does not say that everything is for him, although she knows he knows it.

She is surprised by his request. Has he reverted to some kind of playground infancy, that he keeps requesting from her children's games? Is this part of his breakdown? And she is surprised when, as they say goodbye, he mutters, 'I say, Em, have you ever been down Wookey Hole?'

She denies all knowledge of Wookey Hole and the Cheddar Caves, but in the morning checks her map and sees that they are on her route. On the way back, perhaps?

HINDSPRING

Emily sets off early, the keys to Ashcombe dangling importantly from the car key-ring, and drives westwards. It is a glorious day, one of those brilliant winter days when the sun shines from an azure lightly streaked with small white high faraway tendrils of cirrus cloud. It is cold at first, but she fancies it grows milder and warmer, or is that the car's excellent heating system, which purrs so comfortably around her feet and knees? She feels a powerful disembodiment at the wheel of her father's car, as she crosses the counties. Hitch-hikers solicit her, bearing placards requesting the M5, Plymouth, Exeter, but she ignores them, cherishing her solitude, listening to the radio, flicking channels imperiously from Mozart to Manilow, from Kiss to Classic, from disc jockey and Car Marts to discussions of the clitoral orgasm. The world is hers, and this is England. She eats sandwiches from a plastic box guiltily packed by Patsy, and drops crumbs upon her navy sweatshirt. She is young, she is weightless. She has no cares. She has an admirer, in the ancient city of Florence, who says he adores her, but she is free of heart. She sometimes allows him intimate caresses, but not very often. He is not the one. Technically, she is a virgin, although she is well acquainted with the clitoral orgasm, which she had discovered many years ago with the active participation of Sally Partington. She has liked Florence, and her course in Art History, and her language classes, and her new friends, and the striped buildings. But she lives in an interlude. All things are yet possible to her. She drives on, at eighty miles an hour, to meet them, through the levels, past the headlands, past the glittering high horizon of the sea.

The last stretch of coast road is of spectacular beauty. The sky above is still dazzling, but over the Bristol Channel below her, to her right, lies a fleece of white cloud, sucked up from the sun from who knows where, from the moorland, from the water. It rolls in innocent bundles, sparkling with light, and she flies above it, marvelling. To her left is the browned moorland, pricked yellow here and there with gorse, coloured a paler brown with the dried fawn cusps and bells of the heather, glowing with the bronze of bracken: single thorn trees with a haze of red berries lean here and there from the prevailing wind. To her right is this sea above the sea, this strange and soft illusion. She knows that Wales lies out there across the channel, but although visibility seems infinite, she cannot see it. She feels she has created the world afresh. No one has ever seen this world before.

The road unwinds before her and it glitters blue like water, blue like a thin high flowing river, as the tarmac reflects the sky. High carved copper hedges enclose her for a while and sheep graze unmoved by the roadside. A cluster of ponies lift heads to watch her. Will she see deer on the hillside?

She slows, as she begins to look for the turning, for the track where Will Paine had climbed down from the abattoir lorry. They had warned her, her parents, about the steepness of the descent; she goes into bottom gear, which is so severe that the car hardly moves at all. So this was where Grandma Frieda had hidden herself! She crawls slowly, bumping over boulders, avoiding ruts. Either she must get back up in the daylight, or she must spend the night here. Has she the courage to spend the night in a haunted house? Ought she to put herself to such a test?

The door is reluctant to open, for the wood is swollen, but the key has turned easily, and she yanks and yanks until it gives way. The house is less cold than she had expected, and she discovers some overnight off-peak storage heaters that have been left on permanently. So electricity is still connected. She explores the ground floor, opening the door of the well-stacked freezer, admiring the row of gumboots, touching the skull, the dried orange, the packs of playing cards portraying the defunct monarchy of France. She finds the butler's pantry and the wooden animals and the jewel cases. There are large, thin-legged, small-bodied spiders everywhere: she does not much care for them, though she accepts their claims of residence. And when she opens one of the sidedoors on to the courtyard, she finds a toad sitting patiently upon the doorstep, as though waiting to enter. It is one of the strangest sights she has ever seen. It looks up at her, she would swear with a question. Its head on one side, it leans inquisitively towards her: it sits its ground.

'Hello,' she says, from some profound instinct of politeness. The toad does not answer, but it takes a small hop forwards. She is charmed by this. 'Come in, come in,' she says to the intelligent beast, and it hops in and on to the stone-flagged corridor. Does it know where it is going? Shall she leave the door open in case it wishes to leave? What are her social obligations to this visitor?

The toad hops along the corridor with gainly, neat, jointed propulsion. It is making for a cellar door, which stands ajar. It turns to look at her, before it disappears around the corner.

Emily is enchanted by this meeting. She is on friendly terms with the animal kingdom, and toads and newts and frogs and water-creatures have always given her delight. Many hours of her childhood she had spent gazing into the fishpond at the Old Farm, or with a jam jar by the chalky water-crowfoot-blossoming brook, which runs through the water meadows. She knows the toad is a friend. Was it also a friend of Frieda's?

Carefully she makes her way up the rickety stairway, to search the upper floors: how glad she is that Simon is not with her! For Simon is as afraid of beasts as she is delighted by them. He holds frogs, toads and snakes in especial horror. She knows he has reptile nightmares. Drug dreams are worse than delirium tremens, she has heard, but why in-criminate, why demonize such sweet and mild-mannered fellow beings? Poor Simon, she fears he is lost.

She gazes from the upper floor, over the water. The blanket of clouds has lifted now, and she can see the distant shore. The light is beginning to fade, though it is noticeably brighter here in the west than it would have been at Stonehenge, at Old Sarum. She must be sensible, she must make a quick reconnaissance up here, then get the big car back up the drive and check in at her Country House Hotel with special Four Course Dinner before nightfall. 'Pamper yourself,' the hotel's advertisement had urged her, and she looks forward to a night's pampering. She can come back in the morning, she tells herself. She pushes open Frieda's bedroom door.

Emily Palmer never checks into the Blackmoor Court Hotel. She does not answer her mobile telephone. Has she plunged from the cliff, or fallen down the staircase? Has she driven the car into a ditch, or been murdered by a hitch-hiker?

No, she is sitting in one of the upstairs rooms at Ashcombe. It is late at night and her lofty light shines across the waters from the uncurtained windows. She is transfixed. She is mesmerized by Frieda Haxby's computer and its arcane messages.

She had begun to play with it in the afternoon, and now she cannot stop, although the sky is dark and the North Star shines above her. She has found herself coffee in a jar, and everlasting milk in a waxy cardboard carton, and a tin of baked beans, and sweet soft musty biscuits in a plastic box. She has plugged in a small fan heater which blows hot air on to her booted ankles. She has draped an old plaid blanket round her shoulders. She has poured herself a small glass of Madeira.

Frieda's secrets had been easy to unravel, for Frieda had written herself many messages. The walls of the computer room are covered in messages, attached with drawing pins and tape. Some are in red felt pen – lines of verse, shopping lists. There are lists of operational instructions for the computer – passwords, key words, names of files and documents. There are one or two newspaper cuttings pinned up, over which Emily had paused briefly – an article from *Nature* about the possibility of life breeding without photosynthesis from basalt in deep water, an obituary of the actor Patrick Fordham, which Frieda had decorated with exclamation marks. There is a translated Icelandic rune, which reads

> *Wealth is the source of discord among kinsmen*
> *And the fire of the sea*
> *And the path of the grave-fish*

There is a photograph of Benjamin as a baby, and postcards showing a view of Stockholm, a painting of a death ship with black sails, Napoleon on a beach in a red sunset, a harbour at Tenerife.

Emily had not spent much time on these leavings and jottings, for she knew the important material would be in the computer.

Emily had been surprised to find that Frieda Haxby was on E-Mail. And her family had not even known she was on the telephone. Emily had accessed her E-Mail correspondence without much difficulty, for Frieda's instructions to herself had been easy to follow. For the month before her death, Frieda had been communicating with scholars in Cambridge, in Viborg, in Bellagio, in Uppsala, in Mannheim, in Sofia. In the bin Emily found letters about the Swansberg Stone, about Descartes, about Grotius, about Beowulf. Frieda had been wired, formidably wired. Her mind like a lighthouse, her mind like a beacon.

And Emily has found Frieda's memoirs. She has found various accounts of Frieda's childhood, some of them contradictory, and now she is searching for the story of her Great Aunt Everhilda's death. Emily Palmer's hair glints red-gold in the lamplight. Wrapped in her plaid rug, she is an Iron Age maiden, safe in her hillfort: a Highland lass, the last of her race. She is plugged in, across the millennia.

Frieda writes:

'Now Will Paine has finally been dislodged, I'm going to have one more attempt at writing about Hilda's death. And if I can't do it this time, I give up, and I'll go back to playing patience. Or maybe I'll go back to town, for the winter. Why not, after all? I don't *have* to stay here, do I?

'I can't remember how long ago it was that I realized that Hilda had forced me and Andrew together. She need never have introduced us. But she threw us together. Night after night, in the black-out, when she was on night-shift. I thought I was outwitting her by making up to him, but she was outwitting me. She'd plotted it all. She wanted me to incriminate myself. Remember, I was only sixteen. And the war made people sexually voracious. We didn't want to die before we'd done It. I remember talking about it endlessly at school. And who else was I going to do it with but Andrew? I thought I was stealing him from her, but really she procured me for him. Did she know what she was doing? I don't know. But that's what happened. Andrew seduced me, one night in that room in her digs in Wolverton, in her bed. Or I seduced him. I wanted to prove something. I wanted to prove I wasn't just the clever one. I was sick of being the clever dull one. And I wanted It. I suppose I must have wanted Andrew, though I can't remember what it felt like to want him. Because then I wanted to get rid of him. But by then I was married.

'And to think that for all those years Andrew and Hilda were carrying on behind my back, and that I suspected nothing. Nothing. I swear to God that until those last weeks I had no idea that they ever saw one another, except under my roof. I must have been pig stupid. I must have been bat blind, worm blind. I can't tell you how I hate, even now, at my age, to admit how much I hated to look ridiculous. I was so proud. And they had made such a fool of me. They had deceived me, and I'd been too busy, too indifferent, too stupid to notice. When other people tell you stories like this you don't believe them. And maybe it's not true that they were carrying on all that time. Maybe it was an on-and-off affair. All those years of on-and-off.

'And to think that I thought my sexual life was over. Because that's the other strange thing. While Hilda was alive, I never even thought of being unfaithful to Andrew, although he was such a disappointment, and I was so frustrated. Because, let's face it, he was no good in bed at all, although he wanted it. I had to do all the work. Why did I persist, through three children? Pride, again. I had to prove I could. Those three children of mine are all his, in case anyone ever questions it. Well, you can tell they are from looking at them. And Hilda's baby was his too, if looks are anything to go by. So despite all he must have had a high sperm count. People did, in those days. Even queers like Andrew.

'Hilda's death released me, and I knew it had the moment I saw her. It freed me from her, it freed me from Andrew. So I should be grateful to her for doing herself in. Maybe I am. It pulled the veil from my eyes. Was that what she intended? No, I don't think so. Or not in that sense, anyway. She wanted to hurt me. She wanted to blind me. But my eyes adjusted, and here I am, and she is more than thirty years dead.

'I said I'd try to write about her death, and so I will. I don't know if I can put it in my memoir.

'When Andrew and I were married and living in Romley, when I was slogging my guts out teaching and lecturing and working on Matriarchy and the Iron Works, and getting myself pregnant, and falling asleep upright like a workhorse at the bus stop, Hilda used to come and see us from time to time. The pretence was that we were friends again, but we knew we didn't trust one another an inch. And I used to put on a good front with Andrew, making him put his best foot forward, boasting about his prospects, hiding his drinking, laughing off his drinking. Anyway, I didn't give a damn about his drinking. Hilda was drifting from job to job, she didn't seem to stick at anything. She was jealous of my success, or so I imagined. At last I'd got the upper hand, I'd got a career and a man and three children. I wasn't going to show her that I hated it, that I was empty with dissatisfaction. I'm amazed now I had the energy to feel empty. You'd have thought I wouldn't have had time. But I knew I'd been cheated. I'd cheated myself.

'I used to nag at her for not going to see Ma. I tried to make out that she'd nothing better to do than to go and see Ma. No wonder she hated me. But then she'd always hated me. Since the day I was born.

'I used to wonder why she'd never got married. She, the pretty one. With her which-twin-is-the-Toni permanent waves.

'Then she went off to Rotterdam, to work for a shipping company. Or that's what she said. She'd had such a stupid succession of jobs, like so many women after the war. Genteel jobs, ladies' jobs, though we were no ladies. Tea-shops, photographer's receptionist, the lighting department at Selfridges, answering the telephone at the Halifax Building Society. How could she have gone back into all that, when she'd had some kind of proper job at Bletchley Park? Not that I ever found out what she did there. Official Secrets, she wouldn't say. But they must have trained her to do something, after she was called up. Maybe that's how it was, in those days. The men came back from the war and the women were put out of work. Well, I of all people know that's how it was, because that's what I was working on at the time with my LSE grant, but you don't expect your own sister to behave like a statistic. I thought she was smarter than that.

'So off she went, out of sight, out of mind. That must have been just after I'd had Rosemary. There was still rationing, I think. Fair deals for all. Sweet coupons. It was a mistake, having three children. It was a mistake having any. I can't think why I did. I never really meant to. They just happened. I wouldn't have called myself the maternal type. In fact I know I wasn't. They were a problem. Think what I might have been, might have done, if I hadn't been burdened. It's a mystery. No use my complaining about Hilda not knowing what she was doing when I didn't know what I was doing myself. I suppose if I hadn't had them I'd always have wondered what it would have been like if I had. But I never thought motherhood was all it was cracked up to be. Daniel was a hideous baby. Dark red and blue. I remember looking at him and thinking, "What *is* that?" Grace wasn't much better. Rosemary was the only reasonably pretty one, and look what she turned into.'

(Emily, at this point in the narrative, begins to feel severe restlessness. Will Grandma Frieda never get to the point? Emily wants the lurid death scene, not this dreary and brutal self-questioning. It's slightly depressing, to find that your grandmother wishes your father had never been born. And there's no way of knowing, with this machine, when the death will come, if ever. There may be some means of discovering how long MEM9 is, as a document, but Emily isn't sufficiently familiar with the programme. A PC isn't like a book, when you can tell if the end is nigh from the number of pages. There could be millions more megabytes to go, before Great Aunt Hilda snuffs it. Her fate may be trapped in there, somewhere. Or perhaps Frieda drowned before she reached the big scene? Frieda doesn't seem to have gone in for dating her documents. And anyway, we don't have a death date. For Frieda, or for Hilda.

Emily scrolls rapidly forward, through seamless yards of glowing electronic pale-green characters. Rotterdam, bomb damage, reconstruction, Oxford University Press, Dry Bendish, the North Sea, Uppsala, Sweden, Grotius, Descartes, Hilda, Hilda, Andrew, Hilda, pregnancy, National Health Service, Romley, telegram, Hackney, SOS.

Emily slows down, arrests the lives flowing soundlessly away under her middle mouse finger.)

'She'd sealed the doors and the windows, towels under the doors, sticky tape on the windows. That's how people did it in those days, when domestic gas was still lethal. All you had to do was put your head in the oven and make sure there wasn't too much leakage. It was far and away the most popular method. And that's what she'd done, except she'd put two heads in the oven, instead of one. In fact to be brutal, she'd shoved the baby *right in* the oven. It was a little girl, about a year old, with faintish-red hair, wrapped up in a yellowish crochet baby blanket. Its head was on a pile of folded tea-towels. Hilda was wearing her dressing-gown, but she'd knotted a scarf round her eyes. She was kneeling there, like at the guillotine. I didn't see the baby at first. Mrs Munnings just stood there in the doorway, gasping. We could both smell the gas. We were both so slow, it seemed, but I must have been very quick, because I'd opened the windows, and pulled Hilda out, and pulled the baby out, and seen the envelope on the table, and pushed it down in my coat pocket, and all before Mrs Munnings moved. The windows were sticky, they were old sash windows with dirty cords and sort of corrugated frosted glass. The room looked out over the passage to the house next door. I remember the cold air coming in. Mrs Munnings put her apron over her nose and mouth, I think she thought she'd be poisoned in twenty seconds. I must have turned the gas tap off, but I don't remember doing it. Only the oven was on, not the top burners. The oven was filthy, thick with grease.

'The envelope was addressed to me. She was expecting me, because she'd sent for me. It was so deliberate. What if I'd got there sooner, while she was still alive? It was revenge. She summoned me.

'She'd been living here for months, it turned out. More or less round the corner. I could have got there sooner if I'd recognized the address sooner; if I'd taken a cab, if I hadn't had to find someone to leave with my own lot. But at the inquest they said she'd have been dead anyway. She'd given herself plenty of time, before summoning me. She knew what she was doing. They were quite kind to me at the inquest. The wronged wife. Nobody seemed to blame me.

'That was the end between me and Andrew, as she'd meant it to be. He ran off. He was always a coward. But sometimes I think it was nothing to do with Andrew at all. He was just piggy in the middle. We cooked him up between us. No wonder he scarpered. She'd sealed herself into the kitchen in the small hours. They say that's the time when most people do it.

'She summoned me, and I arrived too late, but not too late to see her there. Now I summon her, but she won't come. Where is she? She was Mummy's favourite. Mummy would never accept what had happened. She refused to believe it. And after Hilda's death, Mummy hated me all the more, and needed me all the more. Hilda had escaped but I would never escape.

'I burnt Hilda's farewell letter. That was the strangest thing I ever did. I took it home, and burnt it. I never told anyone about it. Until this moment. And now I'm only telling myself. I didn't even read it. I didn't want it read out at the inquest. I opened it, in my own kitchen, back in Romley. Was it a letter of reproach? Of hatred? I assumed it was. But maybe it was an apology. I remember thinking, if I burn this, I'll never have to read it. Burning cannot be reversed. Burning is a one-way process. Burning leaves no possibility of a second chance, of regrets. Burning isn't a cry for help. Burning is final.

'So they said at the inquest she didn't leave a message.

'She failed to kill me once. When I was a child. And so she killed herself.'

Here ended MEM9.

Emily Palmer stared at its last sentences, reran the passage, reread it. Well, she'd found Hilda's death with a vengeance. Poor old Grandma, what a saga. How squalid. What a nasty little story to carry around with you for more than half a lifetime. Poor old Hilda. Poor little baby. Poor everybody. Poor Mrs Munnings, whoever she was.

Emily stretched and yawned. A bird was beginning to sing, out there in the darkness. She'd been here all night. Soon it would pale from the East, though the nights were long in December. They had come from the East, the Haxby axemen.

Emily switched off Frieda's machine. Silently its stories were swallowed into its memory.

She thought she ought to get some kip. Suddenly she felt very tired, and her eyes felt scratchy. A long drive, then all this family history. Emily had a hostility to family. Her own was so smug, so blind, so self-righteous. And look what family did to people. Grandma Frieda seemed to blame everything on her mother, who no doubt blamed her mother, and so on for ever, everyone complaining from generation to generation that life hadn't been fair to them, that they hadn't had a good start, a fair deal, the right parents, the right home . . . What a miserable succession.

Emily settled herself down on a broken-down settee, in the big room downstairs, and arranged the blow heater so that it blew warmly right on her. She wrapped herself up in Grandma Frieda's duvet. She hadn't fancied Grandma Frieda's bed at all, nor her bedroom. Both had been unhygienic. Almost worse than the tale of Hilda's death had been the sight of an encrusted china chamber-pot right under Grandma's bed. And in the wardrobe there had been another two chamber pots, luckily empty. How odd of Grandma to have wired herself up to E-Mail and for all Emily knew the Internet, and yet to have disdained the flush lavatory. How could anyone in the late twentieth century choose to use a pot? (Emily Palmer was too young to imagine a weak bladder on a cold night.)

Emily snuggled down. The duvet was clammy, and she felt a bit sneezy. She'd put in a few hours' snooze and then she'd think it all over. She knew she ought to have rung the hotel. She ought to have rung home. Where the hell had she left the phone? Was it still in the car? She dozed, then fell into deep sleep. The heater whirred on, at young Benjamin D'Anger's putative expense. The bird sang in the ash tree.

We are nearing the end. Soon we can go for the kill. Indeed, for the

250

overkill. Frieda has killed Hilda, and we have killed Frieda, and Benjamin has tried to kill himself. There will be one or two more deaths, but not many. Some will survive.

Simon Palmer is easily disposed of. He will come to a bad end. He may be found dead on a bathroom floor, or at the bottom of a lift shaft, or knifed in an alley, or mangled by lions. He may be run down on a dark night by a drunken driver. It is only a matter of time.

Jess and Jonathan Herz will survive, and so will Rosemary Herz, though she will lose her job and be placed on medication for the rest of her life. She will probably remarry, it is thought.

Nathan Herz's prospects, you may gather, are not good.

Neither are Will Paine's. Can we really expect Will Paine to get away with it? I would like him to, for he is a friend of mine, and I like him, but frankly the odds are against him. How can his moral luck last? The odds have been stacked against him all his life. He was born in the wrong place at the wrong time and of the wrong parents. You must have noticed that he has a good nature and an intelligence above the average. Given a little more help, he could have improved his lot immeasurably, but he stupidly drew the wrong lot. I fear that it is very likely that he too, like Simon Palmer, will come to a bad end. The net will close in on him. He is a natural suspect.

We shall hear more of the D'Anger family, before the end. Lily McNab struggles to reclaim Benjamin. She explores his illogical conviction that he is responsible for Frieda's death. She discovers that he is the victim of the grossly exaggerated expectations of both his parents. They had pinned too much on this child, they had expected him to be perfect. Never has he been allowed a normal childhood. He has been asked to fly too high, and in response he has dived too deep. He has been convinced he is a hero and a genius and a saint, and now he is being forced to recognize that he is only a boy. His parents have been much to blame. They have loved him too much. They are humbled now.

The Emmanuel delusion becomes a commonplace, as the millennium approaches. Lily McNab will write a book about it.

Let us wait a little. Let us return to Emily Palmer, the wise virgin, as she wakes on a December morning by the sea.

When Emily wakes, it is already mid-morning, and the blow heater has stopped blowing. Either it has fused itself or the electricity has gone off. Emily is still warm in Frieda's stuffy high-smelling duvet, but she wakes to feelings of guilt and sorrow. She ought to have rung home, she is saddened by the fate of her great-aunt, and she is worried about poor little Benjie, oppressed by this great heap. She realizes that, despite her confidence of yesterday, she is nervous about driving back up that dangerous drive. She fears that she will never get back to the top of the hill, never get back up to the coast road. What if the car won't start, what if it stalls?

This is silly, she tells herself, as she unwinds her bedding, tests the lights, makes her way to the bathroom for a splash. The electricity seems fine: it is just the heater that has overworked itself and conked out. She brushes her teeth, sponges herself, digs clean underwear out of her bag. She could have been pampering herself with bacon and egg and sausage and mushroom and fried tomato, instead of hacking open this tin of beans. She stands in the window, looking out towards the sea, tin in hand, forking out the beans into her mouth. The light is bright and clear and warm and very still. In the far distance she can hear a strange howling, as of wild animals. She opens the tall deep windows and leans out over the low ledge to listen. A howling, a yaffling, a baying. The Beast of Exmoor, no doubt.

She smiles at herself, and begins to feel brighter. She would love to meet the Beast. Where, she wonders, is her friend the toad? She must start to pack. She takes herself off to the butler's pantry and begins to box up the silver, the toy animals, the fossils, the jewels. Then she goes back up to the top of the house to the computer tower, and unpins the instructions from the walls, piles Frieda's discs into cartons, assembles the more important-looking papers. She is a little nervous about disconnecting the machine, for it had worked so perfectly the night before, and what if she unplugs something serious? To move the machine she knows it must be put in Park Mode, but how to do that? She switches it on, one last time, and calls up Frieda's memoirs. Will this be the only copy of them, or are they on hard disc? She thinks they will not have reached a disc. Does she want the rest of the family to read them? She could erase them, now, and they might vanish for ever. She might destroy them, as Frieda had destroyed Hilda's last message. What would Frieda have wanted? Would Frieda have wanted Benjamin, her chosen grandson and heir, to read of these miserable long-ago things? Benjamin is depressed enough without his Great Aunt Everhilda on his back. It wouldn't be good for Benjamin to discover a family history of suicide. On the other hand, if Frieda hadn't wanted it known, why had she tried to write it down? Emily switches the machine off, and decides that none of it is her business. She is only a messenger.

She will go down and load the car. She will brace herself to ring home and face the music.

As she carefully descends the rotten stairs, she can hear the howling and baying. It is nearer now, and there are other curious, unexpected noises – can that be the blowing of horns, and the hoofs of horses, and the grinding of gears? Suddenly the whole landscape is alive around her, as turbulence gathers about her, rushes towards her, thunders and crashes towards her and the house. She runs into the big front ground-floor room where she had slept, where the large window still stands open, and she sees in amazement that the whole of the hillside is pouring towards her in violent turmoil. Trees toss and bend, stones and rocks bounce and roll and splinter at her, a whole avalanche descends towards her, and just as she begins to make sense of this mighty upheaval, a red deer leaps the urned parapet, and crashes across the lawn, and clears the window-sill, and bounds into the arms of Emily Palmer.

The hounds stream after her, and Emily dashes to bar the window, as the deer takes refuge behind the table, putting her hoof through the back of Leland's canvas, knocking the skeleton clock and the red Bristol glass vase to the floor. The hounds throw themselves at the window, in full cry, howling and yelping and lathering, dozens of them, or so it seems to the hind and to Emily. Emily spreads her arms against the window, and screams. 'Stand back, stand back!' she cries into the garden. The hounds leap, then falter, and across the lawn, hoofs cutting the grass, come the horses and the riders, steaming, angry, hot-blooded, maddened by the chase. The riders in the vanguard reign in their mounts when they see the hounds, when they see Emily at the window, but more and more horses crash down the hillside beside them through the bracken, through the rhododendrons, almost tumbling over one another in the pursuit. Soon the lawn is thick with steaming, snorting steeds and horsemen and dogs, gathered as suddenly, and as improbably, as if they had dropped from the heavens. They yelp and throng.

The hind trembles with terror, and Emily is exultant with indignation. She is fearless. As some kind of calm obtains amongst the huntsmen, Emily opens the window and leans out.

'What are you doing?' she demands, in a voice as firm and as clear as a bell. Her hair flames with its own light, and those who were to tell the tale swore that she appeared as an avenging angel. Terror now fills the huntsmen, for who is this maiden, what is she doing here, and where is their quarry? 'Away with you!' cries Emily. 'This is my grandmother's property!'

The scene is majestic, ridiculous. The hounds are subdued, and the Master of the Staghounds approaches to offer a gallant apology. He touches his hat with his whip, he bows like a gentleman. But still he wants his deer. The house and the lawn may belong to her and her grandmother, but the hind belongs to him.

Emily cannot believe her ears. The scene descends into bathos. She turns into a fishwife.

'Are you suggesting I let this poor creature out to those murdering monsters?' she yells. 'You must be mad! I'll have you all for trespass! And get those dogs off my roof!'

For two of the hounds in their excitement have taken the short cut, and jumped from the path above on to the guttering: now they perch nervously, not sure how they got there or how to get off again.

'Get off, get away, get off!' repeats and exhorts Emily. 'You have no right to come here, and I grant the beast sanctuary!'

She is worried about what the beast is up to, behind her: she has heard the crashing of glass, but dare not look round to examine the damage. She must confront these intruders until they sound the retreat. She knows nothing of stag hunting, she knows neither its rules nor its seasons; she does not know that at this season of the year the hunted deer will be a female and therefore fortunately unantlered. But she does know that she must stand her ground. That is the role that has been given to her, and she will not betray it. She is the heroine of the chase, the protectress of the deer at bay. It is a fine role, and one she knows she looks good in: nevertheless she is surprised when a chap in helmet, lifted goggles and leathers drives his motorbike on to the lawn and into the middle of the mêlée and starts to take her photograph. The grass is a sea of mud by now, but then one couldn't have said it was very well kept in the first place. Can the chap on the motorbike be a friend and an ally? Is he, by any happy chance, a hunt saboteur?

Not quite, it proves, but he is good enough for her purposes. He is a press photographer, and he has been following the stag hounds for an article about the League Against Cruel Sports. He cannot believe his luck. This will be the picture of the decade, of the century. It will be reproduced until there are no more hunts and no more hinds and no more hunted, until the moors and woodland are no more. Emily and the hind have made his fortune. He snaps and snaps, as Emily stands there in the window, until he realizes that other cameras are beginning to emerge from the leafage, from the woodwork; hunt followers, even hunters, appear to be equipped with all kinds of photographic apparatus, and the scene is transformed from panic and chaos into a photo-opportunity, as lights flash, lenses dilate, tits are pressed, dogs whine, horses stamp and snort. Nobody wants to miss out, but our professional photographer is not keen to share his prize, and also wakes up to the fact that he badly needs a shot of the deer indoors as well as a shot (which he hopes to God he has got) of it leaping in panic over the window-sill. So he runs forward and rushes across the mangled grass and the one-time herbaceous borders and yells at Emily: 'Let me in! Let me in!'

Emily hesitates, takes in the features of his face, likes what she sees, and opens a pane. He scrambles over, less elegantly than the hind, which is cowering at the other end of the room immobile with shock.

'*Western Press*,' says the young man, who is almost as young as Emily herself.

'Emily Palmer,' says Emily, dazed.

They gaze at one another, astonished. The young man lifts his camera at her, lets it fall. He is open, eager, unwary. He has learnt no guile. Is he, perhaps, the one?

'Sorry,' he says, apologizing for his professional reflex.

'That's OK,' says Emily. She is panting slightly, with excitement. Her nostrils are dilated, her colour high, her eyes brilliant.

'Are you all right?' asks the young man.

'*I'm* all right,' says Emily. 'But I don't know about *him*.'

She indicates the trembling beast, at which she dares not look: she is afraid it is damaged, injured, will have to be put down.

'*Her*,' says the young man. 'It's a hind.'

The manner in which he says this convinces Emily that she has found a friend, and she bursts into tears of shock and relief.

'A hind?' she weeps. 'Do they chase hinds?'

'You bet they do. Hinds in calf, hinds with calf. In December they only chase hinds.'

'Is she all right?' asks Emily.

'I'll have a look,' says the young man. 'Do you mind if I take a pic while I do it?'

Emily is busy shutting and bolting the windows against the milling confusion of the thwarted throng. The young man kneels gently by the frightened animal, speaks to her quietly, then flashes at her. The beast jerks in alarm, then quivers into stillness.

'Don't do that,' says Emily.

'Sorry,' says the young man.

The hind seems to be in one piece, but they agree that they will have to keep her indoors until the crowd has gone. Emily says she is afraid the poor thing will die of fright, but the young man says he thinks she will recover. What next? Shall Emily go out and parley?

'We'll have to get rid of them,' says Emily. 'Can't I tell them just to get off my property?'

'Not as easy as all that,' says the young man, beginning to look around him with interest, taking in not only the beautiful maiden but also the bizarre décor of skulls and bones of the house she inhabits. 'The horses can get out, but there's been an accident in the drive. An Isuzu's gone over the edge and a lot of other stuff is stuck behind it. It's a scene up there, I can tell you. It'll take hours to clear.'

Emily is beginning to calm down, and the animal too seems less distressed. Emily is delighted to hear that the hunt followers have plunged themselves into a muddy impasse, and cross-questions her new friend about how it happened. He assures her there is considerable damage to the drive. 'Somebody will pay for that!' declares Emily, glaring angrily through the window at the crowd. She has triumphed over the hunt in every way: it has been utterly routed and wrong-footed. May all its Land Rovers crash after Frieda Haxby into the sea!

The young man (who has declared himself to be Jim from Bristol) allows her to think that he shares her anti-hunt feelings, which he now does, although he had set out on the day's chase as a neutral observer. He offers to go out and negotiate with the Master of the Staghounds, and, if Emily will permit him, on his return to take some more pictures. Emily assures him that she can deal with the Master herself, and climbs over the window-sill to do so, leaving Jim in charge of the hind. She confronts them all, boldly. She tells them roundly that they are trespassing, that she gathers they have blocked her drive, and that she is about to ring the police. It is no good their telling her that they thought the house was uninhabited. That is no excuse. They had better get out of her grounds as quickly as they can. And to whom should she send the bill for damage to property?

The undifferentiated mass of black-jacketed, white-stocked, fawn-breeched, red-nosed, hair-netted, khaki-jacketed, black-booted folk begins to mumble, thin, retreat. Emily tosses her golden mane and scrambles back over her window-sill.

Jim says it would be better to ring a national paper than the police. He wants to sell the story, and so should she. They compromise: they will ring the press, and the police, and a vet, and Emily will make them both a cup of coffee.

It takes three hours to clear the drive, and two days for Emily to get back to Wiltshire with the spoils of Ashcombe. By then she has become a small-scale national heroine, for Jim's pictures have come out uncannily well. He had been following the hunt since the moment the hounds left their kennels, and he has a whole portfolio covering the meet outside the Royal Oak at Moulton, the pursuit over the moor, the lemming leap down the hillside, the overturned Isuzu, the gathering on the lawn, the damsel with upstretched arms at the window, the confrontation of the damsel and the Master. And indoors, he has portrait after portrait of Emily Palmer and of the shy creature she has saved. The hind had not been persuaded to lie down with her head in Emily's lap, as she had continued to cower behind the sofa amidst the debris of skulls and glass; eventually she had been rescued by a vet from Lynton and an Exmoor Ranger who had managed to coax her into a van, and had promised to release her with the herd. But we were able to see Emily leaning over the back of the sofa, fruitlessly extending an apple; Emily attempting to pat the trembling head; and the delicate head itself, with its lucent, long-lashed, harmless female eyes.

The vet was of the opinion that she had calved within the last three months. The calf, he optimistically assured Emily, would be running with the herd. He did not tell Emily that the hind was probably suffering from myopathy, leading to excess lactic acid and kidney failure, and might well be pregnant again. His heart and local loyalties were with the hunt, despite the pathos and drama of the brave, lone and desperate flight. He would leave the dirt to the League Against Cruel Sports. They would make a mountain out of it, he guessed.

They would, they did, and they do, they will.

Emily does not know what to make of it all. She quite forgets Grandma Frieda in the flurry of her nine-day-wonder notoriety. She is not used to being interviewed, but keeps her cool remarkably well, as a lawyer's daughter should, and indeed the press does itself credit in some of its descriptions of the event. The connection with Frieda Haxby's disappearance is not missed, and for the second time in two months remote Ashcombe is in the news. A place of mystery and drama, of legends in the making. There is a particularly stirring piece in one of the quality Sundays by a columnist who had happily been reared in the neighbourhood and who knew all its stories: he retold the old tale of the noble huntsman who had in ancient times pursued a hind across the brow of the moor, up Countisbury Hill, and down through the thickets of the steep hillside towards the sea. At the perilous spot now known as Hindspring Point the hind had paused, glanced backwards at her lone pursuer – for all save the noble knight had fallen back in the chase – and then with three mighty leaps had bounded down the cliff into the sea. There, legend has it, she swam away to the west, across the channel, and out of sight. The penitent knight had marked her tracks, and at each set of the hoofmarks of the hunted beast had planted a stone – three stones which may be seen to this day. They commemorate her valour.

And what will Emily Palmer raise as monument to the hind which sought sanctuary in her arms? To her grandmother who fell from this cliff?

Emily Palmer is not sure what she thinks about hinds and hunting, about blood sports and cruelty and conservation. She does not tell the gentlemen of the press that for perhaps two years of her life her greatest desire had been to hunt with the Bessborough Foxhounds, and that for two years she and her friend Sally Partington had talked ponies, dreamt ponies, read about ponies, collected rosettes, studied form, and longed to leap over hedges and ditches and smear themselves with the blood of the stump of the severed brush of the red beast. Their bedrooms had been shrines to the show-ring and the stable, and they themselves had smelt of straw and bran and oatcake and manure. How Simon had sneered, how Daniel and Patsy had yawned! And then all this passion had passed away, and both Emily and Sally had been filled with a transitional shame. Yet the shame, Emily begins to guess now, and will believe later, attached as much to her feelings for Sally Partington as to the blood lust of the hunt.

Sally Partington had graduated from ponies and the clitoral orgasm to unsuccessful attempts at the vaginal orgasm with Simon Palmer. Emily Palmer had given up the lot, had deliberately forgotten and expunged the lot. And now everybody seems to be asking her what she thinks about horses and hunting. She answers very coolly, and gives nothing away. She insists that she is neither saboteur nor fanatic.

The field is full of ironies. Some of the arguments of the anti-league strike her as unconvincing, and some of its supporters as insupportable: a few of the hunters and hunt followers seem quite nice. (The chivalrous owner of the crashed Isuzu writes her a charming apology and asks her round for tea.) What is one to do? Does one have to have an opinion?

Animals have no opinions. Animals have no sense of irony. They leap, they run, they tremble.

Emily the heroine is perplexed. She knows the hind had brought her a message, but what was it? And where is the poor creature now? Did she die from the shock? Did her calf die? Perhaps she should advise Benjamin to turn Ashcombe into a bird sanctuary, a deer sanctuary. As human habitation, it is doomed. Those who stay there must stick or leap.

Four roods the hart of legend leaped to Hartleap Well, four roods the hind of legend to the sea, and four roods Frieda Haxby fell to her death. The story of Hartleap Well is told by Wordsworth, and it is set in Yorkshire, but many other counties have such legends. (Lincolnshire has one about a blind horse, and it is commemorated at Bayard's Leap, near Sleaford; Frieda, as we have seen, had been taken to see the giant horseshoes by her father. Brewer says the horseman was Rinaldo, but the locals say he was called Black Jim.) A rood (or a pole, or a perch) is five and a half yards (or five metres) and in early drafts of his ballad Wordsworth had allowed his hart to leap nine roods, not four; in his unromantic, stampmaster old age he scaled down that leap, but maybe he was wrong to do so. In the genre of legend, all things are possible, and exaggeration bears conviction. It is only in this real world that the mud is heavy and sticks.

Let us liberate Will Paine. Let the bird fly free. Oh, there are many plots that could enmesh and entangle and imprison him, we all know that. The police, the hard men, bad company, the dope, they all lie in wait for Will Paine. Are there any plots that will let him free? Not in this country, that is clear. There is no place for him in the country of his birth. We have sent him a third of the way round the globe already, across the Atlantic billows, but he is not yet safe, he is not yet far enough from us. Can he fly further? With one more bound he may cross the Pacific and reach Sydney. If we send him far away, out of sight and out of mind, as we sent our convicts of old, may he survive and know the good life? We dispatch him now not to hard labour but to the fantasy of a good job with a decent wage. Will they let him in? Will they turn him away at Immigration? He is not very black.

Fly, bird. Fly, cryptic bird. Take thy flight, thy Qantas flight.

Sorrow has come upon the Palmers, the Herzes and the D'Angers. They had seemed to be doing so well. It is hard to say which suffers most. Let us ask first for a reckoning of Nathan Herz, to whom we bear no malice, not the least in the world.

Nathan's end comes suddenly, unpredictably, on a mild night in spring. He has had a good day at the office, and has dined not wisely but too well at one of his favoured restaurants in Soho, with one of his favoured clients. They have been made much of by the *patronne*, who loves Nathan, and who has urged upon him perhaps one glass of Armagnac too many. The liquor had rested warmly upon the *ravioli aux trompettes des morts*, the *pieds de porc Sainte-Menehould*, the *Caprice des Dieux*, and Nathan and his friend Baxter, Marketing Controller of Associated British Unit Plan Trusts, sat long over the filter coffee, exchanging notes on the state of the economy, the old days of their youth, their sex lives, their livers, their loathing of exercise. Nathan and Baxter are old drinking companions, bonded by the bottle, and they share a contempt for the nineties cult of self-regarding health, for the regimes of gyms and jogging and personal aerobic tutors and mineral waters. Why pay good money to run up and down a short flight of stairs to nowhere? They know they are in a minority (which is why the *patronne*, herself of an older and more indulgent generation, loves them so much) but they are defiant. They admire the Bohemians of earlier days who drank themselves to death. Why do people want to live so long? It is unnatural. What makes them think it's worth it?

Nathan feels on this good night that he has no worries at all. Even when he visits the gents, pisses copiously, then has to reach for the wall as he senses a sudden constriction in his chest, he still feels no worry. Conviviality courses through him. He loves the *patronne*, and kisses her goodnight. He loves Baxter, and they clasp hands and hug one another at the end of Greek Street, as Baxter hails a cab. Even now, Baxter suggests a drinking club, but Nathan declines – he is feeling a little odd down his left arm and elbow, and although the distant, almost dis-embodied sensation causes him not the slightest anxiety, he thinks perhaps he should be sensible and get himself home. He too hails a cab, and sets off south to the other side of the river.

This proves to be a mistake. He should have stuck with Baxter and the booze.

As the cab crosses the bridge, Nathan asks it to stop, and tells it he'll get out here and walk the last few hundred yards along the river path. This also proves to be a mistake.

He tells himself that he needs a breath of air, that the closeness of the restaurant (which, anachronistically, encouraged smoking) has stifled him. As he tries to count out his money, he finds he is very pissed, unaccountably pissed, for he cannot tell one banknote from another. In the end he hands over a fistful of paper currency and tells the driver to help himself to the fare, keep a quid, and hand back the rest. The driver does as he is told, for he is a thoroughly decent old-fashioned cabbie, and an Eastender to boot. The driver watches with some concern as Nathan weaves his way towards the steps down to the towpath. That is the last time that anyone admits to seeing Nathan alive.

Nathan is fished out quite promptly the next morning, and the events of his last evening on earth are subjected to close scrutiny, even before it is discovered that he had suffered a mild heart attack. The heart attack might explain his death, but how can it explain why Nathan was standing at the bottom of a cobbled slipway with his feet in the Thames when he toppled over? Does it explain why he left his briefcase placed so neatly on the sixth step of the stone stairs leading down to the beach and the slipway, just above the reach of a high tide? No, it does not. There will have to be an inquest.

Rosemary is at first embarrassed by the vast amount that Nathan and Baxter Coldstream seem to have eaten and drunk at their last supper, and by the detailed account from *patronne*, fellow diners and cab-driver of Nathan's staggering last hours. Those pigs' feet, so retro, so gross, so indigestible, so monstrously non-kosher, cause mirth even in a coroner's court, and the coroner makes a point of dwelling upon them. But Rosemary rallies and wins through. Even the laughter had been full of admiration. Rosemary decides to be proud of Nathan, not ashamed of him, and once she had adopted this policy it is as though the lock upon her heart is opened and the flow of her old love for him released. She is proud of his exploits. He has done well.

She is fortified in this position by the sincere and extravagant gestures of affection which greet her on all sides. His colleagues claim they will miss him horribly, and they shower her with flowers and other tokens of esteem. The flat by the Thames is transformed into a conservatory in memory of Nathan Herz. Bouquets with mysterious messages arrive from unknown ladies, and Rosemary decides to greet these too with pride. (The Eagleburgers send a case of champagne: is this or is this not in poor taste?)

Rosemary is invited to dinner by Baxter Coldstream, and they dine in the very restaurant where Nathan had consumed his last trotter. Baxter drunkenly implores her not to blame him, and tells her that he blames himself for not insisting on taking Nathan to Carlucci's.

And it is true that if Nathan had opted for common sense and an earlier night he would not have ended up in the river. What can he have been doing, down there at the water's edge? Can it have been a suicide attempt? This, to the relief of all, is finally ruled out. Nathan had nothing to commit suicide *about*, confirm his boss, his colleagues, his friends, his wife, his mother, his stockbrokers. Since Christmas, life had been looking good for Nathan. He had come up with an acceptably risqué and imaginative plan for health insurance, he had braved the invoicing of the forgotten clients and been warmly forgiven, he had been given a clean bill at his last medical, and he had won five hundred quid on a tip on a horse at Lingfield. What more could a creative director in a rising advertising agency want? Had he known something about the market that nobody else knew? Had he had a secret grief?

Baxter, holding Rosemary's freckled hand over the Armagnac, and squeezing it until her widowed diamonds pinch, assures her that never had Nathan been in better spirits. They had had a cracking evening, a smashing evening. Nathan hadn't had a care in the world. They'd reminisced about their first meeting at Sharp MacManus all those years ago, and about the night they'd spent carousing after it with Nathan's old college pal, the night they'd ended up in Bow Street. And had Rosemary ever heard the story of the Combined Biscuit Christmas Party?

Rosemary, who has for years fastidiously avoided male tales of debaucherie and camaraderie, who has avoided many a company function, listens with new-found longing, with sympathy reborn. He had been quite a lad, her Nathan. She and he had had good times together too. Baxter is right, one must remember the good times. She sniffs, her nose turning pink with emotion, and returns the pressure of Baxter's fingers. She will miss Nathan. Somewhere beyond the comforting pleasures of this wake lies lasting loss.

But Rosemary's sorrow, ameliorated by recaptured love, will be as nothing to the sorrow and horror of Daniel and Patsy Palmer. Nathan Herz's death was one of happy ease in comparison with the violent death of Simon Palmer. How had his parents not seen the warning signals? Where had they been looking, as Simon descended into the pit? Will Paine could have told them, had once even tried to warn them, but he is not here. Emily had observed symptoms, but even the cool, the sensible Emily had not seen how far things had gone. She too had looked the other way. Simon's tutor (who happened, alas, for these crucial weeks to double as his personal tutor) has been too preoccupied with his own worries to pay Simon much attention – and anyway, all that *loco parentis* stuff had seemed to him old hat. If the idle young of the idle rich wanted to spend their time tripping, hallucinating, needling or ghetto-blasting, what was that to him? Half of them were schizoid anyway. Simon Palmer had almost certainly been schizoid. The only papers he'd even managed to turn in had been disorganized and demented. Hardly worth the marking.

Simon's unexpected body had to be identified by its fingerprints. He hadn't washed pleasantly with the friendly tides as Frieda Haxby and Nathan had done; he had been taken out by a lorry as he walked the wrong way along the hard shoulder of the slip-road leading on to the M3 at the exit that leads to Hartley Bessborough and on to the Old Farm. He had been obliterated, smashed, and run over repeatedly, like a fox or a badger, like a cat or a dog or a motorway bird. The lorry had not stopped; nor, it seemed, had some of the cars that followed it. It was a dark wet night with bad visibility – but even so, even so. After the identification of the body, some reports filtered through from motorists who had seen a wild figure walking southwards on the wrong side of the dual-carriageway of the A34, waving its arms like a windmill and lunging occasionally at the headlights of an oncoming vehicle. A drunk, a tramp, a crazed traveller, all had assumed: all, including Judge Partington, who, his licence regained, had been driving himself to a dinner at his old college in Oxford. Greatly to his credit, Bill Partington had not suppressed this sighting, as he so easily might have done, but had reported it as soon as he realized the import of the ghastly apparition: red jersey, some kind of tattered-looking green jacket, dark glasses, fair hair, average height, unsteady gait, carrying a white plastic bag . . . Partington was not a bad witness, though this was in itself little comfort to Patsy and Daniel Palmer.

There was, indeed, little comfort. All they were told, all they could tell themselves, is that he could not have known what had hit him.

Patsy will never recover from the impact of this blow. Mothers, it is said, do not. Daniel, being a man, appears to take the shock more calmly, but he has become even drier than he was before, and finds no solace save in his work. His smile now has the chill of winter frost. He has sustained a double loss: not only has he lost his only son, through what he himself chooses bitterly to describe as his own contributory negligence, but he has also lost his home, in which he had taken such a proper pride. For it is clear within weeks of Simon's death that the Palmers cannot continue to live at the Old Farm, unless they live in it as a prison. There is no way to leave the Old Farm without driving along the stretch of road that killed Simon. This they know they cannot do. So they put the house on the market, and wait. The market remains sluggish, as it has been for years, and property prices are low. They may have to wait for a long time. The pond silts up, the lawn is not mown, bindweed embraces the sundial, and ground elder ramps around the roots of the wistaria. Dock and nettles smother the vegetable garden, and greenfly swarm on the roses. Water drips unnoticed through the leak over the study window. The Aga burns still, but Patsy no longer troubles to cook. The Palmers think they will move east, perhaps to Suffolk, to a smaller house, somewhere without memories, without history.

Patsy's grief is compounded by her fear that Simon had been making his way home as a first and last plea for help. And he had not reached it. Well, a mother, even a bad mother, would think that, wouldn't she? She tells this fear to none save harmless, pallid Sonia Barfoot. Sonia accepts the confidence and offers no comfort. Sonia Barfoot is a connoisseur of pain. She accepts, she absorbs, she forgives.

Would it comfort Patsy Palmer to know that things have turned out better for Will Paine, her surrogate son? Will has fallen on his feet, as he puts it, in Sydney. He is apprenticed to a landscape gardener and he is learning the names of plants. He loves working in the open air. The sun suits him. He is healthier and stronger than he has ever been. He thanks Patsy Palmer for this transformation, and sometimes thinks of sending her a postcard. Without Patsy and Frieda, where would he be?

We may turn, now, to the D'Angers. They are slowly and painfully on the mend. Slowly, with the professional help of Lily McNab, Benjamin D'Anger rises from the depths, and begins to emerge from the decompression chamber she has constructed for him. David and Gogo

266

watch and wait. Benjamin will never be as he was, omnipotent and brave. He will not take the whole globe on his thin shoulders. He will dive no more into the bottomless. But he will survive. Or so says Lily McNab.

Gogo finds herself spending more time with her widowed sister Rosemary, who now has time on her hands. They lunch in the hospital canteen, or in a cheap and crowded little Italian trattoria off Queen Square, or in a vegetarian Indian self-service basement restaurant at the bottom of Tottenham Court Road. They talk about their children, their mother, their husbands. They become friends again. They speak of poor Patsy, poor Daniel, poor Simon, and of the admirable character of Patsy's little Emily, who has grown old before her time. They speak of their strange childhood in the old Mausoleum, and of the damage that it has done to them, and of the games they played in the attic. They speak of poor Aunt Everhilda, whom they had never known, and their poor little nameless half-sister, who had died in a gas oven. They speak, obsessively, at length, of their vanished father, so little mentioned for so long; so many children now are fatherless, but in their day they had been lonely in their special social role. They piece together their fears of the past and for the future, and each time they meet a new pattern emerges, a new seam is stitched. One day they will make sense of their ancestry. Are they unique, are they freaks, are they throw-backs, are they pioneers of a new order? Frieda had left them with so many questions unanswered.

How wise they had been, they agree, to marry out, to alter the gene pool. Nathan is now enshrined in both their hearts as a hero, and Jonathan and Jess show every sign of inheriting his fine qualities. Rosemary, a reformed daughter-in-law, visits Nathan's mother weekly with the children, and learns to make chopped liver. She draws the line at gefilte fish, but she improvises an excellent method of turning herrings from the deli into her own version of chopped herring, with the aid of a few turns in the food-processor, some sour cream, an onion and a hard-boiled egg: she imparts the recipe to Mrs Herz. Mrs Herz is delighted with these new attentions. They don't quite make up for the loss of Nathan, but they certainly do help.

Rosemary puts the riverside apartment on the market, and then, as soon as a prospective buyer comes to look at it, takes if off again. She has decided to stay where she is, for with Nathan's life insurance policies and his company pension she can well afford it. And she has grown fond of the river. It keeps Nathan's memory alive. She watches the tides at night, as he once watched them, and she feels no ill-will. The river keeps her company. And the neighbourhood, despite the recession, is improving – one day the new gallery will be built, one day the new theatre will be finished. Already a smart new restaurant has opened on the ground floor of the Ceylon Quay: it serves oysters and lobsters, sea bass and seaweed, and its shop sells dark sweet balsamic vinegars and an olive oil of the month. How Nathan would have loved it, Rosemary sometimes sighs.

Rosemary Herz is to be seen at low tide, standing on the slipway, gazing at the proud painted cast-iron pylons of the London, Chatham & Dover Railway, at the huge stained green and white stone piers of the bridge, at the twelve strange red granite columns that march across the water, at the pebbles and pots and pans and shoe soles of the shore, at the gulls and cormorants, at the driftwood barges. *Invicta*, claims the bridge, with its heraldic horse and its heraldic lion.

Unvanquished too, in their way, are Gogo and David. Gogo's marriage adventure had been more daring than Rosemary's, and it has weathered storms, but is now in clear water. The relationship of Gogo Palmer and David D'Anger has ever been marked by courtesy and respect; through these dull virtues they have stayed afloat.

David D'Anger prospers. He is now the elected Member for Middleton, and his party is the party of government. Its majority is slim, but it will serve. David is pleased to have been elected, and by a very respectable margin, for the alternative would have been most unpleasant, but it must be said that he is increasingly disillusioned with party politics and indeed with his own party. It seems to have moved far from where it had stood when David, as an ardent student, had first joined it; it is now, as every journalist says five times a week, almost indistinguishable from the opposition. The Just Society recedes over the horizon, in a haze of talk and compromise and phrase-making.

Egalitarianism and redistribution are words to avoid, concepts to deplore. Perhaps, David wonders, he has been wrong all along? Perhaps he should retreat to the cloister of theory, and accept the new Chair of Sociology at Northam University? (It has been offered to him.)

He cannot quit yet: he must serve his time like a man. And anyway, it is all very fascinating. The customs of the House, its intrigues, its gossip, its alliances – who would have thought he would ever make it to here? But he finds the composition and lineaments of his constituency of even greater interest than the House. It is a vast living social research project all his own, attending his examination. He resolves to be a good constituency man, to look after his flock like a good shepherd, to chart its structure like a good sociologist. Even if he can't change much, at least he can record it properly. He will collect statistics that have never been collected before. You can't push a button and wake up in the new world. But you can pay close attention to the bit that you inhabit. And he has been a very lucky man. He has won Middleton, and he will work for it, and it will work for him. He has been given a licence to nose about in its backstreets, its highstreets, its outlying dormitory villages, its pubs and its nursery schools.

He resolves to give up his media persona and his TV slots, for he is finding it increasingly difficult, now he is no longer in opposition, to toe the party line. He does not want to speak out and be dismissed as an ignorant college boy, hijacked by the corner-boys of the hard left. Better to keep his mouth shut, to bide his time. Academe will always take him back.

News of David D'Anger's change of tack reaches the Leader, who accosts David casually one day in a corridor of power and asks if it's true that David has been turning down TV opportunities and discontinued his contract with *Race to 2000*. Yes, says David. That's political suicide, says the Leader, smiling his boyish smile. For me or for the party? inquires David. For you, of course, says the Leader, still smiling.

The Leader is said to be telegenic, but he is not nearly as good-looking as David D'Anger, and he does not have the incalculable positional advantage of being a man of colour.

David is summoned to a more formal meeting, at which he agrees

269

to accept appearances on named programmes on agreed topics. He reserves his right to refuse *Any Questions*, *Question Time*, or anything else that resembles a quiz show. He insists that his manner on such programmes would be in the long run counter-productive – whether for himself or the party, he does not say, and they do not at that point think to ask. But his reply does lead his leaders to wonder what David D'Anger's view of the long run might be. Is he playing a deep game? What are his political ambitions? Nobody with the gift of the gab like David D'Anger ever refuses to appear on TV. Backbenchers queue up to get themselves on radio phone-ins. David D'Anger is a dangerous man, a man to watch. Who does he think he is?

So David's reputation grows, and, as he retreats, he advances.

Plans for the film of *Queen Christina* also advance, and Benjamin D'Anger's fortune augments. It will not be as vast as his parents had at one point feared and hoped, for Frieda, it is discovered, had not invested hundreds and thousands of pounds in high-interest bank accounts, stocks, shares and building societies: the £34,000 in her current account had represented a fair proportion of her liquid assets. The money she scattered so violently upon Will Paine is gone for ever, which is just as well, as it appears to have come from an illegal American bank account on which much tax would have been and indeed may yet be owing. (The position is expensively unclear.) At the time of the sale of the Mausoleum she had already divested herself of various random sums, mainly to old-fashioned, global, respectable charities such as Oxfam and Amnesty International. There were one or two surprises – she had, two years before the sale, and therefore at the height of her dubious relationship with Cedric Summerson, bought £5,000 worth of shares in Grisener International, a conglomerate which owned reputable brand names in the processed food business, and less reputable subsidiaries, including the infamous Hot Snax, manufacturers of Butler's Bumperburgers. These shares, which she had kept, had done spectacularly well, and would bring in a tidy sum for young Benjamin. Less profitable had been her stake in the Severn Barrage, but even here she had not lost much.

The bulk of her wealth lies, putatively, in the value of her copyrights, now extended by European law for seventy years from her death. Benjamin's grandchildren may live to enjoy their profits, and it seems that profits there will be, at least for the next decade. The old classics never go out of print, and continue to appear in several languages. *Queen Christina* has been given a new lease of life, and may become, who knows, a box office hit, a cult text: there are plans for a paperback tie-in. Of course, the whole enterprise may be a flop, as the hardback had been, but at least it can't lose money, or not for the Haxby estate. Movies are a gamble, literature is a lottery. Who can tell what time will bring?

Ashcombe, the trustees agree, is a liability rather than an asset. Are they therefore entitled to dispose of it at a loss? And how much in law and in ethics are they obliged to consult young Benjamin?

It is clearly in young Benjamin's financial interest to sell Ashcombe and keep the Hot Snax shares. But is it in his moral interest?

The trustees discuss this at length, for they do not, it seems, see eye to eye. David D'Anger is in favour of consulting Benjamin, or would have been had Benjamin's mental state been less precarious, whereas Lord Ogden of Grotius takes the view that it is his prime duty to protect the boy's legacy and Frieda's investments. In the matter of Hot Snax, Lord Ogden prevails. David is secretly relieved: nobody can blame him for not standing up to a man of Ogden's weight, and even David hesitates to assert his right to devalue his own son's money. Ogden is famed for his shrewd legal and financial brain, and Frieda's intentions in appointing him had been clear enough. David submits with a good grace, and with a good grace Ogden concedes on the lesser matter of Ashcombe. If David wants to involve the boy in any decisions regarding the house, of course he may.

David and Gogo think it may be good for Benjamin to apply his mind to Ashcombe. They consult Lily McNab on this: she is professionally reluctant to offer anything as clear as an opinion, but she does not disagree.

So we may prepare to take leave of Benjamin D'Anger, rich, clever, wise and sad, as he contemplates the prospects of his ruin by the sea. Twice he revisits it, once with his parents in the spring, and again with his cousin Emily in the late summer. Many a time has Emily rehearsed to him the tale of the hind's flight, and now she tells it once more, as she drives him round the thrilling hairpin bend of Porlock Hill. Benjie listens, absorbed, as he makes his way with much relish through a bag of Maltesers.

A year has passed since Benjamin paid his first and last visit to his grandmother at Ashcombe. So much has happened since then, reflect he and Emily in mutual silence, as the story of the hunt ends and the car gains the summit and the road flattens and unwinds. Deaths, illnesses, elections. Emily has elected not to go to university this autumn after all; she has given up her place at Newcastle, where she had been accepted to study archaeology, and has chosen instead to take a short course in something called Media Studies in a rechristened polytechnic in Glamorgan. Daniel and Patsy were not pleased by this change of plan, but they are too demoralized as parents even to think of arguing with her. She gave them as her reason that she was 'sick of the past', but her real reason is not obvious. (Benjie guesses it; they have an appointment with Bristol Jim the photographer on the way home.)

Benjamin thinks not about the past, but about the future, as he watches the moor for signs of deer or ponies. The future no longer oppresses him with its black pot lid, its cavern roof of horror, but the way forward and out and up to the light and air is by no means clear to him. He is well aware that Lily McNab has been suggesting to him, over the past few months, that he is not as special, nor as responsible, nor as predestined as he had thought himself to be. He is not Benjamin, nor Emmanuel, nor Beltenebros. He can choose to be ordinary. Nobody will blame him if he is not the first and the best. He has pretended to go along with her on this, and he has made the same pretence to his parents. But deep in himself he still believes he has a special destiny, and that if he does not find it he will have greatly failed.

A special destiny, but what shall it be? As squire of Ashcombe, or as saviour of Guyana? There are too many choices.

His father seems to have become bored by Guyana. He is sunk in the parish pump politics of a not very interesting area of West York-shire, or so it sometimes seems. He has abandoned Demerara. (Has Lily McNab, at second hand, been in some way responsible for this? If so, David is not aware of it.) Saul Sinnamary urges Benjamin to return to Guyana, as he himself frequently does, but who wants to spend his one and only life on aeroplanes, in transit, a perpetual tourist, belong-ing neither to one place nor another? Lily McNab seems to believe Benjamin should abandon dreams of returning, and settle, as she has done, in England, and accept that for better or worse he is British. Angels tempt Benjamin from all sides, and he does not know which are the good ones, which the bad. He must not listen to the wrong voices, but which are they?

Benjamin D'Anger stares at the moving moor, and puts another Malteser into his mouth. He sucks it, luxuriously, letting the soft milk chocolate coating melt, and then feeling the honeycomb within col-lapse and crush against his tongue. It is wicked and delicious. It will rot his teeth.

Benjamin and Emily have an appointment to meet the land agent from Taunton at Ashcombe, but when they arrive there is no sign of him. It is a warm and sunny afternoon, so they open the doors and windows for an airing, then wander out on to the lawn. The garden is better kept now than it had been in Frieda's day, for a man comes once a week from Oare to cut the grass, trim the hedges, round up the weeds, poison the creepers. The house too has been tidied: the worst of the furniture has been sent to auction, Frieda's knicknacks have been confined to a tall corner cupboard, and her paintings brought back to London. (They, like Hot Snax, are worth a surprising amount, though unfortunately the Leland was ruined when the hind put her foot through the canvas. Nobody has yet dared to tell the painter of the strange fate of his work, though when, at last, Benjamin comes to confess, he will claim to be strangely flattered. Painters are, luckily, quite mad. Turner used one of his own favourite pieces – a view of Blythe sands – as a cat flap.)

Emily and Benjamin lean on the parapet between the urns and gaze down at the flat and shining water. The ivy has been spray-gunned from the urns, and they have been planted with scarlet geraniums.

'What do you think, Em?' asks Benjie. 'Do you think there's a curse on it? Do you think Frieda put a curse on it?'

'It doesn't feel like it, at the moment,' says Emily, sniffing the salt on the air, listening to the raucous yelping cry of a gull, to the soft distant rattle of pebbles.

'What should I do with it, Em?' asks Benjie.

She puts her arm around him, as they lean together against the warm lichen-spotted stones of the wall.

'A hotel?' she suggests. 'A rest home for old poets? A conference centre? What do David and Gogo say?'

'You know David and Gogo. They don't say anything. They want me to say.'

'Do they want you to get rid of it?'

'I don't know. I'm not sure if they know.'

'It doesn't seem a sad place, to me,' says Emily. 'Despite everything. I think Frieda was happy here, in her own way.'

'Saul says I can turn it into a bird sanctuary. He's got a thing about bird sanctuaries, ever since he started reading up the life of this York-shire explorer called Waterton, who owned acres of Guyana and mar-ried a Guyanese princess and came home and turned his estate into a bird park. Saul's making a T V programme about him. He says we're probably all related. Waterton, and the princess, and the Sinnamarys, and the D'Angers.'

'Well, so what?' says Emily. The ethnic bit loses her.

'I don't see the point in turning this into a bird sanctuary,' says Benjie. 'It's a bird sanctuary already. Look.'

They watch a large black bird – rook, crow, jackdaw? – as it perches in the ash tree. It struts, puffs itself out, settles, hunches up its shoulders, squawks. Various unseen small birds answer chippily. The black one hunches again, squawks again. It is sinister, ridiculous. A robin hops out of a bush and comes to perch on the urn near Benjie's right ear. A blue tit of preternaturally vivid and primal blue and yellow and cream swings provocatively from a twig. A wren scuttles noisily in the undergrowth. These birds are indifferent to people. They think they own the place. They are brazen.

The water shimmers, and a great ruffle of breeze sweeps over it, turning the pale-blue silver to slate and back again. It is irresistible. They have to go down. They abandon the land agent, and answer the call of the sea. They are ill-shod for the expedition, but who cares? They run down the lower lawn, and out of the wooden gate at the lowest end of the garden, and into the steep lane that descends to the beach. They scramble down, dislodging stones as they go, past the high banks studded with the flat green discs of pennywort, straggled with the long leggy green stalks and white stars of stitchwort, pierced by the pale green cowls of arum lilies. They jump down the log-edged steps, which somebody has repaired since Frieda's day, and on to the shingle. A kingfisher hovers, flirts its wings, and darts away from their approach in a flash of pink and emerald-blue.

They begin to pick their way westwards, towards the grey point, over pebbles, over rocks, across patches of mud, across pools, across the living crunch of limpet and barnacle. Benjie's trainers serve well enough, though they are soon soaked through, but Emily's slither and slip, and from time to time she has to take them off to get a grip. Soon her feet are bleeding, but she has no wish to turn back. They reach the point, and there is another point, and beyond it another, headland after headland, reaching on to the open Atlantic. On they go, pausing from time to time to examine a wonder – a striped stone, a shell, a plastic bottle, a viscous amber suckered stump of oarweed, a cork, an ancient lobster-pot. They come across a whole tree trunk, lying above the waterline, of a bright rusted orange, soaked to a chewed fibre, and a great root, four feet across, knobbled and whiskered like a giant celeriac which clings still to the rocks it grew amongst. They find a solitary, shipwrecked Brussels sprout, and a pierced metal barbecue tin. They clamber across sloping diagonal slabs of sliced violet, across rounded fissured boulders of hard blue-green, across beds of burnt sienna that have been scarred by satanic knives. They look up at the wooded crags above them, and listen to the drip of waterfalls. They hear the roar and grind of water rushing down a cleft in the cliff, and come across a miracle – a river which disappears steeply into the shingle, then bubbles up with renewed force and turmoil three yards further down the slope to the shore. They round the second point, but still they cannot turn back, for there, ahead of them, tucked under the hill, is the old kiln, and above it is the third point of Hindspring. So on they go, and onwards, to the next point and the next. They are young, and on they go.

The land agent, when he arrives, may find himself waiting for some time.

'Jump for it!' cries Emily Palmer, as the tide comes in. And Benjamin D'Anger jumps.

January 1996
Porlock Weir